# BARNARD'S GALAXY

## DESCENDANTS OF LEGACY

### D.K. NOVA

First published in the United States of America in 2020 by Elijah Dakota Arend

Paperback and eBook edition published in 2020

www.DKNovabooks.com

Paperback ISBN: 978-0-578-68203-7 eBook ISBN: 978-0-578-68205-1

Book edited by Scooter Ricciardi

Printed and bound by IngramSpark

FOR JORDAN -

THANK YOU FOR YOUR CONSTANT LOVE AND SUPPORT. YOUR BELIEF IN ME KEEPS ME GOING AND WRITING EVERY DAY. I LOVE YOU.

# Table of Contents

# Chapter 1:
# Johthuns- Goodbye Brother

A Johthun family sits on a mountain top watching the sky, their metallic black goggles shimmer as stars soar by. The fur covering them blows in the wind, while an aroma in the air pierces the noses atop their snouts. They smile with their full sets of jagged teeth, enjoying each other's company while their tails whip around behind them. It's a special night for this family. They're celebrating their two sons being accepted into the prestige program to become Elite Protectors—the highest level of the military that any Johthun can achieve.

"I am so proud of you, boys! Tanglor, Ashar, it has truly been an honor raising you both."

The boys nod to their mother, deeply moved. Hiding the tears in their eyes, they motion for their parents to look back at the celestial brilliance lighting up the skies. As the night grows darker, they start to head down the mountain towards their home. Tomorrow they must leave to begin their training as Elite Protectors. Tanglor stops his family. He has something to say.

"Thank you for adopting us. I can't express to you in words how much you have meant to Ashar and me. I didn't know my parents at all, but I'm sure they would be grateful to both of you."

Ashar jumps in.

"Tanglor took the words out of my mouth. We were just two fledglings in a foster home trying to get by before you brought us into your lives. We became brothers because of that, and we will stay brothers no matter what."

Their parents, already emotional, reach out and hug their sons tightly. Noticing the stars have all but stopped shooting by, they hurry back to their home beneath the mountain so the boys can get some sleep.

"You boys get some rest. You have a big day tomorrow!"

Their mother leaves the room, shutting the door behind her. Ashar and Tanglor fall asleep quickly in the hopes that it will make tomorrow come faster. As the night goes on, Tanglor finds himself in a familiar nightmare. One that he's had as far back as he can remember. Locked in the dream, he tosses and turns in his sleep, but, as usual, he is unable to wake up.

The dream is always vivid, but like he's seeing it for the first time. There are Johthun Elders and two other Johthuns, a male Elite Protector and his pregnant wife. They are on a ship headed toward Thoonta, a planet neighboring Joht. A meeting is taking place until a group of six mysterious creatures bursts into the room. They look like the Johthuns, but their faces are blurred out, and they have bright teal eyes. They interrupt the meeting by threatening the Elders and the Elite Protector. He retaliates and attacks two of them, taking one down before getting knocked out by the other. Laughter fills the room as the creatures approach the pregnant female standing in front of the Elders. She pulls out two knives and throws them at the laughing monsters, piercing two of them in the head. They fall to the floor, causing the other four creatures to cease their laughter. The Elite Protector gets off the ground and walks over to his pregnant wife and the Elders. They all stand in silence as ten more of the creatures enter the room. He turns to his wife.

"Make sure you and our child get out of here safely and take the Elders with you; don't look back. I love you so much."

He kisses her and turns to the creatures, pulling out his blades. They charge at him, but he jumps over them and flees the room with them in pursuit. Without hesitating, the pregnant Johthun seals the door behind them. She launches the escape procedures and initiates the self-destruct system. The room they're in detaches from the rest of the ship and begins its route to Thoonta. Tanglor, still in the dream, watches as the Elite Protector takes out the creatures with no hesitation. His blades are covered in blood as he slides between the monsters, carving off their limbs, all except one. He walks over to the last creature crawling away and kicks it over, so it's facing him. The Elite Protector begins to speak, his words the same in every dream:

"I can't believe you would betray me, my family, and the Elite Protectors!"

He kicks the creature again, causing its blurry face to come into focus, becoming a Johthun. Tanglor wakes up, just as he does at that spot every time he has that dream. Ashar sits across from him.

"You have the dream again?"

"I'll be alright; it was the same as always. Don't tell mom and dad. I don't want them worrying."

Tanglor hops out of bed, shaking off the dream. He's eager to get dressed.

"I hope you're still the only one that knows about my nightmare."

"Of course, Tanglor! You know I don't talk to anyone other than you."

They both start laughing as they finish packing. Their parents are already in the caravan, waiting to take them to their shuttle. The shuttle will take them to Joht, where they'll begin their training. The boys rush out with their packed bags and run over to their parents, and the other three Johthun recruits waiting for them. [1] The ride to the shuttle is a quiet one. Different emotions permeate the vehicle. Tanglor sits lost in thought, remembering the dream he had last night. He can't stop thinking about how the blurry face turned into a Johthun.

"Were all of those creatures Johthuns from the start? They betrayed him and the Elders, does that mean all of those creatures were Elite protectors too?"

While he's spacing out, Ashar notices and hits him on the arm.

"Tanglor! We're almost there, you ready?"

"Huh? Yeah, I'm ready."

One of the other Johthuns on the caravan gets up and walks toward them, a female named Ranyana Xantlow.

"You boys better be ready because we're here."

She walks past them, shooting Ashar a smile as she does.

Tanglor laughs.

"Ooooh, Ashar! It looks like you have someone else to talk to now."

Ashar blushes while standing up. He and Tanglor say goodbye to their parents before walking off the caravan towards the shuttle. The enormous vessel in front of them is unlike anything they have seen on Thoonta. It's a massive blue ship with a glass dome on the top and wings on the sides. The eager recruits run as fast as they can to get a good seat and settle in for the brief ride to Joht. Tanglor stops at the door to say goodbye to his parents one last time.

---

[1] Ashar and Tanglor are fifteen. No one over the age of eighteen gets selected to train for the Elites. - *Inevsah Rensul, Johthun Historian*

"Thank you for everything you've done for us. We will see you again."

His parents try but fail to hold back their tears as they wave him goodbye. As he walks in, the doors snap shut behind him. The shuttle starts to rattle and screech, slowly taking off. After a couple of seconds, it blasts off into the sky, breaking through the atmosphere and out into space. Around this time, the recruits realize that they have not seen a single crew member. A voice comes over the intercom.

"Hello recruits, my name is Leazara Luns. I am currently the Colonel of the Elite Protectors; you will be assigned to your trainer when you arrive on Joht. Graduation will be in three days. You are now part of the prestigious Elite Protector program. Whatever you think you know about us is wrong, forget about the history and recruiting you've heard about in the past. We enlist Johthuns based on three criteria: Those who have had their struggles and hardships, those we think we can trust, and finally, we choose based on who we think is strong enough to make it through our Elite trials. Prepare yourselves for the hardest three days of your lives. Your bodies, minds, hearts, and souls will be pushed in these tests. The Elites only take the best of the best. See you soon."

The recruits listen in awe. It's clear how much they admire Leazara Luns. After all, she is one of the greatest soldiers in their history. She's been an Elite Protector since the very beginning. Her courage and fighting skills have gotten her out of tight situations where others perished. Tanglor looks over at Ashar.

"Ashar! Maybe we'll get the chance to spar with her! How cool would that be!?"

Ashar opens his mouth to respond but gets interrupted by a loud bang followed by a blaring alarm and the Colonel's voice.

"This is Colonel Luns, the piloting controls have taken damage from some debris outside. We have no way of controlling the shuttle now. The five of you need to figure out a way to get to Joht, or you will die. There is an escape pod, but it will only fit three of you. Hopefully, it doesn't come down to that."

The Colonel's voice disappears; the five recruits stare at each other in panicked silence. Finally, Tanglor speaks up.

"We just need to think. We have about thirty minutes before we're completely off course and lost. Let's get to the front of the shuttle to see if we can find anything. A couple of us should check out the escape pod and the other rooms."

Ashar gets out of his seat.

"I'll go and check out the other rooms on the shuttle. Ranyana want to come with me?"

She hesitantly smiles at Ashar before getting up and following him. The other two recruits are brothers. Freden, being the oldest, decides he should go and check out the escape pod while Tanglor and Dretzlin go to the front of the ship to look at the controls. Ashar and Ranyana, failing to find anything useful in the other rooms, rendezvous with them in the front of the vessel. Freden radios in from the escape pod.

"Guys, there's nothing in here. I'm heading back to you."

Once they've all regrouped, they pace back and forth—each trying to think of something to do. The time is ticking away, now only ten minutes remain before the ship goes entirely off track. Tanglor looks toward Freden.

"Did you notice how much power the escape pod had?"

"Yes, it was at full charge. Why?"

"Ashar, do you remember when we were playing that exploration game of ours back home?"

"Haha, you mean when we ran out of fuel, and we were drifting in space? Wait. Tanglor, that was make-believe. This is real! If it doesn't work, we're dead!"

"We're dead if we don't try anything!"

Ranyana butts in.

"How about the two of you fill us in? That way, we can decide as a group?"

Tanglor looks around at everyone.

"All right. Since we're drifting in space, we should launch the escape pod with three of us on it. Two of us will stay back to cut the power and work the pulley system on the front of the shuttle. We can use that to attach ourselves to the escape pod, and then it can tow us back to Joht. With the escape pod at full charge, it should be just enough to keep us on the correct path."

Freden is the first one to say something.

"I, for one, think this is a ridiculous idea. It's suicide! If three of us can use the escape pod to get off safely, then we should. I'm sorry, but letting two of us die, so three of us can get off is the best choice we have."

Tanglor gets in Freden's face.

"You need to stop thinking about yourself! Being an Elite protector is about thinking about everyone else; it's about protecting! I'm not letting any of us die today!"

Dretzlin gets between them and pushes his brother away.

"Tanglor's right, Freden! We can't just leave two people here to die when there's a chance for all of us to live."

Freden looks back at his brother and takes a deep breath.

"You're right. I'm sorry, everyone."

The five recruits work together quickly to ready the plan, only five minutes left before they lose full control. Everything is ready, but they still have to decide who gets on the escape pod. Worst case scenario, the three on the pod would still be able to detach from the shuttle and make it to Joht. Tanglor steps away from the other recruits.

"This was my plan, so I am going to see it through on the shuttle. My brother Ashar will stay back with me so that the three of you can travel safely."

"Yeah, that's right... wait, what?"

Ashar starts to walk toward him, but Freden steps forward.

"No, it's okay. Tanglor, in the short time I've known you, you have already shown me what it truly means to be an Elite. I misspoke earlier, and I want to make up for it now. Ashar, please go on the escape pod with Ranyana and take care of my brother."

Ashar nods his head, the three of them get onto the escape pod. Tanglor and Freden go and sit in the front of the ship. Once the pod is in front of them, they'll need to use the pulley system to latch on. The time is down to two minutes, as the pod comes flying from the right side of the ship. It slowly approaches the front as Ashar gets it lined up. Tanglor uses the controls from the shuttle and gets the pulley system connected. His plan seems to have worked; they're back on track heading to

Joht with the escape pod still at over half power. Tanglor cuts the power to the shuttle, wipes his sweaty brow, and lets the pod do the work.

As they get closer to Joht, the pressure from the atmosphere causes the pulley system to loosen. It swings and hits the power cells damaging them. From their position at the front of the ship, Tanglor and Freden watched it all happen. They open the communications to the escape pod.

"Ashar, can you hear me? The pulley system just destroyed part of your power cells! What is the charge at?"

"Yeah, I can hear you! The charge is at twenty-eight percent; there is no way we're going to make it to Joht now!"

"Don't worry! We'll figure something out."

Tanglor shuts off the communications and turns to Freden. Before he can say anything, Freden puts up a hand to stop him.

"I know what you're going to say... Both our brothers are on that escape pod. If us dying means they'll live...."

Tanglor nods his head and uses the controls on the shuttle to detach themselves from the escape pod. He puts his hand on Freden's shoulder. The two watch the others continue their way toward Joht while they start to drift the other direction slowly. Freden touches his hand to the window.

"Goodbye, brother."

# Chapter 2:
# Tralupians- Traditions

A stormy night brings havoc to a palace on a hillside, shaking its windows while thunder roars through its halls. Hooded figures gather around inside its chamber where a ceremony is taking place. The palace sits on a lush planet called TokBellu, where there is more water than land. Trees grow out of the water, reaching so high into the sky; it seems they almost touch the clouds. Creatures walk and swim around the planet; their skin is smooth with no fur. Their arms and legs end in webbed hands and feet. They have long tails with three fins attached to the end—like blades that function as a propeller in the water. Their eyes have two pupils each, and they have a slit on the sides of their necks that allow them to breathe underwater. These creatures call themselves Tralupians. The storm continues to rattle the palace around as Tralupians enter the chamber. All of them walk in, taking off their hoods, before gathering around an elderly Queen on her deathbed. A trident and crown rest on the edge of the cushion next to her. The old Queen sits up, exerting some of her precious remaining energy, and addresses the creatures surrounding her.

"Thank you for coming to the palace today. As you can all see, my time is running short. I only have a small amount of life left before I pass and become one with the RoyalTree."

One of the Tralupians steps forward and sits next to her on the bed.

"Mother, we are all here to watch you pass over to the next life, to join our ancestors in the water, and to grow high into the sky with the RoyalTree."

All the others in the chamber look to their Queen and Princess. The Princess stands up, raising her mother's hand into the air.

"Queen Zelena, my mother, has been a great leader to our people. We gather here today to guide her into our ocean, where she can continue to lead our people from the trees that grow into the sky. Joined with our past leaders, she will evermore watch over us."

The Tralupians fall to their knees, bowing to their Queen. She stands up with the help of her daughter and stumbles up the stairs exiting the chamber. Queen Zelena gets to the top and walks out of the palace, standing at the ledge overlooking the water. Before them stands the tallest tree on TokBellu—RoyalTree. It grows proudly in front of the palace. The others follow behind their Queen, showing their support until the very end. Queen Zelena stands up as straight as possible, looking out at all her people assembled in front of RoyalTree. She sways back and forth in the storm as it rages on, yelling to her people.

"My people, I am sorry that I have to leave you now, and I am sorry that I lost our ways toward the end of my reign. Our army isn't nearly as big or powerful as it was when I took over for my father, but I can assure you that my daughter Zuna will lead us back to that! We will be stronger and more united with her as Queen. She won't lose our ways like I did."

Queen Zelena slowly walks to the edge of the palace ground and looks over the ledge. The giant RoyalTree sits in the water beneath her, its roots twisting into the soil. Zuna walks over to stand beside her and places her hand on her mother's back.

"It's time, mother..."

The Queen turns back around to face her daughter. She takes the crown off her weary head and passes it over to Zuna along with the trident.

"Take this crown and Zembor's Trident; you are the leader of our people now... Lead them to greatness Queen Zuna."

Zuna puts the crown on her head and takes the trident. She holds it up in front of her, basking in its glory. Suddenly, her face turns grave. She thrusts the trident into her mother's gut. Green blood gushes out of Zelena onto it as a flash of Orange light shoots out from Zembor's blade absorbing the blood. Queen Zuna pulls out the trident and drops it, watching her mother stumble backward with her hands on the wound. She gets to the ledge and falls over. Queen Zuna and the other Tralupians rush to the ledge and look down; they see her body splash into the water next to RoyalTree. The water begins to cover her while she stares up at them. She reaches up toward her daughter. Zuna reaches back down to her while the roots from RoyalTree wrap around and pull her under. Zuna stands up and wipes away her tears.

"She is one with RoyalTree now."

Zuna turns around and looks to her people, the trident lying on the ground next to her. She reaches down and grabs it, lifting it above her.

"I, Queen Zuna, promise to bring us back to glory. I swear to all of you that I won't lose the ways of our people like my mother did. I am going to prove to you all that I am a true Wrathfin!"

She thrusts the trident up and down in the air. The Tralupians surround her, cheering for their new Queen while the storm above them rages on. The new Queen walks back into the palace to sit down on her throne and wait for her mother's advisors. After a couple of minutes, two Tralupians walk in. They wear long robes; one is a male named Defunis, and the other is a female named Serel. Her mother's advisors have been around for hundreds of years, advising Zelena and Tez before her. Defunis and Serel both bow to their Queen before speaking.

"Ah Queen Zuna, it is good to see you on the throne."

"Thank you, Defunis, it is good to see you and Serel are still alive and well."

Serel steps forward.

"My Queen, what will be your first order of business as our new leader? There are a couple of different issues we need to address."

"I am aware! Things are going back to how they were when my grandfather was our King. I love my mother and always will, but she wasn't fit to lead our people. My first order of business will be to get all our people training and fighting again. They've gotten lazy, and it's unacceptable!"

Serel stands tall in front of the Queen.

"I agree with you, my Queen."

She clears her throat.

"The Flutinas are eager to speak with you about the crown now that your mother has passed."

Queen Zuna sits forward on the throne.

"The Flutinas? They're the noble family that my mother was supposed to get rid of so that we didn't have to continue dealing with this topic. I will speak to them."

Serel and Defunis bow to the Queen before opening the doors to her throne room. Two Tralupians walk in and stand next to each other. They bow before speaking.

"My name is Tranjora Flutina; this is my wife, Yongrea Flutina. Our family has been next in line for the throne for generations. We have been loyal followers to the Wrathfin family in hopes of working together to one day share the crown. We spoke with your mother many times about it, and, unlike the previous rulers, she listened to us and was considering the idea. Now that she has passed, we want to share the same idea with you. We know you have other things on your mind, so just know that the Flutinas still stand with you and your family."

The Flutinas both bow once more; the Queen stands up and bows back to them.

"Thank you for coming to speak to me. I appreciate your loyalty to the crown and my family. I will think about your proposal, but right now I have other matters that I must attend to."

The Flutinas take their leave and walk out of the throne room. Zuna sits back down while Defunis and Serel continue to talk.

"My Queen, we also have a few things to show you. Your mother kept these hidden since she didn't want to alarm the public with some of this knowledge."

The Queen, intrigued by this, sits up in her seat again.

"Bring them to me; I want to see what my mother was hiding."

Defunis walks over to her with a towering stack of papers. She grabs several sheets from the top and starts skimming them. Maps, star charts, and weird-looking creatures jump out from the pages.

"What is all this? Where did it come from?"

"They have been passed down to all of our Kings and Queens ever since Tez decided our history needed to be written down. He released our general history in the libraries but removed this to keep the people from knowing and panicking. Anyway, he passed the information down to your mother, and now it goes to you. You will do the same with any children you have. The same thing goes with Zembor's Trident. You probably noticed the orange flash that absorbed her blood. That was her becoming one with the trident and RoyalTree."

"I can't believe my mother never told me any of this. What else didn't she tell me?"

Defunis and Serel exchange glances.

"Your mother had an older brother. She never mentioned him because they didn't get along very well."

Zuna stands up with the documents in her hands. She walks toward Defunis while reading through it all.

"My mother had a brother? I remember her mentioning something about someone named Zirk in her stories about Grandpa Tez. But she never said anything about a brother. She told me that Grandpa had to choose between her and another contender for the crown. She didn't say who it was, though. How come he chose her over this uncle of mine?"

Defunis reaches over and grabs one of the sheets containing the information about her family history.

"It was a tough choice for Tez, but ultimately your mother, who was eight years younger than Zirk, won your Grandpa's heart over. Not only that, but she was also just as skilled as Zirk was in combat, and she was smarter than him. Zirk didn't take it well. He left before your mother could finish the passing ceremony. He wasn't seen again for fifty years, but that is a story for another time."

Queen Zuna stares at him, wide-eyed and intrigued.

"Wait, I want to hear more about my uncle and mother!"

"I am sorry, my Queen, but we need to stay on track."

He reaches back into the pile of informative papers.

"Ahh, here is the one I was looking for. Zembor's staff! Here is how the trident was created. Your greatest ancestor, Zembor Wrathfin, the first leader of our people! His staff started as just a normal blade when he lost his arm in an attack from the Ventrians. Zembor was one of the first Tralupians to scout TokBellu. He and his team were ambushed by the Ventrians in 1555, sparking the long war with them. After losing his arm, some of our scientists developed a prosthetic blade to replace it. He used it as his signature weapon when leading the Tralupians into battle. Eventually, he was killed by the Ventrians in 1785, but his arm blade was saved and turned into a staff, then a trident, Zembor's Trident. It is passed down from our leaders to not only show us who is in charge but also to keep our past leaders with us. It is said that their knowledge and part of their soul is stored within the trident."

Queen Zuna lifts the trident up and carefully examines it as he talks; she starts to swing it in front of her jabbing the air.

"I like the feel of it."

Defunis laughs while watching her.

"That is all for tonight. You should get some rest. You have a big day tomorrow now that you're the Queen. Serel and I have hundreds of stories that have been passed down and kept secret. We can tell them to you anytime."

Queen Zuna stops and stares at the papers.

"What about this one? I want to know what happened to Tez's brothers and sisters. Mother told me that Grandpa was the youngest out of his five siblings. There are reports about an orange planet too, what happened to them?"

Serel walks over and hastily bundles the papers into her arms.

"We can go over more tomorrow, but now is the time for sleep. Our Queen can't be tired when she gets introduced to her people!"

Queen Zuna stands up off the throne, nodding her head. She walks down the stairs to her chambers to get some rest. Still, in the throne room, Defunis approaches Serel.

"Do you think she'll be able to do it? She is only fifty."

"Our Kings and Queens always start young, but fifty is a little younger than normal. With that being said, I think she will be all right. As long as she continues to let us advise her."

"She is more suited for this than her mother was. Watching her grow up these past fifty years, Zuna is short-tempered and has a side to her that is unsettling."

"I know what you mean, Defunis, but there is nothing we can do except help her. Her mother made the mistake of allowing the Flutinas to come and talk about the crown. They want it for themselves and always have."

"The Flutinas are cunning when it comes to trying to obtain the crown. Keep your eyes and ears open. Rumors run wild around the palace."

They nod their heads to each other before going their separate ways. Queen Zuna lays down in her new bed, the bed that used to belong to her mother. She closes her eyes and thinks over the events of the day. She tosses and turns, plagued by nightmares. Visions of stabbing her mother with the trident and watching her fall into the water, making a splash, replay on a loop. Zuna's eyes open wide; she sits up in her bed. She looks around in a panic before her breathing slows. She gets out of bed and walks back to the throne room. As she walks through the door, she sees Tranjora Flutina sitting on her throne.

"Hey! What do you think you're doing!?"

Tranjora doesn't move. Slowly, he looks up at her, his eyes glowing orange. He stares at her and mumbles in a language she doesn't recognize. Zuna gradually approaches him. As she gets close, she reaches her hand out to touch him.

"Tranjora? Are you all right?"

"Trabah......... Tra....... Urlonk...... Ur. Tra.... Ur...."

As she places her hand on his shoulder, he jumps up out of the throne and grabs her arms, clenching tightly. His eyes are bright orange as he gets close and screams at her.

"Ahhhhh! They're going to come and take everything from you! Our people, your daughter, everything will be lost!! TokBellu will be in ruins! And their black eyes, nothing but darkness!!!"

Queen Zuna stands in shock, staring into Tranjora's eyes as he shakes her and continues to scream. Finally, Serel comes running into the throne room.

"What's going on here? Queen Zuna!!!"

She runs over and strikes Tranjora on the back of the head. He releases his grip on the Queen and stumbles forward to the ground. He takes a couple of deep breaths before looking up at them, the orange in his eyes fading away.

"What... what's going on? How did I get into the palace throne room?"

Zuna and Serel look at him with disbelief.

"You can't remember?"

"Remember what? I was asleep in my bed with my wife, and then I woke up here with you two staring at me!"

Queen Zuna walks over to him.

"I woke up, and you were sitting on the throne, muttering some unknown language. Your eyes were solid orange. When I tried speaking to you, you jumped up and grabbed me. You screamed at me about losing everything, losing TokBellu and my daughter…. Does that mean anything to you?"

Tranjora puts his hands on his head and starts to rub them around.

"A thousand pardons, my Queen, I don't know anything about that and have no idea why or how I ended up here."

He bows down to Zuna.

"I beg you, forgive me for my behavior."

Zuna lifts him off the ground and asks Serel to escort him off the palace grounds. She walks up the stairs to the throne and sits down, staring off into the dimly lit room, thinking about Tranjora and the words he spoke to her. She closes her eyes for a second and sees his orange eyes staring at her.

"They're going to come and take everything from you! Our people, your daughter, everything will be lost!! TokBellu will be in ruins! And their black eyes, nothing but darkness!!!"

Her eyes open back up in a panic. She takes a deep breath and walks out of the throne room.

# Chapter 3:
# <u>Johthuns- Welcome to Joht</u>

Tanglor and Freden sit in the dark shuttle drifting away from Joht. They watch as the escape pod passes through the atmosphere, Freden's hand still pressed to the window.

"They made it."

Tanglor turns to him.

"Both of our brothers will live on and honor us."

Freden understands the magnitude of their sacrifice and feels at peace with his choice. The two of them sit in silence, accepting their fate. Out of nowhere, the ship turns back on. Freden stands up.

"Didn't you cut the power? How did it just turn back on?"

"Yeah, there's no way."

Colonel Luns voice comes onto the intercom and fills the room.

"Congratulations, boys. You have completed your first test. The ship's autopilot has reactivated; we will see you shortly on Joht."

The intercom shuts off, and the shuttle makes its way toward the planet. Tanglor and Freden heave simultaneous sighs of relief and sit back down while they enter the atmosphere. Freden looks over to Tanglor.

"I don't know if I should be upset or happy about what just happened."

Tanglor laughs.

"Let's just be happy that we're still alive."

They both relax back in their chairs while the shuttle lands on Joht. The doors open, they are immediately welcomed by Ranyana and their brothers.

"Tanglor!"

Ashar stops and shakes his head before Tanglor hugs him.

"I'm glad to see you, too, Ashar."

Ranyana jumps forward.

"It doesn't matter that it was a test. You two saved us. Thank you."

The five of them exit the shuttle to a sight none of them had seen before. Black, brown, and gray fur cover the different sized Johthuns here, some of their tails are missing from loss in battle. They still wear metallic black goggles to help them see through the light, but their clothes vary depending on what rank they are. They wear anything from cloth pants and shirts to leather and metallic armor.

The recruits are swiftly escorted towards the Colonel, staring as they pass by all the different Johthuns. A group of Elite Protectors walks past them; they are in awe at what they see. The Elites wear trench coats or small capes and have bands around their arms and legs to carry their equipment. They carry blasters, blades, and staves that they use for lethal and non-lethal attacks. The recruits step aside and watch them pass, while the Colonel approaches behind them.

"There are my recruits! Follow me to the Parasav, our underground training facility. We aren't going to waste any time. Great job on passing your first test on the shuttle. I was impressed with how you handled yourselves."

The recruits salute the Colonel and bow; they then proceed to follow her to the Parasav, passing through the city of Joht with its massive buildings towering over them. The recruits get distracted, observing the city life of Joht before the Colonel reminds them to keep walking. They get through the city and arrive at a large, open dirt area. The Colonel turns around and smiles at them before she looks back toward the empty land. She pulls out a small, shiny, oval-shaped object with no writing on it; it's not Johthun technology. She presses the gleaming oval; it lights up, emitting a bright teal color. It instantly reminds Tanglor of his dream and the creature's bright Teal eyes. He shakes his head, attempting to dismiss the thought, and watches as the empty land starts to rumble. Abruptly, a small building erupts from the ground. A door opens, and the Colonel walks in.

"Follow me. This way leads down to the training facility."

The five recruits stand watching, four of them glancing at Tanglor for direction. He looks at them and nods his head with confidence. They follow him inside, and the door shuts behind them, followed by a low rumbling. Suddenly, the building plummets into the ground before it comes to an abrupt halt. The doors open to a dim cavern, and the Colonel walks out, taking her goggles off.

"These are the caves our ancestors lived in before making it to the surface. This is where *we* started."

The recruits exit the room and hesitantly remove their goggles. It's the first time any of them remember having taken their goggles off. Thoonta is always bright, so they have to keep them on even when they sleep. Ranyana starts to laugh, and then she begins to cry.

"I'm sorry, I've never felt this before."

The Colonel lets them bask in the moment before asking them to continue following her. They walk behind her through the enormous underground facility. It seems to fill up almost the entirety of the old cave systems. They get towards the end; the Colonel stops and points to different doors.

"Please go into your rooms and change into the Elite uniforms laid out on your bed. Once you're all changed, we will go to the Great Hall for dinner, where you will learn the true history of the Elite Protectors."

As the recruits walk past the Colonel into their rooms, she stops Tanglor to talk to him.

"I saw what you did up there on the shuttle; I was quite impressed with how you took over. The others already seem to look to you as their leader. What was your name again?"

"My name is Tanglor Monite."

"Monite? Hmmm, what was your last name before the Monite family adopted you?"

"Umm, I don't remember. The foster home said they lost that information."

"I see. Get yourself cleaned up and change into your uniform. Once you're ready, we'll be waiting for you and the other recruits in the Great Hall."

Tanglor walks into his room, thinking over the conversation he just had.

"It almost seemed like she knew who I was...."

He gets interrupted by a loud bang on his door.

"Tanglor! Hurry up! We're hungry!"

"Yeah, yeah, Ashar. I'll be out in a sec, just let me get changed."

Tanglor gets changed into his new uniform. It's black with a blue stripe running diagonally across his chest to a blue cape draping over his right shoulder. He walks out of his room to find his friends waiting for him. As they start to walk to the Great Hall, Ashar pulls Tanglor off to the side.

"What took you so long to get ready? Felt like we were waiting forever for you."

"The Colonel stopped me after you guys got to your rooms. She complimented me on my performance on the shuttle and then asked what my last name was. It was kind of weird. I got the feeling that she already knew who I was."

"What do you mean? How would that even be possible?"

"I don't know, but let's just focus on dinner right now."

They arrive at the Great Hall; the Colonel walks over to escort them to their table in the center. Elite Protectors surround them, filling in the room. The table next to the recruits is where six Captains sit. On the other side, the Colonel sits alone. Everyone takes their seats, and the ceremony begins. Loud drums cause the room to shake, while the Elite Protectors stand up and gather around the three tables. The Elite Protectors stop and stand straight with their arms at their sides. The drums stop, and the Colonel stands up.

"You will now see the true history of the Elite Protectors. This is some raw footage Tazlow Raff left behind for us; this is all we have left from his recordings."

The recruits sit in silence, waiting for the footage to start.

A single Elite Protector emerges on the screen, looking into the camera.

"My name is Tazlow Raff; I am the founder and leader of the Elite Protectors. I'm making this video to ensure that the Elites never lose their ways. We are to protect every Johthun regardless of rank or past. We protect, no matter what! I made special blades, staves, and blasters that will do lethal and non-lethal damage. Our further training will provide you with the tools you need to use these weapons. You will be pushed beyond your limits. We are the best of the best, The Elite!"

Tazlow gets interrupted for a moment when a loud thud comes from the door behind him. It gets louder, but Tazlow continues to talk over it.

"Do not forget our ways! No matter what they try to do to us, we cannot forget who we truly are and what we can become!!"

The banging on the door grows louder before it comes crashing down behind him. He pulls both of his blades out and gets into a fighting stance. As he charges the door, one of his blades hits the camera causing the recording to stop. Tanglor sits up in his seat, he can't quite figure it out, but he recognizes the way Tazlow stood there with his blades. Ashar looks over to him.

"Tanglor, are you alright?"

Tanglor gives Ashar a concerned look.

"The Johthun in that video…. He looked like the one in my dreams."

Ashar looks around the room then back to Tanglor.

"The food is getting served; we can talk more tonight if you want."

Tanglor gets distracted by the Elite Protectors, bringing out massive plates with meat piled high on them.

"Ashar, what is that?"

Ashar stands out of his seat and looks with Tanglor at the copious amounts of meat.

"I don't know, but it smells amazing."

Ranyana laughs as she pulls Ashar back down into his seat.

"The meat is from an animal called supsue. They were originally discovered on the planet Conril, but after relocating some of them, they can now be found here on Joht too."

The Colonel walks over, smiling.

"For being from Thoonta, you sure know quite a bit about Joht. How do you know about the supsue? They have never been on your planet, and I believe it's illegal to smuggle any there."

Ranyana looks around at the other recruits before turning to the Colonel with a smile.

"Not only is it illegal, but you can be kicked off-world for smuggling it. My mother and father were some of the first to help with the relocation of the supsue. When I was born, they didn't want to raise me with them, so we moved to Thoonta away from it all."

The Colonel looks around to the other recruits as the supsue gets brought to their table.

"Ahh yes, the Xantlows were crucial to the discovery of the species, but I am sure your parents left out the fact that they were the ones that discovered Conril as well. Everyone eat! Don't be shy. There is no shortage of supsue or the delicious meat that comes off them."

The recruits all reach for the plate and take the meat from it. They all take a bite and look at each other with amazement. Tanglor turns to the Colonel.

"The flavor is phenomenal. How come it's illegal to bring it to Thoonta?"

Ranyana speaks before the Colonel can.

"The Elders can't regulate it from such a distance. Without them having a branch of the government on Thoonta, they can't properly tax and distribute it."

The Colonel stands up; her smile turns into a smirk.

"Your parents taught you well. Ranyana is right, but for reasons, you wouldn't understand. Finish your plates and clean up. "

She turns and walks back to the table in the middle of the room. A couple of seconds pass before she stands on top of it and looks to the recruits.

"Everything you saw is only the start of our real history. Tazlow Raff showed us how to be Elites, and he will show all of you too. Go back to your rooms and get some rest. Training will begin bright and early tomorrow!"

The Elite Protectors surrounding them move to the side, creating a path for the recruits. They get back to their separate rooms and say goodnight to each other. Tanglor tries to fall asleep, but after an hour of tossing and turning goes, he gets out of bed to wander around the Parasav. As he's leaving his room, he can hear giggling going on behind Ashar's door.

"Ranyana must've snuck in there. Hopefully, they don't get caught."

Tanglor walks past and heads to the Great Hall. He sees Colonel Luns sitting by herself at the center table.

"What are you doing, Colonel?"

"Please, when we're alone, call me Leazara. I couldn't sleep. What are you doing, Tanglor?"

"I couldn't sleep either."

"Nightmare?"

"Yeah, something like that? Hey Leazara, can I ask you a question?"

"Certainly."

"Do you know who I am?"

"Of course, I know who all of my recruits are."

"I know that, but it's a different feeling. I don't know anything about my birth parents or even who they were. I don't know; maybe I'm just looking for answers."

Leazara stands up and puts her arm around Tanglor.

"I know you just like I know all of the other recruits Tanglor. I'm sure you'll get some answers soon enough. Now get back to your room and get some sleep. Tomorrow isn't going to be easy."

Tanglor notices Leazara's nervous look, but instead of asking her more, he leaves the Great Hall. Tanglor gets back into bed and falls right into his ordinary dream. Except for this time, after the Elite Protector kicks the downed Johthun the second time, the dream continues, and the Elite stops fighting to look up at Tanglor.

"Tanglor! Talk to Leazara. She can tell you who you are!"

The injured Johthun grabs a blade next to him and pierces it through the Elite. He gets up off the ground and drives the edge down into his chest.

"You think you're a hero saving the elders and your family, but they are doomed just like the rest of the Johthuns. All of their lives end here with yours, Tazlow Raff."

The ship explodes, and Tanglor wakes up. Starting to panic, he takes some deep breaths to calm down. It's time for him to get ready for the next Elite Protector test.

The recruits walk back down to the Great Hall to meet their trainer. The Captains and the Colonel greet them. The Colonel steps forward.

"I've taken great interest in the five of you, so I have decided that I will be your trainer. I will personally make sure that all of you have the proper skills to become Elite Protectors. Follow me to the simulation room."

The recruits try to contain their excitement as they follow behind the Colonel. As they are walking, Tanglor pulls Ashar aside.

"Ashar, the Elite Protector in my dream, its Tazlow Raff. He talked to me last night."

"What? What did he say?"

"He told me to talk to Leazara. He said she knows who I am."

"You're going to have to talk to her then."

"I tried last night, but it seems like she's hiding something from me."

Before they could finish talking, they arrive at the simulation room. Leazara waits outside while they go in, the door shuts behind them. The Colonel walks over to the window and speaks to them over the intercom.

"When I start the simulation, the five of you will be sent into different virtual realities. It's random so that you could be sent into one by yourself or with anyone else in the room. The simulation will be in complete control. The only way out is to finish what it wants you to. Good luck."

The Colonel starts the simulation, sending the room into complete darkness. A faint light starts to return, Tanglor finds himself standing with Ranyana and Ashar. The room has turned into a massive ship floating on an ocean of water with several strange-looking creatures wandering around. They have dark grey skin and long blonde hair covering their faces. The three recruits watch in confusion as the creatures run around with sharp metal blades, killing each other for control of the ship. Suddenly, they stop and slowly turn, noticing the three recruits. Their faces start to warp, and spikes begin to form all over their bodies. The beasts charge at them. Tanglor pulls Ashar and Ranyana down underneath the deck of the ship into a room, shutting the door behind them.

"We need to find some weapons to fight back with. I'm not sure what the simulation wants from us, but I'm pretty sure we aren't supposed to die in here."

Ranyana points to a wall behind them.

"Look, Tanglor! We can use some of their weapons against them!"

They turn around to discover an armory with a variety of weapons. Tanglor takes a blade for each hand, Ashar takes a double-sided sword, while Ranyana grabs a handful of small knives.

Tanglor steps forward with his swords in hand.

"All right, let's take these monsters out and gain control of the ship! Let's show the Colonel what we're capable of!"

Ashar and Ranyana follow behind weapons at the ready. Tanglor kicks the door down and slices his blades through one of the beasts. The wound opens, but no blood comes out. After a few seconds, it vanishes. Without questioning it, the three of them continue to fight their way through the horde. They make it to the top of the ship, where the fighting is most intense. One of the monsters knocks Ashar over and uses its sharp claws to slice his face. Ranyana sees him go down and throws her knives into its back. It vanishes, leaving Ashar on the ground. She walks over and helps him up.

He smiles.

"Thanks, but I had him."

They laugh and continue to fight until all the monsters have disappeared. The three of them stand on the ship, not sure what to do next. Ranyana finds a steering wheel that controls the empty vessel, while Tanglor and Ashar investigate below deck. As they look for answers, they hear Ranyana yelling.

"Guys! You need to get up here quick!"

The two of them run back to the top deck and Ranyana motions to the sky. They look up to see a significant, dark figure forming above them. It begins to rumble and flash. Massive blasts of light start to appear before striking the open ocean around them. The dark mass rains water on them while continuing to rumble and shake. The bursts of light gain speed, and gusts of wind start smashing into them, making it hard to see. Tanglor and Ashar run over to the steering wheel where Ranyana is. More of the creatures emerge from the water, climbing up the ship.

"Ranyana! Do the best you can to get us away from that terror in the sky! Ashar and I need to fight off the rest of these monsters!"

They stand ready to fight as the monsters climb out from the water onto the ship. Hundreds of them fill the deck and start charging at the three of them. Rain continues to pour out of the sky with huge gusts of wind blowing them around. The huge bursts of light continue to strike around them, while the dark figure roars, causing everything to shake. Ranyana sees a light in front of them, shooting up from an enormous hole in the water. She has no choice but to go for it.

"Brace yourselves! We are about to go for a ride!"

Tanglor and Ashar continue to battle the monsters away from Ranyana, while she steers the ship towards the giant hole. As they are getting close, a blast of light hits the ship throwing it off course. One of the monsters pushes Ranyana to the side and grabs the wheel steering the boat away from the opening. A few of the monsters corner Ashar and Tanglor jumping on top of them. Never giving up, Tanglor stabs his blades through the monsters on top of him. He gets up and runs to Ashar and slices through the ones on top of him. He turns to Ranyana and throws his first blade at the monster standing over her at the wheel, piercing it in the head. The ship steers back toward the opening in the water. Tanglor grabs his second blade and throws it at the steering wheel, locking it in place.

"It's going to seem crazy, but we don't have any more time! Follow me!"

Tanglor runs to the edge of the ship and jumps off as it passes the opening. Ashar and Ranyana blindly follow and jump in with him. The opening they jumped through closes behind them as they free-fall down the hole. Light starts to surround them, getting brighter before they're blinded. Suddenly they hit the ground, the light dims. They are back in the simulation room with the Colonel watching them through the window. They turn back around and notice Dretzlin standing there by himself. The door to the simulation room opens, the Colonel walks in.

"Congratulations, you all passed. The simulation put you into extreme situations to see how you would react."

She pauses and looks at Dretzlin.

"I am sorry about your brother. If it weren't for him, you wouldn't have made it out alive. Be grateful and know he would want you to continue moving forward."

Dretzlin shakes his head, and the recruits head back to their rooms. They all follow close behind him, wondering what happened to Freden in the simulation. They get to their rooms, and Tanglor stops Dretzlin.

"Hey, hold up! I don't know what happened in there, but if you need anything, we are all here for you."

Dretzlin has a worried look on his face while walking into his room. He doesn't say a word as he shuts the door behind him, leaving the other recruits looking nervous. Tomorrow is the last day of training before graduation. Tanglor looks over to Ashar and Ranyana.

"We need to be ready for tomorrow, but we can't leave Dretzlin like this. You guys go back to your bunks. I'll stay here to make sure he's okay."

Ashar puts his arm around Ranyana.

"Good idea. I'll come back later to check on you and Dretzlin. Try to get some rest too, Tanglor."

The two of them walk back to their quarters. Tanglor sits outside of Dretzlin's room, falling asleep with the back of his head resting on the door.

# Chapter 4:
# <u>Tralupian- The Queen's Law</u>

The sun shimmers across the ocean on TokBellu, reflecting through the palace windows. Queen Zuna is awakened by the light shining through her curtains.

"No time to waste!"

She jumps out of bed to choose her outfit for the day: brown leggings, a blue robe, and her crown. After placing the crown on her head, she grabs Zembor's Trident and walks out to the throne room. Defunis and Serel are waiting by the throne. She sits down, and Serel steps forward.

"My Queen, we have much to do today. First, we'll begin with the people welcoming you onto the throne. After the celebrations, we desperately need to discuss what to do with the people themselves. Our population has been growing for years now, and your mother refused to help and instead had fifteen children. Sorry to say, but you are the only one that amounted to anything."

Zuna interrupts her.

"I agree with you, but don't you dare speak ill of my family members! I don't care how worthless they are. I have a plan for my siblings, and any other Tralupians cast out of their families."

"What will you have us do?"

"I am implementing a new law starting immediately! Any Tralupian cast out of their family must report to the barracks or *die.* Families that have more than one child will have to put them through a series of tests to decide who is most suitable to live with them. Once you have a decision, the ones who fail will live in the barracks. My siblings will finally have something to do, as they will run and maintain the barracks—training, feeding, and cleaning the infantry that will serve in my army."

Defunis stands next to Serel.

"We will put the law into effect right away. What would you have us do to those who may oppose this new decree?"

"Have the soldiers kill anyone that refuses right away. We need to show them the kind of leader I am; some may need encouragement to listen."

Defunis and Serel both bow. Defunis leaves the throne room to meet with the army about the new orders, while Serel walks over to the Queen.

"We need to get you ready for the people."

Zuna follows Serel back to her chambers. Serel takes her to the closet and pulls out a bright red dress with sparkling rubies on it.

"Here, your mother wore this when she was welcomed as our Queen."

Zuna stares at it for a couple of seconds before grabbing it.

"It's too long. My mother was always a bit of a prude."

She whips around her tail and strikes the end of the dress. The fins on the end of her tail slice the bottom off, making it shorter.

"There, that's much better!"

Zuna puts the dress on and stands proudly. Serel smiles at her.

"You look marvelous, Your Grace. Come now, the people are waiting for you."

The two of them walk out of the palace to the ledge overlooking RoyalTree. They stop and turn around, Serel steps next to Defunis. They look out at the kneeling Tralupians surrounding the Queen; she stands with Zembor's Trident and the crown. The crowd stands up and starts cheering for their Queen as she steps forward.

"Thank you all for welcoming me and accepting me as your Queen. I have decided that I will not rule as my mother did. She was too lenient. I intend to lead with strength and an iron fist. No one will break the laws that I set in motion without suffering the consequences."

Zuna lifts her trident next to her and walks through the crowd of Tralupians back to the palace. She gets to the stairs and walks up to sit on her throne.

"The first decree will be enacted immediately! Defunis will explain it, as the soldiers begin enforcing it."

She sits down with Defunis and Serel standing next to her.

"As you all know, our planet has grown smaller as our population continues to grow larger. Queen Zuna has reopened the barracks, any families with more than one child will have to put their children through eight tests to decide who will stay home with them. The tests are only to be given to children aged seven and older, once your child turns seven, they must compete against whatever sibling previously won, if there is one. These eight tests will determine your children's willpower, strength, intelligence, intuition, hand-to-hand combat, leadership, weapon skills, and politics. The children who lose will be relocated to the barracks to live out their lives as infantry for the army. Your children will be allowed to visit home, and you can visit them. The punishment for refusing to participate is death. If your children don't report to the barracks after they lose, they'll be hunted down and imprisoned. I advise you to take your children home now; the tests will begin immediately."

All the Tralupians look at each other in silent confusion. Whispers start going through the crowd.

"Is she being serious?"

"She can't be..."

"That's crazy; she can't."

The Queen stands up from her throne and smashes the butt end of her trident onto the ground.

"I suggest you do what my adviser says before I change my mind on even opening the barracks."

Zuna stares into the crowd with a crazed look in her eyes. The crowd gradually starts to leave the palace, looking over their shoulders. Her soldiers follow them back to their homes and commence the tests. Hours pass while the trials continue until the silence is broken by a mother screaming for her child. One of the Queen's soldiers has taken the first child to the barracks, while the mother follows behind yelling at him.

"You can't take her away from me!! Please, this isn't fair!"

She reaches out and grabs the soldier. He turns around and pulls out his blade.

"Stay back, or I'll be forced to kill you."

The mother doesn't hesitate and grabs the soldier again.

"Please! Show some mer—"

The soldier drives his blade into the mother's chest; she falls to the ground. Other Tralupians see what has happened and panic, rushing around knocking into the soldiers and grabbing their kids. The soldiers fight back, slaughtering the innocent civilians as they try to protect their children. They ransack homes and rip the young away from their parents, killing those who stand in their way. After the massacre, deemed the Queen's Law, those left stopped resisting the soldiers and let their children get taken away. The barracks fill up with children from the ages of seven to seventeen, while the Queen sits comfortably on her throne, a smile on her face.

"Serel, go and find my brothers and sisters. Who knows where those insignificant Tralupians are."

She bows to the Queen and walks off to find the siblings. Defunis stands next to her waiting for her orders.

"Defunis, I think... I think I'm in over my head. I want to look strong and fierce in front of our people, but I don't know if I can keep it up."

He turns to her and grabs her hand.

"My Queen, you must be, or else the people will tear you apart. Serel and I are here to help you in any way we can, but you must stay strong and keep up what you're doing, whether it's an act or not. Our people need guidance, and they don't listen to reason, they listen to force!"

Zuna wipes away her tears and sits upon the throne.

"You're right. Go and help Serel find my siblings. I need them for the barracks."

Defunis lets the Queen's hand go and leaves the throne room. Zuna, tired of waiting for their return, finds the stack of papers with their secret history. She flips through the documents, looking for the story about the orange planet. As she shuffles through the pages, one falls out. She reaches down and picks it up. It reads...

*Zirk and Zelena Wrathfin- 2180.*

30

Zirk, 24, was the lead candidate set to graduate at the top of his class. He had friends who loved him and would follow him anywhere. As the year progressed, his younger sister, Zelena, beat all his previous records and moved up through every class. She was now in his, and he had to do everything he could not to let her beat him. She had no idea how he felt and thought it was always a friendly competition, but deep down, Zirk hated the fact that she was just as good as him, if not better. The year continued with both excelling, showing great leadership and skills to be the next leader. Zirk's hatred grew when the two of them were named top of their class together. He couldn't stand it, but he wouldn't say anything. He figured he would become the next King since he was eight years older than Zelena. He waited, and finally, the time came. The year was 2200, their father, Tez, had grown very ill. He was to appoint a new leader during the upcoming ceremony in front of RoyalTree. Zelena and Zirk both prepared to receive the crown and trident. They wished each other luck and gave one another a hug. Zirk meant none of it. He only cared about earning the crown and trident for himself. As his father spoke his last words, the decree was finally announced.

"Our next Queen is Zelena Wrathfin."

Zirk stood in shock for a moment before storming away from the ceremony and out of the city. Zelena would continue the tradition taking the crown and stabbing her father with Zembor's Trident. Zelena successfully leads her people, maintaining their army, and continuing the exploration of TokBellu. After fifty years had passed, Zirk finally resurfaced. He had been plotting to come back and steal the throne from Zelena. He gathered a small army and marched on the outskirts of the city where Zelena met him and agreed to a battle to the death. They both choose the trident for their weapon, as expected of Tralupians Kings and Queens. Their people circled them, eager to watch the battle. With their tridents drawn, they charged at each other. Zirk leaped into the air while Zelena slid on the ground, one swinging and the other blocking. They continued fighting for hours, countering everything the other did. The battle was endless; the crowd grew tired. Zirk and Zelena stopped and decided to split their father's land equally. Zirk would stay on his half with his people while Zelena did the same. They would interact only when they needed to. One hundred years went by as the two sides pretended to be peaceful while plotting against each other. Zelena continued to build up her army, hoping to take her brother out with ease, while Zirk took a different route. He had his scientists developing a serum that would let them live past the current lifespan of 300 to the age of 500. Zirk would outlive his sister and her army, watching them rot away. He spent the next ten years hiding his secret and testing it on his people. Hundreds died during the tests before it was finally mastered. Zirk and his scientists were thrilled by their achievement and gathered up their people. They began injecting all of them with the serum increasing their life spans by 200 years.

The procedure took a few hours, distracting Zirk's scientists and causing them not to pay attention to Zelena and her people. Zelena ambushed them and murdered Zirk's people with no hesitation. But, she momentarily spared Zirk's life. Waiting to kill him until he told her *how he made the serum. After realizing what he did, he begged for his life, but Zelena had no further use for him. She stabbed her trident through his neck, leaving him to die on the ground slowly. She went on to create more of the serum and dispersed it out to her people and any of her brother's people that promised loyalty to her. She continued to rule with success for another 100 years until she slowly lost her mind, and the people suffered for it. After she killed her brother, she lived with the guilt of her horrible actions. She wouldn't tell anyone, but it ate her up inside. Zelena loved her older brother, and she hated the fact that he deserted her because her father chose her instead of him. She spoke to her advisers in secrecy, saying that she would have done things differently if he stuck around, but she never got the chance to tell him that. One hundred years went by with her staying healthy, then one day, she snapped and realized she had no children to take over the throne once she passed. Her focus switched from leading her people to having children that would be great Tralupians. There were rumors of her obsessing about an Orange planet that lead to her going mad toward the end of her reign. She forced Tralupian men to come to the palace to try and sire her children, and after years of doing so, she finally succeeded with a Tralupian named Za-Ryan. She would watch some of her children struggle to live in this world; she claimed that the orange planet was to blame for messing with her head and telling her things she didn't want to hear. She would yell to herself when no one was there.*

*"Lies!! Stop lying to me!"*

*Her advisers could only watch with nothing to do other than accept what was happening. After years of seeing their Queen go mad, they decided to tell her about the orange planet's existence and that it was more than just a world. Her advisers told her the story about her aunt and uncle, Zeph and Zaren. They learned of the orange planet from their older sister Hetra, who discovered it while she was out exploring and scouting the planets around TokBellu. After years went by, Zeph and Zaren finally had the resources and time to send scouts to the orange world. There was a violent storm that surrounded it, keeping it safe from any outsiders that tried to get on. When the scouts came back, they had information stating that the storm had finally stopped after hundreds of years and that the planet was covered in orange sand with wind gusts blasting the rocks and caves on the surface. The information they gave to Zelena calmed her mind, finally knowing it was real, but the obsession was still there. She had to understand why she was getting these visions. She had to figure it all out before she passed. "*

Queen Zuna puts the papers down and thinks about the details of the story.

"Why did mother never tell me about any of this? Was she trying to protect me? I wonder if the planet has anything to do with what Tranjora said."

She continues to sit and ponder about it until Defunis and Serel walk into the throne room with four of her siblings.

"I just happened to finish the story about my mother and her brother. It was fascinating. I understand why my mother wouldn't want to talk about Uncle Zirk, but I can't figure out why she wouldn't mention anything about that Orange planet to me, though. Where are the rest of my brothers and sisters?"

She steps down and walks over to her two brothers and two sisters standing in front of her.

"Oryuna? Where are our other sisters?"

Oryuna steps forward.

"Sorry, my Queen, I haven't seen them since mother kicked us out. Ilikso, Musfina, and Siritano stayed with me after everything that happened."

"I see. Very well... I only need four of you to run the barracks. You will train all the recruits as well as feed them, clean them, and give them somewhere to sleep. I will reward you with a home here in the palace, as long as you keep to yourselves and run the barracks without any issues."

They all gratefully accept their sister's offer, then turn to leave and gather their belongings to bring back to the palace. Oryuna stops and turns around before leaving.

"My Queen, sister, we thank you."

She bows again before leaving the palace.

"We will be back with our things and then go straight to the barracks to get our recruits going."

Defunis and Serel walk over to the Queen, sitting in front of the stack of papers. Defunis grabs the stack.

"You said you read about Zirk and your mother? So, you read that your mother wasn't always that way after she had you and your siblings?"

Queen Zuna stands up and grabs the stack of papers back from him.

"I did, and I saw that she was an excellent warrior who led our people to greatness at one point. Uncle Zirk sounded like a lunatic who couldn't handle my mother being better than him."

"That's one way to put it, but your uncle Zirk wasn't always bad. The crown and trident became his obsession, much like your mother's obsession with the orange planet. I assume you read a little bit about that as well then?"

"I did…. I don't understand why my mother never told me about it."

"There is something strange about that planet, my Queen. Your grandfather tried to get Zeph and Zaren to forget about it after Hetra discovered it, but they were too smart for their own good. They couldn't handle knowing the planet was there, but not knowing what was on it. They worked non-stop, coming up with a tool that allowed them to see it from TokBellu. They would watch the storm circle around the planet for hours on end. Tez would get angry with them and try to stop them, but they were hooked. Eventually, they found the resources to set off toward the planet. They waited until after their scouts told them the storm had died down, allowing them to get on the surface. In the year 2150, Zeph and Zaren set out with some of Tez's best soldiers. The planet was on the edge of our solar system, so they knew it would take around seven years to get there. They set off, and seven years later, they reported in saying they had landed on the surface. After that day, we never heard from them again. Another seven years go by; they were supposed to have returned. Tez grew tired of waiting and sent his scouts to search for them. After years of searching for them, the scouts reported back, saying the storm had formed again, making it impossible to land on the planet's surface. On their way back to TokBellu, the scouts discovered parts of Zeph and Zaren's ship. It had been destroyed near our homeworld, but there was no sign of any sort of life. Your grandfather gave up hope and believed they were either dead or stuck on that Orange planet. He turned his attention to his children in the hopes of maybe hearing from his brother and sister again. But it never happened, to this day we still don't know what happened to Zeph and Zaren."

Queen Zuna sits on the throne listening to Defunis in awe.

"That's it? There is nothing else about the planet or about what happened to them? There has to be more!"

"I am sorry, Queen Zuna, but that is all of the information we have from the secrets your mother left behind. The planet is still out there, though. Come with me, and I will show you."

Zuna gets off the throne and follows Defunis to the palace's laboratory.

"This was Zeph and Zaren's lab. They rebuilt it after the war with the Ventrians. They also built this telescope to look out into the night sky. After enhancing it multiple times, they eventually got it to see deep into space and even further. Here, I have it all set up, so you can see the orange planet."

Zuna walks over to the massive telescope; the wall it faces starts to open. She sits down on the chair and positions her face down to look into the lens. It slides out of the open wall and points into the sky. Zuna can see the planets surrounding TokBellu; she uses the knob next to her and zooms in toward the orange world in the distance.

"There! I can see the orange planet! That storm from the story, it's circling the planet at a ridiculous speed! How do we know when the storm stops?"

Defunis walks over to her, sitting with the telescope.

"We still haven't been able to figure out the exact time, but it seems to stop every hundred years or so with it stopping the last time back in 2150. It started back up by 2175, maybe sooner, when Tez was searching for them. Based on those calculations, the storm will continue raging on for close to another hundred years."

Queen Zuna leans back.

"And when those hundred years go by, and that storm stops.... I'm going to find out what's on that planet; I'm going to find out the reason why it caused my mother to go mad and to find out what happened to Zeph and Zaren!"

Defunis smiles at her and puts his hand on her shoulder.

"That sounds like a good plan. We can go over more of it tomorrow if you'd like?"

Zuna looks over to Serel.

"If you'll be there to tell me the stories too?"

Serel smiles at her.

"Of course, my Queen. Now, let's get to bed."

Queen Zuna follows Serel to her chambers, Serel sits with her until she falls asleep. She then gets up and walks back to the throne room, where Defunis waits for her.

"Is she asleep?"

"Yes, she is asleep. Are you ready to go?"

Defunis nods as they both put their hoods up over their heads and walk out of the palace. Queen Zuna wakes up and walks out just as they shut the door. Apprehensive about what she saw, she sneaks behind them. She quietly follows them outside of the palace to where the RoyalTree stands tall, sprouting out of the water. Defunis and Serel remove their hoods and stare at RoyalTree; their eyes begin to glow orange, as it glows orange back. RoyalTree shoots a blast of light into each of them. The tree stops glowing, Defunis and Serel fall to the ground. The orange light surrounds them and lifts them into the air, then they both swirl around the tree and into the water below. Queen Zuna runs and looks over the edge. She sees the two orange lights spinning around RoyalTree to the bottom before disappearing. She waits a few minutes to see if Defunis and Serel return. When they don't, Zuna walks back to her chambers and climbs into bed. She tosses and turns. Night changes back to day as she lies in bed with her eyes wide open. A knock on her door snaps her back to reality.

"Who is it?"

"It's Serel, may I enter?"

Zuna sits up in her bed.

"Come in!"

Serel opens the door and walks in with breakfast.

"Defunis had the cooks make breakfast for you today."

She hands the food over to Zuna while she stares at her.

"Is something wrong, my Queen?"

"What did you do last night after I went to bed?"

Serel clears her throat and walks back to the door.

"I left your chambers and went back to talk with Defunis. We spoke of the future before taking our leave. After that, we went home. Why do you ask?"

"I was just wondering. I woke back up last night, and I swear I saw something weird. I must've been dreaming, oh well."

"Hmmm, I'm not sure what weird thing you would have seen, my Queen. You need to get ready, though. Your responsibilities are waiting."

Zuna starts to eat her breakfast.

"Thank you, Serel. I'll be up in a few minutes."

Queen Zuna continues to eat her food while she thinks about the orange light, she saw last night. She wonders about Tranjora's eyes the night before and how they were orange like that planet. Before getting lost in her thoughts, she finishes eating and gets ready. She puts her robes and crown on before grabbing her trident and walking up the stairs to the throne room.

# Chapter 5:
# Johthun - Becoming Protectors

Tanglor has flashes of Tazlow speaking to him while he sleeps.

"My name is Tazlow Raff; I am the founder and leader of the Elite Protectors. I am recording this video to ensure the Elites never lose their ways. We are to protect every Johthun regardless of rank or past. We protect! You will be pushed beyond your limits. We are the best of the best, The Elite!"

The dream jumps to Tazlow standing over the downed Johthun. Instead of kicking the downed Johthun, Tazlow stops and turns to Tanglor.

"Talk to Leazara. She can tell you who you are!"

The injured Johthun grabs a blade on the ground and pierces it through Tazlow.

"You think you're a hero saving the elders and your family; they are doomed just like the rest of the Johthuns. All of their lives end here with yours, Tazlow Raff!"

The Johthun stands up and drives the blade down into Tazlow's chest. He falls to the ground, and the ship explodes. Tanglor wakes up in another panic before calming himself down, Ashar sits across from him.

"Nightmare again?"

"Yeah, it's different now, though. I hear Tazlow more. He keeps telling me to talk to Leazara, right before he gets stabbed in the chest. Then the ship explodes, and I wake up. I swear the things I'm dreaming happened."

They are interrupted by shouting coming from Dretzlin's room.

"Ahhhhhhhhh! Leave me alone!!"

Tanglor and Ashar jump up and crash through the door. Dretzlin is standing on his bed with his hands pushing against his head.

"No, No, No! I'm sorry, just please, please stop."

He is staring at the wall like something is there.

"I watched you die.... just go away already!!"

Dretzlin falls to his knees with tears running down his face. He starts to shake uncontrollably; his eyes roll around in his sockets. Ashar and Tanglor grab him and hold him down. The Colonel comes running into the room with several Elite Protectors following behind.

"We will take it from here! Get them back to their rooms!"

Before the boys can protest, they're shoved away and escorted to their rooms by two of the Elite Protectors. While they're walking away, they can hear Dretzlin screaming.

"Please, just make it stop!"

The Elite Protectors shove Ashar and Tanglor in front of them and start to talk.

"This is our chance!"

"I was thinking the same thing. He's done a good job not being seen yet."

"Yeah, let's hurry and get these two back so that we can help with the attack."

They both nod and stop talking before looking forward to Ashar and Tanglor.

"Hey, recruits! Pick up the pace and get back to your rooms!"

They both take off into a sprint back to their rooms. They find Ranyana standing by Ashar's door.

"There you are! What's going on?"

Tanglor runs by and goes into his room, while Ashar grabs Ranyana and follows behind. Tanglor and Ashar catch their breath, leaving Ranyana puzzled.

"Guys, what's going on!?"

Ashar gathers himself.

"Something is going on with Dretzlin. He's crazy, or ghosts are attacking him!"

Tanglor shoves Ashar out of the way.

"Seriously, Ashar? Something is wrong with Dretzlin, but we're not sure what's going on with him. We do know that the Colonel is trying to protect us from something that is about to happen."

"What do you mean, Tanglor?"

"The two Elite Protectors that brought us back here were talking about helping in an attack. They didn't say any names, but it's obvious that they're talking about the Colonel. Now that I think about it, they said something about someone not being seen. Pretty sure, Dretzlin isn't going crazy."

Ashar stands back up.

"We need to go and help them...... It could be another one of our tests."

Tanglor looks back at him and Ranyana.

"You're right; it could be a test. Either way, we can't just sit here while our friends are in danger."

Ashar shrugs his shoulders.

"All right, let's go pass another test."

The three of them grab their weapons and leave the room quietly. Ashar and Ranyana follow behind Tanglor as he leads them down the hall to Dretzlin's room. As they approach his room, they can hear four Elite Protectors around the corner. Tanglor slowly peeks his head out; he can see them standing firm watching the door.

"All right, this is going to be pretty tough, but we're going to have to take out four Elite Protectors."

Ashar looks at Ranyana and then back to Tanglor.

"And how do you propose we do that? They're Protectors, and we're still in training."

Ranyana jumps in before Tanglor can reply.

"The Colonel chose to be our trainer for a reason. From what I know, she doesn't just do that for any group of recruits. We need to do whatever we can to save her....test or not."

Tanglor nods his head.

"I say we try to even the odds and use a distraction to take one or two of them out. Ashar and I will take care of the distraction, Ranyana, take out at least one of them."

She pulls her knives out.

"I'll get two of them. We should probably set our weapons to non-lethal, right?"

Tanglor notices both looking at him for an answer.

"Set your weapons to non-lethal. As Tazlow Raff said, we protect every Johthun, no matter what."

The two smile and nod back to Tanglor while changing the settings on their weapons. Tanglor and Ashar walk past Ranyana around the corner. Ashar pushes Tanglor down to the ground to get the attention of the four guards. Ashar puts his hands on his head and starts to run toward them in a frenzy.

"Someone help! They flew into my ears, and I can feel them crawling around!"

He falls to the ground in front of the guards. They look at him confused before one of them walks over and pokes him with his blaster.

"Hey, whatever you got going on here.... take it somewhere else."

Tanglor runs over, pretending to be out of breath.

"Help! There are more of them coming. They almost got me, too!"

The four guards all stand up. The one poking Ashar stops and kicks him.

"All right, that's enough. Take your friend and get out of here."

Tanglor goes over and helps Ashar off the ground. They start to walk down the hallway away from Ranyana. Suddenly, they stop and fall to the ground screaming in pain—the four Elite Protectors rush over, letting their guard down. Ranyana sneaks out from around the corner. Two of the guards watch with their backs turned as the other two crouch down to help Tanglor and Ashar. Ranyana throws two of her knives and leaps into the air behind them. They strike into the back of one of the guards. Before the other one can turn around, she's already on his back with her blade piercing him. They both fall to the ground without making a sound.

Ranyana approaches the other two guards standing above the screaming boys. They lose their focus and turn around to see her, only to be restrained by Tanglor and Ashar. She quickly throws two more knives knocking them out. The four Elite Protectors guarding the door are now unconscious. Tanglor and Ashar stand up.

"Ranyana, that was amazing! Ashar, let's get them cuffed and tied up."

Ashar hugs Ranyana; they get the guards cuffed and head to the door to peek inside. Dretzlin's knocked out on the bed, and Colonel Luns is on her knees, hands cuffed behind her back with a gag in her mouth. Six Captains stand in the room; one of them is pacing back and forth, speaking to the Colonel.

"Ahh, what a sight to see! The great Leazara Luns beaten by me, Captain E'Tormas Flujen! I know I speak for all the other Captains behind me when I say there is no sympathy from us. We are happy to see this little crusade of yours come to an end."

Colonel Luns tries to speak through the gag.

"Mmmbbbmbmmmm"

Captain Flujen smacks her in the face and starts to laugh, the Captains behind him join in. Laughter fills the room before he continues to talk.

"Back in 2400, when Tazlow found that ancient technology—the computer console that set us forward hundreds of years— a lot of us disagreed with using it. But we had no choice; we went along with it. We all followed the Great Tazlow Raff!! What a bunch of SHIT! That computer turned our people into killers, and we lost who we were. I know, I know, you disagree and can say numerous things that would counteract what I'm saying. The thing is, I'm done."

He turns around and gestures at all the other Captains.

"They're done. And almost all those Elders you've infected are done, too. It all ends here with you, Leazara. Make this easy for me and tell me where you hid the computer console!"

He smacks her in the face and removes the gag from her mouth. She coughs and spits up blood before bursting into laughter.

"You think I'd tell you where I hid it. You must be a lot dumber than I thought."

Captain Flujen gets irritated and kicks her to the ground.

"Enough, Leazara!"

He strikes her in the face twice then lifts her back up onto her knees. She sits proudly with a smile and cuts all over her face; blood drips to the floor.

"There's nothing you can do to make me talk."

He gets angry and walks away to regroup with the rest of the Captains. While this is happening, Tanglor comes up with another plan.

"You guys have followed me this far, and I appreciate that. What I'm going to ask of you is a lot, but I need you both."

Ashar and Ranyana look at each other; he reaches out and grabs her hand. They both look to Tanglor and nod.

"We're with you every step of the way."

"All right! The two of you are going to change uniforms with the unconscious Elite Protectors out there. Once you've changed and have your masks on, you're going to take me in as a prisoner that you captured trying to save the Colonel. Because she took a special interest in me, they'll think I know where the computer console is. At this point, I'm hoping they leave one, maybe two, of the Captains behind while the rest come with me to find the console."

Ashar jumps in.

"I'm with you so far, but where are you going to take them? You don't know where the computer console is, do you?"

"Of course not, this is the first I've heard of it too! I'm going to try to take them out of the Parasav—back up to the surface. As soon as we've left the room, you two need to take out whatever Captains are still there and save Leazara and Dretzlin. Once everyone is safe, signal me."

They all look around at each other. Ranyana starts to walk back toward the guards that are tied up.

"Well, what are we waiting for?"

Ashar follows behind her.

"What are we going to do to signal him?"

"I don't know; you'll figure it out!"

Ashar argues as he follows her to change into the Elite Protector uniform. They get back and put Tanglor's hands behind his back. Ranyana ties them together, leaving them loose enough that he can break free easily. Ashar and Ranyana put the masks on, covering their faces, and pick up the blasters. Ashar stops and removes his mask.

"This isn't a test. These blasters are set to lethal. They would've killed us if they hit us with these shots."

Ranyana and Ashar start to get nervous, Tanglor turns around and looks at them.

"This doesn't change anything. We can do this!"

He starts to walk into the room; they follow behind. Ashar shakes off the nerves. He puts his mask back on before pushing Tanglor forward and yelling to the Captains.

"We caught this one trying to save the Colonel! He says he knows where the computer console is!"

The Captains all turn around, Flujen steps forward.

"Ahh, if it isn't the Colonel's favorite recruit! Is this true? *You* know where the console is?"

Ashar lightly hits Tanglor in the back with the end of his blaster. Tanglor convincingly falls forward onto his knees.

"I can take you there if you let them go."

Captain Flujen turns and looks at Dretzlin, then back at the Colonel.

"How about this? The Colonel stays tied up until I get back with the computer console. As for your friend Dretzlin, he is free to go whenever he wakes up. The kid is crazy anyways."

With no choice, Tanglor agrees to his terms. The Captain walks over to Tanglor and looks at Ranyana and Ashar in the Elite Protector uniforms.

"You two stay here with Captain Rawlty. Make sure he gets your names so that I can reward you for this."

They nod their heads. The rest of the Captains follow behind Tanglor and Flujen, leaving Ashar and Ranyana alone with Rawlty. Rawlty walks over to them to find out their names.

"All right, give me your names, and Flujen will reward you both handsomely when he is Colonel."

They both look at each other. Without knowing what to say, Ashar responds with the first thing that comes to mind.

"My name is Freden."

Rawlty give him a suspicious look before moving on to Ranyana.

"And you, what is your name?"

"My name is Rany."

He continues to look suspiciously at them as he writes their names down. He slowly moves toward the bed Dretzlin is knocked out on.

"You two watch the Colonel, I'm going to make sure this kid isn't going to go bonkers when he wakes up again."

Rawlty leans over Dretzlin and pulls out a belt, strapping him down to the bed. He walks around the bed to strap his feet down. As he is walking, he loses his footing and nearly falls, almost as if something ran into him. He plays it off and straps Dretzlin's feet down to the bed.

"There, now if he wakes up, he won't be able to go anywhere. I don't know why Flujen bothers lying about his deals."

Ashar can't stand listening to him anymore. He starts to walk over to Rawlty while Ranyana makes her way to free the Colonel. Rawlty notices Ashar walking toward him.

"What are you doing? Don't make me kill you!"

He pulls out his blade, but Ashar is too quick and fires the blaster into his stomach. It pierces right through him, causing him to bleed and scream in agony.

"Ahh! Stop, you can't do this! I know you're not Freden...."

Ashar grabs Rawlty's hand holding the blade; he redirects it and moves it down. He slowly pushes Rawlty's hand. Ashar backs away and watches Rawlty gasps for air as he sits with a hole in his stomach and a blade in his chest.

Ranyana cuts the Colonel loose and removes the gag from her mouth.

"Thank you! Who are you?"

Ranyana and Ashar take their masks off; the Colonel smiles through her beaten face.

"My recruits! I knew there was something special about you. Where did Tanglor take the other Captains?"

Ashar starts to remove the straps from Dretzlin.

"He's trying to lead them out of the Parasav back to the surface. He has no idea where that computer console is."

Ranyana helps Leazara up.

"There's no way he could know; I'm the only one that does. I will tell you all about it once we get Tanglor."

Dretzlin starts to regain consciousness. While Ashar is taking the last strap off, something stops his hand. He looks down to see nothing, but he can't move his arm. He gets thrown back away from Dretzlin; a body starts to form from thin air. An Elite Protector stands before them holding its blades ready to attack. Ashar grabs his blaster, but the Elite Protector stands down, putting his blades away and removing his mask. Dretzlin can't believe his eyes.

"How is this possible!? I watched you die!"

Freden walks toward him.

"I am sorry, little brother. There is so much you don't know about me. I stayed so that I could say goodbye."

He puts his hand on Dretzlin's arm before turning around. He presses a small button on his left shoulder and starts to vanish right in front of them until he is completely gone. All they hear is his voice.

"Now, stay out of my way. Next time I see you, we won't be brothers."

His voice fades away, and Dretzlin is left sitting in confusion. Ashar runs over to him, while Ranyana gets the Colonel out of the room.

"Dretzlin! We need to get out of here. Come on!"

He gets up, and they follow Ranyana and the Colonel out of the room. They get around the corner and are met by the other Elite Protectors, still in the Parasav. The Colonel hobbles forward and drops her weapon.

"We are still Elite Protectors! Just because one of us has lost their way, doesn't mean we all need to! Stay with me, and we can rebuild. We can be better than we were before. I need all of you to do that, though!"

She looks around at the Elites before limping toward them.

"We need to help each other. The computer console Tazlow found is not the cause of all of this. We were the ones that found it and used it. How we use it is what makes us who we are. The technology on it helped our people thrive, and it's still helping us every day! We need to be grateful for that!"

The Elite Protectors look around at each other, one by one, they start to drop their weapons to salute their Colonel.

"I am honored to see all of you back on my side! We need to stop Captain Flujen; he has Tanglor. Everyone, get out there and get him back!"

The Elite Protectors swarm out of the facility to find Tanglor, as the Colonel falls to the ground. Ashar, Dretzlin, and Ranyana rush to her side.

# Chapter 6:
# Tralupian- RoyalTree

In the early morning, while everyone sleeps, RoyalTree glows bright orange. As the sun begins to shine, the Great Tree flashes, and the orange color disappears. Defunis and Serel stand at the base, looking into the water. The robes they wear flash the same orange color before they change back to solid brown. Defunis looks over to Serel on the other side of the tree.

"How did you sleep last night?"

"I slept alright. There's a lot on my mind."

"I feel the same way, the idea of Zuna being the one is still…unsettling, but she is the only one that has fit the description requested by RoyalTree. None of our past Kings or Queens have come close to resembling our great Leader Zembor like Zuna has. With a push in the right direction, she will fulfill the prophecy."

Serel walks around the tree over to him.

"Indeed, she will. Let us get to the palace before she wonders what we're doing out here. She can't know what we truly are, not yet."

Defunis nods his head to Serel. She latches onto his arm as they walk up the palace stairs. They arrive to find their Queen waiting for them on the throne.

"Where have you two been? Never mind that. I've been waiting to meet with the Flutinas."

Defunis and Serel bow to their Queen.

"My Queen, we are very sorry for our tardiness. We won't let it happen again."

"I don't understand why the two of you refuse to stay here in the palace. There are rooms for each of you, and honestly, I'd be more comfortable knowing you're both here at night."

They exchange a look, then Serel steps forward.

"We have never lived in the palace with any of our past Kings or Queens. We like our home outside of the city, and we would prefer to stay there instead of coming here. Please understand, my Queen."

"I suppose that is okay. I had another weird dream last night. At least I think it was a dream. I just feel a little vulnerable at night with no one else in the palace."

"I know you aren't excited about it, but your brothers and sisters will be staying with you now, and they are more than capable of protecting you."

She stands up with an angry look on her face.

"I don't need protection! I need guards to be on patrol constantly! Something is going on around here that we don't know about. I've seen things at night that…."

Zuna's voice trails off.

"We will arrange to have guards here during the day and at night for you, my Queen. Is there anything else we can do?"

"No, that will be fine, since the two of you won't live here. Is there something about the palace that I should know about?"

Defunis looks to Serel before he answers.

"Nothing has happened in the palace, my Queen. At least, not to our knowledge. It's just that we have grown very fond of our small home outside the city. Once we leave here, we can go and be in solace by ourselves. We like the quiet after being around noise all day. Nothing against you or the palace, it's just not for us."

Queen Zuna accepts their answer and sits back down on her throne.

"Thank you for being honest with me. I trust you two. How could I not after you advised for both my mother and grandfather? Did your parents advise before you two?"

"We don't know much about our parents, but we're told that they advised our leaders before us. We are a noble family in the sense that the adviser role has been passed down within our family. With that being said, we never got the privilege of meeting our mother or father."

Serel joins in.

"Though we have heard many stories about them. They were well-respected among all Tralupians. We have been told multiple times that my resemblance is identical to my mother, while Defunis is identical to our father."

"Interesting, is there any history on the advisers?"

"Unfortunately, there is no written history of us, just the knowledge that gets passed down from RoyalTree."

"RoyalTree? I've heard the legend behind it, but it isn't true, is it?"

"All of the childhood stories you heard about RoyalTree are true. It isn't just a tree, but a life form that started to grow a long time ago. It was planted by Zembor Wrathfin when he had the palace built. No one other than Zembor knew what he planted. After a couple of years, it grew high up into the sky and continued to grow. RoyalTree is as much alive as you or me. It feeds off our life forces and gives back to us in return. We wouldn't have this lush environment without it, and RoyalTree would be dead if it weren't for us."

"So, the blood that absorbs into the trident and the tree wrapping its roots around my mother? That's because of it being alive?"

"The trident absorbs the blood from any Wrathfin that it kills. The combination of Zembor's blade and the wood from RoyalTree gives it life. It's said that the blood that gets absorbed into it keeps our past leaders with us. It is said that if you listen closely to the trident, it will speak to you. I have never had the chance to test that out, but I wouldn't doubt it. As I said, RoyalTree is alive and breathing. The roots moving around are like our arms and legs moving around. RoyalTree reaches out for those who get sacrificed and latches onto whatever life force is left to give it. It is very rare for RoyalTree to call out to someone other than our past King or Queen, but when it does, we have to answer its call or pay the price."

"Pay the price? What do you mean?"

"It only happened the one time when Zembor first planted RoyalTree. After he passed away, RoyalTree knew and started to suffer. It started killing off the environment around us. Water started to evaporate, the green land turned to dirt, and the sky dimmed to an angry, dark red color. Zembor's son, Zalzatine, was too fixated on finding the Ventrians and killing them all, that he ignored what RoyalTree was doing. Zalzatine refused to believe the truth and decided to hunt down the Ventrians, destroying his city and the land himself. Zalzatine ordered his men to set fire to the surface while dropping bombs under the ground. Hundreds of Ventrians climbed out of their homes, only to burn alive. Tralupians suffered along with the Ventrians. It was the Apocalypse that RoyalTree warned Zembor about when he planted him. He made a deal when he was abducted from a ship that was thought to be a massive metal bird at the time. Sorry, I'm getting off-topic. Many Tralupians didn't believe Zembor's story about the incident when he got back, causing Zalzatine to question it himself, even though Zalzatine was there when he and Grundar, the Ventrians leader, returned in a ship from the sky. Anyway, Zalzatine didn't believe in RoyalTree and thought they were just ordinary trees that we Tralupians were blessed with after defeating the Ventrians. RoyalTree has a power that is still a mystery, but we know it feeds and thrives off our life force, and it repays us with this beautiful environment. If we stay faithful to it, it stays faithful to us."

The Queen stands up and looks at Defunis and Serel before she erupts into laughter.

"Hahaha, I'm sorry, but that's ridiculous! You guys have to be messing with me!"

She continues to laugh while her advisers stare at her with serious looks on their faces. She finally stops.

"You're kidding me. Seriously?"

Serel walks over to her and has her sit back down.

"We're serious, my Queen. You have to believe us, or RoyalTree will know as it did with Zalzatine."

She stands back up and tries to walk to her chambers.

"No, I can't. That's too crazy for me; I have already done things...."

Defunis grabs her arm.

"Come with us, and we'll show you."

She follows Defunis and Serel out of the palace. They start to approach RoyalTree. Defunis and Serel lead the way and stop in front of it, both reaching their hands out to her. She looks at them and then RoyalTree. It starts to glow the same orange color she's been seeing over the past few days. She nervously reaches her hands out to grab theirs. Right as they're about to clasp together, they get interrupted by some of the Queen's soldiers. RoyalTree's glow fades away as the soldiers run over The Queen turns away from Defunis and Serel.

"What's going on!?"

"My Queen, we are sorry, but the Flutinas are attacking the city! Our soldiers are fighting them off. Tranjora and his wife, Yongrea, both have strange orange eyes, and they're speaking in a language we can't understand."

Queen Zuna pulls the trident off her back.

"We need to stop those traitors! They won't get the crown!"

Queen Zuna and her soldiers charge off, Defunis looks over to Serel.

"Damn, I guess we'll have to wait until after the battle. Grab our weapons, will you, sister?"

"Don't worry, brother. We will convince her."

Serel reaches over to RoyalTree; her hand passes through it while an orange light shines bright. When she pulls her hand out, she has two specialized crossbows. The light disappears as she stands there proudly.

"Look what I had him make for us! They shoot arrows out in the shape of Zembor's Trident."

She smiles and tosses one over to Defunis. He catches it and smiles back as they hurry toward the battle. The two of them arrive to the Queen yelling over the gated wall to Tranjora and Yongrea.

"Take your people away from here before they die! I'm done trying to speak to you, especially after that stunt you pulled the other night!"

Tranjora and his wife both look back at her with their bright orange eyes. Their heads twitch to the side as they yell back together.

"Tra!........ Ur.... Bah...... Trabah! Dah Urlonk!"

"What is wrong with these two? I told you, Tranjora, when you broke into my palace and sat on my throne. I should have killed you right there. Soldiers, attack!!!"

Her soldiers raise their bows and fire over the wall at the Flutinas and their army. A bright orange flash covers the battlefield blinding everyone for a moment. When the glow dissipates, the arrows launched lay on the ground in front of them, untouched. Tranjora raises his arm in the air and slowly starts to walk toward the wall. As he approaches, he throws his arm down and yells.

"Trabah Dah Urlonk!!"

His wife and their soldiers charge behind him. They have devices that unfold into ladders that they place on the outside of the walls. As the ladders reach the top, so does the Flutinas' army. They overwhelm the Queen's soldiers atop the wall, but they keep fighting and hold them. The Queen and her advisers join the battle to help push them back. Defunis and Serel fire their crossbows as the Queen jumps in with her trident in front of her. She strikes one of the enemies in the chest and pushes him back into a wall. Zuna pulls the trident out and swings it around her head, knocking over three more enemies running at her. She turns around and sees Tranjora and Yongrea trying to flee to the palace.

"Defunis, Serel, help me stop them!"

She points to the two running. They take out the enemies in front of them before chasing the Flutinas down. Queen Zuna follows behind them with her trident ready to strike. She slows down as she approaches the palace and sneaks into the throne room. Zuna stops and hides behind the wall. She pokes her head around the corner and hears whispering. She can only make out parts of what they're saying.

"We...... same side........ RoyalTree...... same."

"No..... leave....... take yourself out of them....... not true noble...... ruin.... over the years."

"You don't tell us......... do.... we...... in control.... she dies."

Queen Zuna grasps her Trident tight and jumps around the corner. Defunis stands in front of Tranjora with his crossbow pointed at his chest.

"What's going on here? What were the two of you talking about?"

Tranjora turns and hits Defunis in the face before running away. Defunis and the Queen chase after him until they hear a scream coming from her chambers. They let Tranjora go and run to the bottom of the palace. Defunis and Zuna get to the bottom of the staircase where Serel is pinning down Yongrea.

"Help, she won't stop, no matter what I say to her."

Zuna walks over to them and looks down at her. Yongrea's eyes glow orange as she stares at her, reaching for the trident.

"Oh, you want this?"

Zuna spins it around and slams it down, piercing it through her arm and pinning it to the ground.

"Ahhhhh! Please... Trabah!!! Urlonk!!!"

Defunis walks over and grabs the Queen.

"Come, Serel can handle it from here."

Zuna slaps Defunis' hands away.

"No! I will be the one to handle it!"

Queen Zuna walks back over to her on the floor. She kneels and braces herself on the trident sticking out of Yongrea's arm.

"Did you say something?"

She moves the trident around, causing Yongrea to scream. As she screams, the orange color starts fading away.

"AHHHHHH, PLEASE, YOU HAVE TO HELP ME! IT WON'T LEAVE US ALONE!"

Queen Zuna jumps up.

"What did you just say? Who won't leave you alone?"

The screaming stops, and the orange color fills her eyes once more. She kicks Serel off her and reaches over for the trident. Zuna grabs it first and pulls it out while kicking Yongrea in the face. She hits her head on the ground before leaning back up and staring at Queen Zuna.

"They're going to come and take everything from you! Our people, your daughter, everything will be lost!! TokBellu will be in ruins! And their black eyes, nothing but darkness!!!"

Zuna jumps back before taking a deep breath. She jabs her trident into Yongrea's face. She pulls it back out, Yongrea sits and stares at her, blood pouring out of her face before she finally falls back to the ground. Defunis and Serel walk with Queen Zuna back out of the palace to the battlefield. She stands leaning on her trident, watching her soldiers finish off the Flutina's army. Tranjora is spotted in the distance retreating with a couple of his men.

"Let him go; we will be ready for whatever he tries next. Defunis, Serel, we need to finish what you were going to show me earlier. I don't know what's going on with the orange colors that have been showing up, but I think RoyalTree has something to do with it."

Defunis and Serel both bow to their Queen.

"Get yourself cleaned up first; we will meet you shortly."

Queen Zuna leaves to her chamber while Defunis and Serel walk through the palace. He turns to her with a concerned look.

"We have to seize the opportunity tonight with the Queen. RoyalTree can't go much longer."

"You don't have to tell me, brother. I know what we must do. Once she is ready, we will take her back."

They continue walking to the throne room, where they wait for their Queen. She enters in, holding her trident.

"I'm ready to go see RoyalTree."

Defunis and Serel lead the way out of the palace. The sun sets as they approach RoyalTree. Serel stands, holding her hand out for her.

"Grab our hands."

Defunis and Serel lift their hands in the air toward RoyalTree, as Queen Zuna grabs onto them and looks toward the Great Tree. RoyalTree starts to glow orange again. Defunis and Serel turn to Zuna; their eyes are solid orange. They clinch their hands tight, holding the Queen's hands. Light from the tree starts to reach out to Defunis and Serel. Queen Zuna can't escape. She watches as the light touches her advisers, consuming them and flowing toward her. She tries to scream but is consumed along with Defunis and Serel. RoyalTree shoots the light out around itself and then brings the three of them in close. They spiral around the Great Tree into the water, its roots unwind, creating an opening underneath it. They shoot through it and up into RoyalTree as more roots appear from the sides and form underneath them, giving them a platform to land on. The orange around them fades away; the Queen jumps back away from Defunis and Serel.

"What the hell just happened!? How are we inside RoyalTree!?"

Defunis steps forward; the Queen backs away.

"My Queen, this is what we wanted to show you. We have shown this to every past ruler since Zalzatine took over for his father, Zembor. We are part of RoyalTree and have been around since it was planted. We answer to the voice that comes from within. Like I told you before, we serve it, and it serves us back. RoyalTree wants TokBellu to thrive, but it can't do that without them."

The Queen looks over to Serel.

"Them?"

Serel stands up and walks over to her.

"Yes, RoyalTree isn't just one. That's why there are so many trees around TokBellu. Their root systems are connected and intertwined within the planet's core. If it dies, our planet dies with it. That is why we advise every King and Queen. To make sure RoyalTree continues to live on as one with our leader."

A voice appears around them.

"I am RoyalTree; it is an honor to meet you, Queen Zuna Wrathfin. I hope you understand and accept these terms your advisers have given you."

Queen Zuna looks up into the root-filled tree.

"It doesn't sound like I have a choice. What happens if I refuse?"

"There is always a choice, my Queen, just different outcomes based on what we choose. Like my servants have said, destruction and chaos will come to TokBellu. I will die, killing the planet in the process. Zalzatine almost made that mistake. If it weren't for Defunis and Serel, TokBellu would have been destroyed long ago. Since then, your ancestors have complied and bonded themselves with me."

"If I am to be Queen.... get on with it!"

Serel and Defunis step away from her as roots sprout out of the walls encasing her in a dome. Her advisers grab onto the dome and start to shake. Their eyes are flooded with the now-familiar orange light, which then bleeds out onto the encased Queen. RoyalTree starts to shake the Queen around, knocking her into the walls. She screams as the light fills the hollow tree. A loud shrieking sound pierces the Queen's ears causing her to pass out from the pain. A burst of orange flashes and fades away. Queen Zuna ends up in her bed asleep; she lays dreaming.

A blast comes flying down from the sky, crashing into the palace on TokBellu. Zuna runs out with Serel and several other Tralupians. They crowd into the city as a rainstorm of missiles flies into the palace obliterating it. Queen Zuna and Serel work together to calm their people down, as they watch unknown ships fly above them. Looking around, Zuna sees thousands of dead Tralupians. RoyalTree is burning, and pieces are crashing to the ground. The Apocalypse she'd been warned about has started in front of her eyes. She turns back to her people and watches as they all catch fire and burn away into ash. She falls to the ground as one of the ships lands in front of her. A slick black panel opens; a tall figure stands in the doorway. The light shines bright behind it, Zuna watches as it lifts a hand and points at her. It slowly takes a step out of the ship. It gets closer to her, and she can start to make out part of its face. Large black eyes sit inside a glass bubble staring at her.

Queen Zuna jolts awake from her dream and opens her eyes. Orange surrounds her pupils, but as she blinks, the light fades, leaving her staring at the ceiling.

# Chapter 7:
# Johthun- The Truth

The Colonel lies on her bed with Ashar, Ranyana, and Dretzlin by her side.

"Thank you for staying with me. I know how badly all of you want to be out there searching for Tanglor, but there are plenty of Elite Protectors doing just that. They'll bring him back soon."

Dretzlin gets up and is about to walk out, but the Colonel stops him.

"Dretzlin wait. Sit back down and let me try to explain everything, to all of you."

He sits back down to listen to the Colonel.

"I had an idea of who Freden was when he got here with Tanglor, but I wasn't sure. When he died in the simulation, I knew. But I didn't want to tell you who he was or that he was still alive. He was trying to protect you; I was trying to protect you."

Dretzlin starts to get emotional but holds back his tears.

"I don't understand."

"He is an undercover agent working with the terrorist organization that killed Tazlow Raff. They call themselves the True Guardians. Tazlow was attacked by them in 2669 while traveling to Thoonta with his wife and unborn child. He was escorting the Elders, who were planning to arrive on Thoonta and expand the government and Elite Protectors. Before they could get there, the True Guardians attacked. They were already on board disguised as the Elites. Tazlow sacrificed himself to save the Elders and his family."

As the Colonel is talking, Ashar interrupts her.

"Sorry to interrupt, Colonel, but I've heard this before. In detail. From Tanglor."

Intrigued, she sits up in her bed.

"What do you mean?"

"Tanglor has a recurring dream where he sees all this firsthand. Tazlow fights off all the True Guardians, saves his family and the Elders, and then stops fighting to tell him, "Talk to Leazara, she knows who you are." Then he gets stabbed in the chest, and the ship explodes. Tanglor tells the story a lot better than I do."

The Colonel jumps out of bed.

"I... I don't understand how he could dream that. We need to find him at once."

She leaves the room with the others following behind her.

---------------------------------------------------------

The ground rumbles as the elevator from the Parasav emerges. Tanglor gets pushed out by Flujen; the other Captains stand behind him.

"All right, Tanglor, get moving. If you waste my time, I will kill you without hesitation."

Tanglor starts to walk forward while trying to figure out the best place to take them.

"Yeah, I understand. Just follow me and try to keep up!"

He starts to run. The Captains look at each other before Flujen yells at them.

"What are you doing!? Follow and don't lose him!"

The four Captains chase after him with Flujen falling behind. Tanglor ducks out of their sight behind a building and takes his cuffs off. With his hands behind his back, he pops out from behind the building.

"Hey! Over here. The computer console is back this way toward the city!"

The Captains see him and continue following. Tanglor still doesn't know where he is going to take them. He starts to think to himself, remembering all the different things he's learned about Joht.

"Where can I take them that they'll think the console is? The Rashintrah! It's the biggest structure in the center of Joht, where the Elders reside. I can easily lose them in the crowd once we get closer."

Tanglor stops running and turns around to the exhausted Captains. Flujen, out of breath, pulls out his blaster.

"No more.... running. Walk, or I'll shoot you!"

Tanglor starts to walk toward the Rashintrah with the Captains following closely. After another mile, they make it to the edge of the city. Tanglor notices an Elite Protector watching from a window. He takes a piece of the broken cuffs and drops it on the ground. Tanglor looks back up to the window, and the Elite is gone. He continues to drop broken pieces of his cuffs while looking around, hoping the Elite Protector would follow them. Captain Flujen starts to notice.

"What are you looking for? Keep your eyes forward and get us to the Rashintrah!"

Once Tanglor sees it, he picks up the pace.

"Hey! I said no more running, or I'll shoot!"

He ducks to the right behind a building and goes into a full sprint away from the Captains. Gunshots start to fill the city of Joht, followed by yelling.

"If you don't come back out here, I'll start killing the innocent!"

Tanglor stops and turns back, making his way toward Captain Flujen. An arm reaches out from an alleyway and stops him.

"Wait, my name is Ucarus. I was sent by Colonel Luns. I've already sent our coordinates back to the Elites. Sit tight, and we'll have backup in five minutes."

Tanglor pushes his arm aside.

"We don't have five minutes; he's going to kill them because of me. I can't let that happen."

He grabs one of the blades from Ucarus and rushes toward Captain Flujen. Ucarus follows, they manage to sneak up behind the Captains. Before Ucarus can stop him, Tanglor jumps out, swinging his blade at Flujen. At the last second, Flujen steps out of the way, letting Tanglor's sword pierce through one of his followers. Ucarus hurdles over the incapacitated Captain and gets behind Tanglor.

"Alright, no more rushing into battle! We need to work together if we want to stay alive until backup gets here. Follow my lead!"

Tanglor nods his head as the four remaining Captains circle around them. Ucarus lunges forward, striking one of them while Tanglor jumps behind him, blocking an attack. Tanglor watches Captain Flujen fire his blaster at Ucarus. He dives and pushes him out of the way, leaving a hole in the Captain's chest behind them. Flujen charges but stops as vehicles approach them.

"Let's get out of here while we still can."

Captain Flujen and his remaining two Captains flee, getting lost in the crowd of Johthuns watching the battle. Colonel Luns and thirty Elite Protectors arrive to get things oriented and calm down the crowd. Tanglor and Ucarus hop into the Colonel's vehicle and head back to the Parasav.

"Glad to see that both of you are all right. Tanglor, you and I have a lot to discuss. Talk to your friends and get cleaned up. I'll come to speak to all of you soon."

The Colonel pulls up to the Parasav and waits for the doors to arrive. The ground rumbles as the elevator emerges. Ucarus and Tanglor walk in, while Colonel Luns drives away. The rumbling continues as the elevator plunges back down. Ucarus and Tanglor stay silent until the doors open. Ucarus walks out and looks at Tanglor.

"I look forward to working with you more in the future. Catch you later."

Tanglor watches him walk away toward the Great Hall, passing the other recruits. He sees them and yells.

"You guys did it!"

They see Tanglor and rush over to him.

"Tanglor! I'm glad to see you're still alive. Ranyana and I were able to save the Colonel and get Dretzlin."

Tanglor walks over to Dretzlin and grabs his shoulders.

"I'm happy to see that you're alright."

He shakes his head.

"Thanks for everything you did for me. Sorry I went a little crazy there. It turns out my brother is alive and has been working with a terrorist organization called the True Guardians. There's still a lot we don't know, though. We've been waiting for the Colonel to get back."

As they are talking, the Colonel walks into the room and sits down. They all give her their attention.

"It's time you heard the truth about everything. I want to start by saying thank you for saving me. If it weren't for you, I would be dead, and the Elite Protectors would be no more. If it's any consolation, there aren't any more tests. I've seen enough. Welcome to the Elite Protectors. Tanglor, while you were gone, Ashar mentioned a dream you've been having."

Tanglor shoots Ashar an angry look.

"Ashar felt inclined to mention it to me because of the history I shared with them about Tazlow and his death. I am curious about your dream because it sounds like you know what happened to him. There is only brief footage of that day, and it was destroyed by the True Guardians weeks after the incident."

"I... I'm not sure how, but I've had the same dream almost every night since I can remember. I didn't know it was Tazlow until I came here. It's like the more I'm around things that have to do with him, the more detailed my dreams become. Since I've arrived here, Tazlow has started directly interacting with me in my dream. Now, he stops mid-fight and turns to look at me; then he tells me to talk to you because you can tell me who I am."

The Colonel stands up and walks over to Tanglor, sitting down next to him.

"I have no idea how this is happening, but he's talking to us through you. I do know who you are because Tazlow and I were good friends. I was supposed to be on that ship with him, but he made me stay back on Joht to watch over the Elite Protectors. He knew the ship would be in danger...."

She stands back up and puts her head down.

"I am sorry that I hid this, but I needed to make sure it was truly you."

She stops and turns back to him.

"Tanglor, that unborn child Tazlow was protecting.... was you. Your name is Tanglor Raff."

Tanglor, filled with different emotions, doesn't respond. He stands up and looks around before leaving the room. Ashar gets up and tries to follow him, but the Colonel stops him. She smiles while looking at the others.

"You are the new Elite Protectors along with Tanglor. He will be a great leader, but he needs our support, especially right now."

Leazara provides them with their brand-new Elite Protector uniforms, handing Ashar an extra one for Tanglor.

"Make sure he gets this. He needs you right now, Ashar."

Ashar takes the uniforms while nodding to her.

"You don't need to worry about him. Tanglor is a lot stronger than you know."

She smiles while watching him leave the room to check on Tanglor.

Ashar walks into the bunks to find him sitting on his bed and shuts the door.

"Check it out! We got our Elite uniforms. I know it's not how we pictured it happening, but we're Elite Protectors now!"

Tanglor stands up and grabs the uniform from him.

"My whole life I've been lied to... Our parents on Thoonta, did they know?"

Ashar sits down on the bed.

"You're still the same Johthun, and you're still my brother. Being a Raff doesn't change that. It just gives you more to live up to!"

Tanglor scoffs while smiling.

"I do have some expectations to live up to now that I'm a Raff, huh?"

Ashar starts to laugh as he puts on his uniform.

"I don't know, Tanglor, I think they made a mistake. I think I'm a Raff. The dark blue stripes that are going up the sides of these grey uniforms, oh, and this cool nova star patch on the chest. It looks way better on me!"

Just like that, all the tension in the room disappears as both boys laugh together.

"Well, you're my brother no matter what, so that kind of makes you a Raff too. And this blue cape going over my right shoulder fits well with this uniform, so I'd think again."

"Yeah, good point. I need to get one of those."

Ashar punches him on the arm.

"You ready to start rebuilding the Elite Protectors?"

"Yeah, ready as I'll ever be."

Tanglor and Ashar walk out of the room to find Dretzlin and Ranyana waiting. The four of them, outfitted in their Elite Protector uniforms, walk together down to the Great Hall to meet with the Colonel.

# Chapter 8:
# Tralupians- Buried Memories

------30 years after the Battle-----

Queen Zuna lies in her bed. Her eyes, bright orange, stare up at the ceiling as random memories that don't belong to her race through her head. She tosses and turns before she can snap out of it. She sits up in a panic, shaking her head around. The light fades from her eyes as she slowly gets out of bed and dons her Queenly attire. She adjusts her crown, turns to her trident, and stops. A transparent orange figure stands next to it. It approaches Zuna, as it gets closer, she notices that one of the Tralupian's arms is missing. In its place is a blade.

"Zembor?"

The translucent Tralupian walks through Zuna and wanders around the room, looking at everything she has. Zuna follows it around until it stops at last and turns to her. Zembor speaks to her in a soft, raspy voice.

"The trident is the key. Use it to keep everyone safe."

Zembor turns back around and walks over to Zuna's bed. He sits down and stares at her. His glassy eyes flash orange before the light fills his entire body. He transforms into a small sphere, flying around the room and stopping above the trident. The trident glows orange then turns to a fiery red. It floats into the air, stabs into the sphere, then whirls itself around before launching the sphere back toward the bed. It crashes into the cushions and bounces back up into the air. A couple of seconds go by, and the sphere hits the bed again. This time it creates a hole and falls through to the floor below. The bed violently shakes just as the orange hue starts to seep out from underneath it. Queen Zuna looks at her feet to see the color crawling up her legs. She screams and closes her eyes, but when she reopens them, everything has vanished, and the trident is back to normal.

"These weird visions are never going to stop. I thought it was because of the trident at first, but now I'm not sure. Where are Defunis and Serel?"

Queen Zuna grabs the trident and leaves her chamber heading towards the throne room. Defunis and Serel sit at the adviser's table with Zuna's siblings. Ilikso,

Musfina, Siritano, and Oryuna stand up and salute their Queen and sister as she walks in.

"Sit back down. What are we discussing today?"

They all sit, except for Oryuna.

"We were discussing the barracks and how we have achieved so much thanks to your Queen's Law."

Ilikso stands up next to her.

"I have given it my all for the last thirty years, sister. I am now the greatest warrior in your ranks."

Siritano and Musfina laugh behind him.

"I am happy to hear the barracks have been a success. Ilikso and Siritano, I have seen the two of you fight, you both have improved immensely. I can proudly say that you are my brothers. Musfina, your intelligence, and strategic mindset have skyrocketed the barracks to success. And Oryuna, your leadership, and responsibility have been surprising and outstanding. Thank you, all of you, for what you have done."

They all bow to their sister before sitting back down. Defunis and Serel stand up and approach their Queen.

"My Queen, we need to discuss the Flutinas. Tranjora has been putting together another army these past few years. He still has followers, and those numbers continue to grow as they march toward us."

"You still haven't explained to me what happened that night thirty years ago when I caught the two of you talking."

Defunis nervously looks to his sister.

"My Queen, like I said that night, Tranjora was and still is in a different state of mind. The same one that his wife was in before you killed her. I was simply speaking to him as he was speaking to me. What he was saying made no sense."

"What about him and his wife's eyes? They were orange like RoyalTree and....."

Serel stands up next to her brother.

"We have been looking into it with no luck. RoyalTree wouldn't bond with anyone that isn't a Wrathfin."

Queen Zuna stands up and walks over to them.

"Why is it that we haven't gone back in since that night? Was it even real? Why does it feel like I'm going crazy!?"

Serel turns around and signals for Oryuna and the others to leave. As they get up and head toward the barracks, Defunis and Serel approach their Queen.

"He hasn't requested to see you again. We can't take you there unless..."

Zuna turns back around and sits on her throne.

"Unless he needs something from me? Who is he anyway? I don't know how much longer I can live this way. I need more answers!"

"My Queen, we only have so many answers about RoyalTree, and there is still a lot that we don't know about him. What we do know is we have to do everything he says and that you need his help to lead your people."

"I don't need his help, nor do I want it!"

Defunis and Serel's eyes suddenly glow bright orange. They run toward the throne and stop in front of her, RoyalTree speaking through them.

"You will change your mind, or you shall perish with the rest of your species!!!"

Queen Zuna stands up; her advisers pull back, the color fading from their eyes.

"He can speak through you anytime he wants?"

Serel falls to the ground and looks up to her.

"Yes, he created us. If we disobey him or fail to complete our mission, we suffer."

Defunis helps his sister up.

"That's enough, Serel. My Queen, you need to listen to me carefully."

She sits up and gives her attention to him.

"RoyalTree is not someone you want to play with. You won't win. Why do you think our past Kings and Queens have obeyed and bonded with it like you did? Zalzatine turned his head after he bonded with RoyalTree, Tez was skeptical about it before he was brought inside of the tree, and your mother, she refused to believe it until she had to."

"What do you mean until she had to?"

"By the time your mother was giving birth to you, she had already birthed twelve other children, which was unheard of for a Tralupian. She was struggling to push you out, after hours of trying, everyone thought that both of you weren't going to make it. Your father wasn't going to let that happen, though."

"My father? Mother never spoke of a father."

"She didn't want to speak of him after what happened since she felt like it was her fault he died. But you were it. You were the one thing he left behind, and your mother would always remember that. She loved you more than your other siblings because of everything that occurred that night."

"What happened the night of my birth? Who was my father?"

"Your father's name was Za-Ryan Zulcis. He was a great warrior that won your mother's heart fighting in her army. He reached the top of the ranks before stealing her heart away from every other Tralupian. He married your mother and took the Wrathfin name while helping her lead our people. As I mentioned before, your mother was struggling to push you out. After a couple of hours went by, she had lost too much blood; her breathing became faint. Your father refused to let either of you die, so he picked up your mother and walked her out to RoyalTree."

While listening, Zuna notices the wood on her trident start to faintly glow orange. She reaches over and grabs it, the light glowing brighter before transferring into Zuna. Defunis and Serel begin to shine the same color. They rise into the sky and form together into a sphere. Gliding towards Zuna, they latch onto the trident and cause a burst of light to shoot into the Queen as well. Her eyes cloud over with orange, as she stands still, staring at the trident. It takes control and sends her into a vision.

Defunis and Serel stand before her. They speak in unison.

"My Queen, can you hear us?"

She looks around. They're on TokBellu still, but it appears to be in the past. Zuna looks through the haze and sees a male Tralupian carrying a pregnant female. Her surroundings are blurry, almost like they're underwater. Everything moving around has a faint orange trail following behind it. She finally turns back to Defunis and Serel.

"Yes, I can hear you. Where are we?"

"We are still in the same place, just a different time. It is the trident's doing. While we were speaking to you about your birth, a memory sparked inside the trident. You grabbing onto it caused it to activate and launch the memory."

"So... we're standing in the same spots we were before I grabbed the trident?"

"Precisely! Well, that is, your mind is currently inside of the trident and RoyalTree. Your body is still where it was, but you are not actually there."

"I see, so how do we get back out of the trident?"

"You need to finish whatever memory the trident is trying to show you, so let us proceed. Follow your parents."

Queen Zuna turns back to the male Tralupian, her father Za-Ryan, carrying her mother out of the palace toward RoyalTree. She follows behind him as he approaches the Great Tree. Za-Ryan gently sets the pregnant Zelena down on the ledge. He reaches out to RoyalTree and places his hand onto it.

"Please RoyalTree, I know that I am not a true Wrathfin, but these two, Queen Zelena and our daughter Zuna, are. They can't die. Please, you have to save them!"

A shimmer of orange appears underneath his palm, a wave of emotion washes over his face as he nods.

"I understand, thank you."

Za-Ryan walks back over to the pregnant Queen, bleeding on the ledge. He reaches down and picks her up.

"Everything is going to be okay."

Za-Ryan jumps into the water with the pregnant Zelena. They land next to RoyalTree, causing a splash, the water ripples toward the tree. RoyalTree starts to glow bright, causing the water to illuminate as well. Zuna runs over to the ledge and looks down.

"I can't see anything now. I'm going in!"

Zuna jumps off the ledge and into the water. There's no splash this time since she's in a memory. She can see through the water now, watching her father swimming down toward the bottom of RoyalTree. Zuna looks over to see Defunis and Serel jumping into the water after her.

"Is he planning on taking her inside of RoyalTree? Hurry, we need to follow them!"

Queen Zuna and her advisers follow the memory of her father. As her father gets closer to the bottom, blood begins to trickle out of his eyes, nose, and mouth. He turns toward the barely conscious Zelena.

"My beautiful wife, everything is going to be okay. You and our daughter, Zuna, are going to make it."

She looks back up at him and wipes away some of the blood.

"What…. What is going on? Why are you in so much pain, my love?"

He holds back his tears as he looks into her eyes.

"Zelena…. RoyalTree is going to take care of everything. He told me he would make sure you and Zuna lived through this."

She tries to keep her eyes open, but they slowly close while her voice fades out.

"Don't leave me…"

Za-Ryan keeps her comfortable as he continues to swim toward the bottom of the Great Tree. As they get closer, the roots move out of the way, causing the door to the tree to open. Za-Ryan swims through it as the roots close behind them. Zuna and her advisers speed up and swim through the door before it can close. They watch as Za-Ryan and Zelena emerge onto a platform. He places Zelena on the ground. Orange lights start to flash around them, revealing a city inside of the tree. Zuna looks around in amazement.

"What is this? There's an entire city inside of RoyalTree?"

Serel looks around with her.

"I was not aware of a city being in here. Defunis, what is this place?"

Defunis stands next to her with his eyes wide open.

"It can't be…. It is TralVent, our first city and military headquarters that Zembor had originally taken from the Ventrians. It was taken aback by the Ventrians before Zalzatine retook it for his father. As you can tell from the name, the city was used by both Tralupians and Ventrians. At one point, they lived together under a peace treaty. Sadly, it didn't last long before fighting broke out again. During the fighting, the city mysteriously vanished, but because of the war, there wasn't any time to figure out what happened. When the war ended, TralVent was gone. Both the Tralupians and Ventrians were unable to figure out what happened, so Zalzatine eventually gave up on trying to find it. It is magnificent, though. How could our lost city possibly end up inside RoyalTree?"

Queen Zuna and Serel stand silently watching her parents. Za-Ryan starts to speak.

"I have done what you asked of me. I know I am not worthy of being here, so I thank you."

RoyalTree roars down at Za-Ryan and Zelena before it responds.

"You have done well, Za-Ryan, and I thank you for bringing Zelena to me. As we discussed before you jumped into my waters, I can only give life if I have one to take."

Za-Ryan looks down at his unconscious wife, covered in blood. He looks back up into the hollow tree.

"We had an arrangement. I don't intend to take back my promise if you do what you said you would."

RoyalTree roars again.

"You dare question me? I never go back on what I say. Get on with it!"

Za-Ryan nods his head and lifts his beloved wife into his arms once more. The city lights up as he walks toward it. They walk into TralVent, it glows even brighter, blinding Zuna and her advisers. The light fades away; they all stand in front of a statue of Zembor. Its eyes glow a brilliant orange. Za-Ryan places Zelena gently down at its feet. He then reaches up and grabs onto the statue. It pulses with light, and after a couple of seconds, the entire sculpture lights up, shining on Za-Ryan. Its arm moves and points toward him, before crumbling away to reveal a blade. Za-Ryan kneels to Zelena on the ground. He kisses her on the forehead and then on her belly.

"I will always love the two of you."

Tears start to run down his face, mixing with the blood, as he reaches out for the blade pointing at him. As he gets closer, the statue comes to life and drives the edge into his chest, lifting him off the ground.

"Ahhhhh!! My Queen, my love, take care of our daughter, and live on in greatness."

The statue drives the blade further into his chest. He struggles for a couple of seconds, swinging his arms and legs in the air before his life fades away. His limp body dangles above the unconscious Zelena, his blood dripping down on her. The blade piercing through him starts to glow. The blood droplets turn from green to the same glowing color as the blade. As the now orange blood trickles onto Zelena, it begins to shine brightly, slowly moving around her body - cleaning off all the blood and healing her wounds. The light starts to flash within her before it bursts out, lighting up RoyalTree. It disappears quickly, and Zelena sits against the statue with baby Zuna crying in her arms. She looks up and sees Za-Ryan with the blade piercing through him.

"Nooo! Za-Ryan!!! Why!? Please, RoyalTree, you have to help him."

RoyalTree's voice reverberates through the statue of Zembor.

"There is nothing I can do. He made his choice so that you and your daughter could live."

She reaches up above her towards his limp body, but as soon as she touches his foot, his body beings to crumble away. A pile of orange ash is all that remains, sitting in front of her and her crying daughter. Zelena tries to get up but is still too weak. The ash lifts into the air and swirls around them, an unseen force helping them up off the ground. A faint voice is heard through it.

"You must live on without me, my love. Take care of our children for me and watch Zuna closely. I can see she is already one with RoyalTree."

Zelena closes her eyes as tears stream down her face. The swirling dust around them moves to the statue, absorbing into it. The light from the blade fades away, and the arm starts to reform. The statue flashes once more before disappearing.

The lost city of TralVent releases a burst of light before completely fading away with it. Zelena stands up and looks around the hollow tree. She lifts her daughter above her head.

"This is the Great Zuna Wrathfin, born from Zelena and Za-Ryan Wrathfin. She is the first of our family to be birthed inside of you, RoyalTree."

She brings her back down and places her on the ground next to her. She then bows to RoyalTree, as he speaks to her.

"Za-Ryan's sacrifice will not go in vain. He gave his life to let you and your daughter live. You must continue leading your people while raising your daughter to be our next Queen. She has more royal blood in her than any of your past leaders."

Zelena picks her daughter up and stands to stare up in the tree.

"How is that possible when Za-Ryan wasn't a true Wrathfin?"

"His blood became pure and royal when he made his sacrifice to save you. I used Zembor's blade to change his blood. If it weren't for what he did, I wouldn't have been able to save you. But in the process, something great has come from it. Your daughter Zuna now shares the same blood as our once great leader Zembor, making her more royal than even you."

Zelena looks to her daughter in her arms.

"You're going to be the greatest Queen in TokBellu's history!"

Zuna and her advisers continue watching as everything around them begins to rumble. Suddenly, orange light comes up from the bottom of the tree, like water flushing them out. They get consumed by it, unable to see anything but orange. Zuna takes a deep breath and closes her eyes. She waits several seconds before opening them again. They are back in the present on TokBellu; she is holding her trident once again. The trident illuminates underneath her hand. She lets go and drops it to the floor, the light fading away.

"I.... I'm not sure what to think about that."

Defunis and Serel stand next to her, looking at the trident. Serel reaches down and picks it up to hand back to Zuna.

"We aren't sure either. Like I said before, there is still a lot we don't know about RoyalTree, but we now understand why you are the 'Chosen One.'"

"Chosen one? What do you mean?"

Defunis jumps in.

"RoyalTree has been waiting for the reincarnation of our great leader Zembor. It is your destiny to be that, and now we finally understand why. You were given Zembor's blood from RoyalTree. That mixed in with your already Royal blood makes you superior to any of our past leaders."

"So, what does that mean? How do I use that to lead our people?"

"That is something you need to figure out on your own. We have never advised anyone like you."

Defunis and Serel bow to their Queen.

"That's enough. I do like the title of being the superior Tralupian, but I still don't understand."

"We trust you will in time, my Queen."

Defunis and Serel stand back up and walk with her to the throne room. As they approach, Zuna notices an orange transparent figure sitting in her place. Zelena Wrathfin sits staring at her. Zuna stops in her tracks, prompting Defunis and Serel to look over at her in confusion.

"Do you see something?"

"Yes... my mother. She's sitting on the throne, staring at me."

"Have you tried speaking to her?"

Zuna holds back her tears and approaches the former Queen.

"Mother, is it really you?"

The trident on Zuna's back begins to glow.

"Yes, it's me. I can't believe I'm seeing you again."

"How is any of this even possible? You're dead."

"Anything is possible with Zembor's Trident and RoyalTree. I know how this all seems, Zuna, but this is what RoyalTree does for us. It took me a very long time to understand it all, and by the time I did, it was too late. I am very sorry I never told you about your father. Za-Ryan was my life. Even after we had twelve children together, it wasn't until you came along, Zuna, that I truly understood. You are so special because of your father. I know you saw the memory from RoyalTree...please forgive me."

Zuna walks over to her transparent mother and sticks her hand out. Zelena reaches back, and the light causes sparks to fly when they touch. Zelena pulls her hand away and sits back on the throne.

"We only have a little bit of time before I have to go."

"What do you mean? Go where?"

"Even though I am gone, I am not completely dead. My body is gone, but because of the bond I shared with RoyalTree, my mind and spirit were saved. I live inside of RoyalTree with the rest of our past leaders. The lost city you saw in the memory, TralVent, is where we reside."

"After I stabbed you in the ceremony, you became one with RoyalTree? What about the pain?"

"There is no pain, only light and warmth. It is hard to explain. I am free to do as I please unless RoyalTree needs me, then we do whatever he asks. That was part of the deal Zembor made when he planted the Great Tree."

"I miss you, mother... Why can't I see you whenever I like?"

"I miss you too, my daughter. I wish it worked like that, but RoyalTree works in mysterious ways. Like Defunis and Serel told you, they were created by RoyalTree, and there is still plenty they don't know."

"Are all of our past leaders in there with you?"

"Yes, except Zembor. The oldest leader here is Zalzatine, but he doesn't know or understand why his father isn't here with us. When we ask RoyalTree, it just roars back at us instead of speaking like usual."

"I saw Zembor the other day; the same way I'm seeing you."

"That's impossible! Where? What was he doing? Did he speak to you?"

"I saw him standing next to the trident before wandering around my room. The only words he spoke were something about the trident being the key to saving our people. Then he turned into an orange sphere and slammed into my bed."

"I don't understand how this is possible. If we haven't seen him in RoyalTree, there shouldn't be any way for him to be outside of it. Unless..."

Zuna notices her mother starting to flicker.

"Mother, what's wrong?"

"My time here is running out. I will be back when I can. You are much stronger than you know, my Zuna."

Zelena continues to flash, and the trident on Zuna's back starts to pulsate with her. As they sync up together, Zelena floats into the air and gets absorbed into the trident. Zuna takes it off her back and investigates it as the flashing slows down.

"Nooo! Mother, come back!"

The trident stops glowing orange and changes to a crimson color. A voice yells through it at Zuna.

"Your mother will come back when I tell her to! You are stronger than the rest of them! So be it! You will still be mine!!"

Zuna drops the trident and looks back at Defunis and Serel.

"That didn't sound like RoyalTree...."

Defunis walks over and picks up the trident. The crimson light pulses through his hand.

"Ahhhh!"

Serel runs over to him and tries to knock the trident out of his hand, but it beats faster as she latches onto it, too.

"Ahhhh, help us! We can't let go! It burns!"

The flesh from their hands starts to melt onto the trident. Queen Zuna tries to get to them, but the trident creates a force field around them, blocking her off.

"I don't know what to do! I can't get to you!"

She continues to watch helplessly, banging on the force field, as she watches Defunis and Serel fall to the ground. Their skin from their hands has burned into the trident. The voice comes through again.

"I never should have created the two of you. You have betrayed me for the last time!"

The crimson light shoots out from the trident, hitting the edge of the force field. Zuna watches helplessly as it consumes her advisers. When it finally dissipates, the trident lies still on the floor—Defunis, and Serel next to it. Their flesh has been disintegrated, nothing but their skeletons remain. The force field blocking her way disappears back into the trident, along with the light. She runs over to the skeletons on the ground.

"Defunis! Serel! No, no, no, no…. Why?!"

The trident flashes red again.

"Because they disobeyed my orders and told you things they had no business telling you. I am the creator of RoyalTree. I am a god on this planet!!!"

"What kind of god does this to his people!? You are no god, just a murderer!"

"Hahahaha…you may be right about that, but I have become a god in the process! Obey me or pay the price like them!"

"You're going to have to kill me then. I will never obey you!"

"I cannot kill the reincarnation of Zembor Wrathfin. You are what we have been waiting for!"

"We!? Who are you? What are you?"

"I already told you. I am a god!!!!"

The trident rises on its own and starts to glow red, shooting a beam of light onto Zuna.

"What is this? Let me go!"

"You need to be punished for not listening!"

The red light hits her in the chest, freezing her in place.

"You will still be in your body, but you will have no control over it. I will be the one in control, speaking for you while you watch, powerless. Let's see how long it takes for you to obey me!"

Zuna stands paralyzed, listening to him. The light disappears, and the trident falls to the ground. She can feel her body moving, but not from her own will. Someone else is controlling her. She speaks out loud to herself.

"See, I have the power!"

Queen Zuna saunters over to the trident, picking it up and staring into it. She strolls over to her throne and sits down. The trident glows crimson as she sits with a malicious smile on her face.

# Chapter 9:
# Johthuns- Honoring the Code

The year is 2700. Twelve years have passed since Tanglor, and his friends became Elite Protectors. Tanglor and Ashar have moved up in the ranks, both becoming Captains. Ranyana and Dretzlin are next in line to be promoted as the Elite Protectors continue to grow. Leazara and the Elders have agreed on new arrangements and established new rules for the Johthuns. Every Johthun is to be trained in combat and exploration. Once they graduate from school, they will have the option to specialize in one or learn both. If they choose the military, they will be trained to fight in the Johthun army alongside the Elite Protectors. Any soldier deemed worthy will be selected to train further as an Elite. The new agreement pushed the Johthuns back on the right track, but there were still those that did not agree. As the Elites grew in numbers, so did the True Guardians. Leazara calls a meeting in their newly established base to address the situation.

Our new base, the Tazruhvah, is located above ground in the city a block away from the Rashintrah. The Parasav is now used as a prison and also houses a rehabilitation center for the injured. The Elite Protectors patrol the city, maintaining the peace.

Tanglor arrives at the meeting and sits with Ashar and the two other Captains, Ucarus and a female Johthun named Neliah. Ranyana and Dretzlin come in with the other Elite Protectors and sit down. Once everyone has taken their seats, the Colonel stands up.

"I called everyone here to talk about the True Guardians. It's time they were stopped. We've waited far too long and let them build their defenses up. They moved their home base to the recently colonized planet of Hontor. I'm going to send in two of my Captains with their squads to eliminate them. Tanglor and Ucarus will be my two Captains leading the charge. Ashar and Neliah, you two will wait with your squads as backup. Be ready to move in if they call you."

They all look around, making sure everyone is on the same page, and then look back to the Colonel.

"Alright, Hontor has only recently been colonized. Consequently, we haven't had the chance to get any Elites onto the planet yet. The True Guardians arriving first and establishing their base further complicates things. We are practically close to being in the dark here. Luckily, Neliah and her crew gathered some footage of the planet when they flew by it a couple of days ago."

She stops and points to the screen behind her. A video starts to play, and the camera zooms in on the planet Hontor, where you can see Johthuns moving supply crates and building different barriers. The clip is quick. It shuts off, and the Colonel continues to brief them.

"That's all we have so far. We know they're on the planet, and we know they're going to be ready for us. The topography is like Thoonta, so it shouldn't be too hard for us to maneuver once we get there."

She looks around the room at the Captains and Elite Protectors.

"We will meet again tomorrow after we are victorious!"

They all stand up and cheer! Tanglor walks over to his brother.

"I trust I will see you soon. Though I'm hoping we don't need that backup."

Ashar and Tanglor hug before going their separate ways, they each have one hundred Elite Protectors and two hundred Johthun soldiers in their squads. The Captains with their small armies pack themselves onto the ships, loading their weapons and supplies. They launch into orbit heading to Hontor.

Upon entry into Hontor's atmosphere, they are greeted by True Guardian ships. They fire without hesitation, causing Tanglor and Ucarus to maneuver their ships before they fire back. Ashar and Neliah are behind ready for cover fire. They shoot their rapid blasters toward the True Guardians. Tanglor and Ucarus expertly pilot their ships, flipping and rolling through the bullets and enemy vessels. They pass through the atmosphere, getting by the line of defenses and landing on the planet. Ashar and Neliah watch from orbit ready to help.

Immediately upon landing, Tanglor and Ucarus have their troops unload their vehicles and weapons. Ucarus looks around then frowns at Tanglor.

"It's a wasteland here. Where are the buildings we saw in Neliaha's video?"

Tanglor takes a careful look around.

"I'm not sure, but we need to be careful. They're around here somewhere."

As they continue unloading their supplies, a loud clicking starts.

"Click, click, click, click, click."

It stops just as abruptly as it began. There's silence in the air before a loud bang rings out.

"Boom. Boom."

Out of nowhere, two massive blasts are seen heading toward the armies. The troops scatter, but the bombing happens too fast for some of the soldiers to react. Tanglor dives out of the way—grabbing two of his men on the way down. They watch powerlessly as their fellow soldiers are taken out. A soldier yells between the loud booms.

"Look, the shots are coming from over there! It's a cloaked building."

The blast fires again, and for a moment, a turret attached to a building becomes visible. Tanglor springs up and starts running toward it.

"Charge!! They're right in front of us!"

He slides down and pulls out his blades, swinging them in front of him. Blood pours out of a cloaked True Guardian. Hundreds of them appear in front of Tanglor. He gets up and continues to run with his army behind him. Some of the soldiers and Elites get into the vehicles and heavy turrets they brought with them. They start firing back, causing the building to be revealed. Tanglor and Ucarus lead the charge, wiping out every True Guardian they come across. Blasts continue to hit the ground around them, causing explosions and fire to fall from the sky. Tanglor reaches the entrance of the building with ten Elite protectors and five Johthun soldiers. Ranyana and Dretzlin are among the present Elite while Ucarus goes for the flank with twenty of his troops.

Tanglor and his squad bust through the front entrance, only to be welcomed by True Guardians brandishing weapons they had never seen before. Their blasters glow yellow with small surges coming from the barrel. Tanglor and his soldiers charge at them while they fire. The first shots miss them, but they fire again, hitting one of the Elites. She screams in pain and starts to disintegrate. She continues screaming as Tanglor, and the rest of them watch, frozen in horror. There is nothing they can do. The Elite Protector has completely turned into yellow ash. Tanglor, unable to contain his fury, charges at the True Guardians. His squad unquestioningly follows behind him. Tanglor uses his blade to slice one of their arms off, taking his blaster. He drops it to the ground and continues to use his blades. Dretzlin picks up the mysterious weapon and starts to fire it at the True Guardians. They all turn into yellow ash with Dretzlin standing over them. Tanglor runs over and tries to grab the blaster from him, but Dretzlin pulls it away and stares at him.

"You can take the other ones, but this one is mine until we are done here. Until I find my brother."

He clenches his hand tight around it. Tanglor backs away.

"Just don't do anything you're going to regret."

Dretzlin turns his back and waits to move on the True Guardians, nothing on his mind but finding his brother and getting some answers. Tanglor walks over to Ranyana while they're destroying what's left of the weapons.

"Keep an eye on him, please."

"Always!"

Tanglor calls Ucarus on the comms.

"We're in the front. Everyone here is gone. What's your position?"

Ucarus takes a couple of seconds to respond.

"Five minutes! Strike in five!"

Tanglor and his squad catch their breath and regroup. As the time hits five minutes, Tanglor runs and jumps through the windows in front of him. His team follows and crashes through, causing the glass to fall with them. They fall straight onto the True Guardians, currently fighting Ucarus and his team. They take them out with ease and meet up with Ucarus and his troops.

"Thanks for that, Tanglor! We can't waste any time. We need to catch up to Flujen before he gets away."

They run down the hallway and are met by more True Guardians appearing from thin air. This time Freden stands before them.

"I was hoping I wasn't going to have to see you again, Dretzlin."

Dretzlin steps forward, holding the blaster in front of him.

"I've wanted to ask you some questions, brother."

Freden charges at Dretzlin with True Guardians following behind him.

"I told you when we said goodbye; we are no longer brothers!"

Dretzlin hesitates and doesn't shoot, letting Freden punch him in the face. He drops the weapon and rolls on top of Freden. He gets a couple of punches in before Freden laughs and kicks Dretzlin off him.

"I'm surprised you fought back. I guess leaving you with Tanglor Raff wasn't so bad after all."

He catches Ranyana sneaking up behind him. Freden jumps out of the way and knocks her out with one blow. Reaching down, he grabs two of her knives. Freden tosses them up in the air in front of him.

"I already apologized, and I need to get past feeling bad if I want to survive this."

He throws the knives piercing Dretzlin in the left arm – effectively pinning him to the wall he's sitting up against.

"I don't want to kill you! Stay out of my way!"

Freden walks over to Dretzlin and punches him in the face, swiftly knocking him out. He turns and looks at Tanglor, fighting off some True Guardians. Freden rushes behind him and tackles him to the ground. He stands above him with the others watching. He raises his blade, but Ucarus comes flying out from behind Tanglor and knocks Freden to the ground. He looks back at Tanglor.

"Get your friends and head to the ships. I will take care of Freden and the base."


Tanglor refuses to leave him. In a blink, he's on his feet and charging the enemy once again. He pulls out his blades and leaps toward Ucarus, who is still on top of Freden. Ucarus notices and waits till the last second before rolling off Freden. Tanglor lands on top of him, his blades resting just above Freden's shoulders, a hair's breadth from his neck.

"It's over, Freden. I'm not going to kill you."

"No...but I am!"

Dretzlin shoves Tanglor aside and points the blaster in Freden's face.

"I'm not letting you leave. Not after everything you have done. Your lies and deception end here!"

His shaking fingers grip the trigger while Tanglor and Ranyana walk over to him. Ranyana looks at Tanglor.

"I got this."

She stands next to Dretzlin, still trembling with the blaster pointed at his older brother.

"I can't imagine how you're feeling right now, but I know this isn't you. Remember who we are, no matter how dire the situation is."

Dretzlin begins to listen to her and slowly puts the blaster down. Freden notices and seizes his opportunity. He kicks out, knocking Dretzlin and Ranyana to the ground. The blaster drops in front of Freden, he rolls over, picking it up and immediately aiming it at Dretzlin and Ranyana. Tanglor and the others all have their weapons drawn and pointed at Freden. He starts to laugh as he stands up over them.

"Look what you've done, Dretzlin. All of this, everything that's happening and about to happen is because of you. You should've let Tanglor have his Elite Justice come and take me away. But instead..."

He moves his finger toward the trigger, aiming for Dretzlin. Suddenly, he moves the blaster and shoots Ranyana. Before anyone can react, he hits the cloaking switch on his shoulder and disappears. Tanglor runs over to Ranyana as she tries to hold back the pain.

"No, no, no. Get back here, you bastard!"

He puts his arms around her, Dretzlin sits next to them, his eyes wide with shock. Ranyana looks over to him as she slowly starts to disintegrate.

"It's not your fault Dretzlin.... remember who we are..."

Her voice fades away as she crumbles into yellow ash.

Tanglor sits covered, crying in her remains. Ucarus and the others watch with nothing to say. They gather their things and leave Dretzlin and Tanglor alone until it's time for them to go. Tanglor scoops as much of her remains as he can and puts them into a jar to give to Ashar. After collecting the innocent, and with one of their ships lost in battle, the flight back into orbit is quite crowded. They watch solemnly as the True Guardian's base explodes. Leazara gets on the comms to talk with Ucarus and Tanglor.

"You both did great out there. I am sorry for the loss of Ranyana. She was one of our best. I made the call to destroy the entire planet because of their cloaking devices. Freden should be the only one with a device now. I know Flujen and Freden got away, but we took out the rest of them. See you back on Joht."

The Colonel shuts her comms off, as a voice appears from behind Tanglor and Ucarus.

"Looks like we can come with you to talk to your Colonel...unless you want things to go badly for the Johthuns on this ship."

They both turn around to find Flujen standing behind them with a detonator in his hand. Freden smirks at him.

"Wait until I find and kill him."

Freden walks out to look for Dretzlin. Tanglor wastes no time before running at Flujen, smacking the detonator out of his hand.

"You fool! That will kill everyone on this ship!"

Tanglor pulls his blades out and swings at Flujen. He dodges and jumps away from him, pulling out his blade. He rushes back toward Tanglor and thrusts his sword at him. Tanglor dodges to the right, letting the blade slide between his arm and body, barely missing him. He gets close enough and uses the blunt side of his weapon to hit Flujen in the face repeatedly until he falls to the ground. Tanglor cuffs him and ties him to one of the seats in the ship. He goes on the intercom.

"Everyone, be careful! Freden is onboard. Dretzlin, he's coming for you!"

Dretzlin sits in his room with his head down, hearing the message on the comms. Before he can look up, a voice appears in front of him.

"No need to hide; Tanglor spoiled my fun."

Freden stabs his blade down at Dretzlin, but he rolls back on the bed, narrowly avoiding the hit. He springs to his feet and jumps over Freden grabbing his blaster off the wall. Dretzlin fires it at him, but he activates his cloaking and disappears. Dretzlin continues to fire, destroying the room and finally hitting him. Freden's cloaking deactivates, and he is kneeling on the ground.

"Do it! Just kill me and end this. We both know I'm not going to stop otherwise!"

Dretzlin puts the blaster up to Freden's head and switches the setting to lethal. Tanglor runs to the door and sees him standing over Freden.

"Dretzlin! You don't have to do this! Ranyana didn't die so that you could get your revenge! Remember who you are!"

Dretzlin's arms shake, his finger on the trigger. He stops and takes a deep breath before hitting Freden with the barrel of the blaster, knocking him unconscious. He stands over him and drops the blaster.

"Whatever you've done, you'll have to live with... While being locked away for the rest of your life."

Dretzlin walks out of the room past Tanglor before he stops and turns around.

"Thank you."

Tanglor nods his head and watches Dretzlin walk away. He goes in and cuffs Freden before tying him up in the seat next to Flujen. Tanglor sits down in the Captain's chair next to Ucarus and gets back on the comms.

"The threat on the ship has been dealt with. Everyone is safe. We will be back to Joht shortly."

Ucarus grabs the detonator that Flujen dropped and smashes it into pieces, deactivating whatever bombs were attached to it. Tanglor picks up the jar filled with Ranyana's yellow ashes and puts it in front of him. He stares at it as the ship enters the orbit of Joht.

# Chapter 10:
# Tralupians- Brothers

"What are you doing!? You're going to get yourself killed fighting like that!"

Ilikso interrupts a fight between some recruits in the Barracks.

"You have to be quick if you're going to swing your blade like that."

He approaches the soldier and pushes him out of the way.

"Watch me and then replicate it. Go on—attack me!"

The soldier across from him charges forward, swinging his blade side to side.

Ilikso smiles as he blocks the attacks with ease.

"See, if you just swing side to side like that, it gives the defender an easy counterattack. You must be quick and swift with your attacks. If you miss on a swing, keep attacking! We're warriors, after all! But you need to stay controlled, like this!"

Ilikso deflects another attack, knocking the recruit to the side. He slides on the ground underneath him, kicking out his legs. The recruit falls to the ground as Ilikso holds his blade to his throat.

"When you are in control of your blade, it gives you more control over your body and mind."

He pulls his blade back and reaches his hand out to help the recruit up. Both rookies bow to Ilikso.

"Thank you, Ilikso. We will fight with more control, and we'll be swift about it."

Ilikso bows back before turning around to see his older brother, Siritano, watching him.

"Some impressive teaching skills you have there, Ilikso!"

"Better than yours, Siritano! What are you doing here? Don't you have your recruits to train?"

"Our training has concluded for today; I'm giving them a much-deserved rest. Zuna has us working them too hard. We can't have an army ready if they're all too tired to fight."

Ilikso looks around the barracks at his recruits' training.

"They do look a bit worn out, I suppose, and they do work hard every day, but what about Zuna? If she sees them resting, she'll be furious."

"I will talk to our sister. She has been acting weird lately."

"What do you mean? How has she been acting?"

"I don't know how to explain it. She just doesn't seem like herself."

Ilikso gives his brother a weird look while Oryuna walks in.

"What are the two of you talking about?"

"Siritano was just mentioning that Queen Zuna isn't acting like herself."

"I noticed that, as well. I didn't want to say anything, but it's almost been a year since Defunis and Serel. Do you think that has something to do with it?"

"She was pretty close with them... It could be a reason. We should talk to Musfina. She has been the one advising our sister since Defunis and Serel died."

Siritano looks to both of them.

"The recruits are all busy cleaning and resting for the day, so it's the perfect opportunity for us to go and talk to her and the Queen. If something is going on, we should know about it."

Oryuna and Ilikso nod their heads to him before following him out of the barracks. They make their way to the palace. As they approach the entrance, Ilikso stops and looks toward RoyalTree.

"Did you guys just hear that?"

Oryuna turns around.

"Hear what? Ilikso, what are you talking about?"

Siritano stops and stands next to his brother.

"Wait, I hear something, too."

Ilikso and Siritano walk over to the ledge next to RoyalTree. Ilikso points down into the water.

"Look! Someone's down there!"

Without hesitating, Ilikso and Siritano jump off the ledge into the water. Oryuna looks over and sees something underneath them.

"Look out!"

She jumps down, splashing in next to them.

"Where did it go?"

Siritano and Ilikso look around and see nothing but ripples of water. Ilikso swims over to Oryuna.

"I swear I saw someone down here. Siritano and I both heard them yelling."

"I don't know what *you* saw, but whatever *I* saw underneath you was not a Tralupian."

Siritano starts to swim over to them.

"I think I saw it go under the water."

Submerging themselves, they look around but still see nothing. Oryuna points to RoyalTree's trunk.

"There's a small orange light. What is it?"

The three of them swim over to the light emitting from the tree. Siritano reaches his hand out and touches it. As he places his palm on the light, it starts to flash. It continues while growing in size; it starts to shoot out from the tree. Oryuna and Ilikso back away as Siritano tries to remove his hand.

"Help, my hand is stuck! It won't budge!"

Ilikso and Oryuna watch as the light starts to surround them. Ilikso swims back to his brother and tries to pry his hand off the tree.

"He's stuck! Oryuna, leave while you still can. Get Zuna. She is the only one that knows what RoyalTree truly is."

Oryuna hesitates before leaving her brothers behind. She starts to swim away as the orange light shoots out at them. She looks back and swims faster, trying not to get consumed by the light like her brothers. Oryuna gets near the surface as it gets closer. She jumps out of the water and looks back to try to see her brothers, but all she can see is solid orange.

"Siritano, Ilikso…. The two of you better be okay!"

Oryuna runs to the palace to find Queen Zuna and Musfina.

-------------------------------------------------

"Ilikso! Hold on to me!"

Ilikso tightens his grip on his brother's arm. The orange around them starts to spin and cause a whirlpool in the water. They get tossed around, hitting the trunk of the tree.

"Ahhhh, Siritano! Swim down!"

Siritano and Ilikso fight the current and swim down toward the bottom of RoyalTree. As they get closer to the bottom, roots come out from the tree trunk and latch onto them.

"What the hell is up with this tree? It's like it's trying to kill us!"

Ilikso tries to swim over to his brother, caught in the roots, but he gets grabbed too. They both fight to break loose, but it's no use. RoyalTree has its roots wrapped around them while they sink to the ground. Siritano and Ilikso lay underwater on the ground, unable to move. As they look to each other, the roots start pulling them closer to the tree.

"Ilikso, what's going on?"

"I don't know, brother. Keep your head up and your eyes on me!"

Right after he says that another root comes shooting out from under them and covers Siritano's eyes.

"Ahhhh! Get off me!"

Ilikso struggles more and manages to get his arm loose. He pulls out his blade and cuts one of the roots off him. A loud shriek comes from inside the tree, followed by a low rumble. Before Ilikso can break free, more roots shoot out around him, wrapping him back up.

"What do you want? You damn tree!"

The loud shrieking stops, but the rumbling continues for a moment. It finally ends, and the roots pull the two brothers against the trunk of the tree. Siritano's eyes are still covered. Ilikso shouts to him.

"I am still here, brother! We're going to get out of this together. I promise I won't leave you."

Siritano is about to respond, but another root swings around from the other side of the trunk and slaps against his mouth, keeping it shut.

"Mmbbmmm. MMMMMMMMMM!!"

"Just tell us what you want!? I know that you're a living entity! Show us what you want!!!"

The trunk of the tree rumbles again. The roots wrapped around them let go and form a path into a door under the tree. Siritano looks over to Ilikso.

"What the hell is going on? We need to get out of here!"

"I don't know what's going on, but there isn't a way out past these roots. We have to go through that door."

Siritano looks around at the encased path they're in.

"Shit, let's go."

The two of them swim down to the door and push it open. A current begins to flow past them. Ilikso turns around and looks up.

"That's not good."

The orange around them shoots through the path, launching them into the door and up into RoyalTree. Vines sprout out from the side of the tree, creating a ledge for them to land on. They stand up and look through the hollow tree. Siritano looks to his brother.

"Really? This is the Great RoyalTree? There's nothing in here. How is it a living entity?"

"I don't know, brother, but something doesn't feel right to me."

As they continue to look around, the inside of the tree starts to flash orange. Ilikso grabs onto his brother.

"Something is happening. Prepare yourself."

The light continues to flash, getting faster, a city appears in front of them. The flashing light stops and shoots up into the tree, smashing into it. Lightning starts to strike down around them, as thunder shakes the tree. Ilikso looks to his brother as he begins to run.

"Siritano, we need to get to that city!"

He runs after his brother. The two arrive at a house with an orange light on the front porch. As the two brothers walk toward it, the door slowly creaks open, welcoming them in. Siritano pulls out his blade.

"You were right. This place has a weird feeling."

Ilikso looks at the sign on the door.

"No way! It says TralVent Inn. This is the lost city that disappeared back in 1737!"

"I thought that was just a legend that mother would tell us. She usually sounded crazy. Unless she was with Zuna."

"How is this possible? We need to look at what's inside."

Ilikso and Siritano walk into the inn with their weapons ready. The inside is dark, and noises come from upstairs. Ilikso approaches the staircase with his brother's back to his. The sounds start to get louder. Siritano turns and stands next to his brother, looking down the hallway.

"Should we split up to make this quicker?"

"Are you going to be okay without me?"

Siritano pushes Ilikso and moves toward the first of four doors on the left.

"We both know it's *you* that needs *me*."

Ilikso smiles at his brother and runs to the only door on the right. He reaches for the doorknob. As he turns it, it locks and heats up, burning his hand. Ilikso steps back and looks at the door.

"I don't think so, you bastard!"

He charges at it and smashes through, landing on the ground. A crimson humanoid figure with sharp fingers, black pits for eyes, two slits where its nose should be, and pointed teeth stands staring at him.

"What the hell are you!?"

He stands up and swings his blade at the creature slicing entirely through it. The beast stands unscathed, still staring at him. Ilikso moves slowly toward it. The beast stands motionless, smiling at him.

"Are you even real?"

Its head turns to the side and watches Ilikso as he moves around the room.

"Okay, that's a little creepy... Can you speak?"

The creature turns its body and starts to walk toward Ilikso. He tries to move out of the way, but a sudden numbness comes over him.

"Why can't I move!? What did you do!?"

The creature gets in front of him and starts to laugh. It reaches its hand out for his head, wrapping its long, sharp fingers around him.

Meanwhile, Siritano opens the door to the first room, his blade ready to strike, but the room is empty. He hears a noise in the next room over. Yet, when he opens that door—there's nothing. The sound grows louder, coming from the third room now. He slowly approaches it. Siritano kicks the door down and sees an orange light floating in the middle of the room.

"Another orange light. Why is it every light in this place is orange?"

The light flashes and flies through the wall, Siritano takes a deep breath before walking out of the room towards the next door. It swings open as he approaches it. The orange light flashes and changes to a crimson color. It then transforms into the same creature Ilikso saw. Siritano runs screaming, back towards his brother.

"Ilikso! Where are you!?"

Siritano gets to the broken door and sees his brother being held by one of the creatures. He pulls his blade back out and runs at it.

"Let him go!"

He swings his blade at the creature's arm slicing straight through but doing no damage. The beast turns around smiling, dropping Ilikso to the ground and advances on Siritano.

"You.... are.... the.... one.... we........ WANT!"

Suddenly, it leaps at Siritano, but he jumps backward, dodging its attack. As he steps back out of the door, he's grabbed by the first creature he saw.

"Let me go, you monsters!"

They both laugh while holding Siritano. Ilikso gets to his feet and charges at them.

"You'll both die before you take him!"

Ilikso swings his blade, but the glowing creatures hold their hands out in front of them. A quick burst of light shoots out, knocking Ilikso back. They continue to laugh as they walk away with Siritano, struggling in their grasp. Ilikso gets up, and trails them back to the hallway, he looks down and sees them standing at the end facing a wall. They place their hands on it, and a portal appears. They walk through without looking back. Ilikso sprints after them, but the door shuts and turns back into a wall as he slams into it. He continues to smash his sword against it while screaming.

"Siritano!!! Bring my brother back!!!"

Ilikso lets go of his sword and falls to the ground. He leans on the wall, staring down the empty hallway, his eyes wide open and tears running down his face.

------------------------------------------------------------

94

"Queen Zuna! Musfina!!"

Oryuna screams as she runs into the palace. Queen Zuna and Musfina are sitting in the throne room discussing TokBellu and its future.

"Help!! Zuna, Musfina!"

The Queen jumps off the throne.

"What! Why are you interrupting us with this outburst!?"

Oryuna kneels and catches her breath.

"I apologize, but its Ilikso and Siritano!"

The Queen, visibly irritated, walks toward her.

"Spit it out!"

"They were consumed by an orange substance under the water next to RoyalTree!"

Queen Zuna grabs Oryuna by the throat. Musfina stands up and runs over to them.

"Sister! What are you doing?"

Queen Zuna turns to Musfina, her eyes glow bright orange. A deep voice comes out of her mouth.

"You have been useful to me. Stay back, or I will exterminate you!"

Musfina steps back and watches the Queen pick Oryuna up off the ground. She continues speaking in a deep voice.

"That is impossible! What were they doing in the water next to RoyalTree!?"

Oryuna struggles to talk with her throat, being squeezed by the Queen.

"We saw something in the water; it was yelling for help. We tried to...."

The Queen throws Oryuna to the ground. Musfina runs over to her, as Zuna falls to the ground and grabs her head. The trident on her back starts to glow orange. It gets brighter and suddenly changes into crimson. Zuna yells as she squirms on the ground.

"Ahhhhh!!! I don't know, leave me and find out for yourself!!!"

She continues to struggle as the light from the trident flows into her body. It shines through her skin, crawling toward her head. Zuna stands up and releases a booming yell!

"Leave!!!!"

The crimson starts to seep out of her eyes and mouth, forming a cloud in front of her. Zuna stumbles away from it and falls backward into Musfina and Oryuna arms. Oryuna moves in front of her and pulls out her specially designed blaster. It's a small, single-handed blaster that fires tiny bullets in rapid succession. She shoots it at the cloud, causing it to spread itself out. It releases a faded laugh before flying out of the palace toward RoyalTree.

Oryuna turns back to her sisters on the ground.

"Are you okay?"

Musfina helps the Queen up.

"Zuna, what was that thing?"

She stands up, holding onto her sister.

"Thank you. You saved me from whatever that wretched thing was. Oryuna, I am sorry for what I did. I've had no control over any of my actions for the past year."

Musfina looks to her, shocked.

"What!? This last year of being your adviser, I wasn't advising you?"

"I'm sorry, but no. RoyalTree had me in its control, or at least that's what I thought. We need to get to Siritano and Ilikso before that thing does. I promise I will explain everything to all of you when we return with our brothers."

Oryuna and Musfina put their arms around the Queen and walk with her to RoyalTree. They get outside to see a Dark Red storm circling it. Queen Zuna stands on her own now, observing it with her sisters.

"We have to hurry, follow me!"

She runs and leaps into the water surrounding the tree. Oryuna and Musfina follow close behind. They swim over to the Queen floating in the water, staring at the bottom of the Great Tree's trunk.

"What is it, sister?"

"We have to go down where those roots are. They're covering up our only way in."

Oryuna looks at her wide-eyed.

"Inside what? RoyalTree?"

Queen Zuna calmly swims toward the roots.

"Yes. Keep your weapons holstered while we enter. I don't think all of RoyalTree is bad, but there's something else going on."

Oryuna and Musfina follow behind their Queen. As they approach the roots, Zuna pulls out her trident. She points it at the base of the tree, and it begins to glow orange. The roots move aside, revealing the hidden door.

"Come close to me and hold on."

Zuna's sisters reach out and latch onto her. Zuna opens the door, the water behind them flows forward, pushing them inside and carrying them up into the tree. The water shoots them up, vines sprout out from the sides, giving them solid ground to land on. The inside of RoyalTree is an assault of orange and crimson explosions. The lost city of TralVent appears in front of them. A war rages on between an army of orange ghosts made up of Tralupians and Ventrians and an army of crimson monsters. Blasts of the two colors can be seen throughout the city. Queen Zuna and her sisters watch as the massive battle plays out, while thunder roars and blasts of orange lightning strike around them. The lightning strikes accelerate and continuously hit in front of them; they back up while the energy creates a Tralupian. It stands before them with a blade for an arm.

"I am Zembor Wrathfin, the first King of our people, your Great-Great-Grandfather."

Queen Zuna, Oryuna, and Musfina stand in shock as they look at the Greatest Tralupian, in their History.

# Chapter 11:
# Johthuns- Repercussions

Dretzlin escorts his cuffed brother out of the ship and onto Joht, Ucarus following behind with Flujen. Tanglor exits with the jar of Ranyana's ashes and catches up to the others heading toward the Tazruhvah. They are stopped by the Colonel and the other two Captains, Ashar and Neliah. Ashar steps forward, looking for Ranyana.

"Where is she? Where is Ranyana?"

Tanglor walks over to his brother with his head down.

"Ashar... I'm sorry."

He hands him the jar of yellow ash. Ashar looks at it, confused.

"What is this?"

"This is what's left of her, Ashar."

He grabs the jar in disbelief.

"No, this can't be. Where is she!?"

He starts to tear up and falls to the floor, cradling the jar to his chest. Dretzlin and Ucarus pass by, escorting the prisoners. As they are walking, Captain Flujen stops and laughs at him.

"Look how pathetic you are! Here, let me help you forget her."

Flujen kicks the jar out of Ashar's hands. It crashes onto the ground, sending ash all over the place. Everyone stops and watches as Ashar slowly stands up. He walks over to Flujen and gets in his face.

"Thanks, now I won't have to worry about how she would have felt about this."

Ashar head-butts him, breaking his nose and knocking him to the ground. As Flujen struggles, trying to get back on his feet, Ashar kicks him in the stomach knocking him back down. Ucarus and Tanglor rush over to them.

"Ashar, that's enough. We will take it from here!"

He turns and looks at Tanglor and Ucarus with a disturbed look on his face.

"No, Tanglor, not this time."

Ashar pulls out his blade and puts it next to Flujen's neck. Ucarus tries to grab Ashar, but he turns and punches him, knocking him into the wall. Flujen sits bloody and barely breathing, staring at Ashar.

"Ok, you've made your point! Please, someone, stop him!"

Ashar pulls his blade back and starts to walk away, Flujen releases a sigh of relief. But Ashar stops and turns back around. He runs toward him, jumping and swinging his blade with full force into Flujen's neck. The bloody Captain falls to the ground. Ashar stands above the decapitated body before he falls to his knees, dropping his weapon. He breaks down and starts to cry. Tanglor walks over and puts his hand on him.

"It's going to be okay."

Tanglor pulls Ashar to his feet, and the two head towards the Tazruhvah. He stops and looks back at the others.

"I'm taking Ashar to his room to rest. Meet in the Great Hall when you are done locking Freden away in the Parasav."

Ucarus follows behind Tanglor while Dretzlin and Leazara take Freden to the Parasav and throw him into a cell. Dretzlin locks the door behind him.

"This is going to be your home for the rest of your life. I hope it was worth it for you."

Freden stares back, speechless.

Dretzlin continues to stare at his brother but can't find any more words to say. He turns away and follows Leazara out of the Parasav. They arrive at the Great Hall to find the room filled with Elite Protectors and soldiers. They all sit staring up at Tanglor, now speaking at the podium.

"Yes, I agree that Ashar went too far by killing Captain Flujen, but he is going to have to live with that for the rest of his life. I think that is enough punishment for my brother. It will take a little bit of time, but Ashar will be fine. We have more important things to worry about right now."

Everyone in the room looks around and murmurs in agreement. The Colonel walks through the crowd of Johthuns toward Tanglor.

"I am glad we are all on the same page. Thank you, Tanglor."

He takes his seat next to the empty chair where Ashar would be. Neliah notices Tanglor sitting by himself and joins him.

"Mind if I sit here while Ashar is gone?"

Tanglor smiles as she sits down. Leazara continues to talk.

"We won a tough battle against the True Guardians on Hontor, but we haven't won the war. There are still many of them out there, and they will want revenge. Before Ashar killed Flujen, we were able to obtain the whereabouts of their home base. A planet they call Nahar. They lured us to Hontor to continue building up their defenses there. They'll be ready for our next attack, so we need to make it precise."

Tanglor jumps up from his seat.

"Colonel, I know how I could get into Nahar without them even knowing it."

Leazara sits down to listen to Tanglor's plan.

"I will escort Freden to Nahar staying undercover with his cloaking device. The True Guardians will let him in and have no idea I'm there."

She is intrigued by his plan.

"It's risky. How can you trust Freden? He's going to give away your cover as soon as he can."

"I'm going to be cloaked next to him the entire time with my blade ready to pierce his back. As soon as he makes any sort of move or says anything to give it away, the blade goes in, and I stay invisible."

Before Leazara can respond, Dretzlin stands up.

"I know I am still just an Elite, but I should be the one to do this. I need to prove myself, and I need to speak to my brother one last time. When we arrive, and they let us pass, I'm going to kill Freden and take down their defenses from the inside. Once I do that, the rest of you can charge in and take them out with ease. We can end this war once and for all."

Leazara motions for Tanglor to sit back down, she turns her attention to Dretzlin.

"Normally, it is not our way to kill a Johthun, but we've all seen that he won't stop. If we want to end the True Guardians, we must remove their best soldier from the picture. I will allow you to go and do this, but remember your true mission is to take out their defenses. If those shields and turrets aren't disabled, we stand no chance. Go and prepare yourself. Meet us in the Parasav when you're ready."

Dretzlin leaves the Great Hall, while Leazara turns to make another announcement.

"Before we go into this battle, I have one more announcement to make! The Elite protectors have grown into a great army—an army that is too big for one Colonel. The time has come. We need another leader up here by my side running the Elites! It is my great honor to announce Tanglor Raff as that leader!"

Leazara stands tall and salutes Tanglor.

"Come and join me up here, Colonel Raff."

Tanglor, surprised by the announcement, gets out of his seat and walks toward her. Everyone in the room celebrates, causing the Great Hall to shake. Tanglor stands in the middle, the noise slowly fades away, and the cheering stops.

"Thank you, everyone. I am honored to be standing here as one of your Colonels, but we must stay focused. We need to prepare ourselves for our upcoming battle. We need to be ready to attack when Dretzlin completes his mission. The celebration will come after our victory!!"

They break into a loud cheer for their new Colonel before marching out of the Great Hall. Leazara and Tanglor make their way to the prison in the Parasav. Dretzlin is standing outside, waiting for them.

"I thought you guys had changed your minds. Congrats on becoming a Colonel, Tanglor."

"Thanks, Dretzlin. You ready?"

They walk into the Parasav and make their way to the prison. As they approach Freden's cell, they notice he isn't in there. Leazara pulls out a shiny oval object and presses it. It lights up a teal color and causes the room to fill with electricity. Over in the corner, Freden starts to appear.

"Ok, stop! I'm here!"

Leazara presses the button turning the electricity off. The teal light on the oval fades away. She turns to Tanglor and tosses it to him.

"That's yours now that you're a Colonel. After our victory, I will take you to the Ancient Computer Console and show you more."

She turns back to Freden, kneeling in his cell.

"You're going to help us whether you like it or not. Try anything, and you're dead. Someone, go in and take away that other cloaking device!"

Two Elite Protectors rush into the room. They restrain him and grab the device. Freden sits in cuffs, ready to listen to Leazara.

"Dretzlin is going to take you to your home base back on Nahar, where he will use your fabulous cloaking device so none of your friends can see him. You're going to go along with this, or Dretzlin will stab you in the back. Kind of like how you did to him."

Freden gets a guilty look on his face.

"I... fine. I have nothing else to lose at this point. I'll take you to Nahar, but when we get there, I get to walk away. You'll never see me again."

Leazara and Tanglor whisper to each other before deciding.

"Alright, we have a deal. Only if you help Dretzlin take down the True Guardian's defenses first, after that, you're free to go wherever you please, as long as we never see you again."

Freden stands up.

"Deal. Joining the True Guardians was the biggest mistake of my life. I'll help, then I'm gone."

Dretzlin takes Freden's cloaking device from the guard and pockets it. He takes the one from Leazara and puts it on his shoulder. Dretzlin presses the device and vanishes while walking over to Freden. He removes Freden's cuffs.

"Walk to the ship. Try to escape, and I'll kill you."

Tanglor and Leazara head to their ships and prepare with the rest of the Elite army. They fly off into orbit behind Dretzlin and Freden, making sure to keep their distance. Freden looks around the ship, unsure of where his brother is. He decides to talk anyways.

"Dretzlin... I didn't want any of this to happen. I know it doesn't seem like it, but I was trying to protect you and keep you away from them. The things they believe in and the things they do to make those beliefs a reality is..."

Freden stops and starts to get choked up.

"The things I've seen."

Dretzlin's voice appears in the distance.

"I could've protected myself from them. You could have too, but you didn't!"

"It's not like that, little brother!"

"Don't call me that! You said so yourself; we are no longer brothers."

Dretzlin's voice fades away.

"Dretzlin! Let me explain. It isn't what you think. I couldn't fight them because our parents were True Guardians. After you were born, Mom and Dad betrayed them. They didn't want us growing up like they did, but they couldn't escape. The True Guardians murdered them and came for us. You were my little brother; I couldn't let them get you. So, I made a deal with them to leave you alone if I became their weapon. I did whatever they asked of me, and if I declined, they were going to come after you. I'm sorry I never told you, but you would have wanted to help and would've gotten yourself in the same place as me."

Dretzlin comes out of his cloaking.

"How am I supposed to believe any of this after all of the lies?"

"I don't know how to answer that... I guess you can't."

Suddenly a voice appears on the comms; they look out the window to see Nahar. Dretzlin hits the device and vanishes.

"Tell us who you are! Get any closer, and we will fire!"

Freden takes a deep breath.

"Calm down; it's Freden. Flujen and I were captured by the Elites. They killed Flujen, but I managed to escape and steal one of their ships."

A couple of seconds go by before the voice responds.

"We thought you were dead! I know Vristen will be happy to hear you're still alive. Alright, you have clearance to enter."

Freden pilots the ship to Nahar and lands next to the base. Dretzlin comes out of his cloaking and pulls out the other device. He pauses before handing it to Freden.

"I don't know why I'm doing this.... don't betray me again."

Dretzlin hits the device on his shoulder and vanishes in front of his brother.

Freden grabs the device and puts it on. The doors open, and the True Guardian leader walks onto the ship. His tail has been cut off, and he walks with a small limp. He wears an orange cap on his head that hangs down, covering one side of his goggles.

"Ahh, Freden, I heard you were still alive! I had to come and see for myself! Walk with me."

"Hey, Vristen, long time no see."

Freden walks out of the ship with Vristen and the other True Guardians. They step on silver dirt covering the ground; massive black rocks make up walls and cave systems around them. Freden looks around to see Johthun technology spread out across the soil and throughout the caves.

"You've done a great job finishing the base while I was gone."

Vristen laughs while walking ahead of him.

"You were gone much longer than anticipated, Freden."

Freden scoffs while walking with him; Dretzlin—cloaked—follows behind. Vristen continues to talk to Freden as they walk past the security systems. Dretzlin stops following them. This is where he can disable their defenses. Freden notices but continues to walk with Vristen.

"So Freden, tell me what happened to Flujen."

"Oh, you know, Flujen. He got mouthy after we were captured and pissed one of their Captains off. He lost it. Beat the crap out of Flujen and cut his head off."

Vristen stands silent for a moment staring at him.

"Holy shit...well, no denying that's the Flujen I know. That's alright. He was expendable, unlike you, Freden. I need you more than anyone if we are to win this war."

Freden stops and salutes Vristen.

"Good thing you have me back, sir."

They continue to walk to Vristen's war room. As they are walking, Freden notices another security system. He stops and thinks to himself.

"Shit! Dretzlin won't be able to shut down their defenses alone; he needs to hit both security systems."

Vristen notices Freden standing there staring off.

"Freden! Let's go! We don't have a lot of time. We believe the Elite Protector army is on their way to attack us right now. I need your help setting up our defenses."

"Of course. Show me what you need me to do."

Vristen has Freden enter his war room to look at his table with a map of their defenses and soldiers laid out on it.

"This is where we are sitting with our defenses. I need your expertise in what the enemy is thinking. Do we have enough troops lined up on these exits to be alright?"

Freden leans over the table and looks.

"This looks solid, but I would move a few more troops over here. You don't want to be surprised if they have soldiers sneaking through the tunnels."

"Ahh, see, this is why I need you, Freden! Thank you. Go and find Captain Atokad; he will put you in a good spot for the fight."

Freden nods his head and walks out of the war room. Once safely out of sight, he hits the device on his shoulder, becoming cloaked. He makes his way back to the second security system and waits for Dretzlin to make his move. Five minutes go by;

nothing has happened. Freden turns and sees Vristen leaving. Realizing that they're running out of time, he uses the security systems in front of him to deactivate his half of the base's defenses. Alarms activate with bright yellow lights flashing. Freden takes off into a sprint back toward Dretzlin. He passes Vristen and other True Guardians running back toward the war room. Freden gets closer to the first security system where his brother is. He sees two True Guardians standing over something. Dretzlin is down on the ground, out of his cloaking. Freden, still cloaked, runs, and jumps onto one of their backs, causing the soldier to stumble around. The other True Guardian watches and laughs as his friend falls to his knees, trying to get what appears to be nothing off his back. Suddenly he stops. Blood trickles out from his mouth before he falls face-first to the ground. His friend rushes over, while Freden stabs him in the chest. The two True Guardians lay dead as Freden comes out of his cloaking and rushes over to Dretzlin.

"Dretzlin! Talk to me. Are you okay?"

He rolls over toward Freden.

"Deactivate the security system."

Freden immediately takes out the second half of the base's defenses. He turns back toward his brother.

"Alright, come on. We're getting out of here."

He picks him up and starts walking toward the front of the base. Before they can get there, Vristen and a group of True Guardians stop them.

"Where do you think you're going? Traitor!"

Freden puts his brother down and activates his cloaking. He charges at Vristen while beginning to vanish. Right as he is about to punch him, he completely disappears. Vristen closes his eyes and kneels to the ground. A couple of seconds pass before he opens his eyes and stands to his feet. Five of the True guardians go down behind him. Blood gushes out of their chests; limbs are cut off as Freden reappears, standing with his blades ready for more. Vristen turns around and laughs before sending more men at him. Freden vanishes again, taking out all the True Guardians rushing at him.

"Leave now, Vristen, or you die with all your so-called soldiers."

A massive blast takes out the top of the base; Elite Protectors come rushing through. Vristen makes a run for it. Freden lets him go and runs over to Dretzlin.

"Brother, are you okay?"

"Yeah, now go get Vristen!"

Freden takes off after Vristen, while Tanglor and the others wipe out the True Guardians still fighting. Leazara and the rest of the army surround the base, taking out anyone trying to escape. Freden catches up to Vristen and knocks him to the ground.

"It ends here, Vristen! This is for everything you've done to me! To my family!"

Freden, overcome by emotions, starts to wail his fists into Vristen. Dretzlin limps into the room.

"Freden! You got him!"

Freden slowly stops punching him and backs away. Dretzlin grabs his brother; the two start to limp toward Tanglor and the others. Behind them, Vristen slowly stands to his feet. He coughs up blood before yelling at Freden.

"It's not over! It'll never be over!!"

He pulls out his staff with a blade at the end and charges at the brothers. Freden gets ready to dodge the attack, but suddenly Vristen stops. Dretzlin is standing in front of Freden, the blade through his chest. Vristen falls back to his knees while Dretzlin stumbles over to him. He pulls out one of Ranyana's knives and tries to speak but can't. He stops and stands over the True Guardian leader. With his last breath, he shoves the knife through Vristen's neck and falls on top of him. They both gasp for air, lying in the silver dirt. Freden watches helplessly as his little brother's life fades away. Tanglor walks over to Freden and helps him up.

"I'm sorry, Freden. He never stopped caring about you. You redeemed yourself and made him proud. Let's get out of here."

Freden, in shock, grabs Tanglor's hand and follows him back to the ship. Leazara and the rest of the Elites wipe out the True Guardians and overtake their base. She has the Elites grab any useful resources or pieces of information to take with them back to Joht. As they are looking around, she finds lost archives on the Elite

Protectors and Tazlow Raff. They load it onto their ships and head back toward Joht. Tanglor sits next to Freden. Leazara approaches them.

"Freden, thank you for helping us out. The loss of your brother is a tragedy for us all. I am sorry. I'm afraid that's the way of war; we have to live with its repercussions. Our deal has changed—you're welcome to stay."

He gets up and walks into his room, shutting the door behind him. Tanglor gets up and heads to the front of the ship to get on the comms.

"This is Colonel Raff. The True Guardians have been defeated. I want to personally thank everyone for fighting and risking your lives for the Elites! We will be back on Joht soon. Please take this time to be with your loved ones and get some rest."

Tanglor leans back in his chair next to Leazara. They sit in silence, staring out the window as the ship gets closer to Joht.

# Chapter 12:
# <u>Tralupians- A Historic Conflict</u>

Blasts of orange and crimson light shoot through the windows, lighting up the dim TralVent Inn. Ilikso sits against the wall where the monsters took Siritano, as he stares down the empty hallway, unconcerned about the battle taking place outside. He can't stop seeing the monsters taking his brother away from him. As he sits agonizing over it, he feels a drop of liquid hit the top of his head—snapping him out of his self-induced guilt. Ilikso stands up and turns around to look at the wall. A dark red imprint of his body is stained on the wall.

"What the hell!?"

He reaches his hand out and places it on the wall where the stain formed around him. It squishes under his hand, creating an indent. He pushes against it even harder and breaks through the wall. Pieces of the wall crumble away, creating a doorway with a mysterious portal. Colors flow through the portal, as Ilikso watches it. He turns and looks out the windows to see war happening around him. Orange ghostly figures fight crimson beings, massive blasts fill the streets of TralVent, and orange lightning shoots down from the sky. He looks closer, examining the figures on both sides, trying to make them out. The orange ones look like Tralupians and a couple of Ventrians. The crimson beings looked like the monsters that took his brother from him. As he watches the battle, he glances toward the entrance to TralVent and spots his three sisters with one of the orange figures. Ilikso, eager to see them, turns to run out of the inn, but he's stopped by a hand reaching through the portal.

"Ahhhh! Let me go!!"

It pulls him inside, and the portal fades away, causing the door to shut and the wall to reform. Musfina hears his screams and looks up toward the window he was looking out of moments earlier, but nothing is there.

"Weird, I thought I heard someone yell from up there in that window."

Oryuna and Queen Zuna look with their sister before Zembor interrupts them.

"It isn't possible for the Remnants to make such a noise."

The three sisters stay close to Zembor, as he approaches the battle. Queen Zuna pulls her trident off her back.

"Remnants, huh? So that's what you call the spirits inside RoyalTree?"

"It is the name we give to the good spirits. As you can see, RoyalTree is at war with itself. The Remnants attack the remains of the evil that came with RoyalTree. We have been at constant war with them since I planted RoyalTree long ago."

Musfina looks back to the window in the inn.

"So, what was the scream that I heard?"

Zembor looks toward the window with her.

"I am not sure. It could be from the storm roaring above."

Musfina looks at the window for a few more seconds before a thunderous boom shakes the entire building.

"It was probably just the storm then."

She catches back up to the Queen and Oryuna. They all stand, watching the ghostly figures battle. Zembor approaches the Queen and reaches his hand out.

"Take my hand and follow me. You'll be safe to cross the battlefield as long as you're holding onto me."

The Queen takes his hand, while Oryuna and Musfina latch onto his arm. As soon as they contact him, orange light shoots out from his arm blade onto the three of them. They turn into transparent ghostly figures, just like Zembor. He starts to walk toward the battle. The Queen and her sisters let go, and the transparency fades away, making them solid again.

"What just happened?"

Zembor turns around and reaches his hand back out.

"As long as you're touching me, I can use my aura to hide you from the Remains. If there is life here, they can easily pick up the scent. They'll eventually come for you and take you away to the unknown. If you're hidden, they won't be able to see you."

Queen Zuna and her sisters grab onto Zembor once again, turning themselves back into the transparent figures. They follow Zembor through the battlefield toward the back end of the city, where his statue rests under a lofty bell tower. The three sisters look around at the battle waging on. The crimson figures tower over the spectral orange Tralupians and Ventrians, but they continue to fight. Queen Zuna looks closer and sees her mother fighting alongside her father, Za-Ryan, and her Uncle Zirk. Za-Ryan flips over Zirk, swinging his blade into one of the red monsters. It falls to the ground before turning into a cloud of ash. Zirk grabs onto Zelena; the two of them swing each other around, becoming a cyclone. They stick their blades out and slice through the monsters. Zembor notices and stops, he raises his arm blade into the air and starts to yell.

"Fight with everything you have! We rest when they're gone!"

All the orange figures cheer and charge at the crimson monsters. Zembor escorts the Queen and her sisters over to his statue.

"Stand here with my sculpture. It will protect you when I cannot."

He charges back toward the battlefield with his arm blade ready to strike. Zuna, Oryuna, and Musfina stand next to the statue as the translucent orange fades away again. The crimson figures stop fighting and notice them standing there. Zuna and her sisters quickly grab onto the statue. They turn transparent again, and the crimson figures' attention goes back to the battle. Zembor sprints past the monsters, striking them with quick swipes of his blade. He makes his way over to Zelena, leaving a trail of the crimson clouds behind him.

"Call your father. We need them."

Zelena nods her head. She turns and yells toward the bell tower above Zembor's statue. Two orange Tralupians jump from the top, landing in front of Queen Zuna and her sisters. Tez and Mazray stand proudly, looking toward the Queen. They nod their heads to her before turning and running toward the battle. A loud boom comes from above them, as Hetra, in her fighter ship, flies over them.

"Take them out with your newly-developed weapons, Sis!"

Zeph and Zaren come rushing out from the bottom of the tower. They run by while nodding their heads. Queen Zuna watches in disbelief.

"I don't understand how this is possible."

Oryuna looks around and sees one of the crimson figures staring at them.

"Aren't we supposed to be hidden from those monsters?"

The three sisters stand as close to the statue as possible. Still, one of the monsters starts to walk in their direction. The battle rages on with the orange army pushing the crimson army back. Zembor runs to the frontlines and holds his blade high.

"Now is the time. We are at full strength! Take them out and reclaim RoyalTree!!!"

Hetra leads the attack in her fighter ship, dropping bombs and shooting down into the red monsters. The rest of them charge in behind her. The army of Tralupians and Ventrians use their weapons to destroy every last one of the crimson monsters. Queen Zuna and her sisters watch warily as the lone crimson monster ignores the battle and approaches them with a smile on its face.

"Your brothers say hello…. HAHAHA!"

The monster gets closer and reaches for Musfina, grabbing her. She lets go of the statue, and her transparency fades away. Musfina struggles while she looks into the creature's evil eyes.

"This can't be… I'm supposed to be hidden from you!"

"Did Zembor tell you that!? HAHAHA, that's priceless!"

The monster pulls his arm back before driving its long sharp fingers through her stomach. She starts to lose her vision when suddenly, an orange transparent trident stabs through her back and into the monster holding her.

'Ugh… what is this!?"

Zalzatine stands behind her; he pulls the trident out of her back, and she falls to the ground. Zalzatine lifts the trident back up and shoves it into the monster again. Queen Zuna and Oryuna run over to their sister, dying on the ground.

"Musfina, are you alright?"

She coughs up a mix of green and orange[2] blood.

"My Queen…. Please don't be angry with me."

---

[2] Her blood has some orange due to being born into the Royal Family. -*Inevsah Rensul, Johthun Historian*

Zuna kneels next to her, tears running down her face.

"My dear sister, you have done everything except make me angry. Thank you for advising me and watching out for me after Defunis and Serel died. You are the reason I kept fighting while I was trapped in my own body. I love you, sister."

Musfina starts to smile, her body slowly turning to ash. Queen Zuna and Oryuna hold onto her until nothing is left. The ash floats into the air creating a cloud. It turns toward them and flashes bright orange before flying toward the tall bell tower behind them. Queen Zuna stands up and walks over to Zalzatine; the trident still pierced through the monster.

"Kill it already!"

Zalzatine turns and looks at Zuna.

"I can't. The monster knows life is here. It isn't leaving until it takes that life with it."

"Life? You mean Oryuna and me?"

The monster squirms as Zalzatine drives the trident further into its chest.

"Yes, you and your sister being here during the war has disrupted the flow. Part of RoyalTree calls upon us to defend you, while the other part wants to take you like it took your brothers."

"What do you know of my brothers!? Where have they been taken to!?"

The monster starts to laugh.

"Hahaha, they're ours now!"

Zalzatine drives the monster further back with the trident, pinning him against the statue. Zembor and the other Remnants walk over. Zalzatine leaves the pinned monster to go and stand with his father.

"Queen Zuna Wrathfin, only you can end this. The monster knows of your life here and cannot be harmed; they have watched us ever since I planted the seed long ago."

The monster lets out a scream.

"Ahhhhh!! If you don't let me leave with my life, then my leader will be very displeased with you, Zembor Wrathfin!"

"Your leader has done nothing but go against the arrangement we made all those years ago! I will not stand here and watch him destroy my family anymore!!"

"You're making a big mistake, Zembor!!"

Zembor detaches his arm blade from his body. He walks over to Queen Zuna and offers the blade to her.

"Take it and rid this monster from existence!"

Queen Zuna grabs the transparent arm blade; it lights up orange in her hands. The light fades away, revealing that the blade is no longer translucent. She pulls the trident out of the pinned monster and brings it forward next to the blade. It and trident start to rattle and shake, before flying up into the air and swirling around each other. The blade inside the trident that was thought to be Zembor's turns into the dark red color and shoots into the air. Zembor's arm blade glows orange and flies into the trident locking in place. The crimson blade continues to swirl around the now complete weapon. A blast of orange energy shoots out of Zembor's Trident; it smashes into the dark red sword, causing it to launch at the monster. It pins the beast back onto the statue. The trident floats back down, landing in Queen Zuna's hand. The Remnants all watch and simultaneously kneel to their Queen. Oryuna looks around and kneels with them. Zembor stands up and walks over to Zuna and the monster trying to break free.

"After all these years, my trident is finally complete. The power is yours, my Queen."

He kneels back down in front of her. Zuna turns and takes the trident over to the monster pinned to the statue. She pulls it back and drives it into the monster's stomach. Bright red energy starts to shine out from its wound. It grows even brighter, as the monster pulls out a small green box with an orange button on it. The monster presses the button, which causes a massive amount of crimson light to shoots out of the box, consuming the beast and creating a wormhole. The light swirls around before getting sucked into the portal and disappearing. Queen Zuna and Oryuna can hear screams coming from the opening. Oryuna turns to her sister.

"I can't lose our brothers, too. Take care of our people!"

She runs toward the portal and jumps through it. Queen Zuna yells for her sister, as she reaches out and runs after her.

"Oryuna, wait!"

As Oryuna jumps through the portal, it closes behind her, leaving Queen Zuna alone in RoyalTree with Zembor and the other Remnants. She falls to the ground in front of the statue, crying.

"Why!? I don't want to be alone again!"

The Remnant of her mother walks over and sits down next to her.

"You're not alone…. You are never alone, Zuna."

Queen Zuna wipes her tears and turns around to see all her ancestors standing over her.

"We are all still here with you, my daughter. Now more than ever."

Zelena points to Zembor's Trident, but before she can lift it, Zembor walks over to them.

"Please, can I see it?"

Zuna hands it to the transparent Zembor. The trident glows solid orange as he walks over to the statue. Zembor places the trident into its hand and turns around, smiling to the Queen. He slowly steps backward and disappears inside of it. A couple of seconds go by, as the light from the trident seeps into the statue. The stone starts to crack and crumble away, revealing the light shining beneath the surface. It completely breaks apart, the orange light shoots out from the broken statue, blinding everyone. As it fades away, a nontransparent Zembor stands tall with the trident in hand. Queen Zuna and the other Remnants stand watching in shock.

"How are you here? You died in 1785 when the Ventrians bombed the military headquarters!"

Zembor walks forward and hands the Trident back to Queen Zuna.

"That is what everyone was left to believe. The explosion caused the command center to implode on itself. The ground underneath us caved in, but RoyalTree grabbed onto us. It saved all of us that were caught in the explosion and then kept us here...."

"I don't understand. I thought RoyalTree was supposed to be good."

"RoyalTree is good! It's those damn monsters that you saw that aren't. We aren't sure what they are or where they come from, but, somehow, they can open portals at will. Your sister and brothers are in the unknown now. There is no way for us to get to them without those monsters opening a gateway for us to get through."

"How long has this been going on?"

Zembor walks over to the Remnants of his people. They kneel as he walks past them.

"Ever since the very beginning.... It all started in 1735 when Grundar and I were abducted by a massive metal beast."

Grundar steps out as one of the ghostly orange figures.

"That day... everything changed for us."

Zembor walks to Grundar and places a hand on his transparent shoulder.

"I can't tell you how sorry I am for what I did that day. If it weren't for me, our people would have been united."

Grundar starts to laugh.

"I appreciate the sentiment, Zembor, but we both know there wouldn't have been peace back then. You were wise to strike first."

"Regardless of what could have been, I am sorry, my friend."

Grundar nods his head back to Zembor.

"I have forgiven you. I know it was hard for you to admit, but we did become friends being locked up on that ship for two years."

"We did indeed, Grundar."

Zembor turns back to see Queen Zuna staring at the broken statue.

"The portal won't be opening back up anytime soon—maybe ever. We aren't sure where the monsters take our people when they go through them, but none have ever returned."

Queen Zuna stands up and turns to Zembor and the Remnants.

"My sister made her choice to try to save them. I have faith that they'll return one day, but…. what now? The people are going to lose their minds when they find out the Great Zembor Wrathfin is still alive after all these years."

"The people can't know. If the secrets about what RoyalTree can do were revealed, there would be chaos."

Zuna gets a confused look on her face.

"Speaking of that, what can RoyalTree actually do? How are you alive after nearly a thousand years?"

Zembor walks back over to the destroyed statue and kneels to pick a piece of it up.

"This is the reason why I live after all these years. Whatever this statue was made from, it concealed my body while my spirit was still able to roam around RoyalTree."

"Who put you inside that statue?"

Zembor looks up to her.

"RoyalTree did…. I brought this all upon my people. When Grundar and I were picked up by the metal beast, it turned out to be a massive spaceship. It took us up into space where we were locked away. We were placed in a cell with others, but none of them were Tralupians or Ventrians. We were the seventh and eighth alien species the monsters had come across. Grundar and I took it upon ourselves to try to get everyone together to break free, despite not being able to understand any of them. As we were trying to put a plan together, a gas was released into the cell, knocking us all out."

Queen Zuna, intrigued by his story, leans in.

"What happened after you got knocked out by the gas?"

"After being knocked out for what felt like a year, Grundar and I awoke in the cell with only two of the other aliens. The other six from before were gone. My arm blade had been removed, and we all had suspicious new scars on the side of our heads. We touched them, but felt no pain, so we carried on. The four of us thoroughly investigated the cell but couldn't find anything helpful. Finally, one of the aliens with us removed its tooth and picked the lock on the cell door. We wandered around the ship in hopes of finding some answers. All we saw were the other six aliens—dead—on operation tables with their chests cut open, and their insides ripped out. They had the same scars on their heads; only theirs had a dark red substance leaking out of them. We couldn't figure out why they were chosen over us or what the material coming out of their scars could be. As we kept searching, I found my arm blade on one of the tables. It was the only weapon we had aboard the ship, so I reattached it immediately.

Grundar and the other aliens followed behind me as we made our way to the front of the ship to the controls. We wanted not only to figure out a way home, but why these monsters had abducted us, run tests on us, and then just abandoned us to die. As we got closer to the front of the ship, the door to the bridge opened, and one of the aliens with us saw something inside. Before any of us could stop it, it ran through the door. A loud bang followed by a horrible screech came echoing through the open doorway. I ran through, my blade drawn and ready to strike, to find the alien crawling toward me, with a streak of blood on the floor behind him. It slowly stopped moving and died.

I followed the blood smear and came across a chair by the control panel. A hand with long sharp fingers slammed down onto the console and started speaking in a language I couldn't understand. Before I could even decide what to do, an alarm sounded through the ship followed by a timer with—what we assumed—were numbers counting down. The monster in the chair must've started a self-destruct system. It tried to move from the seat, but I seized the opportunity and drove my blade down into its head! The monster squealed as it fell to the ground. I stood there looking at the countdown timer. Behind it, we could see TokBellu.

Myself, Grundar, and the other alien took no time and started to search the ship for a way off. We eventually found two escape pods. We decided that Grundar and I would take one back to TokBellu, while the alien took the other one back to its homeworld. Before it left, it tried its best to say its name, but all we could understand was that its species were called Pyronts. It had six tentacle legs and four tentacle arms with a giant eye at the top of its elongated head and a mouth below that. The Pyront got into its escape pod and flew away, leaving Grundar and me to get in our pod. Before I was able to enter the escape pod, the ship started to self-destruct, causing explosions to surge throughout. A blast shot through the wall, launching me into the ceiling and knocking me unconscious."

The transparent Grundar steps forward.

"I had to make the tough decision of letting Zembor die or saving his life. I remember being tempted to leave him behind, almost like someone was in my head telling me to do so, but I fought the urge and saved his life. We had become friends, after all. I lifted him onto my shoulder and got both of us into the pod. I piloted us back toward TokBellu, but it was several hours before Zembor regained consciousness."

Zembor laughs.

"Ahh, yes, I remember waking up and not knowing where I was. Grundar calmed me down, but because neither of us knew exactly how to pilot the foreign escape pod, it took us about two months to reach TokBellu. We grew even closer on that small ship, trading stories about our people and talking about our hopes for the future."

Queen Zuna addresses both of them.

"And when you came back, the fighting stopped—everyone was astonished at your return. But in the end, your talks on that escape pod seemed to mean nothing. When you landed, Zembor made sure to win the war, taking a cheap shot and killing Grundar and his son."

Zembor puts his head down.

"Back then, I thought I was doing the right thing for my people... I didn't realize until it was too late. The scar on the side of my head would speak to me and tell me to do things. I didn't fight it because I didn't understand it. It caused me to kill one of my only friends, and further the war between our people. I should have been stronger, like Grundar, and fought it. I wouldn't be alive if Grundar hadn't fought the voice in his head, but I was too weak, too scared of what it could be."

Grundar looks over to Zembor.

"That voice…. I never mentioned that to you when we were on the pod, did I? But yes, that was the reason why I hesitated. It was inside my head, saying to leave you there! It kept telling me to go home and watch you die in the explosions. I stood there looking at you on the ground with this weird smile on my face before I was able to snap out of it. There should be no guilt left in your mind about what you did to me, Zembor."

They briefly embrace each other, then Zembor turns to face Zuna.

"That strange voice had power over me because I feared what it would do if I disobeyed it. Then one day, I couldn't stand it anymore. The voice had gotten louder, so I took my arm blade and put it up to the scar on my head. I slowly pierced the skin, the voice inside my head screaming, while an orange substance spewed out. It yelled at me, "That's enough!" I finally decided to talk back and said, "What do you want from me? Get out of my head!" The voice screamed again before speaking more calmly. "I want you to obey and do as I say. I didn't ask to be put into your head either!"

I found myself sitting on the throne, talking to something, someone in my head. "You were put in my head on that ship while I was unconscious?" The voice didn't scream this time, but it took a second to answer. "Yes, my people and I were captured just like you; those monsters had never seen the likes of us before and ran countless tests on us. The pain was unimaginable. Our species don't have a body like you or the others on that ship. Instead, we are gaseous elements that form together to create conscious minds. But the pain they caused our minds was…. Inexplicable. They wanted to see what they could do with us combined with other species, so they decided to perform some experiments. That's how I ended up here, inside your head. My gaseous body can spread out on your brain, granting me complete control over your actions."

I sat for a couple of seconds, contemplating everything this thing in my head just told me. "Are you or your people malicious? What happens from here? How am I supposed to trust that you won't take over my mind whenever you want?" The voice takes another couple of seconds. "My people and I were never villainous until those monsters captured us off our homeworld of R'Ang. I don't know what happens from here. I have never been stuck inside someone else's head before. I can say that I won't take control of your mind without your consent."

I started to feel at ease, as much as I could with the circumstances I'd been given. "I would greatly appreciate that…. what do I call you?" The voice responds proudly. "My name is RoyalTree, and I am one of the last living Broncholites." RoyalTree and I conversed for hours every day. My son and my people believed my mind was slipping because of how frequently I talked to myself. Trying to explain it to them made me sound even crazier.

Eventually, RoyalTree and I came up with an alternative to having him in my head. RoyalTree woke me up one morning. "Zembor! Wake up; I figured it out!" I rolled over in bed, still exhausted. "What is it? You've been trying to figure this out now for over thirty years. Just face it, you're stuck in my head for good." RoyalTree screamed at me again. "Don't make me take over your body. Get out of bed and walk out of the palace toward the ocean." I didn't want to argue, so I played along and walked outside the palace to a ledge that sits out over the ocean. "Alright, RoyalTree, what did you want to show me?" RoyalTree caused me a headache with how excited he got. "You're looking at it, Zembor! Just hear me out, I know you've gotten used to me being in your head for the past thirty years, but this could be our chance to separate from each other."

I was very concerned at first. "Separate? Where will you go, and how do we go about doing that?" RoyalTree takes a deep breath. "Well, first, you're going to have to cause some pain to yourself by cutting open that scar, when you get deep enough, you'll find me in a metallic silver box. Take the box and dive down to the bottom of the ocean, dig deep into the ground underwater and plant me there." I stopped RoyalTree. "What!? Why would I do any of that?" RoyalTree started to get frustrated. "Zembor…. If you do this, I become one with your planet, I will no longer be able to control you, and I'll be able to control the environment around TokBellu. With the technology those monsters put me in, I can be planted toward the core and grow. I can grow whatever you'd like, you can have a great environment that makes your world look beautiful, or you can have a dirty one with rocks and no colors. Whatever you would want your world to do, I can make it so. We would still be constantly talking and working together; I just wouldn't be in your head anymore. Which, honestly, I think we both want."

I started to follow what he was saying, and the thought of having him out of my head was hard to pass up. "All right, but you have to make a deal with me and keep to our arrangement no matter what. I will plant you down there and wait for you to grow, but you cannot make any sort of decisions without me. Understand?" RoyalTree took a couple of seconds before responding. "I can do that, Zembor; nothing will happen around TokBellu without you being there. Thank you, my friend." I didn't waste any time and used my arm blade to pierce the scar on my head. After stabbing at it and moving through the orange substance for a couple of minutes, I was able to feel the metallic box. I pulled it out and looked it over. It was a rectangle-shaped metallic silver box. I jumped into the water and swam down to the depths of the Ocean. Using my arm blade, I dug deep under the ground. After digging and digging, I finally planted the silver box with RoyalTree in it. I could hear RoyalTree speaking faintly to me as I swam back to the surface. "See you soon,

Zembor." By the time I reached the surface, RoyalTree had already latched himself onto the core of our planet and started to grow into the Great Tree he is today."

Out of nowhere, Zembor gets interrupted by the portal reopening in front of him and Queen Zuna. They both jump back and stand next to the Remnants. They watch with bated breath, as the portal shoots off sparks of orange and crimson energy at them. Finally, Oryuna, Ilikso, Siritano, and a small creature in a hooded robe jump through. They are all covered in blood and panting. Ilikso stands before them with a scar on his face, holding a bloody blade in one hand and the little creature tightly clinging to the other. Oryuna, covered in blood, supports Siritano, who appears mangled and barely alive.

# Chapter 13:
# Johthuns- The Legacy

Tanglor pushes through the crowd of Elites exiting the ship. He rushes into the Tazruhvah and runs to Ashar's room but can't find him. After frantically searching everywhere Tanglor could think of, he finds Ashar sitting in the Great Hall by himself in his captain's chair. Ashar is staring across the way to where Ranyana always sat.

"Ashar, you alright?"

He takes a second to respond.

"No, not really. I can't stop thinking about her. Every time I close my eyes, I see her face, and then it crumbles away into that yellow ash. I didn't even see it happen, but I should have been there!"

"I can't imagine what you're going through right now, but I do know that Ranyana loved you. She would want you to pull yourself together, not for her, for yourself. Ashar, the Elites need you right now. I need you, brother."

Ashar starts to calm down.

"I killed Flujen, and I don't feel any better for it... Ranyana would hate me for that."

Tanglor walks over to his brother and sits down next to him.

"You and I both know she wouldn't hate you for it. She definitely would have been pissed about it, but she would have been okay with Flujen dying."

They both get a little laugh out of that.

"Thanks, Tanglor, for sticking up for me in front of Leazara and all of the other Elites. Oh, and congrats on becoming a Colonel! I knew you were special when we met back at that foster home."

Tanglor puts his arm around Ashar as they walk out of the Great Hall.

"Thanks, brother. I wouldn't have gotten this far without you."

Leazara comes around the corner and bumps into them.

"Glad to see that you are up and about, Ashar. Sorry to interrupt you two, but we have an emergency meeting with the Elders. They are already on their way and will be here in five minutes. Call all of the Elites into the Great Hall."

Tanglor pulls out the shiny oval that Leazara gave him. He pushes it down and speaks into it. As it lights up teal, his voice fills all the rooms in the Tazruhvah.

"This is Colonel Raff. Everyone needs to report to the Great Hall at once."

Tanglor and Leazara take their seats with the Captains behind them. The Elites fill the tables across from them. The seven Elders enter the room and stand in the middle, looking toward the Colonels. The Head Elder, Elisin, 480 years old, steps forward.

"We have come to talk with all the Elite Protectors. We bear urgent news that needs to be shared. First, we can have no more secrets. The [3]Elders and the Elite Protectors need to be one and work together as we did before with Tazlow Raff. My son."

Whispers fill the Great Hall, as Tanglor looks to Leazara.

"Tanglor, I swear I didn't know this."

Elisin continues to talk.

"Yes, there is a lot that has been kept secret ever since my son was killed by the True Guardians. I was one of the Elders he saved that day, and I will always be grateful for his sacrifice."

She walks over to Tanglor.

"It was a real tragedy losing your mother during your birth. She was truly an amazing Johthun. Your father would not have been as strong or courageous without her."

She turns back around to address the entire room.

"Ninety years ago, in 2650, Tazlow and I combined our resources to build five colony ships. Those ships were sent out into the solar system to search for other life forms and planets for colonization. We have had five major colony ships flying around the solar system reporting on any potential life or habitable planets for our

---

[3] *The oldest recorded age is 507. - Inevsah Rensul, Johthun Historian*

people. We kept this information secret for all these years due to threats from the True Guardians and their spies."

Leazara quickly stands up.

"I don't see how it's possible to go ninety years without anyone outside of the Elders finding out about this... How did you keep those ships hidden?"

"We haven't hidden them at all. They have been just far enough away from our planet that you would have no idea they're out there. I wish we could have shared this information with the Elites sooner, but we had to protect ourselves and our legacy."

Tanglor stands up, shaking off the fact that he just met his grandmother.

"So besides finding out about these colony ships, what's the urgent news you needed to tell us about?"

"We have had reports of an alien species near one of the ships. We sent a few of our scouts out with no response. It has been two weeks since we sent them, and earlier today, we lost contact with Captain Plazerin. We need the Elite's help."

Tanglor takes the initiative and speaks up before Leazara can say anything.

"As Elite Protectors, it is our responsibility to help. From now on, the Elders and Elites will work together for our people no matter what. No more secrets."

The Elders look around to each other before Elisin responds.

"We appreciate your terms and want the same thing."

Tanglor turns and looks at Freden sitting with the Elite Protectors.

"Freden proved his loyalty by helping us defeat the True Guardians. We will send him and my brother on one of our stealth gliders to the colony ship. They can get close without being seen and find out what's going on. Then they can relay the information back to us, and we can either attack or negotiate depending on the situation."

Leazara pulls Tanglor to the side.

"Are you sure we can trust Freden?"

"He has nothing but the Elites now. Plus, Ashar will be there watching him."

Tanglor looks back toward Freden and the Elders.

"Everyone else needs to be ready to attack. Get into position and wait for my signal. Ashar, you and Freden do whatever you need to do to see what's happening on that ship—but don't get caught."

He stands to his feet and salutes Tanglor and Leazara.

"Freden and I got this."

The two of them head for the stealth glider in the docking bay. They waste no time loading up and taking off toward the colony ship. It is stationed the farthest away from Joht at the edge of their solar system.

Tanglor and Leazara order Ucarus and Neliah to take their squads and follow behind. They will set up at the next farthest colony ship, near the recently discovered planet, Conril. As they watch their Captains fly into orbit, Leazara turns to Tanglor.

"It's time. Follow me."

Leazara begins to walk in the direction of the Great Hall. She stops and pulls out another shiny oval. It lights up teal, as she gets closer to the wall outside of the Great Hall. The wall starts to shine a bright teal before it fades away. In its place is an opening where the wall used to be. Tanglor follows her inside, eager to see where it goes. The path is dark, so they take their goggles off to see better. Stone and brick pave the walls, they see a winding dirt path that extends for miles beneath the Elite Protector's Base. As they follow the way, the stone and brick turn into dirt and start closing in on them. Leazara advances in front of Tanglor, as he tries to keep up with her. The soil begins to fall from the ceiling, and the path gets smaller the further they go. Suddenly a teal light begins to shine from a hole up ahead. Their ovals start to pulse the same color. Tanglor can no longer see Leazara ahead of him, a sense of panic sets in. Breathing heavily, he tries to squeeze his way through the dirt, falling in on him. He reaches the hole and shoves an arm through, as the earth fully engulfs him. His breath starts to shorten—he's losing air.

"I got you!"

Leazara grabs his arm and pulls him through. He falls to the ground, the oval flies out of his hand into the air and starts to shake.

"Leazara, what's happening?"

"I'm the only one that's been down here. It's never done that to me."

Tanglor gets onto his feet and reaches up to grab it. He clenches his fist around it, but it starts to shake even more.

"Ahhhhhhhhh!"

He falls to the ground in pain, as the object trembles. The teal light starts to burst out of his hand. Leazara runs over but gets stopped by a wave of light that launches her back. She stands up and watches Tanglor scream.

"Ahhhhhhhhh! Stop!!"

He jumps up and slams his fist onto the ground, trying to get it off. The light rushes through the ground activating computers, lights, and the central console. Leazara runs over to where Tanglor kneels, panting, his fist still on the ground.

"Tanglor! Are you alright?"

He opens his hand and looks at his palm. The oval has phased into his skin, and teal light pulses through it up to his fingers.

"I think so. It feels weird."

"Whatever just happened, I don't think it was a bad thing. You turned everything on—the ancient computer console is working again! Tanglor, none of this has been active since your father died."

She runs through the secret cavern, excitedly checking each computer to make sure things are working correctly. Finally, she makes her way to the ancient computer console, but stops herself and turns to Tanglor.

"You should be the one to use it. It's been seventy-one years. The day Tazlow died, this computer died too."

Tanglor walks over to the seat in front of the computer and sits down.

"So... Any idea of how to use this thing?"

He tentatively touches the keyboard in front of him; the screen quickly flashes before it dims back down. A face pops up on the screen, Leazara jumps back.

"What!? This can't be! Tazlow!?"

The Johthun on the screen turns and looks at Leazara and then to Tanglor.

"This may be difficult for you to understand, but no, I am not Tazlow Raff. However, I do possess his spirit, which connects me to him. It will be the same with his son when he passes from this life too."

Tanglor jumps out of the seat and backs away from the computer.

"Wait, what do you mean!?"

The face on the screen starts to laugh.

"Sit back down; I won't hurt you. As I said, I have your father's spirit, which means I hold his memories and can access the emotions he shared with those close to him. I took his face because of how close he and Leazara were. I thought maybe you'd like to see him. Here, hold on, let me switch faces."

The face on the screen switches from Tazlow to a different species, one they had never seen before. His face -- the same teal color as the lights that led them here. His eyes glow dark blue, while his lips are light green; ears point out of his head like daggers.

"This is what I assume my people looked like before I became this computer. I don't remember much before becoming this knowledge-filled machine, but I do remember that my people lived a very long time ago, a time before any of you ever existed. My real name is Martonamo Jusintar, but you can call me Mart."

Nervous, but intrigued, Tanglor decides to sit back down in front of the computer.

"So, you're the reason my people evolved so fast?"

"Well, I can't take all of the credit. The reason why I'm connected with your father is that he and I shared a bond. He was the one that took the information I possessed and used it for the good of his people. Not everyone would do that. Your father was unlike any of the other species I've come across. When I felt his life slip away, mine did too. The reason why I'm alive again is because of you, Tanglor. You and I share a bond now. I can see it there in your right hand."

The teal light starts to shine through Tanglor's fingers.

"You are just like Tazlow. I felt it as soon as you entered the cavern. It looks like it's time for you to continue your father's legacy."

Tanglor glances at Leazara—she seems just as surprised as him. He turns back to the computer.

"Alright, Mart, show me what I need to know."

"Leazara, I'd take a seat if you're going to be watching too."

She sits down, and Martonamo begins to flash the teal color, starting slow and speeding up to a rapid pace. Tanglor and Leazara get lost in the light, staring at the screen. When it stops flashing, Martonamo has control of their minds.

"Alright, hold on tight."

Mart disappears, and the screen changes to the end scene of Tanglor's nightmare. They see the ship explode, but, this time, the screen zooms out to the escape pod flying toward Thoonta.

Tanglor's mother, Mezriah, sits against the door crying, cradling her pregnant belly in her arms. Elisin walks over to her.

"Tazlow saved us. Your child is what matters most now."

She reaches out and helps Mezriah up. She wipes her tears away and looks to Elisin.

"If anything happens to me, promise me that you will watch over him and make sure he is safe."

"He? You know it's a boy?"

"We found out a couple of weeks ago but wanted to keep it a secret. His name is Tanglor Raff."

"Mezriah, everything is going to be okay. You're going to be a great mother to Tanglor."

A loud crash hits the side of the ship.

"What was that?"

Running to the window, they see debris from the exploding ship coming straight for them. Everyone dives for a seat and buckles up. The ship starts to rumble and roll

129

around, causing Mezriah to shake all over the place. She can't take the pain and passes out. Two of the Elders get out of their seats and rush to her side. As debris crashes into the ship, they take her out of the chair and lay her on the floor. One of the Elders looks over to Elisin.

"She's going into labor. If we don't get this baby out of her, they're both going to die!"

Elisin jumps out of her seat and joins them on the ground. Mezriah wakes up for a moment and grabs Elisin.

"Whatever you do, make sure my baby lives... Ahhhhhhhhh!"

She screams until she loses consciousness. With her unable to push Tanglor out, the Elders know they'll need to cut her open. Elisin checks her vitals—she is barely breathing.

"We don't possess the necessary medical supplies onboard to guarantee she'll survive this, but we can't lose the baby along with her...... cut her open. I'm so sorry, Mezriah. My son and I both love you so much."

The two Elders take their small knives and carefully cut her open. Elisin reaches in and pulls Tanglor out. She gets him cleaned off and holds him tenderly as they walk away from his dying mother.

"Shhh, it's all going to be okay, Tanglor."

The screen flashes and jumps forward to them, landing on Thoonta. Elisin exits the ship holding a bundle close to her chest. They walk past the main village on Thoonta to a small house on the mountainside. It's the Monite's house where Tanglor and Ashar grew up. Elisin is welcomed at the door by Mr. and Mrs. Monite.

"Elisin, so good to see you! Please come in."

The Monites step inside, Elisin follows them in with baby Tanglor. She sits down on their couch.

"I'm sorry to drop by without advance notice, but you both have been close friends of mine for many years. Tanglor here is in trouble. The True Guardians are after him, but I've managed to lose them for now. I came here to ask you to adopt this child on his tenth birthday. I plan to drop him off at the foster home here on Thoonta until that time. He must never know he is Tazlow Raff's son."

The Monites' look at each other before Mr. Monite walks over and plucks Tanglor out of Elisin's hands.

"We owe you our lives, Elisin. Anything you need—we'll do it."

He tosses Tanglor up into the air. Happiness fills his face as he flies up and down, safe in Mr. Monite's strong hands.

"See? It'll be a perfect fit. Hopefully, he still likes me in ten years."

He hands Tanglor back to Elisin.

"Thank you; I know he will have an amazing life here."

She leaves their cozy house and heads straight for the foster home. Elisin thoroughly inspects the household before giving Tanglor up to them.

"Please, this is very important. You must never tell him his last name. Don't even file it as information. If they find him—they will kill him."

The last bit of the recording shows her leaving the Monites' home and meeting back up with the other Elders. The light on the screen flashes again; Martonamo reappears while Tanglor and Leazara snap out of the mind warp.

"I apologize; the first time is always the hardest. Drink some fluids, and it'll pass. I know that was some heavy material to take in, Tanglor, but you needed to know that your family, including your grandmother, sacrificed a lot to keep you safe."

Tanglor sits silently, processing everything he just saw.

"Thank you for showing me, but I need to speak with my grandmother as soon as possible. How do we get out of this cavern? We need to get back up to see if Ashar and Freden have any information on that colony ship."

"The way you came in. You share a bond with me now, so just use your hand the same way you would have used the ovals. It gives you the ability to open any of the doors or operate any machines powered by me."

Tanglor turns around to the stone wall that sealed away their exit. He puts his hand on it and watches it light up, along with his hand. The wall vanishes, and their way out opens back up. Tanglor and Leazara follow the path back to the Great Hall to find Elisin waiting for them.

"It was clever of you to build the base above the cavern."

Tanglor and Leazara stand speechless, staring at her.

"Of course, I know about the cavern and the computer. Tazlow took me there a couple of times. Next time you're down there, would you say hi to Martonamo for me?"

Tanglor puts his hand on Leazara's shoulder.

"Go check the comms to see if Ashar and Freden have gotten close to the colony ship. Elisin, I need to speak to you."

Leazara heads to the communications room, while Elisin and Tanglor walk into the Great Hall and take a seat.

"While we were in the cavern, Martonamo showed me how I was born and what you did when we arrived on Thoonta."

She sits quietly and doesn't respond.

"I'm not mad about what you did. I wanted to say thank you. Both for protecting me and for picking the Monites' to be my parents. Anyone else would have taken me and left Ashar behind, but they saw the connection we had and adopted him, too."

Elisin smiles.

"Thank you, Tanglor, for graciously accepting what we did for you. It wasn't easy for any of us. Especially for your parents. Even though you weren't born yet, they both loved you so very much."

Tanglor reaches over and hugs her. She embraces him as tears stream down her face.

"I have waited for this moment for a very long time, Tanglor."

------------------------------------------------------

Leazara sits in the communications room, talking to Ashar.

"Where are you? Can you see the colony ship yet?"

"No, we can't see it yet. By my estimate, we are still almost a day away. This stealth glider only goes so far."

"Keep us updated and, Ashar, keep your eyes on Freden. I still don't trust him."

--------------------------------------------------

On the stealth glider, Ashar looks over to where Freden stands staring out the window.

"Yes, Colonel, I'm watching him closely. I'll never forgive him for what he did to Ranyana."

"Ashar, don't do anything stupid!"

He shuts off the comms and continues to pilot the stealth glider. He looks over to Freden.

"Hey, if you need to get some rest before we get there, now's your chance. We should arrive at the ship in about eighteen hours."

Freden gives Ashar a thumbs up before turning away and falling asleep. Ashar reaches over to the radio and turns on some music.

"I hate flying in silence."

# Chapter 14:
# Tralupians- The Unknown

Siritano tries to break free from the two crimson monsters carrying him away from his brother. He screams for him.

"Ilikso! Help me!!"

The monsters laugh as they approach the wall at the end of the hallway inside the TralVent Inn. They both reach their hands out and touch the wall. It crumbles away, revealing a door with a portal behind it. Siritano kicks his legs out and tries to escape one last time.

"Brother!!!"

The monsters drag him through the portal and shut it behind them. Siritano watches as his brother runs for the closing portal. On the other side, the portal fades away, leaving nothing behind. The monsters stand with Siritano in a wasteland. Above them, massive dark red clouds release violent storms with raging winds and blinding lightning strikes. Orange sand whips around them from the winds covering the enormous surrounding mountains. The monsters drag Siritano through the sandstorm. The pieces of dirt swirling past are so sharp they slice Siritano as they zoom by, but the monster's skin seems unaffected by it. As they approach the tallest mountain, one of the monsters releases his grip on Siritano and steps forward. It raises both arms in the air and waves them forcefully to the left. The orange sand falls off the front of the mountain, revealing a large metal door. He swings his arms back the other way and then down to his side, and the huge door opens.

The monster grabs back onto Siritano and lifts its sharp fingers into the air. It stares at Siritano before shoving its fingers into his gut. Siritano falls to his knees, but the monsters hit him until he stands back up. He stumbles through the door, the two monsters escorting him. Siritano tries to keep his eyes open and looks around as the monsters walk him through a metal fortress. Metallic walls line the inside of the magnificent mountain, and the floor is made from the same metallic material with a layer of the orange sand covering it. He looks up; the ceiling reflects his image to him. The monsters turn a corner into a corridor. They stop and walk over to a silver metallic light that shines from the top of a doorway down to the bottom. One of the monsters says an unfamiliar phrase, and the light vanishes. They walk Siritano through and throw him into a room with another alien creature. The two monsters leave, uttering the unknown phrase and causing the silver metallic light to shine down again, effectively sealing off the doorway. Siritano gathers his strength to turn and evaluate the alien. It's a small creature, standing on two legs with a robe and a hood covering its face. Siritano reaches out to it, but because of all the blood loss, he passes out as soon as the little creature moves toward him.

A couple of hours go by before Siritano comes to. When he does, the little creature kneels next to him.

"Please tell me you can understand me... what's going on? Where are we?"

The little creature stares, its eyes glowing yellow under its hood.

"I can understand you, and I'm sorry to say, but I don't know where we are. Everyone here calls it the Unknown or the Metal Mansion. I was captured and brought here—I assume in the same manner you were. Those monsters left you here to perish. You are lucky to be alive."

"How am I alive?"

The little creature stands up but doesn't break eye contact.

"I couldn't just sit here and watch you die, so I saved you with my powers."

"Your powers?"

"It is a very long story to tell, but yes. My people developed powers on our homeworld, although they only work when we have the elements around us. Luckily for you, I have trained myself to use almost anything as an element. I utilized the small wind current that passes through here, as well as some of the energy coming from the silver light, to cauterize your wounds and stop the bleeding. I was also able to recycle the blood you lost, which gave you the liquids you needed to recover."

Siritano stands up, feeling a bit sore.

"Thank you for helping me...?"

"Qualt.... My name is Qualt; I am a Remori. What is your name?"

"I am Siritano and I'm a Tralupian."

Siritano looks over to the doorway.

"Do you know what that silver light shining from the ceiling is?"

"Whatever you do, don't touch that light. It hurts very much. I learned by watching the others trapped here."

"Thanks for the heads up. It is good to meet you, Qualt. "

The little creature stands about four feet tall.

"Same to you, Siritano. It's nice to have company for a change. I've watched far too many of the others get taken back into that room over there. I have only seen one return, and she wasn't the same. She didn't even look like the poor girl anymore either."

As Qualt speaks, he points through the silver light at a metal door across a bridge.

"What's inside that room?"

"I haven't had the pleasure to find out. I hope I never do. If you're thinking about getting out of here, there isn't anything you can do."

"I can't just stay here forever. I need to go home! My brother will be coming for me soon."

Qualt turns around and sits on a bed in the corner.

"I'm sorry, Siritano, but there is no way for your brother to get here without a portal opening up. And that's not possible without one of those monsters."

Siritano walks over to another bed on the opposite side of Qualt.

"My family is relentless. They'll figure out a way to come for me. I know they will."

The two of them lie down on the beds.

"If they do come and save you... do you think they could save me, too?"

-------------------------------------------------

Ilikso looks out the TralVent Inn window at the battle going on outside. He sees his sisters enter the city and yells for them. He turns to run out of the room, but a claw appears out of the portal and grabs him—pulling him inside. Ilikso falls through, watching the portal close behind him. He topples over, landing on an orange, sandy surface.

"What just happened? Where am I!?"

He stands to his feet and is instantly greeted by three alien creatures. They stand before Ilikso, with red eyes and black pupils. They have spikes that run from their head down to their tails and crystallized scales that cover their bodies like armor. One of them steps forward and pushes Ilikso against the wall behind him.

"What are you!? What was that thing I pulled you through?"

"Why did you pull me through?"

The alien pushes him again.

"Answer me!"

"My name is Ilikso, and I'm a Tralupian. That thing I was some sort of portal, like a gateway or a doorway to another place. What are you, and why are you here?"

The alien looks around at the orange wasteland.

"We are Dimorians, and we were captured by whatever those monsters are. The three of us managed to escape, but we can't leave our brothers and sisters behind. My name is Razeel. This is Sarwu, and this is Uzatomus."

Razeel lets Ilikso go.

"I am sorry for pulling you through that portal. How will you get back home?"

"I'm glad you pulled me through, Razeel. I think my brother, Siritano, was taken to this place by those monsters. Do you mind if I come with the three of you back to your brothers and sisters?"

Razeel turns to Sarwu and Uzatomus.

"I don't mind. Do either of you?"

They both shake their heads.

"Looks like you're welcome to join us. Here, you might want to equip yourself with a weapon."

Ilikso catches the blaster Razeel throws to him. He reaches down for his blade, but it's gone.

"Shit, my blade must've fallen back at RoyalTree. What kind of blaster is this?"

Sarwu smiles at him.

"Try it out. Shoot that rock over there."

Ilikso turns and aims it at the rock she's pointing at. He fires, but instead of bullets, it shoots out blasts of light that burn whatever it touches.

"This is amazing. How do you have weapons like this?"

Uzatomus pulls out a larger rifle.

"We were blessed by mysterious gods that left behind their technology. We are also able to communicate with other species due to our crystallized scales. We still aren't sure how it all works, though."

Ilikso looks at the rifle.

"That's amazing. Our people don't have anything like that. Well... I guess we kind of do with our Great Tree, but that's a long story. Maybe I'll tell it to you if we make it back out of here, where exactly are we going?"

Razeel points over to an enormous mountain across the way. A storm rages on, causing the sand and dirt to swirl around brutally.

"We need to get over there. That mountain is where they took us, along with all of the other aliens."

Siritano looks through the storm.

"The mountain? How are we even going to get there?"

"There is a giant metal door that leads inside of it. We heard it being called the Metal Mansion."

Sarwu walks over to Siritano. She places her claw on his shoulder.

"We have to go through the storm to get there. The three of us will form a triangle around you, blocking you in, so the storm can't hurt you. The crystallized scales will protect all of us."

Razeel and Uzatomus walk over to them and form the triangle around Siritano. The four of them slowly cross through the storm towards the mountain. They reach the other side, unharmed. Siritano stands looking at a metal door dusted with the orange sand.

"Thank you for protecting me. This door barely has any sand on it, so it must have been opened recently. How do we get inside?"

Razeel walks over and gently pushes Siritano aside.

"Step back. I don't know if this will work."

Razeel takes off a piece of the crystallized armor and places it on the metal door. He lifts his hands into the air and swings them to the left and then to the right, before bringing them back to his side. The crystallized scales on his body start to shake; a light comes out from one of them and reflects off the one on the door. It shoots back at him and reflects again and again off each scale. The power accumulating from the scales reflecting the light causes the door to begin to rumble. The rumbling turns into violent shaking, as the piece of scaled armor grows, covering the massive metal door. Razeel places his arms forward in front of the door and pushes them to the side. The door starts to tremble before shooting open.

"Hurry, get through! I can't hold it for long!!"

Sarwu, Siritano, and Uzatomus all run through before Siritano and Uzatomus turn back to hold the door open with their backs pushing against it. Razeel runs and jumps through; the door closes with all four of them on the other side. They've made it inside the Metal Mansion. Ilikso looks around in amazement.

"The name makes perfect sense now. This is fascinating!"

The three Dimorians move ahead.

"No time to see the wondrous Mansion. We need to get our people before it's too late."

Ilikso catches up to them, as they run through the Metal Mansion. They get to a corridor with cells on both sides. Silver metallic light shines down, blocking the entrance to the cell doors. Uzatomus looks to Ilikso.

"Those silver lights hurt. We need to learn the phrase the monsters use to turn them off."

"Thanks, glad you told me that."

Ilikso looks around to see if any of them are coming. He notices a Tralupian behind one of the silver lights.

"Siritano!"

Siritano jumps up off his bed and looks over to see Ilikso on the other side of the silver light.

"I knew you would come for me! How did you get here?"

"There is no time for that right now, brother. How do I get you out of here?"

"The lights only go away when the monsters say a strange phrase. Qualt and I have been trying to figure it out."

"Qualt?"

Siritano points to the metal door across the bridge.

"They took him through that door. He saved me, so I have to save him!"

Razeel yells to Ilikso.

"Ilikso, someone is coming. Hurry, we need to hide."

"I'm going to get you out of here."

Ilikso turns around and runs back over to Razeel and the other two Dimorians. They hide behind some pillars just as three monsters come out from a metal door across the bridge. They walk over to the corridor with the cells, stopping to look around before splitting up and going to different cells. The monsters enter the three rooms causing the silver light to disappear from the entryway; one of the rooms is Siritano's. Ilikso waits for the right moment, as he looks to his newly acquired Dimorian friends.

"Ready to do this?"

Razeel stands up and starts to walk toward the cell on the right where one of the monsters went.

"We are ready."

Ilikso makes his way to his brother's cell. He pulls out the blaster Razeel gave to him. He enters the cell and sees the monster holding Siritano down on the ground. Ilikso points the blaster at the beast.

"Let him go!"

Ilikso fires the Dimorian weapon, the light shoots out, hitting the monster in the leg. It turns to run at Ilikso, but the light from the blaster causes its leg to disintegrate. It falls to the ground. Ilikso walks over to it and shoves the blaster right up against its head, firing it again. The monster's head melts away as its body twitches for a couple of seconds. Ilikso reaches down to his brother.

"Are you okay?"

Siritano takes his hand and stands up.

"I'll be fine, but we need to move quickly... I have to help Qualt!"

The two of them leave the cell to see the Dimorians still fighting the other two monsters. Razeel is fighting one back, but his blaster has been knocked away from him. Uzatomus has been knocked out of the battle, while Sarwu struggles to fight the other monster on her own. Ilikso looks to his brother.

"We need to help; I wouldn't have found you without them. Siritano, help Sarwu; I'll get Razeel his weapon and get Uzatomus up. Take the blaster!"

Ilikso throws the blaster to Siritano as he runs toward Sarwu. Siritano jumps over the monster and punches it in the face. He lands on the other side with the blaster aiming towards it. He fires, hitting the beast in the arm. It lets go of Sarwu; she hurries over to Siritano. He takes another shot, but it misses as the monster moves to the side, its arm melt away. It stands up and starts to walk toward them. Siritano fires again, but the blaster does nothing. He hands it to Sarwu.

"It needs to be reloaded, but it'll take too long!"

The two of them rush over to Ilikso and Razeel. They kneel next to the unconscious Uzatomus. Razeel stands up and steps in front of them. The two monsters walk toward them.

"Stay behind me. I think I can hold them off."

Suddenly the monsters stop; the metal door across the bridge opens. Twenty more of the creatures run out, standing ready behind the other two. They smile and start to speak in the unknown tongue before it changes to a language they can understand.

"Yu olluk trog zando around the Metal Mansion anymore. You all need to get back into your cells. Stop resisting, and this will go much easier for you. We don't want to have to kill you after spending so much time collecting our specimens."

Razeel starts to pull his crystallized scales off his body.

"I hate when someone thinks they can just do whatever they want... I know a lot of creatures like you, and it disgusts me."

He turns back and looks to his companions.

"I'm not letting us die here today. I'll hold them for as long as I can. You better fight your asses off!"

Razeel turns back around and screams at the twenty-two monsters facing him. They charge at him, but he screams again while advancing on them. The scales he pulled off his body start to float around him. They gather speed creating a whirlwind. Razeel screams again, the creatures charging him are pushed back. The whirlwind around him releases shockwaves, knocking some of the monsters off the bridge they stand on. They fall into darkness as Razeel blocks the way to his friends. Uzatomus regains consciousness.

"What's going on? Razeel, no!"

Sarwu grabs him and helps him up. They head for where Razeel continues to hold the monsters off. Siritano and Ilikso follow. Razeel notices them behind him; he continues to walk forward, pressing the monsters further back. Fifteen of them still stand, blocking the only way out of the Metal Mansion. One of the monsters breaks free from the rest and runs toward Razeel. He jumps over the shockwave, landing on top of him. It takes a bite out of his shoulder before Ilikso can knock it off into the darkness. Razeel's whirlwind begins to slow, and the scales swirling around him crack and break. He falls to the ground, leaving them vulnerable to the monster's attacks. Ilikso looks up to see the remaining creatures charging at them once more.

"Everyone, look out!"

The fourteen monsters tackle Razeel to his knees and tear him apart. Sarwu and Uzatomus rush over to him, screaming, and fire their blasters into the crowd of monsters. Ilikso tries to get them to move ahead, but they refuse to leave without Razeel. Ilikso turns back to his brother. Siritano has started to make his way toward the metal door across the bridge.

"Siritano! Where are you going!? We need to get out of here!"

Siritano continues to walk toward the door. He sneaks past Sarwu and Uzatomus, who stand on top of the torn apart Razeel firing their weapons.

"I'm not leaving without Qualt. I would already be dead if it weren't for him!"

Uzatomus gets tackled to the ground; his rifle slides over to Siritano. He swiftly picks it up and fires it at the monster taking a bite out of Uzatomus. It releases a loud screech as its body starts to disintegrate. Uzatomus gets back up. He stands covered in blood and pulls out a smaller blaster.

"Thank you, Siritano. We'll hold them here as long as we can. Take the rifle and go save your friend!"

Siritano makes for the metal door, holding the rifle in front of him. Ilikso runs to catch up with his brother, passing by the two Dimorians still engaged in battle. Sarwu smiles at him as he runs by.

"Get the two of them out of here…. We're staying here with our brothers and sisters."

Ilikso gets through the doorway and stands next to his brother. They look around the empty, eerie room. It's filled with metal tables lined up in rows. On some of the tables lay the remains of dead aliens, but they can't make out what kind because of how bloody and distorted they are. They are in an examination room where the monsters took the aliens they captured. Siritano starts to slowly walk through, looking at the dead aliens on the tables.

"None of these look like Qualt. He is too small to be any of these aliens."

Ilikso walks behind him.

"This Qualt might not be alive anymore.... Brother?"

"I know he's still alive!"

An ear-splitting scream comes from behind a blocked entry. They look through the silver light and see some of the creatures moving around—another cry echoes through the room.

"Ahhhhh! Somebody, please help me!"

Siritano looks through the light.

"That's Qualt; he's still alive!!"

Ilikso runs over to the light with his brother.

"We can't get to him. That silver light blocks the way!"

Siritano turns back and surveys the tables holding dead aliens.

"There has to be something here that we can use to shut it off!"

As he looks around, Ilikso spies one of the monsters making its way toward the entryway.

"Siritano, here comes our chance to get through!"

Siritano runs back to his brother. They both hide under the tables closest to the doorway. The monster speaks its unknown language, the light vanishes. Ilikso jumps out from under the table and tackles it into the wall. Siritano runs through the entrance as his brother knocks the monster to the ground.

"Hurry, Ilikso!"

Ilikso grabs one of the knives next to him on the table and shoves it into the monster's head. It screeches and falls to the ground. Ilikso grabs the knife and stabs the beast again before taking the knife with him through the door. He stands next to his brother; the silver light shines back down behind them, trapping them inside this new, unfamiliar room. The screaming continues and gets louder as the two walk toward a glass window. A light flashes from orange to crimson behind it. The light begins to flash faster. Gradually, the orange fades away until the light is a solid dark red. Siritano stops and looks through the glass window. Qualt stands with his hands chained to the ceiling, he jumps and kicks his feet around.

"Please, make it stop!"

Ilikso joins his brother and watches through the glass, as two of the monsters walk over to Qualt and examine him carefully. They take their long sharp fingers and press them against his head; blood starts to drip out of his wounds as he continues to scream. One of the monsters moves to a table and lifts a jar with an orange mist floating inside of it. Ilikso puts his hands on the window.

"That orange color is the same as the Remnants from RoyalTree!"

The monster shakes the jar around before throwing it to the ground in front of Qualt. It breaks and releases the cloud. It floats up toward Qualt's face, hidden beneath his hood. Qualt whispers to the cloud before it funnels itself into his hood. His eyes turn orange, and he screams again—the monsters back away from him, waiting to see how he reacts. Ilikso discovers a way to get into the room. He takes his knife and jumps through the doorway, stabbing one of the monsters in the neck. The other monster—startled— swipes its sharp fingers at him, raking him across the face. Ilikso stands back, staring down the beast, while Siritano runs behind him to free Qualt. The monster turns away from Ilikso and jumps at Siritano.

"Siritano, look out!"

Qualt's eyes turn back to their natural yellow color, as the orange cloud shoots itself out of Qualt and onto the monster. The cloud flashes brightly and yells at them.

"The three of you need to leave here at once! Go!!"

Siritano releases Qualt from the chains and rushes him out of the room. When they get back to the silver light blocking the doorway, Qualt steps forward.

"I finally learned the phrase they use.... Olluk tras dah umbar!"

The light shining down fades away, allowing them to pass through. They run by the dead aliens on the table and make it back to the metal door. Ilikso kicks it open. As they run through, they see Sarwu and Uzatomus covered in blood with bodies piled up next to them. Sarwu turns and sees them.

"Don't worry about us. Get them out of here!"

Ilikso, Siritano, and Qualt run past them, as more creatures come from across the bridge, tackling her and Uzatomus to the ground. Siritano and Qualt stop to help, but Ilikso grabs them both and urges them forward.

-----------------------------------------------------------------

"I can't lose our brothers, too. Take care of our people."

Oryuna jumps into the portal and watches it close, as Queen Zuna reaches for her. She falls back and lands in a chair with a highly advanced computer console sitting in front of her. She hears voices coming from behind her. Oryuna gets out of the chair and hides behind the door, just as the monsters enter the room. She stays hidden, trying to make out the unknown language they're speaking, but it's no use. The language is like nothing she's ever heard before. She stays hidden and watches them. They seem to get frustrated with the console, but just as they start to get violent, a face appears on the screen and speaks back to them. Before Oryuna can get a good look at the face, she hears another voice from behind her. Quickly, she ducks into a closet to avoid being seen. Another monster walks through the doorway and changes the screen to some security camera footage. Oryuna pokes her head out to see the video of both her brothers fighting some of the monsters assisted by other alien creatures.

Oryuna sees the monsters getting up from the computer console. She hides back in the closet, as they run out of the room. Exiting the closet, she approaches the screen and to watch more of the footage. A large group of monsters starts to overwhelm two of the aliens and take them out, while her brothers and another alien escape out of the corridor. The cameras switch to follow them, running through the halls toward the only way in and out. Oryuna looks around the room and notices a green box with an orange button on it. She remembers seeing the creature back at RoyalTree use something like it to open the portal. She grabs the box and runs out of the room toward her brothers. By the time Oryuna is within sight of them, they've been cornered by a pack of the monsters. Before she can make it to them, they attack.

Ilikso and Siritano fight back while the little creature with them sticks its arms out in front of him. The ground beneath him shakes, hands made from the dirt fly up from underneath them, smacking some of the monsters into the ceiling. Six more come and overwhelm him. The ground continues to rumble, followed by a bright yellow light emitting from the cracks. The light shoots the monsters off. The little creature grows from only four feet to seven feet tall—sparks of blue and yellow shoot off him as he floats into the air. The monsters charge at him again. The sparks fuse around each other to create an electrical surge that launches toward the approaching monsters, while the hands from the ground shoot up again, creating a wall behind the monsters. The surge of blue and yellow light hits the first monster.

The current shoots through it, hitting the other five creatures, electrocuting, and killing them all. More monsters flood the room, focusing on Siritano. They begin to overpower him, scratching up his body with their sharp fingers. Ilikso tries to make his way over to him but gets cut off.

Oryuna fights her way through the horde with her blades. She throws one of them toward Ilikso, piercing a monster in the head.

"Take one of my blades, brother!"

Ilikso pulls the blade out of the dead monster and swings it around, evening the odds. He takes out ten of the creatures while making his way to Oryuna and Siritano. Oryuna slices the monsters away from Siritano, but one of them latches onto his arm with its sharp teeth. Ilikso jumps over and slices into its side. The beast lets out a loud screech as it grips onto Siritano's arm. He pulls his blade out and slices down again, cutting through its neck—the monster's body thuds to the ground, followed by its head. Siritano, bloodied and mangled, falls into Oryuna's lap. She looks at Ilikso.

"Hurry and get over here!"

Ilikso turns and runs over to her, as the monsters circle them.

"Let's hope this works!"

Oryuna pulls out the little green box and presses the orange button. The three of them watch as a portal opens in front of them. They pick Siritano up off the ground, He looks to Ilikso and tries to speak.

"Q...ua....lt."

Ilikso looks over to the little creature shooting off sparks of blue and yellow energy. Ilikso runs toward him, jumping over monsters and slicing into them.

"Qualt!"

Qualt's surge of energy starts to die down, as he turns and floats to the ground in front of Ilikso. One of the monsters jumps up and lands behind him. Ilikso shoves his blade forward toward Qualt. It goes by his head and pierces into the monster behind him. The beast falls to the ground, as Ilikso reaches his hand out to Qualt.

"Time to go."

Qualt's eyes glisten as he takes Ilikso's hand. They fight their way back to Oryuna and Siritano, then the four of them stumble through the portal. On the other side, their sister, Queen Zuna, an alive and well Zembor, and all the Remnants of RoyalTree stand looking at them. Siritano, marred and bleeding, falls to the ground. Qualt runs and leans over him, as Ilikso turns around and looks at the portal with his blade ready. Oryuna looks at the little green box. The orange button is now flashing red. It gets faster and starts to beep. Oryuna throws it back through as it explodes, causing the portal to shut. Oryuna and Ilikso help Qualt pick Siritano back up off the ground. Queen Zuna runs over to them and hugs them.

Siritano uses what strength he has left to smile at the Queen.

"Did we just get a hug from the great Queen Zuna?"

The Queen laughs as she wipes the tears away from her eyes.

"We will discuss everything that happened later over dinner. Right now, we need to get Siritano cleaned up and to a doctor."

Zembor walks over and helps Ilikso and Qualt carry Siritano out of TralVent. Oryuna walks behind them with Zuna.

"How is Zembor alive? Wasn't he...”?

"As I said, sister, we will discuss everything over dinner."

Queen Zuna smiles and walks ahead to catch up to Zembor and Ilikso. They reach the outskirts of the city. Queen Zuna turns to Zembor putting Siritano down.

"Come back with us. We don't need to tell the people you're back. You can stay in the palace with me and disguise yourself if you need to."

Zembor looks over to her.

"I... I couldn't do that to you."

She embraces him.

"I never knew my father. It would be nice having you around, and you could help me lead our people. Plus, I want to know more about you and RoyalTree."

Zembor looks around the Great Tree.

"I have been stuck in here for the past thousand years... I would be happy to come with you back to the palace."

Queen Zuna and the others stand looking toward the city, with the Remnants of their ancestors looking back. Orange light starts to flash around them. Getting faster, it turns to a solid light, blinding all of them. The light fades away, the six of them stand outside the palace on the ledge by RoyalTree. Oryuna and Ilikso take Siritano straight to the doctors.

"Qualt, come with us. We might need your help."

Qualt follows behind Oryuna and Ilikso, as Zembor and Queen Zuna stand looking out into the ocean. Zembor takes a deep breath, looking at the sunset.

"Thank you for saving me. I thought I was going to be stuck inside RoyalTree forever."

Zembor kneels to the ground and grabs Zuna's hand.

"I will do anything you ask of me. I am here for you, Zuna."

He kisses her hand as the sun sets behind them. Queen Zuna blushes and pulls her hand away from him.

"Thank you, Zembor. It is nice to have friends like you."

He stands up and watches her walk back into the palace. Night begins to fall, as Zembor stares up at RoyalTree. His eyes flash orange before he turns around and follows Queen Zuna into the palace.

# Chapter 15:
# Johthuns-Unlikely Friends

Freden tosses and turns. He's unable asleep with Ashar's listening to music. He can't take it anymore, so he gets up and turns the radio off.

"Sorry, but I can't listen to that music anymore."

Ashar shrugs it off.

"What would you like to listen to?"

Freden sits down next to Ashar.

"Nothing... I wanted to talk."

"I have nothing to say to you."

Ashar turns the music back on. Freden waits a couple of seconds before turning it off again.

"Just listen then... I need to say this to you before I disappear. I can't be around the Elites. I don't belong here, not after the things I've done."

Ashar nods at Freden to let him know he's listening.

"Ashar, I know you hate me for what I did. I don't blame you; I'd hate me too. And I know there is nothing I can do or say to make it up to you, or her. I truly am sorry for taking Ranyana away from you. She was a great soldier and an even better Johthun."

Ashar stops piloting the ship and hits Freden in the face, knocking him to the ground and giving him a busted lip.

After a second, he reaches his hand out to help Freden up.

"I appreciate the apology, but words aren't going to fix what you did."

Ashar lifts Freden back into the seat next to him.

"You don't need to leave, Freden. You need to serve the Elites. If not for yourself, then for the ones you've hurt."

Freden takes what Ashar says to heart. He is about to get up, but he notices debris from some wrecked ships ahead of them.

"Those are probably the scouts Elisin was talking about."

Ashar turns on their comms to radio in for Tanglor and the others back on Joht.

"We found the scouts you lost, Elisin, or at least what's left of their ships."

The comms are silent.

"Hello? Tanglor? Leazara?"

Nothing but silence... Ashar and Freden sit in their glider, staring at the destroyed Johthun ships.

"There has to be something interfering with our comms. Guess we're on our own for now."

Freden activates stealth mode on their glider as they pass through the wreckage. Ashar slows it down to a stop. They both look ahead to see ships that aren't Johthun. Crystallized panels surround the unknown vessels, as they speed around the floating Johthun colony. The colony ship is intact, with just a few dents and scrapes to the outer hull. It looks like they survived a small attack, possibly from this alien species. Freden and Ashar try the comms one more time, but still no response. Ashar gets out of his seat and looks to Freden.

"It's just you and me. We're going to have to infiltrate the colony ship and save our people."

As they start to gather their equipment, Ashar stops and speaks to Freden.

"I'm counting on you here, Freden. We're going to have to sneak past all of them and pull up right next to the colony. Once we're there, we'll activate the doors and sneak in. We don't have any cloaking devices available for this mission. Our scientists are still trying to duplicate it and make more for the Elites."

"I know. You can trust me, Ashar. I have your back."

Once they finish getting their equipment, Ashar pilots the stealth glider toward the colony. He maneuvers through the alien ships without being spotted, pulling up to the docking door on the side.

"Alright, Freden, I can hack into the door system. It's only going to give us about fifteen seconds to get through, then it closes. Ready?"

Freden nods his head as Ashar unlocks the door. They both run for the entry as it slowly opens. It's only halfway open when an alarm sounds; it begins to close. Ashar jumps, only getting the front of his body through. He is stuck between the shutting doors, Freden grabs his legs and starts to pull.

"I got you. We can figure out another way in."

"No, push me through! This is our only chance."

Freden lets go and backs up to get a running start. He charges and hits Ashar's legs, launching him through the door as it closes behind him. Asher swiftly gets up. He turns around and bangs on the door to Freden.

"Get back into the stealth glider and wait for me to radio in. I'm going to figure out what's going on here. Quickly, someone's coming!"

Freden runs back into the glider, shutting the door behind him, causing it to be hidden from sight. The entrance to the colony ship opens again, a creature appears, looking out. It has crystallized scales covering most of its body. Spikes run down its head down to its tail, and it has red eyes with dark black pupils. It looks around for a couple of seconds before turning back and walking inside, shutting the door behind it—Ashar radios into Freden.

"Did you see that thing?"

"Yeah! What was that?"

"I'm going to go ahead and say that's the alien species we were looking for. From what it looks like, they took over the ship. I'll have to get to the upper deck and find the Captain. Hang tight, Freden. I'll let you know what I find."

Ashar shuts off his comms and sneaks past the creature. He moves to the hallway away from the docking bay. Two more of the aliens come around the corner, causing Ashar to jumps into a room, closing the door behind him. He waits and listens for the footsteps to fade away before leaving the room and heading for the upper deck. A stairway leads him up to a room where he finds the Captain lying on a bed. One of the creatures stands over him. Ashar pulls out his blade and sneaks up behind it.

"Move away from him!"

The startled creature turns around and moves away from the Captain with its hands up. The Captain leans forward and sits up on the bed.

"Ashar!? Where did you come from?"

"Captain Plazerin, what's going on here!? We've been trying to get through to you and the ship for the last two weeks. Elisin sent me to check on things."

"Lower your weapon, Ashar. This is one of their doctors; she was taking a look at me. I suffered an injury from an asteroid storm that hit our ship. If it weren't for them, we would have taken more damage."

Ashar puts his weapon away; the creature puts her hands down and reaches out to shake his.

"Nice to meet you, Ashar. My name is Dr. Sunize."

He takes her hand and shakes it, noticing the sharp nails on her fingers.

"Likewise, Doctor. If I may ask, what species are you, and how is it that we understand each other?"

"Well, for one, I'm a Dimorian. My people are from a planet outside of your solar system called Dimastus. As for understanding you, I believe it is because of a metal-like substance, we discovered a long time ago. It fell from the sky inside an empty spaceship; we were able to use it as a resource for everything. It helped reshape our species and gave us technology beyond our dreams. We have yet to discover all its uses, but we wear it over our skin and on our vehicles. I believe it helps translate our languages. It's helped so far with the other species we discovered."

Ashar stops and thinks about their technology but decides not to share.

"Other species?"

"A while ago, we were attacked by a species called Ventrians. We were able to understand them, too. When they decided to talk."

"I'm glad you and your people are here. Do you mind if I speak with the Captain for a moment?"

Dr. Sunize nods her head and walks over to an injured Dimorian across the room. Ashar sits on the bed next to Captain Plazerin. He keeps his voice down while talking to him.

"You really got hit by an asteroid storm, and they happened to come out of nowhere and save you?"

The Captain hesitates before responding.

"No, not exactly...We had a run-in with them before the storm. I was meeting with their leader Calaido. He's currently with our engineers trying to figure out how to start the ship back up."

"Hmmm, I don't know. Something doesn't seem right to me. I'm going to head over to the engine room to meet this Calaido."

"Be careful. He can be aggressive."

Ashar leaves the Captain to go and find Calaido. As he approaches, he can hear shouting in the engine room. The door opens, a Dimorian with a black eye walks out. Ashar watches him slowly walk by before entering the room. A Dimorian much larger than the rest of them turns around.

"I said to get the hell out of here!"

He stops and looks down at Ashar.

"Who are you?"

"My name is Ashar Monite; I am a Captain of the Elite Protectors. I have come to see why we lost communication with our colony ship."

"Well, as you can see, there was an asteroid storm that hit the ship, causing quite a bit of damage. It must've knocked your comms out."

"Why didn't our people radio us before the storm? You were meeting with Captain Plazerin, weren't you?"

Calaido drops his tool; they hit the deck with a loud clang. The other Dimorians and Johthuns in the room back away as he approaches Ashar.

"What are you getting at? Are you implying we caused this?"

Ashar stands as tall as he can in the shadow of the towering Dimorian.

"I'm just asking questions. How you take them is on you."

Calaido starts to laugh and rubs Ashar on the top of his head.

"I like this, Johthun! Yes, I was meeting with the Captain of your ship before the storm hit. We had nothing to do with it if that's what you're concerned about."

Ashar pretends to laugh with the Dimorian leader.

"Glad to hear you and your people aren't here to fight then... Can I ask what you *are* here for?

"We got tired of staying around Dimastus. We wanted to explore and expand the great Dimorian Kingdom! Before the storm, Captain Plazerin and I were discussing the different resources we have available to trade. I offered him some of our fine metal for some of your intriguing tech he mentioned."

Ashar gets a little nervous.

"What kind of tech did he mention?"

"I want to see that ancient computer console your people have back home."

"There are tons of Johthuns that have never even seen it. What makes you think you'll be able to?"

Calaido's laughter fills the entire room.

"I can be pretty persuasive, and I have more to offer than most! Now go and get some rest while I fix this damn engine. Hey, you two!"

He looks over to two Dimorians working on the console that controls the engine.

"Escort our new friend to an open room to get some food and rest."

They walk over towards Ashar and escort him down to the end of the hallway to an open room. Ashar walks in, the door closes behind him, leaving them standing outside. He walks over to his bed and checks in with Freden on his comms.

"Freden, you still there?"

"About time! Is everything okay in there?"

"I'm still figuring that out. These creatures call themselves Dimorians. They seem peaceful for the most part, but I don't know. Something doesn't feel right. Captain Plazerin seems like he's hiding something. I need to stay here, but you should take the stealth glider and head for Conril to meet up with Ucarus and Neliah. I'm going to get the ship's communication system working and let Tanglor and Leazara know what's going on."

Silence sits over the comms before Freden responds.

"I can't leave you here. I can find a way in and help you."

"Help me do what, Freden? There's no point. Hurry and go before they find you out there."

"Damn! Alright, I'll let you know as soon as I get to the others. You need to radio in as soon as you get it working again!"

"That's the plan. Talk to you soon."

Freden shuts his comms off and sits down in front of the pilot controls. He hesitates one more time before he takes off away from the colony ship. Once the glider is far enough away from the Dimorians, he deactivates stealth mode and flies faster to Conril.

Ashar sits on the bed, holding his communication device tight. A knock on the door startles him to his feet. He quickly pockets the device as Captain Plazerin enters the room.

"Don't say a word. This is the only chance I'll get while they aren't listening."

Ashar shakes his head and sits back down on the bed.

"Calaido is a monster! He has control over everything on this ship. It looks like nothing is going on, but he's slowly taking everything from us. He's not interested in anything except our technology and our scientists. There are a couple of Dimorians that don't agree with his ways, but if they speak out, he kills them without hesitation. He's killed three of them in front of us because they didn't follow a simple order."

They hear Calaido storming down the hallway. Captain Plazerin starts to speak faster.

"You have to get out of here while you still can and warn the others. He's planning on heading for Joht and our surrounding planets to take everything from us."

The door flies open and Calaido steps in.

"Ahh, there you are, Captain. I believe we've fixed the engine, so we need you back up piloting the ship. You said we could make it to Conril in a couple of days, correct? We better get moving. I can't wait to see what it looks like with all your fancy technology."

Plazerin leaves the room with Calaido. Ashar follows behind.

"Hey! What about the communication system?"

"Oh yes, that's working again too. Feel free to use it."

Calaido and Captain Plazerin walk together to the front of the ship, while Ashar takes off toward the control room to use the comms. Once he gets there, he reaches out to Tanglor and Leazara.

"Colonels! Can you hear me? The comms are back up on the colony ship."

Leazara sits in the control room back on Joht in the Elite Protector's base.

"Ashar is that you!? Are you on the colony ship right now? What's going on?"

"The alien species Elisin was talking about is on the ship. They call themselves Dimorians. They didn't attack. Instead, they helped our people survive an asteroid storm. Their leader helped fix the engines, but he wants to see what Conril looks like. Captain Plazerin shared knowledge about the ancient computer console; he wants to see it. It hasn't happened yet, but I think he will start killing people if we don't go along with what he wants. Freden didn't make it onto the ship, so I sent him to meet up with Ucarus and Neliah."

"Thank you for the report. Excellent work, Captain. Keep us updated on everything going on. We will let Ucarus and Neliah know that you're all headed their way. Keep an eye on Calaido, but don't do anything rash unless you have to. Keep our people safe."

Leazara turns the comms off and runs out of the control room to find Tanglor and Elisin walking out of the Great Hall.

"I just spoke with Ashar. We need to start preparing for a potential invasion. Get everyone into the Tazruhvah and start training the recruits at once. These Dimorians and their leader, Calaido, sound like trouble."

# Chapter 16:
# Tralupians- The Reality of RoyalTree

Queen Zuna tosses and turns in her bed. The apocalypse, prophesized to her by Tranjora and RoyalTree, takes over. Zuna tries not to think about it, but it starts to consume her. She sees it every night in her dreams, and the same thing happens. She watches as her people burn to ash, while missiles rain down onto the palace and city. As she sits on the ground helplessly, a ship lands in front of her. The door opens, revealing a humanoid figure backlit by a bright, shining light. The figure starts to approach her, lifts his arm, and points to her. All she can see are big black eyes looking at her through a glass bubble. The dream ends when the being reaches out and grabs her. Overcome with fear, Queen Zuna bolts upright in her bed. She looks over and notices Zembor sitting in a chair next to her bed. He stares at her.

"You seem to be plagued by nightmares every night. Is everything all right?"

Queen Zuna blushes in embarrassment.

"Have you been sitting there every night after I fall asleep?"

Zembor gets out of the chair and sits next to her on the bed.

"Yes, and for your whole life too. This is just the first time I've physically been here in the room."

Zuna scoots closer to him.

"There is so much more that I want to know about you, Zembor. Before anything else, I want to hear the rest of the story about you and RoyalTree."

Zembor stands up, smiling at her.

"I will tell you everything you want to know, but first, get yourself dressed and ready for the day. I will meet you in the throne room."

Zembor walks out of her chambers and heads toward the throne room. Zuna, with a smile on her face, gets out of bed, and dresses carefully. She grabs her crown and trident before eagerly walking to the throne room.

She walks through the door and sees Zembor talking with her brothers and sister.

"What was on the other side of the portals you went through?"

Siritano, still recovering from his wounds, sinks into his seat, looking scared. Ilikso glances at him and sits up.

"It's okay, brother."

Ilikso stands up and addresses Zembor.

"We were in the Unknown. That's what the captured aliens called it, along with all of the Remnants in RoyalTree."

Zembor's eyes open wide.

"No one has ever before been to the Unknown and returned to talk about it. What did you see?"

"Darkness and evil…. The place was murky, and the planet was a wasteland. Everything was covered in abrasive, orange sand from a seemingly unending storm. Dark red clouds covered the sky, while lightning struck the ground around us. The storm clouds moved the sand around so violently it caused the particles to pierce your skin if you were caught in it."

Oryuna stands up.

"That's not all of it either. Enormous mountains covered the vast landscape. The orange sand hides it well, but there's a massive base inside the mountains. The Metal Mansion—metal walls, floors, and ceilings spread throughout the base giving it its name. When I jumped through the portal, I landed on a chair inside the monsters' base. After hiding and observing the monsters, I could tell I was in their control room. They spoke a language I couldn't understand, but I could tell they became frustrated watching the security camera footage where Ilikso, Siritano, and some other alien creatures fought the monsters. The creatures that fought with Siritano and Ilikso were able to speak and understand us. Three of them were called Dimorians, and the other one, Qualt, was the Remori that came back with us. Unfortunately, the Dimorians perished before being able to make it out of the Metal Mansion. Had it not been for them, we would still be there."

Siritano sits up in his seat; the scared look turns to a hopeful one.

"We don't know that they died! Sarwu and Uzatomus were still alive when we left them."

Siritano slides back down in his seat. Zembor shows his condolences to the siblings.

"I am sorry. Watching friends die can be excruciating. I have seen my fair share of that. From what you're describing, it sounds like you were on the planet R'Ang, RoyalTree's homeworld. How did you make it back?"

Ilikso looks around to the others.

"RoyalTree's homeworld? RoyalTree isn't from TokBellu?"

Queen Zuna walks over to them.

"Precisely. RoyalTree is an alien that was captured by those monsters, just like the others. Except for one big difference is that he and his people don't have solid bodies like us: instead, they're gaseous. They call themselves Broncholites and RoyalTree maybe the only one left of his kind. He and his people were discovered on their homeworld of R'Ang by those monsters. It sounds like they completely took over the planet and started experimenting on them. After figuring out they could use the Broncholites to their advantage, they created those silver metallic boxes that allowed them to be placed in other alien's heads. They were able to use their gaseous bodies to flow out of the silver boxes and into whatever creature's brain, giving them control over their thoughts and actions. This is what happened to Zembor."

Zembor walks around the table and stands next to Queen Zuna.

"RoyalTree was put into my head when Grundar and I were abducted by the metal beast. I wasn't aware of it until I returned here to TokBellu…. After I killed Grundar and continued the war with the Ventrians, time went by, and RoyalTree started to speak to me. We became friends, instead of hostiles sharing a body. After thirty years of living with RoyalTree inside of me, he finally came up with a way for us to separate. That is how the Great Tree came to be in front of the palace."

Queen Zuna sits down at the table with her siblings and smiles.

"And that is where we pick back up. You were cut off by them coming back through the portal. I told you that I had a lot of questions about it. Please continue…. I believe you had just planted RoyalTree deep into the ground under the ocean. By the time you made it back to the surface, RoyalTree had already latched himself onto our planet's core and started to grow."

Zembor chuckles as he takes a seat in front of the siblings listening intently to him.

"Queen Zuna is correct. After planting RoyalTree into the ground under the ocean, he took no time in finding the core to our planet and growing into the massive tree we all know today. As I swam back up to the surface, I watched as RoyalTree continued to grow high into the sky. I wasn't sure if he was ever going to stop, but after he rose hundreds of feet into the air⬚—he finally did. I approached the ledge next to his rapidly growing trunk, and, as I looked, I noticed a spot where this orange color was leaking out. I got closer and reached out to touch it. It was the same orange substance that came out of my head due to the silver metallic box. As I touched the substance with my hand, it started to glow; I could hear RoyalTree speaking to me.

"You and your people can live in whatever world you would like now. Come and look at what you have done."

The spot my hand had touched glowed brighter before opening up into a doorway. I walked through it. As I entered, vines sprouted out of the inner walls of the tree, creating a path for me to walk on. Once I was inside, RoyalTree's voice grew louder.

"The Great Zembor Wrathfin, to think of how this relationship started…. Thank you for allowing me to live on inside of you and for becoming my friend. The arrangement we made will live on. What are your orders?"

I looked around the utterly hollow tree and thought carefully before answering. I asked RoyalTree to make our planet a lush and beautiful environment. Moments passed, then the Great Tree started to rumble. I looked down and could see the roots being sent out of the tree into the ground. The roots spread across the entire planet before sprouting up into huge trees—though none as tall as RoyalTree. The ocean waters warmed as steam rolled off the top of the water. The dirt around the tall trees sprouted abundant, green blades of grass. The air became more comfortable to breathe as RoyalTree extended its roots throughout our world. As I watched from inside the tree, a bright orange light floated in front of me. RoyalTree was moving—he was alive and had free will to travel around TokBellu as he pleased. I wished to be able to talk to him whenever I wanted like we discussed, so he had some of the orange light—part of his gaseous body—enter me through my mouth. He spoke again.

"I have done what you requested of me. TokBellu has grown into a wonderful environment with a lavish landscape. The rest of our arrangement will continue each day. You and I will speak about whatever you would like, and I will help you lead your people."

I left RoyalTree and looked around at the fantastic environment that he had created. I couldn't believe my eyes."

Queen Zuna stands up and walks over to her throne. She sits down and looks over to Zembor.

"So, what happened? How did everything become, well, like this? It seems like RoyalTree was peaceful, so where did the other dark red gaseous creatures come from? The monsters from inside the Great Tree were the same monsters my brother and sister saw on that planet, R'Ang."

Oryuna looks over to Siritano, sitting with his eyes closed.

"The monsters we saw on this planet, R'Ang, were the same ones as those monsters inside RoyalTree.... How is that possible?"

Zembor gets upset and sits down with the siblings at the table.

"I feared it was true, but I didn't want to believe it... if that is the case and you saw those monsters on R'Ang, then they have indeed taken over RoyalTree's homeworld. Did you see any orange or crimson Broncholites floating around while you were there?"

Ilikso looks over at his brother—his eyes still closed. As Zembor is about to say something, Siritano's eyes snap open, he jumps out of his seat.

"The red clouds in the sky, the ones that were causing the storm!"

Zembor stands up with him.

"That's it! The rest of the Broncholites make up the raging storm! RoyalTree told me that most of his species were taken captive and held against their will in a Metal Mansion."

Siritano continues to look toward Zembor.

"Where is RoyalTree? Why are you telling us all of this and not him?"

Zembor sits back down.

"I'm afraid RoyalTree has been under attack ever since I planted him. Those monsters somehow knew when I removed him from my head; they watched him grow, becoming part of our world here on TokBellu. When I was "killed" by the

Ventrian explosion, the ground opened underneath us. We were left to suffocate in the dirt. As we clung to life, RoyalTree used its roots and brought us inside of its trunk. I remember laying on some dirty vines looking around. I watched as the Ventrians that got caught in the blast tried to stand up and continue to fight my people. As one of them pulled out a small knife, a dark red figure quickly ran by grabbing the Ventrian. More and more showed up, taking away the Ventrians and my people. I was left standing by myself, as a horde of those dark monsters surrounded me. I remember waiting there, accepting my fate. I closed my eyes and welcomed death.

Upon opening my eyes, the red monsters had all been turned to ash; three orange clouds hovered in front of me. Before I could speak, they surrounded me. I tried to fight it, but I was paralyzed. Their aura lit up bright before turning into stone— encasing me into that statue. After being trapped for so long and being one with RoyalTree, I was able to send my spirit out as one of the other Remnants. The voice that you heard when you were inside the Great Tree was me. RoyalTree has been missing for over a thousand years, and I haven't been able to find him. I became RoyalTree while I was trapped in there for all that time. That is why it has been a tradition among the Wrathfins. I was only able to accept those with royal blood in them. Without it, RoyalTree would slowly die away, leading to an apocalypse. The legend is that Zalzatine didn't believe in RoyalTree, but that is wrong. My son was devoted to it because he knew RoyalTree had disappeared. I told him everything while I was trapped inside that statue. Without a sacrifice, RoyalTree would wither away and die, and because of how he was connected to TokBellu, it would wither away with him."

Oryuna stands up next to him.

"So, you're telling me that RoyalTree is gone and you've been acting as him for a thousand years? What will happen now that you're gone?"

"That is correct. RoyalTree disappeared around the same time that I became that statue. Don't worry about the Great Tree now that I am no longer inside of it. That's what the Remnants are for. They were recruited by me and then sacrificed to join the Great Tree. As a Remnant, they were able to fight off the evil within it and defeat those monsters, or, as we call them, the Remains."

Ilikso stands next to Oryuna.

"If RoyalTree is gone and you're alive and not inside of the Great Tree, then how is it still living and providing us this lavish environment?"

"It all still works the same as before, because of the Remnants. They are still alive in mind and spirit, just not in physical bodies like us. They can do the same thing I was doing and act as RoyalTree. With all this new knowledge of the Unknown, I have no doubt that RoyalTree is back on R'Ang."

Queen Zuna leaves her throne and rejoins her siblings at the table.

"What do we do now? If RoyalTree has a chance of being alive, we can't just leave him to die. He's done so much for the Tralupians and TokBellu!"

Zembor nods his head.

"RoyalTree is the only real friend I had besides my family. Even then, he was more loyal than anyone. RoyalTree was taken from his homeworld and made a new home here with us on TokBellu. If he left to go back to R'Ang, it would be to save his people. That's why he put me into that statue—that bastard!"

"He knew you wouldn't have let him go without you. He also knew that if he took you with him, then the Great Tree and TokBellu would have perished."

Zembor sits down at the table and puts his hands over his face.

"After all these years, I finally understand why he left…. Yet, I am still lost and broken about it."

Queen Zuna walks over to him and places her hand on his shoulder.

"We can talk more once you go and get some rest. I still haven't seen you sleep since you've returned."

"I slept for a thousand years in that statue. I don't need more sleep!"

He turns to the Queen and notices her looking at him with irritation on her face.

"Yes, my Queen. I will go and get some rest."

He starts to walk out of the throne room toward her chambers.

"Thank you."

Queen Zuna turns back to her siblings, sitting at the table.

"It is hard to wrap my head around all of this. I don't know what to think. Please, I need the three of you to help me understand. Is he crazy?"

Before any of her siblings can speak, Qualt enters the throne room.

"Zembor Wrathfin is not crazy. Everything he says is the truth. I was in the Unknown for many years before Siritano arrived. The things I saw those monsters do to the other aliens was……"

Siritano stands up and limps over to Qualt.

"I still can't thank you enough for what you did. You saved my life, thank you."

Qualt laughs and punches him lightly on the arm.

"You saved mine too. If it weren't for you, Ilikso, and Oryuna, I would be lost like those Dimorians. You and Ilikso found me and got me out of that experiment."

Qualt's yellow, glowing eyes get brighter.

"The experiment! There was that orange gaseous cloud!"

Ilikso jumps up.

"That's right! It spoke to you before going inside of your hood. What did you whisper to it?"

"All I said was that I would follow its lead. When the cloud approached me, it flashed orange and spoke to me, saying to remain calm and wait for the right moment."

"It had to be one of the Broncholites. Maybe it was RoyalTree!"

Qualt helps Siritano back to his seat and sits down next to him.

"It is quite possible… now that I think about it. I had to have been on R'Ang for more than a couple of years. I remember arriving with the red monsters, but at that time, that storm you were speaking of didn't exist. There was green grass and water flowing around the mountains. When I was put into my cell, there were many other aliens—but they eventually disappeared. Those floating orange clouds filled up most of the cells. As time went on, they were replaced with different aliens. I didn't think anything of it when I saw the same floating clouds later, but instead of orange, they were that crimson color. We watched the monsters escort them out of the Metal Mansion; I never saw them again. That one that helped you guys save me was the first one I had seen in a long time."

Queen Zuna looks at all of them before sitting down on her throne.

"Sounds like Zembor isn't crazy…. Regardless, we have a lot more to do to get ourselves ready in case another one of those portals opens. Qualt, how were you captured by those monsters? We haven't had any portals open outside of the Great Tree. Do you think one can appear here in the palace or anywhere else on TokBellu?"

"I was captured by those monsters when they landed on our planet. I had just set up a new colony with a group of my people. We greeted the creatures with the hope of them being friendly, but they killed some of us and took the rest hostage. If we didn't go with them, they would have killed us all. I and ten other Remori boarded their ship and flew off into the stars. After months of flying, we arrived at the bright orange planet. I didn't see any of the portals open until a couple of years later when I was in a cell. A monster, much bigger than the ones we knew, came out of it. It stuck around for a couple of days before leaving through another portal. It never came back, but the monsters you saw started using portals too. I'm guessing that was the reason for the big monster's visit. He was teaching them how to use portal technology. Thinking of all the alien creatures they're capturing and bringing back to the Metal Mansion, I would guess that they're close to being able to open a portal just about anywhere they want."

Queen Zuna puts her head down before she grabs the trident off her back and places it in front of her. As she looks around, the trident starts to flash orange. The others stand up and look to her.

"My Queen, what is wrong with your trident?"

Zembor reappears, standing just outside of the doors.

"My trident is trying to speak, which means RoyalTree is alive!"

He runs over to the Queen and kneels before her.

"My Queen, may I see the trident?"

She looks at him and notices an orange shimmer in his eyes.

"Show me."

She hands the trident over to him. As he latches onto it, the trident's glow brightens. Light shoots out from it, enveloping everything in the room. Queen Zuna and Zembor stand in the throne room, suspended in time. Qualt, Ilikso, Siritano, and Oryuna are frozen next to the table. Zuna turns to Zembor and sees a massive orange cloud floating behind him.

"RoyalTree?"

Zembor turns around and backs up toward Zuna.

"He was never that big…. R.T, is that you?"

The cloud moves closer to them and beings to flash. Zembor holds the trident out in front of him, the tip of the trident touching the cloud. It slowly changes to a deep red color. Bolts of light start to shoot out of it, as it grows bigger. Gusts of wind develop out of thin air and push the two of them around. Strikes of lightning start to shoot out, as a thunderous roar comes from the cloud. Zembor puts the trident onto the ground and walks closer to it. Zuna reaches for him.

"Zembor! What are you doing!?"

"It's okay! R.T, it's me, Zembor Wrathfin. I haven't forgotten about you, and I know you haven't forgotten about me! Please! We're here to help you! I want to know where my friend is!!!"

The cloud calms and starts to shrink back to average size; its color changes back to orange. The cloud continues to move towards them hesitantly. Zembor looks over to Zuna.

"It's okay, let him come to us. He wants to show us something."

Zuna nervously stands next to Zembor as the orange cloud wraps itself around them. The two stand inside the mist as it expands, showing them TokBellu from space. It zooms in and moves time forward to when the Ventrians blew up the Tralupian's city.

"This is fascinating. Have you ever seen this before?"

Zembor looks at Zuna with amazement in his eyes.

"I have not. I didn't know RoyalTree could do something like this."

A voice appears around them.

"I have left this message behind for Zembor Wrathfin. I am sorry for confining you to that statue, but I knew you wouldn't let me leave you behind to go and help my people. I promise I will only be gone for a year; then, I'll be right back here with you on TokBellu. Take care of the Great Tree while I'm gone. I will see you soon, my friend.

Now that the message has been heard, I am no longer needed."

The cloud starts to shrink back down. Before it completely vanishes, Zembor yells to it.

"This was recorded when I was put in the statue?"

"Yes."

The cloud completely vanishes, as Zembor falls to his knees.

"No, this can't be...."

Qualt, Ilikso, Siritano, and Oryuna are released from suspended time to see Queen Zuna standing over Zembor. Ilikso slowly walks over to them.

"What is it? What has happened?"

Queen Zuna picks the trident back up off the ground; the light stops flashing.

"RoyalTree, it was him.... he left a message for Zembor when he put him in that statue. He told him he was going back to his homeworld, and he would be back in a year.... It's been over a thousand years, and he still hasn't returned."

"The orange light on the trident, it's gone?"

"RoyalTree was the orange light. It continued to flicker to let us know there was a message that had not been heard. I don't know if we will ever see it light up again."

Zembor stands up and turns to them, with tears running down his face.

"He is still alive; I can feel him. He must've forgotten about the part of him that was still inside of me. He is in trouble and in a lot of pain.... That crimson color he started changing into..."

Qualt interrupts him.

"Dark red cloud? Those monsters must've done something to the Broncholites to take away their natural orange color."

Siritano limps to them.

"That's what they were trying to do with you and that Broncholite back on R'Ang!"

Oryuna finally jumps in.

"We need to figure out a way to get back there. This is bigger than us. Whatever those monsters are, they're causing turmoil to other sentient species! If we do nothing, then we are just as bad as them!"

Queen Zuna sits back down on her throne.

"I agree, Oryuna, but there is no way for us to get back without a portal. Even if we fly our ships back to R'Ang, we have no way to get through that storm. Hetra, Zeph, and Zaren discovered R'Ang long ago. A storm was always around it until one day, Zeph noticed from the telescope that the storm had stopped. They took a team to examine the planet, and they were never heard from again. Tez eventually gave up hope when he found pieces from their ship floating close to TokBellu. We need to watch that storm to see when it stops again. If it ever does, that'll be our chance."

Ilikso looks around before looking back to the Queen.

"What about going back inside of RoyalTree? There has to be more answers there, plus all the Remnants could help us. They knew about the Unknown before we did."

Queen Zuna stands up from the throne. She can see everyone is tired and worried about RoyalTree.

"That is a good idea, brother, but first everyone needs to get some rest. We can't do anything to help RoyalTree if we kill ourselves. Clean yourselves up and meet me back here in an hour. I will have the cooks prepare us some dinner."

They all nod their heads and leave Queen Zuna and Zembor alone in the throne room. Zembor sits wide-eyed, staring out at RoyalTree. Zuna sits down next to him.

"We're going to figure out where he is. We're going to help him."

Zembor turns to her and tries to hold his tears back. He falls into her lap, crying. The light from their moons shines down onto them, as they stare out at RoyalTree and the ocean.

# Chapter 17:
# Johthuns-A New Life

Thousands of Dimorians follow behind their leader in the Johthun colony ship. Calaido sits in awe as they approach Conril.

"Dimastus is always dark. We maybe get four hours of light a day if there are no clouds! Move quicker; I want to see the land!"

Captain Plazerin looks to Ashar before speeding up the colony ship. Ashar gets up and tries to leave the room, but Calaido stops him.

"Where are you going?"

"I'm going to let everyone know of our arrival."

"Sit back down. I'll announce it over the intercom."

Ashar does as he's told, as Calaido grabs the intercom from the Captain's chair.

"We're arriving at Conril in fifteen minutes. Prepare yourselves!"

He shuts off the intercom and throws it back over to Captain Plazerin, piloting the ship. Ashar stands up and looks at Calaido.

"There are a bunch of innocent Johthuns down there doing nothing but living their lives. You are to leave all of them alone while we are visiting Conril."

"Visiting? You mean I can't stay here?"

"What?"

Calaido starts to laugh and stands up, towering over Ashar.

"If I decide I like it, I'm going to stay here.... with my people. If you and the Johthuns don't like that, well, then this is going to be fun."

He walks past Ashar hitting him with his shoulder and knocking him to the ground. Ashar gets up, ready to strike, but Captain Plazerin holds him back.

"You're going to get yourself killed. Now isn't the time. His army is just as big as ours, and I'm pretty sure there's more lurking in the shadows."

Ashar takes a deep breath to control his anger.

"I need to let Tanglor and the others know."

Captain Plazerin gets back to the controls.

"I think they already know we're here."

Ashar turns and looks out the window to see hundreds of Johthun ships ready to escort them to the planet. Ucarus and Freden fly across from them. Ucarus points to the comm.

"We're going to fly you and your new friends down to the surface. That work for you, guys?"

Calaido comes barreling back into the room and grabs the comm from Ashar.

"That works for us, but let's make it fast! I need to get out of this ship and see the planet!"

Ucarus looks around.

"You got it."

The Elite ships fly them down to the surface of Conril. Dimorian and Johthun ships land on the planet's surface along with the Colony. Ashar, Captain Plazerin, and Calaido exit the Colony ship, followed by hundreds of Dimorians and Johthuns. They're welcomed by Neliah, who is acting as the representative for the Elders and Elites. She steps forward to greet them.

"You must be Calaido."

Neliah bows to him to show respect.

"My name is Neliah. I welcome you to our planet, Conril. We will have a dinner tonight for both Johthun and Dimorians to share. In the meantime, follow me to where you and your people can stay."

Calaido decides to play along and bows back to her.

"Thank you, Neliah. My people and I are grateful for your hospitality."

They follow along behind her, walking through the Johthun city. Calaido and the Dimorians look on in amazement, as they pass the tall buildings and stores lining the street. Some of them begin to run through the city, taking whatever they want. Neliah notices, just as Calaido steps forward.

"Whoever decides they want to take what's not ours will have to deal with me!"

The Dimorians slowly drop whatever they took and continue following Neliah. She turns to Calaido and smiles at him. They come to a group of run-down houses that the Johthun explorers first used upon their arrival to Conril. Calaido and the Dimorians don't mind the appearance and start to settle in quickly. Neliah finds Calaido before she leaves.

"We will see you all back in the city for dinner when the sun sets. Please let me know if you and your people need anything in the meantime."

She walks back into town to meet up with the others. Ashar, Ucarus, and Freden stand in the center of the city waiting for her.

"Have you guys been waiting for me?"

Ashar grabs her and looks at her.

"Are you okay?"

She laughs and pushes him away.

"Yes, I'm fine. Why? What's going on?"

"Sorry, Calaido is dangerous. The way he's acting, he's up to something."

A weird feeling goes through everyone before Ucarus says something.

"We need to have some sort of backup plan ready in case Ashar's right."

Freden paces back and forth, kicking the dirt. He stops and turns to the group.

"Is the stealth glider back up to full charge?"

"Yeah, why?"

"We should use that as our backup plan. Someone can leave in that if everything goes to shit."

They all look around at each other. Neliah breaks the silence.

"That's not a bad idea, but I can't leave because I'm the representative here."

Ashar interrupts her.

"I'm staying back, too. I was the first Elite to deal with Calaido; I'm going to be the last."

Ucarus looks to Freden.

"Looks like you and I get to go to the glider. We'll be ready if anything happens."

Freden and Ucarus make their way towards the stealth glider, leaving Neliah and Ashar to prepare for a dinner with thousands of Johthuns and Dimorians. They get together several Elites to hunt for some supsue. Ashar, Neliah, and the Elites grab their blades and spears before entering the forest.

After a couple of hours of hunting, they leave the forest with over a hundred supsue to eat. They return to the city to slice off the skin and gather the meat off the bones. Ashar starts a giant bonfire, lighting up the city, as Johthuns and Dimorians begin to arrive and huddle around the warm fire. Neliah mixes a giant bowl of Luhdva, a Johthun specialty. It's clear the Dimorians are enjoying the food and drink. They mingle with the native Johthuns and share conversations about their history and families. Neliah and Ashar watch as the two different species celebrate meeting each other. As the night goes on, they find themselves conversing alone, Neliah takes a liking to Ashar. He leans in to make a move, but once again gets interrupted by Calaido.

"There you two are. I've been looking for whoever is in charge here."

Neliah scoots away from Ashar and stands up.

"That would be me, Neliah."

"Right, Neliah. Thank you for the food and drink!"

He raises his mug of Luhdva high in the air.

"To our newly found friendship with the Johthuns."

All the Dimorians raise their mugs high and cheer with their leader. Calaido stumbles away from them and sits down next to the fire with the Dimorians. Neliah sits back down next to Ashar.

"I'm cold, but I don't want to go over to the fire with Calaido there... He creeps me out."

Boldly, Ashar puts his arm around her and pulls her close to him.

"Here, this should help warm you up."

She looks up at him and smiles before melting into his chest. They continue to watch their people drink with the Dimorians. As the fire slowly starts to burn out, so does the celebrating—beds are welcomed by drunk bodies. Ashar and Neliah are the last two left awake, so they put the fire out. Ashar smiles at her.

"Let me walk you back to your room."

She smiles while nodding to him."

They get to her door, he says goodnight and starts to walk away, but she quickly comes up with an excuse to get him to stay.

"Ashar, wait! Will you stay here tonight? I don't feel comfortable with the Dimorians here, mainly Calaido. I don't trust him; he scares me."

Ashar looks around outside of her room and sees nothing but darkness. He looks back at her.

"Of course I'll stay here with you tonight."

Ashar looks outside one more time as he walks into her room. A chill crawls up his spine as he closes the door behind him. Neliah's room is spotless and sparse. Believing her stay on Conril would be short, she didn't bring much with her. She sits on her bed.

"Come sit down on the bed with me, Ashar."

The chill hasn't gone away; Ashar is overcome by a weird feeling going through his body.

"Ashar, are you okay?"

Neliah gets off the bed and helps him sit down. Sweat starts to drip down his face and body. His temperature suddenly rises, and he pukes on the floor. Neliah jumps back away from him, as he slumps to the ground and passes out. She gets him into the bed and cleans everything up. Worried, she lays next to him, icing his head and making sure he's alright. Neliah fights to stay awake, but sleep claims her.

She wakes up to screams and the sound of shattering glass. She turns and looks out her window to see a flaming bottle of Luhdva fly by. It hits the ground and explodes. She runs to the door to see what's going on. Outside is chaos. Dimorians run around the city, pulling Johthuns out of their homes and taking whatever they want. All resisting Johthuns are being taken prisoner by Calaido himself. Neliah stares in horror at Calaido standing behind the flames, watching it all. He's the one responsible for this. She clenches her fists, preparing to charge at him. Ashar's hand grabs her shoulder. She turns and sees him fall to the ground.

"Ashar!"

Neliah helps him back onto the bed. He uses the little breath he has to talk to her.

"You can't stop him...just help our people stay alive. I'll be fine, but I can't lose you too."

Tears start to fill her eyes; she wipes them away and walks out the door, leaving Ashar to rest. She immediately yells out to all the Johthuns.

"Do what he says, and it will all be okay! Leave your houses, shops, and valuables for the Dimorians. Come stand by me, and I will protect you."

Johthuns begin walking out of the smoke and fire to stand by Neliah. Calaido and the Dimorians continue their pillaging and scavenge Conril, leaving the Johthuns to watch helplessly. Off in the distance, Freden and Ucarus hide away from the destruction. Ucarus wants to run and help, but Freden jumps on top of him and holds him down.

"We have to get to the stealth glider! That was the mission, and we have to stick with it!"

"No!! Let me go! We need to help them!"

"Ucarus! If we don't go, then a lot more of our people are going to die."

Ucarus stops struggling, Freden gets off to help him up. They look at the chaos one more time before they take off for the stealth glider. A group of five Dimorians notices them running for the docking bay and begins to chase after them. Freden stops and shuts the door behind him. He uses one of his knives to break the control panel.

"That'll hold them off for a couple of minutes. Let's go!"

They run for the stealth glider as the Dimorians break through the door. Ucarus stops and lets Freden on first. He shuts the door.

"Go, get out of here, and get back to Tanglor and Leazara."

He turns around and pulls out his blades, ready to fight the Dimorians. Two of them charge at him. He blocks one of their attacks, while the other hits him in the leg. He falls to the ground, but swings back, hitting the Dimorian in the stomach. The other one strikes again, but he dodges it and stabs one of his blades through his chest. The wound on his leg makes it hard to get up with the dead weight of the Dimorian still on his sword. The remaining three charge at him, he closes his eyes, accepting his fate.

"Clink, Clink, Swoosh, Urg, Huh, Clink, Clink, Swoosh, Swoosh, Swoosh!"

Ucarus opens his eyes to find Freden standing over three dead Dimorians. He reaches his hand out to him.

"I'm not leaving you here to die. Come on; we're both getting out of here."

He helps Ucarus up and onto the stealth glider. Before they get onto the ship, Ucarus turns back and grabs some of the crystallized scales off the dead Dimorians. He runs into the glider just as the door closes behind him. Ashar activates the cloaking. Another group of Dimorians comes running through the tunnels to see their dead comrades, but Freden and Ucarus have already taken off for Joht.

Neliah and the other Johthuns are huddled into a group, as the Dimorians finish destroying the city. Finally, Calaido stops his soldiers and orders them to surround the Johthuns.

"Here's what's going to happen. Come over here!"

He points to Neliah with his signature scythe. He presses the switch on it; green energy starts to flow around it.

"You're going to help me with your friends here."

He shoves her in front of him. They start walking toward the tied-up prisoners that tried to stand up to the Dimorians.

"You see them. You're going to help me punish them for not obeying."

"No, I won't help you!"

He takes his scythe and puts it right next to her face.

"You'll do as I say, or I'll show your people what my scythe can do!"

Neliah walks over to the first Johthun tied up and slowly takes her over to the elevated stage in front of everyone.

"Good. Now put her hands behind her back and put her head through that little loop up there."

All the Johthuns watch as Neliah grabs the tied up Johthun. She puts her hands behind her back and slowly lifts her to the rope hanging down. The imprisoned Johthun looks down at Neliah.

"It's okay; this isn't your fault."

Neliah starts to cry as she continues to walk the remaining prisoners to the other ropes waiting for them. Whispers fill the crowd as they watch Neliah put Johthuns on stage to die. After all the prisoners are placed in the hanging loops, Neliah falls to the ground. Calaido walks up and immediately gets everyone's attention.

"That was way more of a show than I thought it was going to be. It makes me worried about how the finale is going to go. From now on, you all answer to me. You're going to share your tech with us, and eventually, we're going to invade Joht and get that computer console of yours. Until then, I want to enjoy this beautiful world we destroyed!"

Calaido grabs the rope hanging in front of him, taking control of the fates of the Johthuns behind him. He jumps off the stage, causing the rope to pull the floor out from underneath the prisoners. They all drop, and their bodies fall under the stage while their heads stay above for everyone to see. Their lives slowly drain away as the ropes suffocate them—the crowd watches in fear. Neliah beings to lose control, her cries turn into screams that fill the crowd with panic. The remaining Johthuns start to run, pushing and shoving against each other. A couple of them get knocked to the ground and trampled on, while others get forced into Dimorians, who instantly shoot them down with their blasters. Calaido jumps back onto the stage and starts to yell.

"Everyone calms down, or we will kill all of you!"

The crowd of Johthuns slowly stops and looks toward the Dimorian leader.

"You all allowed to go home now, but I expect you back here tomorrow with a better attitude. Together we will rebuild the city that you let us destroy. Otherwise, you can join your friends up here."

The lifeless Johthuns are pulled back above the stage behind Calaido. Everyone can see their bodies dangle behind him, as he stands proud.

"Now go before I change my mind! See everyone tomorrow and be ready to work!"

He walks over to Neliah and tosses her over his shoulder. She stares petrified at the five Johthun bodies as he walks her back to the house. He kicks the door open to find Ashar still passed out on the bed. Calaido puts Neliah on the bed next to him and grabs her some water. She reaches for the glass, but he throws it in her face. She snaps out of her trance and lays down with her head on Ashar, staring at Calaido. He covers her up with a blanket.

"You get some rest and make sure he survives that poison I gave him."

He walks out of the house and shuts the door behind him. The room goes dark, except for the reflection from Neliah's eyes. They're wide open, staring at the door, the only sliver of light illuminating her and Ashar on the bed.

As night turns to day, Ashar awakes. The poison has passed through his system, but Neliah is finally asleep. He brings her a glass of water with some breakfast. The smell wakes her up; she grabs the food and starts to eat. She chugs the water but stops abruptly when she remembers what happened last night. Overwhelming guilt fills up inside her, Ashar wraps his arms around her and pulls her in close.

"What happened last night?"

She pulls herself together to tell him.

"I killed them. He made me do it, and they all watched me! My own people think I'm a murderer now because of what he made me do!"

"What did he make you do? Neliah, it's alright."

"He made me help him hang five of our people because they disagreed with him. If I didn't do it, he was going to kill me too. He threatened me, and they all just sat there and watched! I could have done something different!"

Ashar pulls her closer and puts her head against his chest.

"It's alright, you're not a murderer and anyone who thinks so—especially after seeing that—is lost. Everything is going to be okay. Lay down and get some rest. I'm going to go out there and find Calaido."

"Thank you, Ashar."

She hops off the bed and kisses Ashar. He stands and stares at her, a smile on his face, before turning to walk out of the house. She climbs back into the bed and passes out as Ashar shuts the door. He looks around the city to find it destroyed. He sees Johthuns being escorted by Dimorians towards the stage where the five dead Johthuns still hang. Calaido stands in front of them as everyone gathers around. Ashar runs and hides behind a building to avoid being caught. He watches as Calaido starts to speak.

"Today, we are going to get started with the rebuild. My squad leaders are going to split up with different groups of Johthuns. Whatever you need, tell them, and maybe they'll get it for you. Get started!"

Ashar watches as the Dimorians take the Johthuns and start rebuilding the city. Some of them walk toward him. He begins to panic, stuck in a corner with nowhere to go. At the last second, he sees an opening in the building in front of him that he can reach. He jumps up and crawls inside before they see him. The interior of the structure is starting to crumble; he has to be careful if he doesn't want to be buried alive. As he is crawling around, he can hear a Dimorian outside yelling to the Johthuns.

"This building right here. Just take the whole thing down, we'll rebuild from the ground up."

They start to hit the walls, and the building shakes, with Ashar still inside. He runs for an exit, but part of the roof falls in front of him, sealing it shut. He turns and heads for a window, right before he gets there, the floor falls out from underneath him. He swiftly jumps and grabs the ledge, pulling himself up. The building starts to lean to the side, so he runs on the wall as it becomes the floor. He jumps, straightening his body, to fly through the window as the building collapses. Ashar shoots out from the crumbling building onto the streets where some Dimorian guards happened to be standing. With nowhere to run, he puts his hands up; they escort him to Calaido.

"Ashar! Glad to see my poison didn't kill you. What are you doing being dragged up here by my guards?"

Before he can speak, one of the Dimorians talks for him.

"We caught him hiding in a destroyed building."

Calaido walks over to the Dimorian and slaps him in the face, cutting him with his sharp nails.

"I didn't ask you!"

He walks over to Ashar.

"Is this true? Were you sneaking around?"

"Honestly, I was. I woke up in shock from the poison and had no idea what was going on. It looks like you took over Conril and killed some of my people!"

"Only the ones that didn't cooperate! You should thank Neliah; she did a great job last night. Leave him here with me."

Calaido gets rid of the Dimorian guards and has Ashar sit next to him on the hill he calls a throne.

"You see, Ashar, I like you. I don't want to have to kill you or Neliah if I don't have to. Your people are cooperating now, and I need you to do the same thing if you want them all to continue living. You're going to help me rebuild things here, the way I see fit, and when we get to Joht, you're going to help me get to that ancient computer console. If you're going to try to argue with me, I will kill you now."

He pulls out his scythe; the green energy starts to flow around it.

Ashar looks at him and shakes his head.

"If we have an understanding, then you and Neliah get to live in that house. If I catch either of you helping your people with my chores, then I will kill them. Oh, and don't try to use your comms to reach your Colonels. I already took care of that. Now, get out of my sight."

Ashar doesn't risk saying a word and walks back to the house. He opens the door to find Neliah is waiting for him. He falls to the ground, defeated. She runs over to him and grabs him.

"What happened?"

"We're his slaves, so we have to do whatever he says. If we help our people, they die. We have to watch them suffer while we get to live here! He forbids us from using our comms to get in touch with the rest of our people."

She sits next to him on the floor, holding him close. They both fill up with emotions as they realize their new reality.

Calaido gets on the comms.

"I want to speak with the leader of the Johthuns!"

Seconds go by before Tanglor responds.

"This is Tanglor Raff. What is it you want, Calaido?"

"Ahh, so you know who I am? I like not having to introduce myself, haha. I wanted to let you know that Conril is mine! The Dimorians have taken over. We are pleasant to your people unless they stop cooperating. If you send reinforcements or try to stop us, I will kill them all, starting with Ashar and Neliah!"

Before Tanglor can respond, Calaido shuts the comms off. Tanglor turns to Elisin and Leazara.

"What do we do?"

# Chapter 18:
# Tralupians- Home

Siritano's wounds cause him pain as he dreams about getting captured that day. The monster opens the door to the Metal Mansion, then turns around to drive its sharp fingers into him. His eyes shoot open as he sits up in discomfort. Looking around the room, he notices Qualt isn't in the guest bed he set up for him. Siritano stumbles out of bed and limps into the throne room to find Queen Zuna sitting on the throne, alone. She looks at him as he hobbles in.

"Brother, what are you doing awake?"

He glances around the room.

"I was looking for Qualt; he wasn't in my room when I woke up. Why are you awake?"

Zuna stands up and walks over to him.

"Anytime I close my eyes, I see…. darkness and evil. I suppose it's just bad dreams, but they always seem so real!"

Tears start to form in her eyes as she puts her hand on Siritano's shoulder.

"I will be okay, though. I can handle a few nightmares."

Siritano, wanting to comfort her, searches for the right words to say. Before he can figure them out, the Queen speaks again.

"Come, I see Qualt has walked out to RoyalTree."

She takes Siritano by the arm; they walk outside of the palace. The moonlight shines down on Qualt, sitting over the ledge next to RoyalTree. Siritano and Queen Zuna make their way to him and sit down.

"I am sorry. It was not my intention to make you worry."

Qualt doesn't move and continues to stare out over the ocean. Siritano addresses him.

"Are you okay, Qualt?"

His serious face blooms into a smile, as Qualt turns to Siritano and the Queen.

"I just miss my family and friends, and I miss being home on Rembor."

"Your homeworld? How long has it been now?"

Qualt stands up.

"Longer than I can remember. I stopped keeping track after I accepted my fate in the Metal Mansion. I am sure my people have forgotten about me."

Queen Zuna stands up and puts her arm around him.

"I doubt that, Qualt. They may have stopped looking for you, but that doesn't mean you've been forgotten."

Qualt puts his arm around her and then his other one around Siritano.

Siritano smiles at him.

"Let's see, if you were captured and taken to R'Ang before the storm started... it had to have been back before 1990. Hetra discovered the planet on a scouting mission, and that storm was circling it, so it had to have been before that."

Qualt jumps into the air in astonishment.

"That can't be... You said the other day that we are in the year 2683. There's no possible way that I was a prisoner there for 693 years!"

Queen Zuna and Siritano watch as he paces back and forth in front of them.

"I mean, there were many times that I woke up and felt like my body hadn't moved for years.... No, that can't be right!"

He finally calms himself down, stops, and turns to the two of them.

"Thank you for everything you have done for me, but I have overstayed my welcome. I need to try to get back home to my people."

Queen Zuna looks to Siritano; he nods his head.

"As Queen of TokBellu, I will do everything I can to help you get back home. What can we do?"

Qualt bows to the Queen.

"All I would need is a ship that would get me back to Rembor. If it is okay with you, I would like Siritano to come with me."

Siritano, surprised by Qualt, stands up straight and salutes his sister.

"If it is alright with you, my Queen, then I would like to go with him. I owe him this much for saving me back on R'Ang."

Queen Zuna smiles at her brother and signals for him to stop saluting her.

"If that is what you want to do, the choice is yours, brother."

He lowers his arm and smiles back.

"Thank you. I will keep records of everything that happens on my journey. I can't wait to see your homeworld, Qualt!"

Qualt bows to the Queen again, before helping Siritano limp back into the palace. She gazes out at the ocean but gets distracted by the Great Tree beginning to glow next to her. She looks at it and thinks to herself.

"The light is back!"

She pulls her trident off her back and sticks it out in front of her towards the Great Tree..., but nothing happens. The trident doesn't flash or glow orange. She takes her hand and punches the tree in frustration, causing the bright spot to get bigger. She hits it again, nothing happens. She continues to watch as the bright spot starts to shrink. Out of anger, she pulls the trident back and thrusts it into the tree. It sinks into the bright spot, causing a crack to shoot up the side of it. Zuna watches in horror, as the glowing crack spreads across the trunk. Parts of the Great Tree's bark starts to fall off next to her, while she stands watching with tears in her eyes.

"What have I done!? I'm so sorry!"

The bark crumbles away faster, revealing more of the orange light. The Great Tree starts to sway back and forth before it begins to plummet toward Queen Zuna. She stands there looking at the Tree as it falls at her. Zuna wipes away her tears and yells.

"Just tell me what you want! I can't take this anymore; I'm losing my mind!!!"

The Great Tree comes crashing down onto her with a tidal wave of orange light following behind it. Queen Zuna finds herself standing inside the Great Tree, surrounded by orange. A dark red cloud appears in front of her, sparks flying off it as it moves closer to her. She backs away as it speaks to her.

"Please don't be afraid, Queen Zuna."

She stops and examines the cloud closer.

"RoyalTree?"

The crimson cloud forms itself into one of the monsters.

"No, I am Zalzatine Wrathfin. I am here to give you the answers you seek."

"That's not possible. Zalzatine is one of the Remnants."

"He is indeed, but that isn't Zalzatine. None of the Remnants are what you think they are. And Zembor…. well, that isn't Zembor. Everything he has told you about RoyalTree missing is true, but that is the only truth. Zembor Wrathfin is dead and died in the explosion like you and your people thought. His spirit lived on, but it was taken over by the other Broncholites."

"Other Broncholites? I thought they were good before being captured."

"That was true, but after being captured, they were turned evil by the monsters… Everything you were taught by Serel and Defunis was correct. The Broncholites killed them so that they couldn't expose them further. RoyalTree didn't leave to save his people either. He was captured and taken back to his homeworld of R'Ang. We aren't sure if he is still alive."

"If that thing in the palace isn't Zembor, then who is it? And what does it want? What are the Remnants in the Great Tree, and why do you look like one of the monsters?"

"I can only assume that Zembor is one of the Broncholites that took over his spirit. The Broncholites can use their gaseous bodies to surround life and then control it. They kept his body safe by encasing it inside that statue and then used his spirit to control it. I am not sure what it is they want, and I don't know if Zembor's spirit can return after being used like that. It has taken us a long time to figure out who and what we truly are after being sacrificed to the Great Tree. You wake up confused and, in another world, so it's easier to believe what you're told. My spirit was the first one here, besides Zembor's, so I had to go off what the voices told me, what the orange clouds told me. What Zembor told me."

"What was it they told you?"

"They told me the same thing they told everyone that arrived. They told us that we were recruited to fight the evil that was within RoyalTree. That we were chosen by the Great Zembor Wrathfin to keep his legacy alive, which I eventually discovered was a lie. We were used to bring life to the Great Tree and keep it alive. The Broncholites started to lose control of our spirits, as we fought their will and went against them. They disguised us as these monsters and made the Remnants look like our ancestors that have passed away or been sacrificed to the Great Tree. They created that statue of Zembor and used his spirit to lead the Remnants, pretending that they were good, to confuse you and keep control of TokBellu."

Queen Zuna stares at Zalzatine in confusion.

"The truth is so scattered. How am I supposed to believe any of this?"

Zalzatine walks closer to her and puts his sharp claws on her shoulders. He stares at her as his face slowly changes into a Tralupian.

"That is why the Broncholites did what they did…. It isn't their fault either, the Broncholites are no longer themselves."

His face fades back to the monster's, he backs away from her, holding his arms out.

"You have to help us. Our spirits are trapped within the Great Tree. We can't leave until this has all been stopped and finally put to an end."

He starts to transform back into the dark red cloud. Zuna yells to him.

"Wait, if I destroy the Great Tree, then it will destroy TokBellu!?"

The cloud flashes and then disappears, leaving the orange light shining around her again. It fades away, she stands back in front of the tree, her trident poking it. The Great Tree stands unbroken in front of her. She puts the trident on her back again and turns around to find Zembor staring at her. His eyes flash orange.

"Did you have another vision from the Great Tree?"

Queen Zuna remembers what the monster just told her; she steps away from him.

"No…. I was trying to listen to it. I thought I heard a voice coming from the trunk."

Zembor looks at her with suspicion.

"Oh, okay then. Are you sure? You seem a little out of it?"

"Yes, everything is excellent."

She gives him a strange look before walking past him into the palace. The orange in his eyes flashes again as he looks over to the Great Tree smiling.

---------------------------------------------------

Qualt stands in the doorway, watching Siritano get ready.

"Do you really need that much stuff?"

Siritano turns around in excitement.

"I just want to be sure I'm prepared! I've never been to another planet!"

Qualt smiles under his hood.

"What about R'Ang? That was a nice trip, huh?"

"Very funny, Qualt. You know what I mean."

"I know. Okay, Siritano, I think you've packed enough. You won't even need all of that on Rembor, you'll see. We don't have material items like you do here."

"Okay, okay. If you say so, let's load our supplies onto the ship."

Qualt starts walking out of the room as Siritano limps behind him, a bag full of his belongings in hand.

"Is it just the two of us going?"

"Yes, my people will already be nervous with you accompanying me. My planet is sacred; no other sentient life has ever walked on the surface, other than the Remori—and now those monsters that captured us. They will be nervous to see a ship, especially since we didn't have anything close to a ship 693 years ago."

"Are you sure they won't mind me landing on your planet with you then?"

Qualt turns around to him.

"It will be okay, as long as you are with me. And once I tell them about how you and your siblings saved me—they'll welcome you with open arms."

Siritano limps ahead to catch up to Qualt. He puts his arm around Siritano and helps him walk onto the Tralupian ship. It's one of their smaller vessels with blasters on the front, so it flies at faster speeds. It's a sleek silver color with two little wings attached to the side and a big window to see out of the front. Before they take off, they get stopped by Zembor, Ilikso, Oryuna, and Queen Zuna. The four of them squeeze onto the small ship as Zuna walks to the front and puts her arms on their shoulders.

"The two of you travel safely. Siritano, I expect you to come back to us!"

He smiles at her and nods his head. Qualt stands up and offers the Queen a hug.

"Your majesty, I can't thank you enough for what you have done for me."

She smiles and squeezes him back.

"You are always welcome back here on TokBellu. Thank you for saving my brother."

Qualt also embraces both Oryuna and Ilikso.

"If it weren't for the two of you, Siritano and I would both be dead on R'Ang. There is a place in my heart for both of you. Thank you."

They hug him back before exiting the ship behind the Queen. Zembor is left standing there, staring at the two. Siritano walks up and puts his hand out in front of Zembor.

"Take care of my brothers and sisters while I'm gone. Please, take extra care of the Queen."

He reaches out and takes Siritano's hand, grasping it tightly and looking into his eyes. He smiles at him, his eyes glow orange.

"I will make sure to take care of all of them for you, especially the Queen."

Siritano tries to pull his hand back, but Zembor holds it tight—not letting go. A soft laugh comes from within him as he continues to stare. Qualt sticks his hands out; his eyes radiate yellow as his palms face Zembor.

"It is time for us to go now."

Zembor releases Siritano's hand and slowly walks off the ship, staring at the two with his orange eyes. Siritano closes the doors to the vessel; Zembor's eyes go back to normal. Qualt looks to him as he sits back down.

"There is something familiar about Zembor, his eyes, and that laugh."

Siritano sits down next to Qualt.

"I know what you mean. He gave me a peculiar feeling just now. His glowing eyes were pretty strange too."

Qualt starts to pilot the ship off the ground.

"It is a feeling I got from him before, but I didn't want to say anything since he is family."

"He is our Great-Great-Grandfather who was supposed to be dead for over a thousand years…. It's going to take a lot more than him just coming back to life to be part of the family."

"Hopefully, the Queen feels the same way."

Qualt and Siritano look out the front window of the ship as they fly toward TokBellu's atmosphere. Once they blast through into space, Qualt steers in the direction of his homeworld. Siritano looks around in amazement.

"I have never seen anything like this, and honestly, I never thought I would. These ships are only for our scouts, so no one else is allowed to use them. I am truly honored to be flying with you."

Qualt looks over to him with his yellow eyes glowing through his hood.

"I am honored, as well. I know it is bad to say, but I am glad you got captured that day. If you hadn't, I would not be alive. I still don't understand how I could have been there for 693 years…"

"They must have done something to those cells we were in, released an undetectable gas…. gas! The Broncholites! RoyalTree is one of them, and his powers are indescribable."

Qualt stares out the window as he pilots the small ship past undiscovered planets.

"You said you were going to record your travels, right? Get the coordinates of these planets for your people. And I think you're right about those Broncholites. I remember being stiff every time I woke up, almost like I was stuck in the same place for a very long time. But I never left that cell, so being able to figure out the time, or day became impossible after long."

Siritano grabs a star chart and attempts to map out everything he's seeing.

"I can't even imagine... I'm sorry you had to be there for that long, Qualt. What did you eat or drink? How old are you? Sorry, I'll stop asking so many questions."

"No, it's okay. I haven't had conversations like this for quite a while. I don't remember eating or drinking, so they must've fed me while I was asleep. I do remember frequently waking up feeling like I just had a big meal, though. I was 285 when I was captured. I still feel like it, too."

"285 is pretty old for my people. How long of a lifespan does your race have?"

"I was one of the first of my people. No one died while I was around, so I honestly don't know. I feel healthy and young if that helps at all. How old are you, Siritano?"

"I am eighty years old, three years younger than the Queen. Our people can live up to five hundred years now because Zirk, our grandfather, developed a serum. It was only three hundred before that."

"A serum?"

"A special liquid that he had his scientists develop. They injected it into our people so that we could live longer. Because the serum was in our parents, the younger generation has those genes already developed within us."

"That is amazing that your scientists can do that. We don't have anything like that. The Remori live off the nature around us, as well as the Berembian."

"What's Berembian?"

Qualt stands up.

"Can you pilot the ship for a bit?"

"Of course."

Siritano sits in the pilot's seat while Qualt walks around the small cabin behind him.

"Berembian is a special mineral that Rembor makes for us. My people treat it as if it's a God. We worship it, and it gives us these powers."

"Do all of your people have powers?"

Qualt sits down next to him and nods his head.

"Yes. All the Remori are different, though. Our strength comes from within as well as the elements surrounding us."

"Back on R'Ang, I saw you create hands out of the dirt and shoot lightning at those monsters. That was awesome!"

Qualt laughs.

"That was nothing. There were barely any elements to use in that Metal Mansion. Once we get to Rembor, I will show you what I can really do!"

Siritano continues to fly the ship, as he calms down from his excitement.

"So, where are we going? How do I get to Rembor from here?"

Qualt looks out the window.

"I have never been on a ship, other than when I was captured by those monsters, and the prison cells didn't have any windows to look out of... I'm not sure how to get there from here either.... I don't recall what my planet looks like from space."

"What are we going to do? We don't have enough fuel just to fly around looking."

"I *have* to get home, Siritano. My people will never leave Rembor to try to find me. If we need to, we can stop at one of these planets to see if we can find fuel or directions."

Siritano nods, while Qualt chuckles underneath his hood. Siritano's worried look changes to a happy one as he starts to laugh with him.

"I'm with you. We're getting you back home!"

They continue to laugh as they soar through the stars.

-----------------------------------------------------

Queen Zuna sits on her throne, speaking to Oryuna and Ilikso.

"We need to keep it quiet since I'm not sure what to believe."

Ilikso steps forward.

"If what you said is true, then we need to act before he does. What if he's been planning something this whole time?"

Oryuna stands next to her brother.

"I am undecided as well. I can see what Ilikso is saying, and I am worried about him as well, but what if we do something, and we're wrong?"

"I would rather be wrong than dead!"

The Queen stands up.

"All right, that is enough. We will keep quiet about this for now, but stay alert and watch out for each other."

As the Queen sits back down on her throne, Zembor walks in and bows to her.

"My Queen, what were the three of you discussing so fervently?"

"We were just speaking about Siritano and his journey with Qualt."

"Ahh, yes, that is an inspiring journey. I wish the very best for him and his little friend. On a different note, I was hoping to speak to you in private."

She looks to Ilikso and Oryuna and nods her head. They both bow before walking out of the throne room.

"What is it, Zembor?"

"I have thought about it some more; I want to be revealed to the people.... with you by my side."

He walks up to her on the throne and kneels in front of her grabbing her hand.

"You and me, the rulers of TokBellu. I will be with you by your side for everything."

Queen Zuna stands up. Zembor stands with her, not letting go.

"Let go of my hand. I don't want you as my King!"

Zembor's grip on her hand tightens as he pulls her closer with his other arm. She struggles as he stares at her, his eyes changing to a solid orange color. He smiles and opens his mouth; a little orange cloud spews out and floats toward Zuna. She screams for her brother and sister, but the cloud covers her mouth and slowly creeps inside. Zembor lets go of Zuna and steps back. She stands staring at him, and her eyes flash orange.

"I would love for you to be my King. We can introduce you to the people tomorrow. What will we say about you being Zembor?"

Zembor walks behind her and puts his hands on her shoulders. She stands still, the orange light flashes in her eyes again.

"We will tell them that I am someone else. How about Ozem? You can say I am from the poor side of the city; no one will know!"

Queen Zuna stares off at nothing.

"That is a great idea. Tomorrow King Ozem will be introduced."

"Perfect! Oh wait, we need to arrange for a wedding first! I can't be your King if we aren't married."

"I will arrange the wedding for us, Zemb... Ozem."

He leans over and kisses her on the cheek. A tear runs down her face as she continues to stare off blankly.

"Have our wedding set for the end of the week. I will be introduced at the end of our wedding ceremony. It shall be the greatest Tralupian wedding ever!"

His eyes stay orange as he walks away, laughing. He leaves the throne room; Queen Zuna falls to her knees, the orange in her eyes fades away. She sits on the throne room floor with tears dripping off her face.

# Chapter 19:
# <u>Johthuns-The Start of War</u>

A light breeze comes through the window waking Ashar up. His eyes open to find Neliah asleep on his chest. He eases his way out of bed to make breakfast. The aroma of supsue meat ruins the surprise and awakens her.

"Mmmm, nothing like waking up to you *and* supsue."

"Ahh damn, I wanted it to be a surprise. It's just about ready."

Neliah gets out of bed and walks over to Ashar, kissing him. She helps him finish cooking and sets the table. They both sit down to enjoy their meal.

A loud knock sounds at the door.

Ashar gets up to see who's banging on their door. He looks through the hole to see three Dimorian soldiers standing there. They knock again before Ashar opens it up.

"Is there something I can help you with?"

One of the Dimorian soldiers steps forward.

"Calaido calls for you!"

They wait as Ashar looks back to Neliah, she nods her head. The Dimorians escort him to Calaido; he sits on his throne, which is now bigger than he is.

"Ahh, Ashar, it's good to see you out of the house."

Ashar stays quiet.

"Okay fine, I just wanted to let you know that I am bored of Conril. I think it's time we start heading toward Joht. If I remember correctly, one of your people mentioned something about a place called Thoonta."

Ashar doesn't let him say another word.

"No! You need to stay away from Thoonta and Joht. The Elites won't let you or your army land without a fight."

Calaido gets off his throne and walks toward Ashar.

"Don't you think I know that? As I said, I'm bored. Fighting your people sounds like much more fun!"

He walks past Ashar, yelling to his people.

"The time has come! Gather your things and load the ships! We're going to Thoonta!!"

He turns back to Ashar.

"Plus, five years of being on this planet is way too long. Grab Neliah; you two are riding with me on the Colony ship. And find Captain Plazerin. He better not be drunk again!"

Ashar goes back to his house where Neliah sits, all their things packed and ready.

"I had a feeling."

Ashar sits next to her and puts his hand on her leg.

"No matter what, we will get through this together. We need to find Captain Plazerin, though. Any idea where he is?"

"He is probably off drinking again at Varshinora's, that Dimorian club."

"Alright, you stay here while I go and get him. Don't leave until I get back.

He leaves the house and heads for the Varshinora's. As he approaches, he sees a Johthun get thrown out of the building, shortly followed by a Dimorian who lands on top of him. Ashar walks around to the door to find a Dimorian bouncer checking people in and out.

"Lift your arms. Got to do a pat-down."

Ashar lifts his arms as the Dimorian pats him down.

"Alright, you're good to go, man."

Ashar walks into the club. Dimorian and Johthun slaves dance on the stage while free citizens get drunk and watch. He finds Captain Plazerin in the corner, his face down on the table. He walks over and sits down next to him.

"Plazerin, wake up. It's time for us to go. If Calaido finds you drunk again, he's going to kill you."

Plazerin leans back into his seat and burps.

"I've been dead for the past five years."

Ashar grabs a glass of water, splashes it on him, and then slaps him in the face.

"Get your ass up and go clean yourself. Be at my house in ten minutes!"

He gets up and leaves Captain Plazerin to sulk. Ashar walks back to the house. When he opens the door, he discovers Calaido sitting on the bed with Neliah.

"About time!"

He runs over to Neliah and grabs her away. Calaido laughs.

"Hahahaha, take it easy. We've just been waiting for you and Captain Plazerin to get here so we can leave. Where is he?"

"He is on his way right now. He forgot something back at his house."

Captain Plazerin comes walking up behind Ashar.

"Alright, I'm all set!"

Ashar looks at him and scoffs. As long as Calaido doesn't know he's drunk, then he'll be fine. Calaido jumps off the bed.

"Finally! Time to get to Thoonta!"

They grab their things and follow Calaido to the colony ship. Captain Plazerin sits down and pilots them into orbit. All the Dimorians follow behind, taking the prisoners, but leaving behind the remaining Conril civilians.

As soon as Calaido's army makes it to the outskirts of Thoonta, Leazara and Tanglor call him on the comms. He smiles while answering.

"The Elite Colonels, so glad you decided to call. Is this a welcome to Thoonta call?"

Leazara, being the higher-ranking Colonel, speaks to him.

"Welcome to Thoonta. Now turn around and leave!"

"What about all your people I have with me?"

He grabs Ashar and Neliah and puts them in front of the screen.

"What about these two? Don't they mean anything to you?"

"What do you want, Calaido?"

He shoves the two of them roughly aside.

"I want more technology, more knowledge, and power for the Dimorians! I hear you have an ancient computer console; I want it!"

"You will never get your hands on that! We are willing to share tech with you, but that console is ours."

"I'm not interested in your other tech. I'm coming to Thoonta whether you like it or not. The question is, will I see you there?"

She hesitates before responding.

"Yes, you'll see me down there.... if you can make it that is. Ashar, Neliah, if you can hear me, prepare yourselves and remember your training!"

She shuts the comms off and turns to Tanglor and Elisin.

"I'm taking my soldiers to Thoonta. Tanglor, you're going to bring yours as well, but stay in orbit. I need you to leave at once and initiate the attack on the Dimorians. Take out the colony ship. Ashar and Neliah will hopefully be prepared, and you can swoop in and pick them up among the debris. It's risky, but it's all we've got if we want to try and save all our people. It should give my soldiers and me enough time to get to the surface and set up our defenses. Elisin, I need you to stay here. If anything is to happen to Tanglor or me, I need you to run the Elites. I know you have the experience and knowledge."

Tanglor hugs Leazara and walks out of the Great Hall to gather his soldiers. He sits at the top of the docking bay, looking over the ledge. His soldiers fill the entire room. Four hundred Elite Protectors and one thousand Johthun soldiers await his orders. Tanglor stands tall with Ucarus and Freden standing behind him.

"We are to take out all of the Dimorian ships in Thoonta's orbit—including our colony ship. Ashar and Neliah are on board, but, once we destroy it, Freden and Ucarus will fly in on a stealth glider to recover them and any of our other people left alive. Thanks to our scientists and engineers, our gliders can stay cloaked for thirty minutes straight before they need to be recharged. Our armor has been equipped with cloaking as well, but because of our movements, it only lasts for two minutes.

It will automatically reveal where you are if you go over that time frame, so use them both carefully. Our fighters will fly in and be a distraction while our stealth gliders get behind the enemy. We will be victorious!"

Tanglor raises his fists into the air; his soldiers cheer loudly before heading towards their fighter ships and stealth gliders. Tanglor gets into a more advanced ship with his crew. His and Leazara's ships are faster and more reliable than the rest, equipped with weapons and cloaking. Tanglor's ship takes off with his army following close behind.

As they approach Thoonta, they can see the Dimorian army flying toward the surface. The Johthun stealth gliders activate their cloaking and start flying behind them. Tanglor cloaks his vessel and leads his fighter ships straight toward them. Calaido notices the fighter ships coming for them and orders the Dimorians to attack. Lasers zoom by, as Tanglor's Tanglor comes out of cloaking, firing at Calaido and the colony. He flies straight at the window, getting close enough to make eye contact with Calaido, before soaring over at the last second. He sails over the vessel, dropping some of his bombs on top of them, it starts to crumble. A few Dimorians stop fighting the Johthun army and switch their focus to Tanglor. He maneuvers his way through them as they fly at him. He flips around and faces them, launching his missiles straight at them and destroying their ships.

Suddenly, the Johthun stealth gliders reveal themselves and overwhelm the Dimorian army. Freden and Ucarus swoop by in their gliders, firing their blasters and hitting the colony ship. Tanglor watches it explode and fall into pieces, hoping that Ashar and Neliah make it out alive. Freden and Ucarus fly back around, looking for them. The Dimorians follow and fly towards them, but they activate their cloaking, causing the Dimorian ships to fire blindly. The stealth gliders stay cloaked while they barrel roll and flip, dodging their attacks. Ucarus gets close to one of them, his wing clips the Dimorian vessel, causing his cloaking device to fail. He continues to maneuver his way through their shots, while Freden searches through the debris of the colony ship.

Calaido and a group of Dimorians flee the debris on escape pods. Tanglor radios into Leazara.

"We took a good amount of them out, but Calaido and a few surviving Dimorians are still heading toward the surface!"

"Thanks, Tanglor! We're ready for them!"

Freden moves through the wreckage. He finds an escape pod stuck underneath debris and bodies. Inside his glider, he attaches himself to a rope on a pulley system. He turns a knob on his goggles, and it becomes a mask with a filter that transforms the space particles into oxygen, allowing him to breathe in space. Freden opens the door and jumps out toward the escape pod, pushing his way through dead Johthuns and Dimorians. Debris covers the escape pod, so Freden pulls out his blaster and starts to fire at the metal beam holding the pod down. He pulls his blade out, and with two swipes, he breaks it in half. Ucarus flies over in his damaged glider and uses it to push the beam away from Freden. There's an opening on the escape pod that allows Freden to see through the glass. Ashar and Neliah are on the floor, passed out, and running out of air. Freden uses his blade to break the glass. He slides himself into the pod and wakes Ashar up.

"Ashar! Are you alright?"

Ashar coughs and catches his breath.

"I'm okay, but Neliah... we need to get her to a doctor."

Freden rushes over to her. He can hear her barely breathing through her mask. Ashar stands to his feet and helps Freden get Neliah through the opening. Ashar holds Neliah close as he grabs onto Freden. He activates the pulley attached to his rope, and it reels them back to his glider. As they get inside and close the door, Ashar looks over to Freden.

"You need to take her back to Joht to our doctors."

"What are you going to do?"

"Take me over to Tanglor's ship. I'm finishing this fight. I want to be here when Calaido loses."

Freden takes him over to Tanglor's ship and then flies off back to Joht with Neliah passed out behind him. Ashar stands next to Tanglor, waiting for his order.

"Ashar, it's been five years since I've seen you, but there is no time to talk and catch up. Calaido is heading for the surface of Thoonta. We need to prepare ourselves and our soldiers. We need to be ready for Leazara's order to attack."

"I am glad to see you too, brother. I will go and speak with the rest of your crew and let everyone know of the plan."

Tanglor takes his ship and pilots it over to where the rest of his army lies waiting around the planet. They form a barrier to keep the Dimorians from leaving. Leazara sends out a message to Tanglor.

"We have them pinned down right now. If we can get him to surrender, then this will be easy. Don't count on it, though. Be prepared and wait for my order!"

Out of nowhere, a massive explosion erupts from the surface. Tanglor and his army watch from orbit but are unable to go down and help until they hear from Leazara. Tanglor sends a message back to Leazara.

"Stay safe down there, Colonel. We have your back if you need it."

Another explosion goes off as Leazara sits behind one of their defense barriers listening to Tanglor's message. She turns and looks over to some of her soldiers.

"We need some cover fire. Get those Dimorians off our asses. We need to move!"

Her soldiers jump from cover, firing their weapons at the Dimorians. Leazara uses the opportunity and retreats further behind their defenses. Calaido comes running up the stairs taking shots from the Johthun soldiers. He fights through and knocks the Johthuns to the ground, stopping and screaming over them.

"Come back here, Leazara! I will tear this whole planet to the ground if I have to!"

Leazara steps out from behind a wall.

"I'm right here. Come and get me!"

She pulls out her blade with her right hand and holds several knives in her left hand. Leazara charges at Calaido while he pulls out his scythe. She stops and dodges his swinging attack. She jumps off the side of the wall and slashes his arm with her blade. He turns and swings again, but she is too fast. She throws three knives at him, managing to pierce both his legs and one arm. Calaido roars as he rushes at Leazara. She slides underneath him, but he grabs her. He lifts her in front of him, squeezing tight. She squirms in pain before finally loosening his grip with a kick to the side of the head. He drops her to the floor, she doesn't hesitate and jumps onto him, stabbing her blade into his back. He falls to his knees with her still on top of him. She relentlessly punches him in the face until a burning sensation starts to overcome her. She stands up and turns around to find a Dimorian aiming a blaster at her. She looks down and sees an electrical current running around her body. Leazara falls to the ground, while Calaido stands over her and laughs.

"You almost had me beat.... too bad you didn't have help."

He punches her in the face, knocking her out. The Dimorian soldier ties her up and throws her into a cell. Calaido walks back toward the battlefield.

"Let's go and kill the rest of these Johthuns. Call in the secret weapons."

Tanglor and Ashar wait in orbit, surrounding the planet. From the shadows behind them, more Dimorian ships appear. They waste no time and start firing at the Johthuns, breaking up their barrier. Tanglor and his army scatter and fire back at the Dimorians. They fly past one of the ships and look into the windows. They notice that these Dimorians have helmets on, whereas none of the others—including Calaido—ever wore helmets. Without time to wonder what it means, Tanglor swerves through the Dimorian ships and takes one out. The ship explodes and out from the debris, a Dimorian with a helmet floats, staring at them. It slowly starts to drift toward them. Tanglor fires more shots at it, but the dead Dimorian takes every shot and continues to move toward them. It hits their ship and bounces off. They turn around and watch as it floats away, noticing that all of these other dead Dimorians do the same. The battle continues around the dead Dimorians floating away. The Johthun army starts to take casualties from the new Dimorian fighters, Tanglor gets on the comms to talk to his army.

"We stand our ground and continue to fight!"

Suddenly the Dimorians stop fighting and fly to the surface of Thoonta, leaving Tanglor and his army to form another barrier around the planet.

"Stay on guard and wait for Leazara's order!"

Leazara sits bloody and tied up in the Dimorian prison cell on the surface.

"I'm sorry, Tanglor...."

She falls to the floor and passes out.

# Chapter 20:
# Tralupians-Secrets, Love, Despair

Zembor sits on Queen Zuna's throne, looking out at RoyalTree, a smile on his face and eyes glowing orange. Ilikso walks in and sees him sitting there, but before Ilikso notices, the orange in his eyes disappears.

"Zembor? What are you doing on the Queen's throne?"

He stands up and walks toward Ilikso.

"You will address me as your King from now on. It is my throne to share with the Queen."

Ilikso notices his eyes quickly flash orange.

"Queen Zuna hasn't mentioned this to any of us…. What's going on with your eyes?"

"She will be mentioning it to you later today since she has been busy as of late. And my eyes? They're fine. I am just tired."

Ilikso continues to look at him.

"I will find the Queen and speak to her about this. Our people will be in disbelief when they find out you're still alive."

"We have figured that out already. I am going to be introduced in as King Ozem instead of Zembor. The people will believe me to be from the poor side of the city."

"If these are the Queen's wishes, then we will abide by them."

Zembor smiles at him and sits back down on the throne.

"That is a smart decision from you, Ilikso. Now, go and find your Queen."

Ilikso walks out of the throne room in disappointment. He walks toward Zuna's chambers and hears sobbing coming from down the stairs. He listens carefully and can tell it is the Queen. Ilikso slowly walks down the stairs and turns the corner to see Zuna crying on her bed.

"My Queen, what's wrong?"

She quickly sits up on her bed and wipes her tears away.

"Oh Ilikso, I didn't see you there…. I am fine, just overwhelmed by everything going on."

He approaches the bed and sits down next to her.

"You mean overwhelmed by Zembor…. or should I say King Ozem?"

She leans her head against his shoulder; he puts his arm around her.

"Zem…. Ozem will be King with me. I don't know how to explain it, but when I'm around him, I have no control over my actions anymore. I thought I told him I didn't want him as my King, but then I clearly remember telling him that I would love to have him, that I would arrange the marriage and introduce him to the people as King Ozem. I was on the throne, and then everything went orange, but that's all I can remember. Then I woke up here, in my bed, feeling helpless."

Ilikso pulls her closer and squeezes her tight.

"I don't know how that's possible… It isn't like you to have memory problems, especially from something that happened just last night. No matter what, I am here for you. And if Zembor or Ozem⸮—whatever he wants to be called now—tries anything or gives you a bad feeling, I will take care of him. I don't care if he *is* our Great-Great-Grandfather. He was dead for the last thousand years, and we were doing just fine."

Queen Zuna looks up to him as he holds her close. She smiles at him and laughs.

"Thank you for saying that, brother. You have been…."

She blushes as she continues to look at him.

"Just thank you for sticking with me and being there for me."

He smiles back at her.

"I will always be here for you."

Queen Zuna can't help the feeling coming over her, she leans in and kisses him. He embraces her and kisses her back. Zuna stops and moves away from him.

"I.... I am sorry. I don't know what came over me. We can't. You're my brother."

"You're right; I shouldn't have."

Ilikso stands up off the bed. Zuna continues to stare at him as he starts to walk out of her chamber.

"Wait!"

Ilikso stops and turns around. He is met by the Queen. She kisses him again, Ilikso can't resist it. He throws her onto the bed, and they take their clothes off. Ilikso crawls on top of her, they continue to kiss, rolling around the bed.

---------------------------------------------

King Ozem walks out of the palace towards the Great Tree overlooking the ocean. He approaches the trunk of the tree and places his hand on it.

"It is only a matter of time before the planet is ours. Once I get my hands on the trident, things will go much smoother. Have you heard from Tranjora?"

The trunk of the tree starts to glow orange around his hand. It flashes multiple times, like a secret code. King Ozem turns his head to the side and watches carefully.

"His army is marching this way? That won't work if I am to be married and become King. He will interrupt the ceremony and ruin everything!"

The light flashes again under his hand.

"Tranjora has had enough time! It is me who will bring it to you!"

The light flashes violently at him.

"I... I am sorry. I understand. I will be here to make sure he succeeds."

The light fades away, Ozem removes his hand from the trunk of the tree. He looks around to see if anyone saw him before walking back into the palace. Oryuna waits at the adviser table.

"Where is everyone? I've been waiting for the Queen, and no one has been here all day. Have you seen her or Ilikso?"

Ozem walks past her and sits on the throne.

"I saw Ilikso a little bit ago, but I haven't seen him since he left. The Queen is probably in her chambers. She wanted to get some rest after everything that has happened."

Oryuna gives him a strange look.

"Why are you sitting on the throne?"

"I don't want to have to explain it again, so go and retrieve the Queen from her chambers. She will explain it all to you. I am King now!"

Oryuna heads swiftly toward the Queen's chamber. As she gets closer, she can hear voices coming from the bottom of the stairs. She tries to listen but can't make out what they're saying. After a couple of seconds, Queen Zuna turns the corner to walk up the stairs, followed by Ilikso.

"My Queen, my brother. My apologies, I wasn't trying to eavesdrop…. Why was Ilikso with you in your chambers?"

The Queen slightly blushes before answering her sister.

"We were having a private discussion about the situation with our new King, Ozem."

"Ozem? You mean Zembor?"

"Yes, but he will now be known as Ozem. This way, he can be introduced to the people without causing them shock over Zembor being alive after a thousand years. We'll say he is from the poor parts of the city."

"Is this what you want?"

King Ozem sees them talking and walks over. Queen Zuna notices him; her eyes quickly flash orange as he smiles at her.

"Yes, this is what I want. It is also what's best for our people. He will help lead us back to greatness, just like when he was King."

Oryuna looks at Ilikso. He gets a weird look on his face as he stares at Ozem, which then turns to displeasure as the Queen walks over and grabs the King's arm.

"Brother, what's wrong?"

Ilikso doesn't answer Oryuna and walks past her out of the throne room. King Ozem escorts the Queen over to the throne. She sits down as he stands behind her. Queen Zuna puts the trident down in front of her and speaks to Oryuna.

"I need you to help me plan the wedding. King Ozem wishes it to be the greatest Tralupian wedding in our history."

King Ozem's smile gets more prominent as he stares out at RoyalTree.

"Yes, our wedding will be one for the ages! We must have it outside next to the Great Tree. It would be a shame if we didn't include it in our festivities."

Oryuna bows to Queen Zuna. She looks at Ozem standing behind her and notices both of their eyes quickly flash orange before she leaves the throne room to find Ilikso. As she leaves the palace, she can see Ilikso making his way toward the city.

"Ilikso! Wait up!"

He turns around and sees his sister running over to him.

"Sorry, I was hoping to get some time away from everything."

"I don't understand what's going on…. Everyone in the palace is acting weird."

"Tell me about it…. This whole King Ozem thing is a bunch of crap. I can't believe she is going along with it."

Oryuna looks at him and can see the frustration in his eyes.

"Why is it bothering you so much, brother?"

"I…. There is something off about Zembor and this King Ozem, as he wants to be called."

"Is that really the reason, brother?"

He looks at his sister and tries not to blush.

"Yes!"

She smiles at him and nudges her shoulder into his.

"Are you sure you aren't in love with our Queen?"

Ilikso's face gets bright red.

"Of course, I love her. She is our sister and our Queen!"

"I won't judge you, brother, but I can see it in your eyes, especially after I caught the two of you in her chambers…. I do agree with you, though. Something is up with King Ozem; I noticed both his and the Queen's eyes flash Orange. I never noticed hers do that until he came around."

"I…. we were just talking down there and…. Alright, you caught me. I am in love with her."

He puts his head down and stops walking.

"I know it's wrong for us to act on it, but I can't help the feelings I have for her and her for me…. Except when he's around. Every time he shows up, she changes."

"Changes?"

"Yeah, her emotions change, and she says things to him that she normally wouldn't say. I have seen the orange flash too. Something has to be happening that's making her act this way."

They continue walking toward the city.

"We just need to keep a close eye on her from now on. I will head back to the palace while you blow off some steam here in the city."

She turns around to start walking the other way.

"And brother, don't be ashamed of the feelings you have for her. No law says the two of you can't be together."

She walks away, leaving him to his thoughts as he wanders through the lively city. Tralupians walk and swim around him as he follows the path. He hasn't taken a stroll around the city since he was running the barracks with his siblings. He makes his way over there to see how it has been without them. As he approaches the barracks, a small Tralupian gets launched through the opening. A large one follows behind him, yelling.

"You have no place in the army! Get back to the slums and live out your life there!"

The smaller Tralupian gets back on his feet. He is about to leave the barracks, but Ilikso stops him.

"Is this how we run our barracks now? We don't ever turn away a good soldier."

The bigger Tralupian sees Ilikso and salutes.

"This is *not* a good soldier, sir!"

Ilikso walks over to him.

"No? Is there something wrong with him? Any ailments or disfigurements that I should know about?"

The instructor starts to get nervous.

"Well, no, sir. None that we know of."

Ilikso gets in his face.

"Then, I suggest you do everything in your power to train this soldier properly!"

The instructor salutes him again and has the soldier reenter the barracks. The soldier speaks up as he walks past Ilikso.

"Thank you, sir. I will not let this opportunity you're giving me go in vain."

He salutes Ilikso and leaves them alone. The big Tralupian stands still, avoiding eye contact with Ilikso.

"Go back in there and do the job that was given to you. If that is too hard for you, I will find someone else to do it!"

He bows to him before entering the barracks. Ilikso smiles and continues his stroll through the city. The sunlight starts to disappear behind the three moons that are beginning to rise. Ilikso looks up and takes a deep breath, fully taking in the beautiful sight. A high-pitched scream interrupts his moment of peace. He looks over and sees three Tralupian children in the water. As he looks closer, he notices one of them struggling to keep its head above the water while the other two scream for help.

"Help! Help! Something's in the water!"

Ilikso runs and dives into the water, swimming as fast as he can over to the children. When he gets there, the child has been pulled under. He dives underwater, frantically looking for where she went. Off in the distance, he sees the child fighting something off. She kicks and punches around, trying to break free. Ilikso swims over to her as roots and vines shoot up from the ground underneath the water. They latch onto her and pull her down to the ground toward an entrance. Ilikso pulls out his blade and slices the roots and vines holding her. They retract back down into the open hole, but the entry doesn't close. As Ilikso swims back up with the Tralupian girl, he looks back down and sees orange eyes glowing in the darkness, staring at them. He takes the little girl safely ashore and jumps right back in. As he looks back down at the open hole, he notices more than one pair of glowing orange eyes looking back at him. He looks closer and sees a knife flying toward him. He moves out of the way just in time. The hole opens wider, Tralupians with orange eyes pour out of it, their blades at the ready. Ilikso retreats to the surface. He leaves the water, yelling to the Tralupians in the city.

"Everyone! Get to the palace! We're being attacked!!"

All the civilians in the city start to panic as the orange-eyed Tralupians emerge from the water. The girl Ilikso saved falls to the ground, crying, her parents nowhere to be found. Ilikso runs by and picks her up as he makes his way back to the palace.

"If you can get back to the palace, the Queen and her soldiers will protect you."

He looks back to see the orange-eyed Tralupians start to slaughter the innocent civilians in the city. Tranjora emerges from the water with more of his followers. He lets out a loud screech while pointing his blade into the air. The rest of his soldiers run onto the surface while Tranjora walks behind them. Ilikso, still carrying the Tralupian child, picks up the pace as he runs toward the palace with the other Tralupians that made it out of the city. Queen Zuna, Oryuna, and Ozem stand at the palace entrance, letting everyone in. Zuna spots Ilikso and yells out to him.

"What's going on? We can see the city being destroyed!"

Ilikso runs over to her with the Tralupian child and places her on the ground next to them. He pulls out his blades and turns back to the city under siege.

"Tranjora and his army came out from an opening under the water. They're slaughtering everyone that didn't make it out! We have to help them!"

Ilikso starts to run back toward the city, but an arm reaches out and grabs him. Ozem stands proudly behind him.

"I will go with you. It has been too long since my last good fight."

Ilikso looks past him at Oryuna and Zuna. Oryuna nods while the Queen looks back concerned. Ilikso smiles at her before making his way back to the city with Ozem. The Queen yells out to her soldiers.

"Go with Ilikso and save our city! Kill Tranjora!"

Hundreds of the Queen's soldiers march behind Ilikso and Ozem back towards the city. It's in ruins. Orange-eyed Tralupians wreak havoc, as they tear through buildings—killing anyone left inside. They burn down homes while Tranjora stands watching. Ilikso yells to him.

"This ends now! You're dead!"

Tranjora turns around and stares back at him, his orange eyes glowing. He lets out another loud screech before he speaks in the same unknown language.

"Trabah Dah Urlonk!!!"

His soldiers stop pillaging the city and focus their attention on Ilikso, Ozem, and the Queen's army. Ozem begins to smile and laughs.

"This is going to be fun!"

He pulls out a blade and runs at the charging army. Ilikso follows behind him, yelling to their soldiers.

"Attack! Kill them all!"

The Queen's soldiers pull out their weapons and follow behind their two leaders. Tranjora's army meets the Queen's army head-on, bashing into each other as their blades clash, blood spills onto the ground as battle cries turn into screams. Ilikso stays close to Ozem to keep an eye on him. He swings his blade around, taking out the orange-eyed Tralupians. He looks over and sees Ozem jumping and sliding around the battle, taking their enemies out with ease. He makes his way toward Tranjora, but Ilikso loses sight of Ozem as he runs behind the enemy army. Ilikso feels a rush of anger flow through him. He goes ballistic and uses both of his blades to annihilate the enemy soldiers surrounding him. Arms and legs hit the ground covered in blood, followed by dismembered bodies. Ilikso stands, breathing heavy, covered in blood, as he looks around at the battle unfolding. The Queen's soldiers have made their way back into the city and are keeping the enemies at bay. Ilikso runs through the rest of the enemy crowd with his blades cutting into them as he passes by. Some of the Queen's soldiers follow behind him and finish off the surviving enemies. Ilikso makes it through and sees Ozem standing in front of Tranjora. The two of them are speaking in the unknown language.

"Trabah Dah Urlonk! Zu ollu tah!"

Ozem's face changes to anger.

"No Trabah ezia buhtah!"

Tranjora lifts his blade and yells again.

"Dah Urlonk! Trabah Dah Urlonk!"

Ozem reaches for his blade while Tranjora screams at him.

"I can't believe that they would send you! I did everything for them. I will finish this and show them I'm still more than capable of leading!"

Ozem drives the blade into Tranjora's chest. He falls to the ground and looks up to Ozem, the orange in his eyes starts to fade away.

"Tra……bah…. you have saved me. I am no longer in pain or under his control."

Tranjora grabs onto the blade in his chest and pushes it further in. Ozem stands over him as he falls to the ground and dies. All his soldiers cease fighting, and the orange in their eyes fades away. The ones still alive drop their weapons and look around in confusion—Ilikso notices.

"Soldiers, stop fighting! They have surrendered. Tranjora is dead!"

The Queen's soldiers begin to cheer, while the Tralupians that were possessed look around at them. Some of them drop to the ground crying in disbelief over what they've just done. Ilikso walks over to Ozem.

"You did it. Let us head back to the palace. We need to discuss all of this with the Queen."

Ozem takes a couple of seconds, as he stands, staring at the lifeless Tranjora. He turns to Ilikso and nods his head before following him back to the palace.

"What were you and Tranjora talking about before you killed him? It sounded like that weird language again…. Could you understand him?"

As they walk, Ozem looks around at the city in ruins.

"No, I didn't understand anything he said to me. I got tired of listening to it and decided to end it right then and there."

Ilikso examines him carefully.

"I see…. Well, we won't have to worry about Tranjora anymore. You and the Queen shall have your grand wedding with no interruptions now."

Ozem smiles at him.

"That is what I was hoping for. Tell me, Ilikso, are you okay with me marrying your sister?"

The question catches Ilikso off guard; he answers nervously.

"What? Yeah, of course, I am… I don't have a problem with it, as long as you don't hurt her…. If you do, then you will be dealing with me."

Ozem laughs as they approach the palace.

"That could be fun."

Before Ilikso has a chance to respond, the Queen and Oryuna run over to them. Zuna hugs Ilikso before Ozem—he takes notice but keeps to himself. Oryuna hugs Ilikso.

"I am so glad to see you alive! Is it over?"

"Tranjora is gone. Ozem killed him during the battle. I got there right as it happened—just in time to hear Tranjora's last words."

Queen Zuna lets go of Ozem and gives Ilikso her full attention.

"What did he say?"

"After speaking some of that unknown language, he said…. You saved me. I am no longer in pain or under his control."

"What do you think he meant by that?"

Ilikso looks over to the Great Tree.

"I'm not certain, but I think everything going on has something to do with the Great Tree. His eyes were orange, just like the trident, RoyalTree, and the Remnants. Ozem, what do you think? You were part of RoyalTree for so long; you must know something we don't."

Ozem walks up to Great Tree.

"I have told you everything I know, holding nothing back. I can't do what I did before as a Remnant, so I know as much as you do."

Ilikso doesn't buy it.

"I don't believe you! I heard you speaking the unknown language to Tranjora before you killed him!"

Queen Zuna steps in between the two. She looks at Ilikso and is about to say something, but her eyes flash orange, she stops.

"Ozem isn't lying, and if I trust him, then all of you need to do the same! If you can't—then I suggest you leave!"

Queen Zuna turns around and grabs Ozem. They march back into the palace, leaving Oryuna and Ilikso standing next to the tree. Oryuna glances worriedly at Ilikso.

"Is this true, brother?"

"I wouldn't lie. That thing isn't Zembor; it's up to something. He spoke to Tranjora, and right before he killed him, he switched back to our language. He kept saying "them" like someone sent both of them here on a mission. He said that he would show them that he was more than capable of leading again."

"I don't know what came over Zuna right there, but I think you've been right about Zembor or Ozem all along. Her eyes flashed that orange color again right as she was about to speak to you...."

Ilikso gestures to his sister, and they stroll out of the palace.

"We need to be careful. I don't know what's controlling Zembor's body, but it's dangerous."

The two of them find a place in the shadows to talk.

# Chapter 21:
# Johthun-A Home in Despair

Calaido bangs his hands against the cell Leazara sits in. He opens the gate and walks in.

"Alright, it's been a couple of days, and you reek. Time to go rinse off."

He walks over and takes the chain attached to her, pulling her off her feet. Calaido drags her behind him. Suddenly a voice from the darkness appears.

"Let her go!"

Three Johthun soldiers walk out with blades, ready to attack. They charge at him, but he runs and uses the chain attached to Leazara to clothesline two of them. The third one jumps over and stabs Calaido through the arm. He pulls out his scythe and takes the Johthun's head off in one swipe. The other two get up to try and run, but he throws Leazara into them, knocking them back over. Calaido turns on the green energy around his scythe and throws it at one of the Johthuns. It hits him in the back and starts to shock him. The Johthun shakes uncontrollably with the scythe in his back. He reaches over to get help from the other Johthun soldier, but the current from the scythe shoots over and shocks her too. The green energy runs through their bodies until it kills both of them. Calaido picks up his scythe then grabs Leazara once more.

"It's admirable that you still have soldiers fighting to save you. Any Dimorian here would love if I got captured. There would be riots until someone new came out on top."

Leazara walks behind him, laughing. They get to the showers, and Calaido swings the chain launching her in. He turns the water on, and it pours onto her. He laughs at her and starts to swing the chain back and forth, causing her to lose her balance and fall to the ground. She stands back up, and the chain swings again, knocking her into the walls. Water continues to pour over her, washing the blood down the drain. When Calaido has had enough fun, he shuts the water off.

"There, now you're all pretty for everyone to see you!"

He takes her outside, where the rest of the Dimorians stand watching, waiting for their leader. She looks to the crowd and sees other Johthuns tied up as prisoners.

Calaido pushes her forward, and she falls to the ground. The crowd sits down and looks up to them. Calaido steps forward and lifts Leazara off the ground with one arm, holding her in front of him.

"This is one of their so-called leaders! We can take everything from them if you continue to follow *me*—Calaido!"

The crowd stands up and starts to cheer. He tosses Leazara behind him.

"There are still Johthuns here that are not our prisoners, and there are still the ones in orbit surrounding us. Our next move will be to raze their city. Burn their towns down—kill them all!"

The Dimorians in the crowd stand up and start to cheer. Some of them pull out their weapons and kill the prisoners sitting next to them. Leazara helplessly watches while Calaido laughs.

"HAHAHA! Such a pleasant sight! Let's get you back to your cell."

Calaido grabs her chain and pulls it back to the cell, throwing her inside and slamming the gate behind her.

"I'll see you again once Tanglor and Ashar have come down to save you. I want them to watch you die."

Calaido joins the rest of the Dimorians destroying the city. They burn the buildings down and kill any Johthuns they find hiding.

Tanglor and his army watch from the planets orbit, the surface starts to get brighter.

"What's going on down there?"

"I don't know, Ashar, but we need to get down there. Get Elisin on the comms."

Ashar calls back to Joht. Her voice shoots out to Tanglor.

"Tanglor! What's going on? Have you heard from Leazara?"

"No, it's been three days since we last heard from her. I can't wait any longer. It's time for us to go down there, take out the Dimorians, and rescue her!"

Elisin stops and takes a deep breath.

217

"Okay, but be careful. If she is still alive, then you need to get her out of there. Otherwise, the mission is to eliminate the Dimorians and save our people."

"Understood."

Tanglor looks to Ashar.

"Are you ready? We need to get Leazara and make sure our parents are okay."

Ashar nods his head. Tanglor gets on the comms to talk with their army.

"Ucarus, you're going to stay up here with half of our army while Ashar and I go down to the surface with rest. We need to take out any Dimorians we find and save any of our people that we can."

Tanglor and Ashar take off toward the surface, with half of their army following behind. The Johthuns land to find the Dimorians destroying everything in their path. They've taken out the central city, and now they're moving through the towns— getting dangerously close to Tanglor and Ashar's childhood home. Tanglor and Ashar watch as the city burns in front of them. The sound of crackling fire surrounds them as they walk through the burning city, dead bodies from both sides of the battle filling the streets. Tanglor comes across a wounded Dimorian, filled with anger and hate; he grabs him.

"Where is she?!"

He punches the Dimorian in the face. It coughs up blood and replies in a raspy voice.

"Your Colonel is still alive and with our leader. Calaido will never let you have her back. He will kill you a....."

Tanglor punches him again, knocking him out.

Ashar looks off into the distance and notices their old house is in flames. They run over as fast as they can while Ashar shouts.

"Mom! Dad! We are coming. Please be okay!!"

They get to the house but don't see their parents anywhere outside. As it's starting to crumble, Tanglor jumps through the flaming door.

"Where are you guys?"

218

He hears coughing and runs toward it with Ashar close behind. They find their mom and dad lying on their bed, stuck underneath debris from the caved-in roof. Their mom looks them both in the eyes.

"Tanglor, Ashar, there is no time... I love you both, you have made me so proud."

Their dad looks up at them.

"You two are the greatest things that have ever happened to us. Take care of each other......"

His voice gets softer.

"We love you both so much."

His voice slowly fades away. Ashar grabs Tanglor.

"Come on; we have to get out of here!"

They run out of the burning house just as it completely collapses, turning into a ball of flaming debris. They sit and watch as what's left of their parents and old home burns away. Tanglor stands up.

"Let's go."

They slowly walk together back to their ship. Ashar looks at Tanglor.

"It's time to save Leazara and kill that savage."

The fighting continues behind them as the Johthun army begins to push the Dimorians back toward their ships. Ashar spots Calaido running through the battle carrying Leazara over his shoulder. A massive vessel looms over them.

"Hurry, we need to stop him from getting on that ship!"

Ashar and Tanglor take off through the battle. Dimorians fight Johthuns on both sides of them as they run toward Calaido. Some Dimorians spot them chasing after their leader and start to fire explosives in their direction. Tanglor dives out of the way, nearly getting hit by one.  Ashar helps him to his feet, and they continue to run. Explosions continue to fill the battlefield around them as several Dimorians jump out to attack them. Ashar stops, Tanglor slides underneath his legs, striking both Dimorians in the chest. Ashar quickly shoves his blade through their necks.

They catch up to Calaido just as he gets on the mother ship. It takes off right before they can manage to grab on, he looks down at them laughing.

"HAHAHAHA! See you on Joht!"

Calaido shuts the door and takes Leazara to the prison cell on the new ship, tossing her inside. Ashar and Tanglor get to Tanglor's ship and take off after them.

"Ucarus, they're getting away on some kind of Dimorian mother ship. Stop them!"

"I see them. I'm sorry, Tanglor, we can slow them down, but it's going to take a lot of firepower to take that ship out."

Tanglor and Ashar catch up to Ucarus and the rest of the army. The Dimorian mother ship is plowing through the Johthuns, but they continue to fight while Tanglor comes up with a plan. He tells Ashar to lead an attack against Calaido while he and a small team sneak onboard through one of the hatches underneath the ship. Ashar and the large fleet begin the attack on the mother ship. He and three other crews manage to land and start fighting on the massive Dimorian vessel. Tanglor and his small team, pilot a stealth glider underneath the battle and park next to a hatch they find. Tanglor hacks into their systems and unlocks it. They go through the open path and sneak past the fight. Before they can change their minds, the hatch shuts, leaving them to go down underneath the ship. As they're walking, Tanglor notices prison cells and sees Leazara locked up in shackles with a long chain attaching her to the wall. She's barely conscious but able to look up and see him. She tries to get up, but before she can say anything—Calaido steps out from the shadows.

"If you want to set her free, you'll have to get the key from me!"

Tanglor smiles while running forward and jumping over him. Calaido catches his leg and throws him to the ground. He moves past Tanglor and takes out his team with ease. Tanglor flips back up onto his feet and goes over to his injured crew.

"Leave the ship now."

Tanglor turns back to Calaido and tries another move, but he jumps to the right and dodges the attack. He goes again and hits Calaido in the face, knocking him back. Leazara yells to Tanglor.

"Don't let him hit you! His attacks are strong. Be quick, and he'll tire out."

Tanglor acknowledges her advice with a nod. Calaido takes his scythe off his side and switches it on; the green energy starts to flow around it. Tanglor pulls out his blades and evades Calaidos attacks, jumping off walls and dodging underneath him. Finally, he sees an opening and cuts Calaido's left eye. Tanglor grabs the key and runs toward Leazara. As he's unlocking her chains, Calaido starts to laugh.

"You puny Johthun. I will crush you like I crushed your parents! But this time, I will use my hands instead of a house!"

Before Tanglor is done unlocking the chains, he drops the key and slowly makes his way to Calaido. He kicks him down to the ground and grabs the scythe, still flowing with energy. He raises his arm and starts to bring it down to strike the Dimorian.

"Tanglor, noooo! He will pay for what he's done. Right now, we need to get off this ship before it explodes!"

Tanglor stops and runs over to Leazara. He strikes the chain with the scythe, setting her free. Calaido sits there, still laughing.

"You will never make it off the ship in time."

"What are you talking about?"

"You think I would just let our mother ship be taken? I have bombs placed throughout the ship—and I've just detonated them all! The only way to stop it is to use the code. Hahahahah!"

"You bastard, you're going to kill everyone—including your people!"

Calaido continues to laugh.

"Let's continue our fight. We're all dead anyway!"

He charges at Tanglor. Out of nowhere, Leazara whips the chains that are connected to her hands. The chain-link swings and wraps around Calaido's neck, stopping and choking him.

"Run, Tanglor! Get all of our people out of here!"

Before Tanglor has a chance to say anything, explosions begin to go off throughout the ship. Refusing to let Leazara go, he runs and jumps in the air, kicking Calaido down to the ground. He looks at Leazara.

"I will not let you die."

He helps her off the ground and removes the shackles and chain attached to her. She smiles at him before they start to run for the front of the ship, where Ashar is fighting. As they get closer, explosions begin to blow apart the path in front of them, breaking the ship into two pieces. Tanglor runs with Leazara following behind him. He jumps off of the walls and swings from the ceiling, trying to get to the parts of the ship that are still intact.

"Somebody is going to die with me!!"

Calaido screams as he catches up to the two of them. Ashar sees him and starts firing. Shots zoom past Leazara and Tanglor, as they evade and continue across the ship. Calaido gains on them. A massive explosion goes off, breaking their half of the vessel away from Ashar's. With no other options, they run and make an enormous leap across to the other side of the crumbling ship. While in the air, Leazara gets caught by Calaido. She can break free but instead chooses to take him back down to the other half of the vessel.

"Go Tanglor; he won't stop. Make me proud and be a great leader!"

Ashar grabs Tanglor and pulls him up. They watch as Leazara and Calaido continue fighting. She is injured but manages to jump around and hit him in the back of the head. Calaido turns around and gets a good hit in, knocking her back into what's left of the ship. He picks her up and turns to Tanglor and Ashar as they slowly float away.

"You're just going to leave her here to die? Fine, have it your way!"

He takes her body and swings her into the broken wall, where she falls to the ground. He walks over and grabs her by the face, lifting her into the air. He smiles and laughs at Tanglor and Ashar before he takes a bite out of the side of her head. He continues to whirl Leazara around, smashing her against walls before he decides to take another bite out of her. Tanglor's about to go back, but Ashar grabs him.

"It's too late. We need to go. It's what she wanted, I'm sorry."

Ucarus flies up in his nearly destroyed ship.

"Hurry! Mine still flies, but that thing's going down!"

Tanglor and Ashar run and jump off the crumbling vessel heading toward the atmosphere of Thoonta. They land on Ucarus' ship. Tanglor looks up.

"Thanks for the ride."

They fly away, unable to watch as Calaido continues to mutilate Leazara. Tanglor zones in and whispers to himself.

"I will honor and remember you, Leazara. I promise you; your death will be avenged. I will kill that monster."

Tanglor turns back to Ucarus and Ashar.

"We need to get some soldiers to follow them. I have a feeling he isn't going to die from that crash. Head to Joht at once."

Ucarus stands up and salutes Tanglor.

"I'm sorry for the loss of Colonel Leazara Luns. The Elites would be nothing without her. Colonel Raff, you are the Leader of the Elites now. We'll do whatever you ask of us! We will head to Joht at once, and Colonel? Let me know if there is anything else I can do."

He sits back down and pilots the ship back to Joht.

Ashar goes to the back and lays down, thinking about Leazara. He knows there was nothing else they could have done. He gets lost in his thoughts until he remembers Freden took Neliah to Joht. He jumps up and runs over to the Comms.

"Freden! Freden, come in!"

"Hey, I'm here. Stop yelling. Glad to hear your voice, Ashar."

"Sorry for being so short, Freden, but where is she? Did you make it back to Joht in time!?"

There are some footsteps in the background, followed by the crinkling of static from the Comms getting passed around.

"Ashar! Freden got me back here in time, and the doctors expertly patched me up. I'm still healing, but I'm okay and looking forward to seeing you when you get back."

Ashar blows out a big sigh of relief.

"I love you, Neliah."

"I love you too, Ashar. See you soon."

He passes the comms to Tanglor.

"Neliah, is Elisin around?"

"Yeah, hold on. I think she is in her room. Let me go and get her."

Freden jumps back on the comms before Elisin gets there.

"I'm happy to hear you all made it out of there...... Colonel Luns will be missed."

Elisin walks into the room, and Freden hands the comms over.

"I heard, Tanglor...... I'm devastated. Leazara was a great Johthun and a great leader."

"It is a loss for the Elites, but I will step up and be the leader the Elites need."

"Glad to hear that. Did you kill the Dimorians?"

"There were too many of them, Calaido fell back into the atmosphere of Thoonta. We sent soldiers to the surface to kill any Dimorians still there, and to locate his body in the crash."

"Keep us informed with any additional information you receive. See you soon, Colonel Raff."

They disconnect the call and continue the flight to Joht. As they approach the planet, they receive an incoming call from one of the soldiers that Tanglor sent to Thoonta.

"Mac-Ran, tell me what you found."

"We found nothing, Colonel. They took whatever they could and left. We can't find Calaido's body anywhere in or near the crash. There are very few survivors down here, but enough to start rebuilding. We're going to stay here and help. Can you have the Elders send some food and supplies?"

"Great idea, I will let the Elders know as soon as we get back. I'm going to make sure you get the food and supplies you need. Take care of our people; we will talk soon. Thanks for the information, and keep your eyes out for any Dimorians hiding. Take them prisoner and lock them up. We aren't going to kill them anymore. Unless you find Calaido."

Tanglor sits down in the seat behind Ucarus and stares out the window. Tears start to run down his face.

"Ucarus, get us home."

Ucarus uses what's left in the ship to get to Joht. They arrive to find Freden and Neliah standing in the docking bay waiting for them. The rest of their army lands behind them as they exit their ships. Tanglor, Ucarus, and Ashar are stopped by Neliah and Freden. Neliah steps forward.

"We thank every one of you for risking your lives for the Johthuns. You gave us the chance to keep living."

Thousands of Johthuns come out of cloaking from behind Neliah and start clapping and cheering for them. The crowd opens a walkway toward the stage; Tanglor and the others walk through it. He walks up the stairs with Ashar, Ucarus, Freden, and Neliah following behind him. A portrait of Leazara sits behind them next to a giant covered figure. Tanglor walks over to the podium and speaks into the microphone.

"Leazara would have been honored to walk among us through that crowd. She loved every one of us. Even if she didn't know you personally, she still had a place in her heart for you. She was one of the greatest Johthuns I have ever met and was like a mother to me. She took me under her wing, along with a lot of her recruits, and gave us everything we needed to succeed as Elites and as Johthuns."

Tanglor gets choked up. He fights through the tears and keeps talking.

"I wouldn't be standing here if it wasn't for Leazara. She risked her life to stop Calaido and his army. We need to do everything we can to honor her every day and remember who she was and what she sacrificed for all of us."

He turns around and removes the cover, revealing a statue of Leazara with her iconic blade in one hand and knives in the other. She stands in a fierce pose, ready to strike her enemy down. The crowd starts to cheer as Tanglor walks offstage. The roaring continues as the crowd marches around the city of Joht in her honor. The city lights all turn off, and the Elite's light torches. The city of Joht is filled with beautiful flickering lights. They continue to march through the streets, knowing their Colonel will always be watching over them.

# Chapter 22:
# Tralupians-King Ozem

Ilikso sits at the adviser table with his sister, Oryuna. Together they listen to the commotion and laughter that comes from the Queen's chambers. Oryuna notices her brother is annoyed.

"The more you hear them, the more it is going to irritate you. Get some fresh air.... There is no need for you to sit here listening to them."

Ilikso stands up and smashes his fist down on the table before leaving the palace. Oryuna sits by herself, waiting for the King and Queen. Another thirty minutes pass. The laughter continues as King Ozem starts to walk up the stairs to the throne room. He arrives to Oryuna sitting alone.

"Sorry to keep you waiting for so long... Where is your brother?"

Oryuna stands up and bows to the King.

"Ilikso had some other matters to attend to this morning, but he will be back shortly."

King Ozem smiles.

"It wasn't because of the Queen and I being so loud, was it?"

"Loud? I could barely hear the two of you."

King Ozem's laugh gets louder as he sits on the throne. Ilikso walks into the palace and joins Oryuna at the table.

"Ahh, there he is! Ilikso, come here."

Ilikso looks to Oryuna. He takes a deep breath and approaches Ozem. He stops in front of him and stands still.

"Yes, my King?"

"Kneel, when you speak to your King!"

Ilikso stands firm, staring at him. He stands up off the throne.

"Do as I say! Kneel before me!"

"I would gladly die before I knelt before you. You are not my King!"

King Ozem jumps down and gets in Ilikso's face.

"Are you sure about that?"

Ilikso stands his ground and pushes him away.

"You will never be my King. I see what you truly are."

Ozem gets an angry look on his face and pulls his blade out.

"I'm ending this now. I won't let you ruin everything I've done here!"

Before Ilikso can respond, Ozem charges at him, swinging his blade. Ilikso pulls his out and slides underneath the charging King. Their blades clank and clash together, their skills matched. Oryuna yells to both of them.

"Enough! Stop this madness!"

Ozem looks over to her, and his eyes flash orange. He smiles and turns back to Ilikso.

"Does it feel good being so helpless? Watching me with your precious sister, your Queen, who you love so much. Too bad, she's mine!"

Ilikso charges at him, screaming. He jumps in the air with his blade pointing down at the King. Ozem steps to the side and swings back at Ilikso. He moves and grabs his arm. The two stand with their arms locked together. Ilikso drops his blade and punches the King in the face. He holds onto Ilikso and drops his sword too, hitting him back. The two exchange fists to the face while Oryuna tries to break it apart. Finally, the Queen walks in from her chambers.

"What is going on!? Stop this at once!!"

Ilikso lets go of the King and stands, saluting the Queen. King Ozem continues to fight and punches Ilikso in the face and stomach. He keels over, and King Ozem pushes him to the ground.

"There. Kneel before me!"

Queen Zuna runs over and pushes the King off Ilikso.

"What is wrong with you? If you're going to act this way, I will find someone else to be King!"

She reaches down and helps Ilikso off the ground. He takes her hand and looks up to her. She smiles at him, but suddenly her eyes flash orange, she lets go, causing him to fall back to the ground. Oryuna runs over.

"Zuna! What's going on with you?"

Queen Zuna looks at both of them with her eyes flashing orange. She turns and stands next to Ozem while he smiles.

"I have had enough! If the two of you can't accept him as your King, then there is no place for you here in the palace!"

Oryuna helps Ilikso off the ground as Ozem and Zuna make their way to the throne. Zuna sits down with Ozem standing behind her.

"Brother, sister, come here."

Ilikso and Oryuna slowly approach the King and Queen. As they stand before them, Queen Zuna pulls her trident out and points it at her siblings.

"Kneel to your Queen and new King! I am to be married to him by nightfall, and he is to be introduced to everyone as King Ozem. If you have a problem with it, then you are no longer family. Live your lives out in the city and stay away!"

Oryuna looks at Ilikso and nods her head. She kneels and bows to the King and Queen. Ilikso stands staring at Queen Zuna; her eyes flash orange as she furiously stares back. Ilikso stands tall, as a tear runs down his beaten face.

"I will not kneel to a fake King! Ozem is not who he says he is, and you're not yourself. Whatever he has done to you has transformed you into his pet. The Wrathfin name doesn't mean anything to me if I am to be his slave while he treats you like his...."

"Enough!!"

Queen Zuna gets off the throne and walks toward Ilikso, her trident pointing at him. Her eyes flash orange again.

"I will not hear you insult him again. Now, leave the palace. Oryuna will pack your belongings for you. You are no longer welcome here."

Ilikso steps closer to the Queen, the tip of her trident grazes his neck.

"Strike me down... You know what I'm saying is true."

"Go!"

Her eyes continue to flash orange, as tears drip down her face. Ilikso shakes his head and turns around. He looks over to Oryuna, kneeling on the ground, but she looks away from him as he walks out of the palace. Queen Zuna returns to her throne as Ozem watches—a big grin on his face. Oryuna stays knelt before them.

"Queen Zuna, King Ozem, we need to get both of you ready for your wedding. You have to look the part if it's going to be the greatest Tralupian wedding in our history."

Queen Zuna looks to the King.

"She is right. We need to look our best, and no peeking! You can't see me until the ceremony begins!"

"Since when is that a tradition? I don't want to take my eyes off you today!"

Queen Zuna stands up in confusion.

"Since when? Zembor started the tradition when he was married. I know you're Ozem now, but you're still Zembor."

He looks back at her, nervously playing it off.

"Oh... that's right. I'm sorry, it has been a very long time since my first wedding."

Queen Zuna turns back to Oryuna.

"Come, sister, let's go to my chambers and prepare. Ozem, you'll have to find someone else to help you. Oryuna is going to help me."

"Who am I supposed to find to get help from? Why can't Oryuna help me after she helps you?"

"Oryuna is my sister and maid of honor for our wedding so that she will be with me all day. You are King, so go and find someone in the palace. All of them have to help you if you ask."

Oryuna and Queen Zuna retire to her chambers. Ozem waits until they are gone before he walks out of the palace to the Great Tree. Orange sparks shoot off the tree as he approaches it. He sticks his hand out, the sparks shoot at him and create a doorway on the trunk. Ozem walks through, and it closes behind him. He stands inside the Great Tree with his arms in the air, yelling.

"I'm getting married, and I need to look good!! Come and help your father!"

Ozem stands smiling, as the lost city of TralVent appears in front of him. He starts to walk through while the Remnants form around him. He walks through the Remnant-filled city until he reaches the crumbled statue and tall bell tower. He turns around and looks at the Remnants gathered around.

"Where are the Remains? None of them decided to come back after that last battle?"

Zelena's Remnant steps forward.

"Glad to see you back, father. None of the Remains returned after we took out their forces from that last attack. It will be a little while before they can attack again. Is it finally time?"

Ozem walks to the tall bell tower with the Remnants following him.

"You will know when it's time. I know all of you are eager, but you have trusted me this long. Just trust me a little bit longer, and I promise you—it will all be worth it!"

The Remnants cheer as Ozem walks into the bell tower. Ozem makes his way to the top where a spiral staircase circles up the tall tower. It leads up to a giant bell with a hidden room behind it. He opens the door; a gateway sits in the back it. Ozem reaches up and smacks his hand against the bell. It blasts back, causing Ozem to fall to the ground, covering his ears. The gateway in front of him activates, and a portal appears. Ozem climbs to his feet as the bell rings and shakes him around, his eyes flashing orange as his mouth opens. An orange mist starts to come out of his mouth, forming in front of him. As the last little bit of the cloud comes out, Ozem falls to the ground lifeless. The cloud floats through the portal as the gateway shuts, and the portal disappears.

---------------------------------------------------------

Queen Zuna shuts the door to her chambers and turns to Oryuna.

"You have to listen to me while he isn't around."

Oryuna sits down on the bed.

"I'm listening."

Queen Zuna sits down next to her.

"When he isn't around, I have control over what I say and do... I don't know what he did. I can't remember. Whenever I am around him, he can make me say and do what he wants. I can hear him in my head, and then his words come out. What happened with Ilikso...."

Oryuna interrupts her.

"I know, that wasn't you. Ilikso knows that too... He just couldn't take it anymore, watching him with you..."

"I wanted to be with him, but now I've exiled him from the palace. He needs to know that I will always love him. He also needs to know..."

Queen Zuna gets off the bed and lifts her shirt, revealing a bump just under her stomach. Oryuna reaches out and places her hand on it.

"It's his? Ilikso must know... Ozem can't find out. Have you two..."

Zuna pulls her shirt down and sits on the bed.

"That is why I am going to send you to tell him. You have to get him to come back. I need him here with me; you two are the only ones that can stop Ozem. And no, we have not... I made an arrangement with him, but soon there will be no way to hide it."

Oryuna stands and grabs a cloth to wipe away her tears.

"I will do everything you ask. Ilikso and I will stop this wedding from happening. There is only so much time, though. Let's get you ready, so Ozem doesn't get suspicious. How will you explain my absence?"

"I will tell him that you went after Ilikso. He'll believe that and won't care that you aren't here for the wedding. You have to hurry! And please tell Ilikso everything. As soon as Ozem gets within eyesight of me, I won't be able to control what I do..."

Oryuna hugs her sister.

"We're going to end all of this tonight before it's too late. Your child won't be raised in chaos."

Queen Zuna smiles and embraces her sister. Oryuna helps her get cleaned up and into their mother's elegant wedding gown. The emerald color and black lining on the edges looks striking against her skin.[4] After getting Zuna ready for the wedding, Oryuna hurries from the palace to go and find Ilikso.

-----------------------------------------

Ozem's body lies lifeless in the bell tower, as the gateway opens, the portal appears again. The orange cloud floats back out of the entrance and over to the motionless corpse. It hovers over him, and the portal disappears, causing the gateway to close. Sparks begin to fly out of the cloud and shoot Ozem's body, turning his clothes into a nice suit. A crown now sits on top of his head. The cloud floats down into his mouth and nostrils, completely vanishing. Ozem's eyes flash orange, and his body starts to twitch. He stands back to his feet, and the flashing in his eyes slows down.

"It's harder controlling a dead one... Huh, that's not right."

Ozem looks down at his all-white suit and waves his hands across it. The suit changes from white to all black with emerald lining on the edges.

"Much better."

He walks back down the spiral staircase to where the Remnants wait. He stands before all of them, as they watch with smiles on their faces.

"I wouldn't be here if it wasn't for all of you. Thank you for sticking by my side for these past thousand years. You will all be rewarded soon enough."

The Remnants cheer, kneeling for him as he walks past. Ozem gets back to the side of the tree and places his hand on the trunk. Sparks shoot off, and the doorway opens. He stops and looks back at the Remnants.

---

[4] Traditionally on TokBellu, the groom will wear the same colors, but reversed. In this case, black with green lining. - *Varaksha Tinlasp, Tralupian Historian*

"The wedding will be in the palace today; I will order the doors to be left open so that you can see from the tree."

He steps through the doorway, and the bark forms back around the tree. Ozem looks out over the ocean at the sun slowly starting to set. Queen Zuna walks over to him and puts her head on his shoulder.

"Are you ready to get married and officially become King?"

He turns and looks to her. Their eyes both flash orange.

"More than ever."

She grabs onto his arm, and they walk into the palace where thousands of Tralupians have gathered to watch the ceremony. Together they walk down the aisle while the crowds toss flowers, grass, and drops of glistening water onto them. They reach the steps leading up to the throne, where a Tralupian cleric waits. Queen Zuna and Ozem stand in front of the throne, holding hands as everyone watches. The Tralupian cleric steps forward and reads from the stone carving in his hand.

"It is my great honor to be standing here today to wed the beautiful Queen Zuna Wrathfin to Ozem Plidins. The title of King and Queen is not one to take lightly. Queen Zuna, do you wish to have Ozem as your King?"

She looks at Ozem, her eyes flashing orange.

"I do."

"Ozem, do you accept Queen Zuna's wish for you to join her side in ruling TokBellu?"

Ozem smiles at the Queen.

"I do."

The cleric turns around and faces the crowd.

"Now, I'll ask the two of you to sit and prepare for the blood ceremony. There cannot be a King without Royal blood running through his veins."

Ozem and Zuna's faces register shock. Zuna grabs the cleric roughly by the arm.

"No, you can't be serious! That procedure has only been done once on my father. I was told that both my mother and father were in agony for weeks after that. I don't want either of us to have to go through with it!"

Ozem gestures to Zuna to release the cleric's arm.

"What does this procedure require?"

The cleric walks over to a bag he has on the ground. Four Tralupian soldiers walk out from the crowd and stand behind him.

"We have to cut both of you open and pump blood from one of you back into the other. We use this long tube here and run it from your side into hers. Another one runs opposite you, completing the blood transfer."

Ozem looks to Zuna.

"If it's the only way for me to be King... then do it!"

Zuna starts to panic, but Ozem stares at her. Her eyes flash orange as she turns back to the cleric.

"If it's the only way for him to become King, then we do it."

The cleric nods his head; the soldiers escort Ozem and Zuna to chairs. They sit down and get strapped in. Zuna starts to panic again and tries to break free.

"Stop! I changed my mind! Let me out."

Ozem tries to turn his head to look at her but is restrained by the equipment. He yells out to the soldiers.

"She is just scared! Leave her be!!"

The soldiers stop and turn to the cleric. He signals them to leave her. Queen Zuna continues to scream as the cleric starts to cut into her side.

"No!! Please stop!!! He isn't Ozem!! Zembor Wrathfin has been alive inside the Great Tree!!!"

The cleric stops cutting into her, and the crowd goes silent as all their attention shifts to Ozem.

He nervously looks around, as he is stuck strapped into a chair with a knife ready to cut into him.

"It's true! I am the Great Zembor Wrathfin, so there is no need for the blood transfer. Release me from this chair, and I will explain everything."

Two of the soldiers walk toward him, but Zuna yells out again.

"Leave him! He's lying about everything. Zembor is dead! Whatever that thing is has taken over my Great-Great-Grandfather's body. Please, get these straps off me."

The soldiers rush over to her instead. They take the straps off, and Zuna keeps out of his sight.

"It's over, Ozem! Tell us what you really are and what you want!?"

Ozem starts to laugh. He looks up at all the bewildered faces in the crowd.

"I wanted this game to continue, but I suppose this is a pretty good way to end things. It should show them how much I'm still capable of!"

Ozem's laugh gets louder and carries through the palace. The orange light glows brightly in his eyes as he stares toward the Great Tree. It starts to flash, and sparks begin to fly out of it. The bark begins to crumble away, revealing a doorway with darkness behind it. Zuna knows what's about to happen. She runs forward, moving Tralupians out of the way, as orange eyes appear through the darkness.

"Shut the doors to the palace! We have to hurry before they......"

Zuna's eyes begin flashing orange. She stops and turns around, looking into Ozem's eyes. She starts to walk toward him as all the Tralupians watch her. The soldiers run in front of Ozem and stand with the cleric. The cleric steps forward.

"My Queen, please... We can't let you take the straps off."

Her eyes continue to flash until they finally stop and turn solid. She smiles and starts to laugh. Ozem is laughing behind them. They both stop and then speak at the same time.

"Move out of the way or die!"

---------------------------------------------

Oryuna runs through the city looking for Ilikso. She has already searched in the marketplace and slums with no luck. She pushes through Tralupians heading toward the palace for the Queen's wedding and notices a small crowd surrounding the barrack entrance. She makes her way over to find Ilikso fighting the instructor. Ilikso takes a punch from the left and another from the right, but he stops the next one by grabbing his fist.

"Got you now."

Ilikso kicks the instructor's legs out from under him before bending his arm the opposite way, breaking it as he hits the ground. Ilikso drops the broken arm and jumps over him, jabbing him in the throat. The instructor lays on the ground grabbing at his arm and gasping for air. Ilikso kneels next to him.

"I warned you once, and you didn't want to listen. I better not see you around here anymore. The barracks are no longer your business."

He barely stands to his feet and hobbles away, as Ilikso walks over to a recruit with two black eyes and an injured leg.

"He won't hurt you anymore; you will get the proper training from now on. I will personally come and check on your progress."

The recruit smiles and salutes Ilikso. Oryuna walks over as the small crowd disperses.

"There you are. I've been looking all over for you."

Ilikso starts to walk away from her.

"Ilikso, stop! Zuna needs your help. She sent me to find you."

Ilikso stops walking and turns back to her.

"She had plenty of chances to tell me that herself. Plus, she exiled me out of the palace."

"That was Ozem. You were right; he is controlling her somehow. She told me that she can hear him in her head whenever she's within sight of him. He controls what she says and does. We had some time away from him today, and she told me everything. She also told me...."

Ilikso gets closer to her.

"Told you what!?"

"She's pregnant... with your child, Ilikso."

"That... how? What about Ozem?"

"She says they haven't, and that's why she is even more worried about him finding out. They had some sort of arrangement. Either way, we have to get back there and stop that wedding! She wants to be with you, brother, and you and I are the only ones that can stop Ozem."

Ilikso steps back and takes a couple of seconds to process everything.

"My child... Zuna... Alright, let's go!"

The two of them run back through the city toward the palace. A massive crowd of Tralupians blocks the way in. Oryuna and Ilikso try to look over them to see.

"The wedding is starting. We need to get through!"

"Oryuna, up here!"

Oryuna looks to her right and sees Ilikso climbing one of the tall trees. He reaches his hand out for her. She grabs on, and he pulls her up. They look down at the crowd of Tralupians and the palace.

"That's our only way in, Oryuna!"

She looks to where Ilikso is pointing.

"That's water!"

"Exactly! It won't hurt for us to jump in. With the crowd blocking the way, we need another way in. The water takes us around the Great Tree to the other side, away from everyone."

Oryuna nods her head, and they jump into the water. Ilikso and Oryuna stay underwater as they swim next to the Great Tree. As they start to circle the Tree, they notice an orange light flashing on the trunk above the water. They quietly stick their heads out and watch the tree light up with sparks. Once the sparks stop, a doorway appears with darkness behind it. Oryuna and Ilikso hear screaming coming from the palace. They see the Queen running to the doors overlooking the Great Tree.

"Shut the doors to the palace! We have to before they...."

Ilikso is about to get out of the water, but Oryuna grabs him.

"Wait, look."

She points to the tree; they both watch as the Remnants from the Great Tree materialize out of the doorway. Ilikso swims closer.

"They shouldn't be able to leave the tree. How is this possible?"

Oryuna swims next to him. They watch as their Remnant ancestors walk out of the tree and stand in position waiting to attack the palace.

"Something isn't right here. If they were our ancestors, they wouldn't want to attack us or the palace they built."

As the two of them watch the Remnant army stands, waiting for orders, Ozem and Zuna walk out of the palace doors with their eyes glowing solid orange. They both stop in front of the Remnants and speak in unison.

"The time has come! Kill them all. We can use their bodies after!"

The Remnants cheer and lift their weapons high into the air as their Tralupian, and Ventrian bodies fade away, revealing the crimson monsters. They charge into the palace to attack the helpless Tralupians. Queen Zuna and King Ozem stand in the doorway, watching the massacre. Ilikso draws his blade and sneaks behind them. Oryuna follows behind. He gets right behind Ozem and gets ready to stab him, but before he can, Ozem turns around laughing.

"Haven't you figured it out yet? I watched you sneak out of the water. The Great Tree has eyes too. Some of you, Tralupians, really are dumb."

Ilikso thrusts his blade forward, but Ozem jumps back and pulls his sword out.

"Do you really want to lose again?"

"Let's find out."

The two charge at one another, swinging their blades and clash against each other. They stand face to face with their blades pushing against each other. Oryuna tries to help, but Queen Zuna gets in the way, her eyes glowing.

"Zuna, you have to fight it!"

She walks toward Oryuna with her trident, ready to strike.

"I don't want to fight you, please!"

Oryuna pulls out her small blaster and fires it at Zuna, but she spins her trident around deflecting the bullets. She pushes Oryuna back against the Great Tree with nowhere to move.

"If you can't fight it, then you'll have to kill me."

Zuna starts to blink, and the orange begins to fade away slowly.

"I.... am trying.... it hurts! Oryuna help!"

Her eyes go back to the solid orange, and she drives the Trident into her sister's stomach, pinning her against the Great Tree. Oryuna looks down at the Queen with blood dripping out of her mouth.

"Zu...na... Fight... it..."

She reaches out for Zuna walking over to Ozem and Ilikso. She approaches the two squaring off in a heated duel—they exchange blows, not being able to better the other. Finally, Ilikso jumps over an attack and kicks Ozem in the face, knocking him back. He rolls on the ground and grabs Ozem's blade. As Ilikso gets up, he stands with both edges at Ozem's neck. Ozem starts to laugh. The Queen stands behind him and joins in on the laughter. Ilikso looks around to a graveyard, the dead lay around the destroyed palace, fire burns around them as a river of blood flows toward the ocean. Ilikso yells to the Remnants.

"Kill me if you want! He dies with me no matter what!"

Queen Zuna walks around to face Ilikso.

"Make the right decision here, brother. What happens to the Great Tree—our planet—if you kill him?"

Now Zuna stands next to Ozem, the three of them circling each other. Ilikso finds himself with his back against a wall, Queen Zuna and Ozem have their backs to the Great Tree—ready to retreat with their army of monsters surrounding them. Ilikso keeps the blades close to Ozem's neck.

"I don't know what you want here. I'm not letting Ozem leave here alive. Killing him is all that matters to me. Besides you, Zuna."

Zuna looks to Ilikso and tries to fight off Ozem's control. The orange light starts to dim in her eyes.

"Ilikso... help..."

Ozem notices Ilikso's distraction and takes advantage. He cuts himself on one of the blades, moving out of the way before diving and tackling Ilikso to the ground, knocking the blades out of his hands. Ozem sits on him, beating him with his fists, punching with the left, then the right, repeatedly. Ilikso puts his arms up and tries to block what he can, but Ozem doesn't stop. Right as Ilikso is about to give up, the Queen's trident pierces through the Ozem's back. He stops attacking and looks down at it.

"No, this can't be..."

Ilikso pushes Zembor off him to see Oryuna standing over them. A giant wound sits in the middle of her stomach. She falls to the ground, blood pouring out of her.

"Keep... Zuna.... safe.... pl... ea... se...."

Oryuna's life fades away in Ilikso's arms. He shuts her eyelids and lays her down on the ground. Ilikso walks over to Ozem, still on his knees with the trident in his back. He pulls it out and kicks him to the ground.

"Kneel!"

Ilikso lifts the trident in the air and drives it down into Ozem's neck. The palace starts to shake, as the monsters around them turn into orange ash. The Great Tree outside begins to crumble and break apart. Ilikso runs over to the Queen, sitting on the ground.

"What have I done?"

"Zuna, we have to get out of the palace!"

He grabs her, and they run out as part of the roof caves in behind them. They both fall to the ground as the Great Tree continues to fall apart. The orange light starts to shoot out from the tree as the bark falls off into the water. Leaves and branches fall from the top of the tree, crashing down beneath it, causing the tree to rock back and forth. As they watch the tree collapse, a mangled Ozem stumbles from the ruins of the palace with the trident in his hand. He makes for Ilikso and the Queen. Ilikso grabs his blade, ready to strike, but Ozem falls to the ground. He starts to convulse, and sparks fly out from him. His flesh is completely ripped apart, revealing an orange cloud. It floats toward them and flashes at the Queen. She starts to cough and gag, as an orange mist flows out of her mouth and floats back towards the more significant cloud. It flashes again, and the cloud turns into the spirit of Zembor and a Remnant of a bigger, slightly different looking monster than the ones inside RoyalTree. The Remnant laughs as it walks over to the dying tree.

"That was fun. You Tralupians are tougher than any of the others! I have what I came for, so I leave TokBellu to you."

The Remnant disappears into the tree, as Zembor's spirit looks at them.

"I am sorry for everything you've had to go through, but I am afraid it isn't over. The Great Tree is dying and will take TokBellu with it if we don't do something. This was the burden I placed upon us when I brought RoyalTree back here with me. I am eternally sorry for that. You beat him. He can't return now that we have regained control, but the Great tree is tired and weak. It needs more life force to live, a Wrathfin's life force."

Queen Zuna stands in disbelief.

"There is nothing else we can do?"

"With RoyalTree still gone, we must carry on the ways of sacrificing our lives for all of those on TokBellu. You will still be alive in spirit, my Queen."

She turns to Ilikso.

"No, I can't! I'm pregnant!"

Zembor's spirit starts to walk toward the Great Tree.

"I am sorry, but we don't have time to wait for your child to be born. We need to go now."

Ilikso grabs Zuna and looks into her eyes.

"You have to stay strong—no matter what. Take care of our child and lead our people back from this. Return us to the greatness you promised."

Zuna starts to cry.

"Why are you talking like this? We just got each other back."

"I know... and we will always be together. This has to be done, or our daughter will never get a chance at life. I have to do this. I love you, Zuna."

She holds him tight and kisses him. Tears run down their faces as they embrace each other for the last time. He reluctantly releases her, heading toward the Great Tree. Zembor's spirit reaches out for him, a doorway opening behind him. Ilikso takes his hand, and together they walk into the Great Tree. Queen Zuna falls to the ground in tears as she watches the tree stop shaking. Broken pieces fly out of the water and form themselves back into the tree. The broken branches get absorbed into the trunk while new ones form at the top. The roots run underneath the palace, reaching up and grabbing onto the dead bodies—pulling them under. They clean the blood and restore the palace to its former glory. As she sits by herself, Zuna watches, amazed, as TokBellu rebuilds itself. She glances back at the Great Tree. It flashes a lighter orange and Ilikso's face appears on the trunk of the tree smiling at her. She smiles back as his face fades away. The trident on the ground starts to shake. It stands itself up, and the orange light shines out of it once more. Queen Zuna walks over and grabs hold of it. She smiles while watching the sun rise over the ocean.

# Chapter 23:
# Johthuns-Our True Purpose

Tanglor stands in the Great Hall, looking out the window. He watches his troops march around the city—lighting it up for Leazara. Ashar, Ucarus, Neliah, and Freden walk in and stand with him. They all watch in silence as the city glows brightly. Finally, Elisin walks in behind them all and breaks the silence.

"Sorry for the intrusion, but we need to talk."

She approaches them; they turn away from the window to sit down.

"Colonel Leazara Luns was a great leader, but there are still many things she hid from you and the Elites. She always did what she thought Tazlow would have wanted. In the end, she lost those ways and went away from the path Tazlow truly wanted us on. Not just as the Elites, but as Johthuns."

Tanglor gets out of his seat.

"I believe that she was hiding more things from us, but I don't believe she lost her way. She was a great leader and a great Johthun. My father would have been proud of her!"

"I have no doubt about that, Tanglor. Your father would have been so proud of her and you, but he also would have let her know when we needed to stop fighting and turn our focus back to who we truly are."

"And who are we truly?"

"We dug our way out of the underground caverns and built our cities for one reason. We are explorers! We used to thrive on one question alone—what else is out there? We've lost our way due to all this fighting. Your father started the Elites because he wanted to send them out to discover new worlds and new species. They trained more than the other soldiers because he wanted them to be prepared for whatever they found out there."

They all sit, waiting for Tanglor to say something, but he just stares at Elisin.

"Colonel Raff, you need to listen to me. We cannot continue down the path we've been on. Even after that war with all of our casualties, our people are still building and still expanding every day. We are becoming overpopulated and need to find other habitable planets for our people."

"I understand, but our people on Thoonta and Conril need all the help and support they can get right now."

Ashar gets out of his seat.

"Neliah and I will go to Thoonta to help. We can be active Captains on the planet, watching out for it. It would help the civilians there feel safe while they rebuild their lives."

Neliah stands behind him, waiting for the decision. Tanglor nods his head and looks to Elisin.

"I think that is a great idea, Ashar. I will put it through to the other Elders. Leave at once, and they won't be able to tell me no. Ucarus, will you go to Conril and help with their rebuilding efforts?"

Ucarus stands up and salutes his Elder and Colonel before he walks out of the Great Hall. Neliah follows behind him.

"Ashar, let's go?"

"I'll meet you in the glider. I want to talk to Tanglor."

He walks over to Tanglor, standing at the podium where Leazara used to stand. Freden and Elisin walk to the other side of the room to give them some space.

"I'm proud of you, Ashar. Our people on Thoonta need you and Neliah. I know both of you will do great things there."

"Thank you, brother. This isn't goodbye. We will see each other again soon, especially when you come and visit us."

Tanglor puts his arm around Ashar.

"We will see each other very soon. I will come to check and see if you actually helped there."

They both laugh before Tanglor gets a serious look.

"Ashar, rebuild their house.... make it the way mom and dad had it before."

Ashar smiles and gives his brother one last hug. He strolls down the Great Hall, taking a careful look around at everything.

Elisin and Freden walk back over to Tanglor.

"You and Freden need to come with me. I need to show you something. Well, Martonamo needs to show you something. More lost history."

"Why does Freden need to come?"

"As I said before, there are many things that Leazara hid from you. Please Tanglor, lead us down to the ancient cavern."

Tanglor hesitates before leading them over to the wall that seals the passage to the cavern. He puts his hand onto it, and the teal light bleeds through. The wall lights up and disappears. Tanglor walks through, lighting the way up in front of him. The dirt on the ground and walls move to the side, creating an easy path for them to walk on. They reach the end, and the way opens to a cavern. The wall closes behind them—Martonamo powers on as soon as Tanglor enters the cavern.

"Good to see you again, Tanglor. Is that Elisin? It's been a long time since I've seen you."

"Good to see you, too, Martonamo."

"Come and sit down. Have a seat with your friends."

Tanglor and Elisin sit down in front of the computer screen. Freden hesitates before taking a seat next to Tanglor.

"My name is Freden. Happy to meet you, Martonamo."

"Nice to meet you, Freden. There must be a reason that you're here with them. No one can describe the feeling or prepare themselves for what I'm about to do. I am going to show you and Tanglor some lost history that I have saved. You two can view it because of your connections with Tazlow and Colonel Luns."

Tanglor and Freden look at each other in confusion, but before Freden can question what Martonamo just said, he flashes a teal light at them, starting slow and speeding up until it's rapidly flashing. Tanglor and Freden get lost in the light. As the flashing stops, they stare at the screen. Martonamo has control of their minds.

"We are going to go back to when your parents met each other. Where your father discovered me."

The Teal light flashes and they zone in on the screen. A young Tazlow Raff is seen with a team of explorers wandering around a less civilized Joht where dirt covers most of the land. As they search for an entrance into the caverns, Tazlow sees a hill and races to the top.

"Isn't this exciting?! We're going to be the first ones to get back down into our ancestor's caverns! Think of all the things we might learn!"

Suddenly, the hill starts to shake, and Tazlow loses his footing, causing him to roll down the front of it. He hits the bottom and locks eyes with his team looking at him from above.

"Tazlow! Are you okay?"

"Yeah, I'm going to climb back up."

He approaches the hill, but the ground starts to rumble again. The dirt moves from underneath him, revealing a silver door unlike any he has ever seen before. The rumbling gets more substantial, and the door he stands on starts to open. Tazlow jumps off to the side and watches as a dark metallic vehicle is revealed inside the open door. The light shines off its sleek metal, blinding Tazlow and his team. The rumbling turns into a thundering shockwave, causing everything to shake. The dark metallic ship shoots off into the sky and disappears in the blink of an eye. A second shockwave follows behind, causing Tazlow to fall through the door as it shuts. His team rushes down and tries unsuccessfully to get in.

"Go back and get help. There's no reason you should waste your time here with me. I'm going to look around and see what I can find down here."

His team tries to argue with him, but Tazlow won't be swayed. Finally, they agree to go back for help. Tazlow turns around and investigates the dark, mysterious cavern. He removes his goggles to see better, and from what he can see, the cave wasn't built by any previous Johthuns. The walls are made from some sort of unknown metal. Tazlow continues to walk down the hallway, eventually finding a massive room with a giant screen facing him. He sees all kinds of strange machines and devices lying around the room. Lights start to appear from behind him, as he turns around to look, they disappear into a room.

"Hey! Come back!"

Tazlow chases the lights. He turns the corner and gets hit by a flash of teal, knocking him to the ground. He looks up and sees two shiny ovals floating over him. They flash teal over and over before shooting into both of his hands. The ovals tremble inside his palms before causing a burst of light to shoot out from them. The pain is unbearable, and he passes out.

He wakes up to see teal flashing all around him, the lights in his hands are pulsating. The pain has subsided, allowing him to stand back up. Tazlow notices that the giant screen is on in the other room. He walks in and sees a giant face looking back at him.

"Ah, you must be Tazlow Raff. My name is Martonamo Jusintar. Because of you, I have been brought back to life. Thank you."

Tazlow tries to turn and run, but Martonamo shuts all the doors, locking him in the room.

"I'm not going to hurt you. Wherever you go—I go. Those ovals that flew into your hands – sorry about that – mean that we share a bond now. Normally I ask for permission, but I've had some bad experiences. I'm sure you saw the ship that flew away, that was one of them."

"That ship... Who was inside of it?"

"You know, I'm not sure. They never spoke, and their faces were always covered. When I saw you and your team approaching the facility, I used some of the doors and machines inside to cause a shockwave. I destroyed most of the structure, but it caused them to leave. Afterward, my ovals sensed you and deemed you worthy of sharing my bond. This bond with you allows me to access my full range of powers."

"I see... So, what does that mean for me now?"

"Hmmm, the last couple of creatures I bonded with weren't as friendly as you. We didn't communicate much; they just used me for my information."

Tazlow is interested in the thought of other sentient creatures.

"Other creatures? Could they talk? And what kind of information do you have, Martonamo?"

"They could talk, but they only talked about war and conquering. The desire for information is what made them want to. Please don't do the same, Tazlow."

"You don't have to worry about that, Mart. The Johthuns are peace-loving folk. We are explorers at heart, and one day I will lead us to other planets, not to conquer or to kill, but to expand our culture and learn of others out there."

Martonamo starts to laugh.

"Tazlow, I am glad it was you that found me. I have information that will amaze you; It will expand your mind and give you the ability to build ships and vehicles like the one you saw. The Johthuns can be more technologically advanced than you've ever imagined. Sit down and watch."

Tazlow sits down, and Martonamo starts to flash. He gets lost on the screen, seeing all kinds of blueprints and plans for buildings and vehicles. Different types of technology fly by before it finally flashes again, releasing Tazlow.

"I don't want to give you too much at once. Are you alright?"

Tazlow takes a couple of deep breaths and looks back to the screen.

"I have to share this with my people. Is there a way to get you out of this facility? Would you want to come home with me?"

"I would be honored to go back with you and help your people. It would be the first time I'd be used for good. If you go over to that mainframe behind you, the machine shaped like a star, that is what needs to be moved. The consoles and screens can be rebuilt. Now that we share a bond, I can communicate with you wherever you are."

"That'll be convenient. I will fetch my team, and we will come back with tools to relocate you to our home. I will be back, Mart."

"See you soon, Tazlow Raff."

Tazlow walks back to the door he came through and opens it up to find a member of his team still trying to get in. It's a female Johthun. It's clear to see she's running out of water and is barely breathing.

"What are you still doing here?"

Tazlow runs over to her side and gives her water.

"Leazara, you could have killed yourself."

"I wasn't going to leave you behind."

She catches her breath and drinks some water. Leazara jumps up and hugs Tazlow before looking at him and kissing him.

"Thanks for staying and waiting for me, but you should have gone with the others."

She ignores what he says.

"What happened in there?"

"There's no time to explain. We need to get our strongest Johthuns and drill into this hill to get my new friend out of the facility back there."

"Your new friend? What are you talking about?"

Tazlow stops and tries to figure out how to contact Martonamo. He squeezes his hand together into a fist, and it lights up. Leazara backs up.

"Hey, Mart! Can you hear me?"

"I am here, Tanglor. What can I do for you?"

"Say hi to my friend Leazara."

Leazara nervously walks over to his glowing hand and touches it.

"Hello Leazara, my name is Martonamo Jusintar. I can't wait to meet you soon."

The light fades away, and Tazlow opens his hand back up. Leazara stares at him with a blank look on her face.

"What did I just see and hear?"

"Leazara, this is going to sound crazy, but that was a computer console! I found it down in the facility; he's practically alive! We share some sort of bond now. The things he showed me, the information he has stored on him, it will push our people centuries into the future. I will show you all of it when we get back, but we have to hurry before the things in that dark metallic ship come back!"

Leazara doesn't know how much of this she believes yet, but she would follow Tazlow anywhere. She goes back to the city with him to gather tools and their strongest Johthuns. Tazlow walks over to one of the drills that still works. He and his team pull the drill behind them as they make their way back to the facility. They approach the closed door, and Tazlow reaches out and puts his hands on it. Teal light comes out of Tazlow's palm—opening the door. His team follows behind him, down the hallway to the room where Martonamo is.

A bright teal light flashes on the screen, causing the memory to jump to a much older Tazlow. He is talking with Leazara in front of the docking bay door. He pulls her through the doorway to hide behind one of the ships.

"Sorry to pull you away like that, but we need to talk."

"What is it? I'm supposed to meet my sister. You know how she gets if you're late."

Tazlow laughs.

"Haha, you don't have to tell me how Mezriah gets. She'll be fine waiting a couple more minutes for you."

Tazlow reaches his hand out and touches Leazara's belly.

"Have you come up with a story yet?"

"I have a couple of things in mind. It happened right around the war when we were caught by the True Guardians. I can say that one of them forced themselves on me, and this is what I'm stuck with."

She shoves Tazlow's hand away.

"Leazara, I am sorry... We both thought we were going to die over there on Conril. It shouldn't have happened; you and I both know that."

Leazara turns and walks away from him.

"*You* think it shouldn't have happened."

She walks down the corridor to find Mezriah waiting for her at her door.

"Hey, sis! How are you?"

"I'm alright, Mez. How are you?"

The ladies continue to talk as Mezriah shuts the door behind them. They sit down, and Mezriah grabs some tea from the leaves in her garden.

"Wow, Mez, this tea is great! You grew this outback?"

"Yes, with Tazlow's help, of course!"

The door to their house opens, and Tazlow walks in.

"Sorry to interrupt you and your sister, but we need to talk."

He sits down next to both of them. Leazara looks at him and shakes her head; he ignores her.

"I can't anymore, I'm sorry. Mezriah, your sister and I have been hiding something from you, and I can't take the guilt anymore."

Leazara stands up and backs away from her sister.

"Leazara, what's going on?"

"I..... I'm so sorry, Mez. We were trapped on Conril with nowhere to go. They were going to kill us and well. Tazlow and I took a moment for what it was. I'm sorry, Mez."

Tazlow jumps in.

"There is nothing that I can say to make this better, but you need to know.... especially because Leazara is pregnant."

Leazara lifts her shirt, showing her sister the slight bulge in her stomach. Mezriah sits stunned—speechless. She recovers within moments and walks up to her sister, embracing her. Releasing Leazara, Mez turns to Tazlow next. She cocks her hand and punches him in the face, letting him stagger back before grabbing and hugging him.

"I am very upset about this, but there is a life being made from this mistake... We will all move past this, and no one will know. Leazara, Tazlow, and I will be there for your child if you ever need anything."

She turns and looks back at Tazlow.

"We have a lot to discuss."

Martonamo flashes the bright teal light again; the screen jumps to Leazara lying on a bed, going into labor. Tazlow and Mezriah are in the room with her. The doctor walks in.

"Alright, are we ready to get this started? Is everyone here... Is the father here?"

Tazlow looks at Mezriah and Leazara. Mezriah adopts an angry tone to help play it off.

"If you think a murdering rapist should be around a child... No, the father won't be coming."

The doctor gets nervous and turns away from them to start the procedure. A couple of hours go by before the room is filled with a faint cry. It's a baby boy. Leazara sits with a smile on her face as her son is placed into her arms. Mezriah and Tazlow can't help but smile as they walk over to her.

"He is beautiful. What are you going to name him?"

Leazara looks back to her sister, Tazlow standing behind her.

"I'm going to name him... Freden Fornlor Luns."

Another flash of light and Martonamo's face appears on the screen in front of Tanglor and Freden.

"Sorry, I know it's a lot to digest, but there's one last thing to show you."

The memory jumps forward a couple of years. Tazlow, Mezriah, and Leazara stand in the docking bay. Freden, just two years old, runs around them as they talk.

"Mezriah and I have to go to Thoonta. If we want the Elites to succeed, we need to do this. Martonamo is in danger on Joht, and this is the only option we have. We need to show the Elders that we don't want to fight. Exploring is what we were meant to do, and Martonamo gave us the ability to do that. We know there are other species out there, we just need to go out and find them! I need you to stay here to protect Freden and our second child. Have you thought of a name for him yet?"

"I'm going to name him Dretzlin Taz Luns."

Mezriah walks forward with her arms encircling her pregnant belly.

"That is a beautiful name, sister. Hopefully, he'll get along great with Tanglor Lezar Raff."

Tazlow pulls them both in tightly and hugs them. He kisses Mezriah before he turns and kisses Leazara.

"I love both of you so much."

He grabs Freden and lifts him onto his shoulders.

"Take care of your mom, buddy. See you soon."

He puts him back down by Leazara. They wave goodbye as they walk onto the ship with the Elders and Elite protectors. Leazara grabs Freden and takes him back to their house to discover the door broken down. She slowly walks in and sees everything destroyed. She hears footsteps upstairs and tries to run, but her water breaks. She crawls into the corner underneath the stairwell with Freden following behind. The steps get louder until they stop right above her. A True Guardian walks down the stairs and notices little Freden sitting in the corner.

"Hey there. Where are your parents?"

Freden crawls over to the darkness under the stairs and hides behind Leazara.

"Please... If you help me, I'll do whatever you want."

The True Guardian looks around. He puts his weapons down and crawls underneath the stairs to help her.

"Are you... You're having a baby under here!?"

"Please just help me."

The True Guardian pushes Freden out of the way and helps Leazara breathe and push the baby out. He catches the baby and cuts the umbilical cord. He hands the baby boy over to her.

Leazara cradles the baby and softly murmurs his name.

"Dretzlin."

The True Guardian stands, staring at them in shock.

"I can't believe I just helped deliver a baby. What are we supposed to do now? I can't just leave you here like this."

Leazara starts to close her eyes.

"You have to take them... Say you found them together and leave me here to die."

The True Guardian stands over her, trying to decide.

"Damn it; I can't let these kids die. Alright, sorry to leave you here like this, lady, I'll make sure these kids have a place to grow up."

Leazara passes out as the True Guardian takes Freden and baby Dretzlin. He runs down the street, not wanting to further risk the chance of anyone seeing him. He enters the house where his wife is waiting for him.

"Honey, please don't be mad, but I couldn't let them die. If the other True Guardians see us, they'll kill all of us."

His wife stands up and sees him carrying a baby in one hand and a two-year-old standing behind him, holding his other hand.

"You did the right thing. Let's start packing and get out of here."

The teal light starts to flash before slowing down and going black. Tanglor and Freden regain control of their minds and shake off the weird feeling. Martonamo appears back on the screen.

"Your parents were great, Johthuns. Some don't agree with their ways, but that doesn't change who they were and what they did for their people and for you two, their sons."

Tanglor and Freden turn and look at each other. Freden jumps up and backs away.

"No, there is no possible way... You're telling me that my little brother and I were her kids this whole time? Why didn't she come for us afterward? I don't understand why she hid this from me!"

He runs back to the entrance where the door used to be and bangs on the wall with his fists.

"Martonamo, open the door and let me out!!"

The wall disappears, and Freden storms out. Tanglor turns and sees Elisin waiting for him.

"I only knew so much too, Tanglor. I am sorry you had to find out this way. Should we go after him?"

"No, he needs some time to process all of it. He's been through a lot. I can imagine how hard it would be to find all of that out. Martonamo?"

"Yes, Colonel Raff?"

"How many more of those lost history lessons do you have hidden away?"

"I have millions, but I can only access so much of it. I haven't been able to figure out why, but the stronger a bond I share with someone, the more memories I can get to. You also don't want to watch too much at once. Today was cutting it close."

"Thanks, Mart. We will be back once Freden has calmed down."

Tanglor and Elisin walk out of the cavern back toward the Great Hall. Elisin hugs her grandson.

"Get some rest. You have a big day tomorrow. The Elders want to meet with you, so you can tell them the direction you want our people to go in. They will listen to you."

She walks away, leaving him alone to think. He walks over to the podium in the great hall and looks out over the empty seats. He closes his eyes. When he opens them back up, Leazara, Tazlow, and Mezriah stand before him. He smiles at them. Teal light shines through their goggles as they smile back at Tanglor before disappearing.

# Chapter 24:
# Tralupians-The Princess of TokBellu

Queen Zuna sits on her throne, waiting. One of her new advisers, a trainer from the barracks, walks in.

"Werfon, where is the Princess?"

"I thought she was here with you already…. I will go and look for her."

Queen Zuna stands up off the throne.

"No, it's fine. Today is her birthday, which means she doesn't want to do her training. Will you accompany me through the city to find her?"

"Of course, my Queen. Lead the way."

Werfon bows as she walks down the steps past him. They leave the palace and head towards the city. Queen Zuna stops and stands next to the Great Tree for a moment; she turns to it and places her hand on the trunk.

"I miss you more and more every day…. Our daughter is a handful, and doesn't like to follow orders, sound familiar?"

The Great Tree flashes underneath her hand. She smiles and laughs.

"She's eighteen today… I wish you were here with us. She needs her father."

The light underneath her hand fades away, Zuna turns back to Werfon. He sticks his arm out for her to grab onto.

"Let's go and find the Princess."

Queen Zuna and Werfon make their way to the bustling city. Since the defeat of Tranjora and Ozem, there haven't been any more threats to TokBellu. Queen Zuna and Werfon walk past the barracks and see Tralupian soldiers vigorously training.

"Good, we need to have all of our people trained and ready to fight. We can't be surprised again."

Werfon nods his head in agreement as they continue to walk. They get to the marketplace, where Tralupians gather around a small shack with a tent covering the top of it.

"What's going on over there?"

"That is what the civilians call the Carousel."

"The Carousel?"

They walk towards it, as Werfon explains it to her.

"The Carousel is where Tralupian civilians go to blow off steam. You enter the shack, and it leads underground into a club or a bar if you will. The name, Carousel, is based on a stimulant they smoke. It enhances your thoughts and emotions. As you relax, it takes you for a ride, like a carousel. It is hard to explain since I have never done it. If the Princess is in there, she is most likely trying to use it."

The Queen gets a concerned look on her face.

"She better not be down there!"

Werfon and Queen Zuna walk into the Carousel. Inside the little shack, a staircase leads to the underground bar. Upon descent, they find themselves at a doorway covered by a cloth. A bodyguard stands in front of it.

"Codeword?"

Werfon steps to the side, revealing the Queen behind him. She steps forward.

"I am the Queen. Let me through or face your demise!"

The bodyguard, clearly intimidated, steps to the side.

"My Queen, of course. Please enter."

He bows to her as they walk through the doorway. A haze of light green smoke lingers throughout the entire bar, dimly illuminating the crowd dancing and lounging on furniture. Tall glass cylinders with hoses coming out of them sit on the tables. She can see a green substance smoldering inside that produces smoke as a Tralupians draw breath from it. Queen Zuna and Werfon glance around the hazy room looking for the Princess. They hear some commotion near the bar and look over to see the Princess arguing with the bartender.

"You need to leave! I don't care who you are. You can't have any of the Kustifil. It's not meant for underage Tralupians!"

"I am the Princess, and I just turned eighteen. Let me have some, or my mother will hear of this."

The bartender looks nervous.

"Princess Zebe? What are you doing down here?"

"Don't worry about me. Just give my friends and me some of the Kustifil!"

The bartender looks around and notices the Queen standing behind Princess Zebe.

"I…. I can't do that. I am sorry, Princess."

Zebe notices the look on the bartender's face. She turns around to see her mother and Werfon standing there.

"Mother, Werfon…. What are the two of you doing down here?"

The Queen steps closer to her.

"We were worried about you when you didn't show up for your training. We came to look for you. I didn't expect to find you here of all places…"

Zebe tries to walk past her, but Zuna grabs her arm.

"Do not walk away from me when I am talking to you. Werfon and I are worried about you, Zebe. You've been slacking off on your training and…"

"There is no need for you or Werfon to worry about me…. He isn't my father… I don't even know who my father is! I'm eighteen now, Mother. I can walk away from whoever I want to!"

Queen Zuna's face darkens with anger, as she stands to her full height.

"I AM YOUR MOTHER, AND YOU WILL NOT TALK TO ME LIKE THAT! GET BACK TO THE PALACE AT ONCE! WHEN I RETURN YOU BETTER BE WITH WERFON TRAINING! IF YOU ARE NOT, THEN YOU WILL NO LONGER BE THE PRINCESS!!"

Zebe turns around and looks to her mother. She stares back at her, thinking about what she should do. A silent moment goes by before Zebe breaks into tears and runs out of the Carousel. Queen Zuna and Werfon follow behind, she stops and turns to Werfon.

"Let her blow off some steam and then continue the training when she is ready. I need to go to the Great Tree to clear my head."

He nods his head and bows before making his way back to the palace. Queen Zuna walks back into the green, smoky room towards the bartender and sits down at one of the bar stools.

"Get me some of that, Kustifil."

The bartender walks over with one of the glass cylinders and a hose attached to it. He puts some of the gooey, green Kustifil into the bottle, followed by a lit match inside.

"There you go. Just breathe in through the hose, and it'll work its magic."

Queen Zuna grabs the hose and starts to inhale, the light green smoke forming inside the cylinder. She blows the smoke out and coughs a little.

"What is this supposed to do?"

The bartender smiles.

"Just relax and let the Kustifil do its job. Settle into your chair and try to only think of the good things that make you happy."

Queen Zuna slowly sinks into her chair with a smile on her face, as she enjoys the Kustifil.

-------------------------------------------------

Princess Zebe runs inside the palace to her chambers, slamming the door behind her. She jumps onto her bed and shoves her face into the pillows, crying. Werfon knocks on her door.

"Zebe…. Can I come in, please?"

Zebe doesn't reply. He knocks again. After a couple more knocks, she finally gets up and opens the door for him. Zebe turns around and lays back on the bed with her face covered. Werfon walks over and sits down next to her.

"I know I am not your father, but I am an adviser to your mother and your trainer…. and hopefully, your friend."

Zebe's head lifts off the pillows as she continues to listen to him.

"I have watched you grow since you were two years old. Your mother asked for my help after your father…. He would have loved you so much, Zebe. Your mother will tell you all about him when the time is right, but you can't keep fighting her. She wants what's best for you. You will be the Queen of TokBellu after she is gone."

Zebe sits up and wipes her tears away.

"What about what I want? I don't want to be Queen after her."

"You are a Wrathfin. We have never had a King or Queen that wasn't part of your family's bloodline. There would be an uprising if someone other than a Wrathfin became our leader. We wouldn't even know where to start. The Great Tree would die without the Wrathfin blood being sacrificed to it."

"I know how all the stories go, but I don't want to be Queen. I don't want to lead our people like my ancestors have done. I want to be free and explore! I have heard stories of the different species we have encountered! I want to leave TokBellu and see their worlds!"

"Your mother will never allow that. She has encountered some of those aliens herself, and more often than not, it was bad for TokBellu…."

Zebe stands up and walks over to her mirror. She pretends to put on a crown.

"I know there are good ones, too……Werfon, did you know my father?"

"I did."

"Could you tell me a little bit about him?"

Werfon walks over to her.

"I will only say that he was a great Tralupian who loved you and your mother more than anything else. He was kind, loyal, and *very* stubborn…. Your father is a topic for you and your mother to discuss, not me. I'm sure Zuna will tell you everything when she feels the time is right. But she will be reluctant to tell you about him if you keep acting up."

Zebe puts her head down.

"I know…. She is so difficult, though! She forces me to train every day and become this vision of her Greatest Tralupian. I don't want to be that!"

Werfon puts his hand on her shoulder.

"You and your mother will have to talk to each other. Be nice to her and try to do what she says. She will come around."

Werfon walks out of Zebe's chambers. Queen Zuna stands in the hallway, waiting for him.

"Did you get to speak to her?"

"I did. She is going to take a moment to regroup before coming out to train."

"Thank you, Werfon."

They enter the throne room. Zuna sits on the throne while Werfon takes a seat at the adviser's table.

"My Queen, I know it isn't my place... the Princess."

Queen Zuna leans forward, trident in hand.

"The Princess, what!?"

Werfon bows down to her.

"My apologies, Queen Zuna. I don't mean to offend you. Your daughter has told me that she doesn't want to lead after you, but I told her she needs to speak to you about this."

Queen Zuna sits back down.

"I am aware of this already. It isn't hard to figure that out with how she has been acting. I know she wants to know about her father. I don't know if I can tell her, though.

"What is keeping you from telling her about Ilikso?"

"I... I don't want her to know about the Tree yet, and that's the only way she will ever know who her father truly is."

Queen Zuna's eyes start to fill with tears.

"I don't want her to have to go through any of the things I have. That tree still gives me a bad feeling. I know Ilikso sacrificed himself to save us, meaning his spirit lives on inside like the rest of my ancestors, but there's something about how it all ended. The thing that was controlling Ozem and Zembor just disappeared back into the tree, and that was it."

"I thought Zembor's spirit said it couldn't return after Ilikso and Oryuna defeated it and regained control of the Great Tree?"

"He did say that, but I don't know. I get this weird feeling when I'm around it. I can feel Ilikso and Oryuna inside of the tree, but there is something else with them, something lurking in the background, watching."

"Have you gone back inside?"

"I haven't been able to. It's been a little over eighteen years since all of it happened, and I can't seem to find the strength to go in."

"You will soon enough, my Queen. Right now, you need to focus on your daughter. Maybe having that discussion with her will give you the strength you need to reenter the tree."

Werfon bows again to the Queen and walks back to the adviser's table. Princess Zebe ambles into the throne room and approaches her mother. She bows to her.

"Mother, I am sorry for the way I've been behaving. I was afraid you would never listen to what I want, so I thought acting out would be a good way to get your attention. I should have just spoken to you."

Queen Zuna waves her hand, encouraging her to walk up the stairs to the throne.

"I am sorry too, Zebe, I should have listened to you and tried harder to have a civilized discussion. But there is no choice when it comes to leading our people. You have no brothers or sisters, and I am afraid you never will, which brings me to your father..."

"What do you mean? Are you never going to have another King? You will still be Queen long before I have to be crowned."

"Zebe... I can't answer that question right now. Your father and I had a special connection that most don't get the chance to share with anyone. I don't think I'll ever be able to replicate that feeling again. He... He gave his life to save ours. He saved all of TokBellu."

"I don't understand... I know what love is, what connection did you and father share? And stop making this so difficult, mother. Please, just tell me who he was."

Zuna braces herself to finally tell Zebe, but they are interrupted by soldiers running into the palace. They stop and bow to the Queen and Princess.

"What reason do you have for barging in here like this?"

"We are very sorry, my Queen, but we come with an urgent message from the scouts. They found this old disc with a message on it. We were instructed to get it to you at once."

The soldiers run up the steps and hand the Queen the disc, before bowing and running out of the palace. Princess Zebe looks over her shoulder at the small disc.

"What is it?"

"Looks like it's a message from one of our older scouting ships. We haven't used these discs in about eighteen years. Close to when..."

Queen Zuna jumps off the throne and starts to walk down toward her chambers. Zebe looks at her with confusion.

"Mother? What is it?"

"Hurry and follow me!"

Zebe runs down the steps after her mother. They enter her chambers; she sits on the bed, while Zuna rummages around, searching for something.

"Where could it be... Do I even have it anymore? Here it is, scoot over!"

Zuna walks over to Zebe with a computer screen and a bundle of wires attached to it. She sits down next to her.

"What is that clunky looking thing?"

Zuna laughs.

"This is what we used to use when we were communicating with the scouts. We have since upgraded to ones that are much smaller and easier to use."

Zuna plugs the wires in and presses a button on the bottom left corner of the screen. A slot opens at the top, and she drops the small disc in; a couple of seconds go by before a Tralupian appears on the screen. The message starts to play.

"Hey there, sis. I hope everything has been well for you, Oryuna and Ilikso. I miss all of you so much! Qualt and I are having a great time, but we still haven't been able to locate his homeworld. We have searched as far as we can go, but we're running out of fuel and only have about a day's worth left. We're setting course for a small, red planet in the distance. Hopefully, we can make it there. I don't know what we will find since we haven't had any luck with the other planets we found before this. Qualt did some serious damage to these crazy, creepy crawly things on one planet—you would have loved it! I honestly don't know if this message will ever make it to you. We've traveled far from TokBellu. We passed R'Ang, and that storm was still raging away. There were all kinds of wrecked ships floating around the edge of the storm. They must've tried to get past it to save their people that were captured. Don't let any more of our people get taken by those monsters."

Qualt walks onto the screen next to Siritano.

"Hey Zuna, Ilikso, Oryuna! Miss you guys. Thanks again for everything! Siritano and I have seen amazing things in space and on some of these planets we've visited. No sentient life like you or me, but interesting things, to say the least. Like Siritano mentioned, we're about to be drifting in space with no fuel since I wasn't able to find my planet, Rembor. We won't have the exact coordinates of the small, red planet up ahead until we get there, and who knows if this message even makes it back to you guys."

Silence takes over as the two sit together on the screen, trying to keep their tears back. Qualt stands up and walks off-screen while Siritano's cheerful look turns into a grim one.

"We're going to be okay, big sis. I love the three of you and miss you so much. We will meet again someday, back on TokBellu, or in passing."

Tears start to run down his face.

"Take care of each other."

Siritano reaches forward and shuts off the transmission. Before shutting off, the year 2690 pops up on the screen. Zebe looks over to her emotional mother, tears falling from her eyes.

"Who were they? He said, sis... You never told me you had any brothers or sisters."

Queen Zuna looks to her daughter and stands up off the bed.

"Come with me. It's time you knew some of the truth."

Zebe follows her mother out of her chambers and through the palace. They walk through the doors leading to the Great Tree.

"What are we doing out here?"

Queen Zuna walks over to the ledge and sits with her feet dangling off.

"Come and sit with me. Isn't the ocean beautiful? The Great Tree gets this view all day, every day."

Zebe sits down next to her mother.

"The tree is a tree all day. It overlooks anything in front of it."

"You are correct, except this tree isn't just a tree. I have kept the stories away from you. Everything has been kept from you for your protection."

"My protection? From a tree?"

Zebe starts to laugh and stands up to look at the tree.

"Are you being serious right now? Are you trying to tell me that the Great Tree is alive and has a mind of its own?"

Zuna stands up and walks over to Zebe, standing next to the tree. She reaches her hand out and places it on the trunk.

"I had the same reaction as you when I was told the truth. I shouldn't have kept this reality from you."

An orange light appears underneath her hand. Zebe takes a step back.

"That isn't right. Step away from the tree!"

"It's okay, Zebe. There is much you need to know."

The light under her palm grows and flashes again, followed by a voice coming out from the tree.

"No, it isn't time. You have been gone for too long, and things have changed; it isn't safe here. I've been able to keep them from getting out again, but they won't stop. She can't know yet!"

Before Zuna can respond to the voice, a blast of orange light shoots out of the tree at Zebe. It surrounds and overwhelms her, knocking her unconscious. The light on the tree fades away, Zuna runs over to her daughter. She picks her up and carries her back to her room. Zuna puts her on the bed and tucks her in before leaning over and whispering into her ear.

"It was all a dream, my love."

She kisses her on the forehead and walks out of Zebe's room. She returns to the throne room, where Werfon sits at the adviser's table, waiting for her.

"Queen Zuna? What is it?"

"I'm going inside the Great Tree. It's time I faced my fears. The tree needs me, Ilikso and Oryuna need me."

Outside, Zuna looks at the Great Tree. The sun descends, while the three moons rise behind her. She walks toward the tree, pulling the trident off her back and pointing it at the trunk. She stabs it, and orange light shoots out of the tips of the trident onto the tree. Bark falls off, opening a doorway for her. She walks in, and it closes behind her. A massive battle takes place in a now-destroyed TralVent. The only building left standing is the tall bell tower behind the city. Orange Tralupian Remnants lead by Ilikso fight off orange gas clouds with dark red sparks running through them. Two familiar Tralupians float down next to Zuna as she stares in awe at the battle.

"My Queen, it is terrific to see you again."

"Yes, we never thought we would have another chance."

Queen Zuna takes her eyes off the battle and looks over her shoulder.

"This can't be! Defunis, Serel!!"

She grabs both of them and pulls them in for a hug.

"How!?"

Defunis smiles at her.

"Even though that creature created us, he used the Great Tree. So even after we were killed, our spirits returned to the tree, and our bodies were reanimated."

Serel jumps in.

"It took a little longer for our bodies to fully return because of how we were torn apart.... but we're back and can return to the palace with you after this battle concludes."

Queen Zuna smiles back to both of them.

"I would love to have the two of you back, but why do you need to wait until the battle concludes?"

"If those Broncholites win this battle, they win the war, which will allow that creature to return."

"Where did he come from?"

"We aren't sure, but we saw him travel to that tall bell tower over there multiple times. And he was always up there for a while before returning."

Zuna looks over to the tower behind the battle taking place.

"Can we get inside the tower?"

Defunis and Serel look to each other before they look back to the Queen.

"We have never been inside, but we have never tried either."

Queen Zuna lifts her trident in front of her.

"I guess it's time to find out."

She starts to walk toward the battlefield with Defunis and Serel following behind her.

-------------------------------------------------

Princess Zebe tosses and turns in her bed, dreaming about the Great Tree. Her mother stands in front of the tree with the trident, and her eyes are glowing orange. She lifts the trident and screams.

"Stay away from the Great Tree!!!"

Zebe springs forward and sits up in her bed with her eyes wide open.

"What the... I don't remember going to bed last night. That dream."

She sits thinking about her dream and how she got into bed. After a little while passes, she decides to leave her chamber and check the throne room. She arrives to an empty room; the moonlight reflects off the roof and shines down on the throne. Zebe stands quietly, staring at it as a breeze comes through the open doors behind her, gently pushing her toward the throne. She slowly walks up to it and sits down. She looks around the room and embraces the moment of silence. She gets comfortable and falls asleep.

# Chapter 25:
# Johthuns - New Beginnings

Tanglor sits atop the Great Hall, watching the Elites take their seats. He notices the Elders approaching, Tanglor and the Elites stand as they walk in. They get to the center of the Great Hall before Elisin steps forward.

"Thank you for welcoming us today. Please, everyone, take a seat."

They all sit back down as she continues to speak.

"The Elders have called this meeting with the Elites because a new day is upon the Johthuns. With the True Guardians gone, and the losses we suffered in the war, the time has come for us to move in a different direction. The Elders have always made decisions for our people, but we want that to change. The Elites have done so much for us. Tanglor, we want you to not only lead the Elites but to lead all of us. Your father was right when he wanted all the Johthuns to come together with the discovery of Martonamo. We weren't ready then, but we are now."

Tanglor walks over to the podium in front of him.

"Thank you, Elders, for calling this meeting. I am honored that you think I should lead our people, but this is not something I can do on my own. The Elites were not brought together by only me. I cannot accept the position of leading our people, but I do think we should work together and be united like my father wanted. I never met my father, but from what I have heard and seen from Martonamo, I know he would not have wanted to lead the Johthuns by himself."

The Elites and Elders begin to talk amongst themselves while Tanglor stands at the podium. Elisin quiets everyone down.

"What is it you propose we do then, Tanglor? The Elders can't be the ones making the decisions anymore. It has already taken a very long time for us to realize this."

"I am going to elect five more Colonels for the Elites. They are to be stationed at our colonies on each planet. They will act as the leaders of the Johthuns who live there. You and the Elders will still be stationed here on Joht to lead our people and communicate with the other Colonels. No matter what, we will all have a part to play in this."

"And what about you, Tanglor? What will you be doing?"

"I will not be here."

The Elites jump out of their seats in a panic, while the Elders whisper among themselves.

"Everyone, calm down. I am not abandoning you. My father did dream about uniting the Johthuns, but he also dreamt about uniting us with other intelligent creatures. We know they're out there! The Dimorians aren't the only other species. They came from outside our solar system, meaning there are other solar systems out there—other sentient life! My father intended for the Elites to be explorers with training to fight and defend themselves against enemies we ran into along the way, just like the Dimorians. With the technology Martonamo has given us, we can't just sit here and wait to be discovered by others trying to take it from us. We need to be the explorers we used to be! Please trust me. This is what I need to do."

Elisin turns to speak with the Elders. Tanglor and the Elites watch as they huddle in the center of the Great Hall. Finally, Elisin steps out of the huddle.

"Having you away from our people would make things hard, but you have earned the chance to do this. We will need the time to prepare for your departure. We also think you should take one of your Colonels with you, as well as a crew to start this Galactic Community."

Tanglor, surprised by their answer, gets a smile on his face.

"Thank you; you won't regret this decision. I will let my Colonels know of their new positions and get my crew together. The Galactic Community. I like the sound of that."

Elisin smiles back to him before exiting the Great Hall with the other Elders. The Elites leave their seats and follow behind. Tanglor wastes no time and gets on the comms to call Ashar on Thoonta.

"Ashar, how's it going? The rebuilding coming along, okay?

"Hey, Tanglor! So far, everything is going great over here. The rebuilding efforts are going faster than expected. Everyone is happy, Neliah, and I are here helping them out. How is everything going on, Joht?"

"Glad to hear it. The Elders called a meeting in the Great Hall to discuss our future."

"Good or bad?"

"Good, really good. Ashar, they approved my mission. I'm leaving on an expedition that will make history for our people!"

"Expedition? What expedition?"

"To discover the other species out there beyond our solar system. I want you to come with me, Ashar. It's what we've always dreamt of."

"Wow, Tanglor! That's amazing, but I can't go with you. Neliah is pregnant!"

Tanglor takes some time to respond.

"Tanglor, you still there?"

"Yeah, I'm here. Congratulations, Ashar. I'm happy for you and Neliah. With that being said, you two have both been promoted to Colonels of the Elites. Wait for further orders to where you'll be stationed. I'll tell the Elders to keep you two together, especially now."

"Thank you, brother. It's a hard choice for me to decline your offer."

"No need to say more, I completely understand. Tell Neliah congrats. We'll see each other before I leave."

Tanglor gets back on the comms to call Ucarus on Conril.

"Tanglor, glad to hear from you. I was just about to send you a message."

"How's everything going on, Conril?"

"Things are going great over here. Everyone's working hard to get things done. It's nice having people look to you for answers."

"Well, get used to it. You're now a Colonel of the Elites and acting leader of Conril! Stay close to your Comm for further orders."

Ucarus begins celebrating into the comms. Before turning it off, Tanglor laughs. He sits in the Great Hall for a little while, looking around at everything. He glances at the exit and sees Leazara standing there looking at him. She turns and walks into the wall where the secret cavern is. The door opens as she vanishes. Tanglor jumps to his feet and runs over to see nothing but darkness. Suddenly, teal lights start to flash down the path near the cavern. He runs down the pathway to find it open, with lights flashing around the room. The lights stop moving and hit the ground, erupting, and surrounding him. Tanglor tries to shield his eyes, but it's too bright, even with his goggles on. Finally, it disappears. Leazara, Mezriah, and Tazlow stand before him. They walk toward him and give him a hug. Tanglor embraces them.

"What is this? What's going on?"

Mezriah starts to cry.

"My son, we finally get the chance to meet. You've grown into an incredible Johthun."

Tazlow grabs his hand and puts his arm on his shoulder.

"The great Tanglor Raff, you have made me so proud. This expedition you're about to go on is crucial for our people, but you know that already. I've watched you grow up, and I've seen the things you've done. You were meant to do this."

Tanglor starts to cry with his parents. Leazara hugs him one more time.

"I'm sorry I had to keep everything from you, Tanglor. I hope you know that I love you. We all love you so much."

She stops and glances behind him.

"It's okay. Come here, my son."

Tanglor turns around to see Freden standing by the wall with his eyes wide open in shock.

"How... I don't understand."

He slowly approaches Leazara and reaches out to feel her hand.

"I am so sorry for everything, Freden. I never stopped trying to rescue you and your brother from the True Guardians. They were always watching and killed your foster parents when they found out they were helping me. I had to stop, or they were going to kill the two of you too. When you both arrived for the Elite program, I had to keep my guard up. I knew they had sent you to infiltrate our base. I wish I could have done so many things differently."

Freden starts to tear up, so she pulls him in for a hug. Tazlow walks over to them.

"Hey there, buddy. Remember me?"

Freden starts to laugh and hugs his father.

"I'm sorry, father. I wish I were more like Tanglor. Dretzlin would still be alive."

Suddenly another teal light shoots out from Martonamo's mainframe, crashing into the ground. It fades away, and Dretzlin stands before his brother. Freden runs and hugs him.

"I'm so sorry, Dretzlin. I'd take it all back or switch places with you if I could. It's my fault you're gone."

Dretzlin smiles and hugs his brother back.

"Freden, it's not your fault. None of it is. I know about everything. What our mom and dad did for us and what you did for me. I love you, Freden, and I always will. Time to get rid of that guilt."

Freden wipes his tears away and stands back, next to Tanglor. Leazara opens her hand up, revealing the second oval. It starts to rumble and glows before it flies at Freden. It phases into his right hand, just like it did with Tanglor. The pain goes through his body, and he drops to the ground. Tanglor reaches his hand out, which glows as Freden grabs it. Tazlow, Mezriah, Leazara, and Dretzlin flash and turn back into teal lights. They soar around the room, flying past Tanglor and Freden. One by one, they fly back into Martonamo's mainframe. Afterward, his face lights up on the screen.

"Mart, what just happened? How were they all here?"

"That has never happened before. I can only assume that because of the deep connection your father and I shared, his soul found me after his death. He must be guiding his loved ones here after their deaths as well. I didn't think it was possible, but he had a great love for those close to him, including me."

"Is it possible to do that again?"

"I didn't do anything, so I'm not sure. It seems as though they can hear us and see everything that I've been able to see, so I'm sure, in time of need, they'll come back."

Freden interrupts them.

"What about this oval that shot into my hand?"

He lifts it, and it starts to glow again.

"Well, it's the same as Tanglor's. You can now control doors and machines that I have control over, as well as speak to me from anywhere at any time. Because you and Tanglor both have one, you should also be able to talk to each other from anywhere. I do not know what else it does. There has only been one other time where this situation has happened. They were not nearly as cooperative or understanding as you Johthuns, though."

Freden clenches his hand into a fist and opens it back up. The light fades away.

"It is pretty cool. We'll have to figure out what else these things can do."

He looks over to Tanglor.

"I want to go with you on the expedition. I can help you, and we can try to figure out more about these things in our hands."

Tanglor reaches his hand out to him.

"Alright, Freden. Let's go and start the Galactic Community!"

Freden reaches out and grabs his hand, causing the light to shine bright again. It pulses slowly before getting faster, lighting up the cavern. The flashing stops and Tanglor and Freden are frozen, their hands locked together. Their eyes are filled with the teal light, as they stare at each other.

"Martonamo, what's going on!?"

"I don't know. I can't get control of your minds like normal."

Their surroundings start to change around them. The cavern disappears, and a shooting star flies past them. They turn to watch it soar by, eventually crashing into an asteroid. Tanglor and Freden turn in circles, surrounded by stars and planets they've never seen before. A body starts to form next to them, floating in space. They back away and watch as a face is revealed. It's Martonamo's face, but this time his face is teal, and his eyes glow dark blue. His lips are light green, and his ears point out like daggers. They watch as the rest of his body forms. He is just as tall as Tanglor and Freden, with broad shoulders and small wings on the sides of his arms and legs. His feet have four long toes with sharp nails on them. The clothes he wears look formal like he was some sort of royalty in his lifetime. A blue top with a cape and black shorts covers his torso.

"Whoa... This hasn't happened before, either."

He shakes his legs out in front of him and wiggles his arms. The wings on his arms and legs straighten, becoming sharp blades.

"I believe this is what I looked like before I got stuck in that computer. Still not remembering much else."

Tanglor and Freden walk toward him with caution. Tanglor reaches out and touches his hand.

"Martonamo... Do you know where we are, at least?"

"We are clearly in space, but I'm not sure exactly where."

He starts to walk toward two planets connected by some sort of tube. The one on the left is dark blue, and the one on the right is bright green. The tunnel connecting them is half the size of the planet and has windows across the sides. You can see creatures walking around inside of it, but it's too far to see what they look like. Martonamo starts to run toward it. Tanglor and Freden chase behind him.

"Mart! Slow down!"

Suddenly, a black hole appears next to the planet. Time starts to speed up around them, and more shooting stars soar by as they watch the black hole grow. It finally stops, but it's too late. The dark blue planet starts to break off, getting sucked into the darkness. Bodies pour out of the broken tunnel, following the planet into the black hole. The piece still connected to the bright green planet fires a missile out toward the dark abyss. A couple of seconds pass by, and it explodes, causing the planet to be pushed away from the black hole. Martonamo, Tanglor, and Freden watch as time continues to speed past them. The planet starts to lose its brightness and turns to a darker green color. Martonamo falls to the ground and screams in pain.

"Ahhhh, the memories! They hurt!"

He continues to scream and squirm around the floor before his body fades away and vanishes in front of Tanglor and Freden. With nothing else to do, they start to walk toward the green planet. Time still hasn't slowed down; the planet turns brown as they get closer. They finally stand above the dying world and notice a shimmer of teal coming from its surface. Time eventually slows back down as they approach the light. Freden and Tanglor walk on this now desolate planet. The land has completely died and buildings far more advanced than their own, are all destroyed. Tanglor looks over to Freden as they continue walking.

"It looks like war swept through here. Whatever weapons they had must've been devastating."

"Yeah, I've never seen destruction like this before."

The teal light in their hands illuminates. They see a flash of the same light coming from up ahead, followed by a loud bang. They sneak around the destroyed buildings to get a closer look. The light continues to flash, but the noise stops. Tanglor peeks his head out to see a creature like Martonamo sitting in an open field. Freden peeks out behind him.

"Wait, is that Martonamo?"

"We can't be sure. Let's keep watching."

The creature looks over in their direction; its eyes have been removed. It stands up and starts to walk over to them. Tanglor and Freden get back behind the building, trying not to make a sound. They peek back out and see the creature has stopped moving, trying to listen for them. It turns around again and speaks in a feminine voice.

"Come out. I can hear you. Please... I can't see! They took my eyes from me."

The creature falls to the ground. Tanglor walks out from behind the building.

"Tanglor, what are you doing?"

He continues to walk toward the creature, staring into the dark holes that used to be its eyes.

"See, I knew someone was there."

It stands up and walks toward him. Tanglor stops, but the creature keeps walking, going straight through him. Surprised, he turns around to see another one of the same species walking over. Freden comes out from behind the building, and it runs right through him as well. The creature yells.

"Nevrahniah, are you okay!? I'm here."

She falls into his arms.

"No, no, what did they do to you? I'm so sorry. I got here too late."

"It's not your fault. I tried to hold them off, but they were too strong. They didn't kill me, but instead took my eyes, so that I could never truly see you again."

He slams his fists onto the ground.

"They're going to pay for this. I'm sorry, Nevrahniah."

He lets go of her as she reaches out for him.

"No, Martonamo! They will kill you!"

He leans over and kisses her on the forehead.

"Wait here for me."

Martonamo walks away from her as she cries and screams for him to come back. Tanglor and Freden walk past her and follow behind Martonamo. He takes off into a sprint and jumps into the air, his wings taking him into a quick flight before a smooth glide. Tanglor and Freden try to keep up, but Martonamo separates himself by going over a mountain into some sort of coliseum. They climb after him, arriving at the top to an overlook of a massive arena. Martonamo stands in the middle with hundreds of his people surrounding him. A voice comes over the intercom as Tanglor and Freden get closer.

"It ends here, Martonamo. You and your wife can't stop us. We've already become gods and destroyed most of the life in the universe! There's nothing more you can do now. Either join us or die like the rest of them!"

"You'll never be my gods, and I'll never stop fighting you! Not after what you did to Nevrahniah!"

"If you cooperated with us, she was going to get them back, but I guess not. Here, you take them."

Two eyeballs come falling from the sky. Martonamo catches them.

"You bastard!"

He flexes his body, causing his wings to turn into blades, and rushes into the crowd.

"Don't kill him. Take him hostage!!"

Martonamo jumps over them, swinging his bladed wings down. Tanglor and Freden rush over to his aid. They pull out their blades and attempt to slash through Martonamo's enemies, but nothing happens. Martonamo is finally overwhelmed as they jump on him and hold him down. Suddenly Martonamo appears next to Tanglor and Freden again and watches his past self struggle to fight his people.

"I guess this is why I don't remember... I've put so many memories away because of how terrible they are, but it's time I start facing them to find out the truth. I think it's time we got out of here."

Tanglor and Freden put their hands onto Martonamo. They stare up at the open doors, waiting for something to come out. Light starts to flash out of Tanglor and Freden's hands, as it pulses, a massive figure flies down from the sky. It wears a hooded robe that covers its face and body. The figure starts to speak while the light flashes around the three of them. The voice is like thunder, piercing their ears. It hurts for a brief second before their surroundings start to change again. The walls around them go from the dirty arena back to the cavern. Tanglor and Freden's eyes turn back to normal, and their hands release, shooting them away from each other. Tanglor stands up and reaches his left hand out to Freden.

"We're going to have to be more careful with these ovals in our hands. You okay?"

"Yeah, thanks."

Martonamo appears on the screen with his full body. Tanglor watches with a smile on his face.

"Tazlow was right. You are alive in there."

Martonamo smiles back.

"I am. Thank you for helping me remember."

Tanglor looks back to Freden.

"We're here with you every step of the way, Mart. Freden and I have a lot more we need to see, too, and I know how hard that can be. You're not alone in this."

Martonamo stands up off the chair he's sitting on and salutes them.

"Thank you, Colonel Raff and Colonel Luns."

He opens the wall behind them.

"I think it's the first time I've said this, but I definitely need some rest after that. Come back when you can, and we can go over some more memories together."

Tanglor puts his arm around Freden, and they walk out of the cavern, shutting the door behind them.

"Tanglor. He said, Colonel Luns."

Tanglor smiles and continues to walk with Freden.

"Let's go, Colonel Luns. We've got a Galactic Community to build!"

Freden smiles back and puts his arm around Tanglor as they walk back up the path to the Great Hall.

# Chapter 26:
# Tralupians-Fifty Years

Zebe's eyes snap open at the sound of the palace doors shutting. Queen Zuna walks from the Great Tree. She has two Tralupians following behind her that Zebe has never seen.

"Zebe, get off the throne and go sleep in your bed."

Zebe rubs her eyes and looks at her mother and the two Tralupians again.

"Why are you covered in ... Is that blood? Who are they?"

Zuna looks down at herself and wipes the orange dust off her clothes.

"No, it isn't blood. Just some ash from.... Go to bed, and we will talk more in the morning."

Zebe gets up of the throne and stumbles toward her room, half asleep. Queen Zuna walks up to the throne and sits down, addressing Defunis and Serel.

"Will Ilikso and the other Remnants be okay in the Great Tree?"

Defunis sits down at the adviser's table.

"Ilikso leads the others to a victory, and you destroyed that bell in the bell tower. The portal behind the gateway can no longer be opened."

Serel sits down next to her brother.

"The bell was what opened and closed the portal behind the gateway. Without it, that creature will no longer be able to get back, but I fear that might have been our only way to find RoyalTree too."

"I know Zembor will be displeased about that, but it had to be done. We will find a different way to save RoyalTree. If he is even still alive."

Werfon walks in and notices the two advisers at the table.

"My Queen, is there something I need to know?"

"Werfon, these are my first two advisers, Defunis and Serel. They were created and then killed by that creature that was posing as Zembor and Ozem. They have since been reincarnated within the Great Tree and returned to help us."

Werfon bows to them before taking his seat.

"It is nice to meet the two of you."

Queen Zuna leaves the throne and walks to the table where they all sit.

"I need to speak to my daughter. She has too many questions that need to be answered."

The three advisers nod to her and stand up. Zebe appears behind the Queen.

"Mother? I need to know what happened last night."

The three advisers bow to the Queen and Princess, then walk out of the throne room. Queen Zuna sits down at the table, and Zebe joins her.

"I know you have questions. I am going to try to answer all of them, but I need you just to listen. Okay?"

Zebe sits back in her chair.

"You have all of my attention."

"Alright, let's start with that video message we watched yesterday. That message was from my brother, Siritano. He mentioned two other names on the transmission, Oryuna, and Ilikso. Ilikso was another brother, and Oryuna was one of my sisters. My mother had thirteen kids in total. Out of the thirteen children, I was selected to be Queen after my mother passed. At first, my siblings hated me for it, and it drove them away from my mother and me, but eventually, four of them came around. Ilikso, Siritano, Oryuna, and Musfina, all of them are dead now, except for Siritano. I sent him away on a special mission to take his friend back to his homeworld. His friend, who you saw in the video, is named Qualt—a Remori from the planet Rembor. They've been gone since before you were born and haven't returned or found Rembor as far as we know. They're either on that red planet they spoke of or dead."

"I know you said to just listen.... but how did Qualt and Siritano become friends?"

"This is where things start to get a little crazy, so just stick with me. I didn't believe any of this until I saw it for myself. Last night, when you were asleep on the throne, you asked if I had blood on me. It wasn't blood; it was the remains of these aliens called Broncholites. They're sentient life forms, but their bodies aren't like ours. They have gaseous bodies that they use to get inside other creatures and control them.

Our Great Tree was once alive and was created from one of those Broncholites. Zembor Wrathfin accidentally brought it back to TokBellu after being abducted by a mysterious ship over a thousand years ago. While he was up there, the creatures that seized him knocked him out and put a Broncholites in his head. After returning to TokBellu and figuring out something was inside of his head influencing his choices, he was able to talk to it. RoyalTree is what he was called. They lived together for close to thirty years before RoyalTree figured out a way to split from him. Zembor planted him in the ground under our ocean, allowing him to use his gaseous body to spread across TokBellu. RoyalTree grew into the Great Tree and helped our planet thrive by producing a luscious environment.

Eventually, Zembor was killed, and his spirit was absorbed by the tree. The tradition of our kin taking over as leader and ending their predecessor's life was started by Zalzatine after Zembor was killed by the Ventrians. We came to find out that RoyalTree latched onto Zembor and saved his spirit and body, but, after doing so, RoyalTree was captured by the other creatures and the Broncholites became their slaves. They killed Zembor and encased his body in a statue, preserving it for the creature's leader to take over. He stayed inside the tree as one of the Remnants and forced the other Remnants to become his slaves, turning them into dark red monsters. The Broncholites took the form of the other Remnants and started to wage war inside the Great Tree.

With RoyalTree still missing, we must continue the sacrifice and provide the Great Tree with Wrathfin blood. Otherwise, it will die and take TokBellu with it. Prophecies of the Apocalypse are always prevalent because of similar scenarios in our past. My brother, Ilikso, and sister, Oryuna, were killed in the last war against the fake King Ozem, which occurred right before your birth. They gave their lives to save yours and mine, but because they are Wrathfins, they live on as the Remnants in the Great Tree. You and I will have that honor in our passing too."

Zebe sits quietly, her eyes wide open staring at her mother.

"I know it is a lot to take in Zebe, but..."

"I don't know what to say to any of this... Why do Wrathfins have to be the ones to sacrifice ourselves?"

"It is because of the bond Zembor Wrathfin first shared with RoyalTree. RoyalTree lived inside of Zembor's body with him for over thirty years. My best guess is that they eventually shared a soul and combined their spirits as one. When RoyalTree was captured, the Great Tree started to die. Zalzatine entered the tree and discovered his father's spirit. After speaking with the Remnants inside, Zalzatine ended his reign early and made the sacrifice. The Great Tree sprung back to life and TokBellu with it. Since then, this responsibility has been passed down through our family as a shared burden. If we ever stopped, then the Great Tree would slowly die, taking TokBellu with it."

"What if we found RoyalTree and brought him back?"

"That was what Zembor was trying to do, but no one knows where he is exactly. We think he is on the planet R'Ang. That is where my brother was taken after being captured while we were inside of the Great Tree. The monsters were able to open portals that took them to their planet. Siritano was captured and placed in a cell where he met that Remori, Qualt. They barely made it out of the prison alive. Luckily, Ilikso and Oryuna entered through different portals and were able to save them. It is a story I don't know the full truth to since I wasn't there."

"That's that planet Siritano was talking about on the transmission. It was the one with that storm circling it."

"And that is the reason we can't get back there without a portal...but, since I destroyed the bell that accessed the gateway in the bell tower, I don't think any more portals will be opening up anytime soon."

"Is there any way for us to replicate the portals ourselves? If this RoyalTree had that much influence on us, then we need to try to save him if we can."

"We all feel the same way about it, Zebe, but it's not that simple. There is still more for you to learn from the Great Tree, and from Werfon and me. But before I tell you, you have to promise me that you will listen to what I say and go through your training and studies like before."

Zebe stands up and bows to her mother.

"I am sorry for acting the way I have lately. I just wish you would have told me all of this sooner. I will promise under one condition."

Queen Zuna stands up next to her.

"What is this one condition?"

"You have to promise me something too. When I show you that I'm the best and finish top in my class—you have to tell me everything about my father."

Queen Zuna turns her back to Zebe and walks toward the throne.

"I…. I promise. I will tell you everything about your father once you finish at the top of your class. The next fifty years are going to be rigorous and painful, but you will learn everything you need to know about leading our people and the secrets that have been stowed away from the public."

Zebe smiles warmly at her mother.

"Thank you; I will work hard and prove to you that I deserve to know who he is. Mother, I hope you know this doesn't change my mind on how I feel about being Queen."

"I know, Zebe…. Go and get ready for your training with Werfon."

Zebe heads back to her room. Defunis and Serel re-enter and sit at the adviser's table.

"Zebe took it really well. I think she is going to turn things around and focus on her training and classes again."

Defunis stands up.

"That is great to hear, that will surely make things easier for us."

Queen Zuna stands up.

"Us? What do you mean?"

Serel stands up behind Defunis; their eyes flash orange at the Queen.

"It will be much easier for us to do what we want with the Princess busy."

Queen Zuna pulls her trident out, but it is too late. Her adviser's eyes continue to flash orange at her. She falls to the ground, trying to crawl back on the throne.

"How...that orange cloud isn't inside of me anymore. He's gone.... This can't be possible."

Defunis and Serel walk behind her as she continues to crawl toward the throne.

"Did all of the cloud make it out of your body? Even the tiniest amount gives us a small amount of control over you..."

Serel reaches down and helps the Queen on the throne.

"You're right, though. He is no longer here and you destroying the bell makes it, so we are safe from him and in control of you!"

Tears run down the Queen's face as Serel and Defunis help her onto the throne.

"Why are you doing this? I loved the two of you. When I watched you get torn apart..."

Defunis starts to walk away from her and Serel.

"I am sorry for that, my Queen, but we have no remorse. We watched from inside the Great Tree and saw everything. We saw how you and your people acted, as well as Ozem and the Remnants inside. It's all a big mess! Serel and I are going to be the ones to fix it. I mean, we are technically Tralupians since we were created this way."

Serel takes her hand off Queen Zuna and turns away from her.

"I.... I am sorry, Zuna, but we can't sit back and watch this continue. TokBellu needs us to be more than advisers. We're going to lead TokBellu back to greatness through you. We won't be able to fully control your body like Ozem, but we will have influence over you, we will be voices in your head at all times. It will take some getting used to."

Defunis and Serel sit back down at the adviser's table while Zuna sits on the throne, crying. They stare at her, and their eyes flash again.

"Stop crying and wipe those tears away... You are a Queen!"

Queen Zuna sits up and immediately stops crying. She wipes her tears away, and her eyes flash orange at the two advisers as she stands up.

"Sorry, but this overwhelming feeling of fatigue just came over me. I'm going to go and get some rest. Come and get me if there is anything I am needed for."

Defunis and Serel watch her walk to her chambers. Defunis has a smile on his face while Serel sits with a worried look on hers.

---------------------------------------------------

The sun rises above the Great Tree overlooking the ocean, as a breeze blows through the window onto the sleeping Queen. Werfon rushes into the room and wakes her.

"It's a big day! Zebe is graduating as number one in her class. She beat out every other warrior yesterday by a landslide!"

Queen Zuna opens her eyes and rolls over to look at him.

"It is still so early. Why do you insist on waking me up like this?"

Werfon laughs as he opens the curtains, letting the sunlight in.

"Because you can't miss your daughter's big day! She has worked very hard every single day for the last fifty years. The least you could do is be enthusiastic about it!"

She rolls out of bed and starts to get ready.

"I am enthusiastic about it, just still half asleep. I will get my things together and meet you and the others in the throne room. We can head to the barracks together to see her graduation ceremony."

"Do you want me to get Zaren and Zelray, or would you like them to stay in the barracks and wait for us there?"

"They are old enough to live in the barracks now. They can wait there for their sister's ceremony."

"Then, I will await you in the throne room with Defunis and Serel."

Werfon bows to the Queen and walks out of her chambers. She finishes getting ready and makes her way to the throne room. Defunis, Serel, and Werfon all wait for her.

"I want to stop by the Great Tree before going to the barracks."

The three advisers bow to their Queen and follow her out of the palace to the Great Tree. They stand behind her as she approaches it. She pulls her trident out and places the tip of it against the tree's trunk. Orange sparks shoot out from the tree and the trident, opening a doorway. Zuna doesn't step through. Instead, Ilikso appears.

"My Queen, I am glad to see you."

She reaches out and touches his transparent orange body.

"I am always happy to see you. Our daughter is graduating today—top of her class. That means it's time to finally tell her about you."

"I have watched her grow up into a great Tralupian. Telling her about me should have happened long ago. Zuna, I have waited almost seventy years to meet her."

"I know. I am sorry, Ilikso. It's been hard without you. I tried to remarry and had two more children, but it didn't help. I miss you more and more every day. I know if I tell Zebe the truth, she will resent me for not letting her see you sooner."

"It wasn't safe for her to enter the Great Tree, and it still isn't. Zembor has been working nonstop to try and find a way to open a portal to R'Ang. His obsession with saving RoyalTree won't falter. He is convinced that if we save RoyalTree and bring him back, all of us can be brought back to life. He thinks RoyalTree will stay inside the Great Tree and help TokBellu prosper like before."

"That's why you haven't been letting me inside? You have to be honest with me about everything with the Great Tree!"

"I don't want you or Zebe coming inside the Great Tree until Zembor gives up on trying to save RoyalTree. He has been gone for too long, and we don't know if he is even alive. Plus, if you were in here, you would be working just as hard with Zembor to try and bring me and everyone back."

Queen Zuna puts her head down.

"You are right…. If there is a chance to bring you and the others back, why would I not try to do that?"

"None of us know if what Zembor says is even true… There is too much you would have to sacrifice to accomplish that. By the time you did, you wouldn't be yourself anymore. Do not concern yourself with it, Zuna. I will take care of things inside the tree as I have been for the last 68 years. Just remember that I love you and Zebe both so much. I am so proud of her… and you."

Ilikso reaches out to Zuna and places his hand on her shoulder before he fades away. Zuna takes the trident off the tree, and the doorway closes. She turns around and looks at her advisers.

"Ready to go?"

They all nod their heads and lead the way to the barracks with Queen Zuna following. When they arrive, they see Tralupians crowding the entrance, trying to get in to witness the graduation ceremony. This Tralupian ceremony is one of the most exciting things to see in the city, the students that have proved themselves take the next step in becoming warriors. The ritual consists of them engaging and testing the skills they have learned in a final free-for-all of intellect and strength. Since Princess Zebe is one of the warriors, all of TokBellu has come to watch the battle. As Queen Zuna and her advisers approach the barracks, the crowd of Tralupians steps out of their way, revealing the entryway. Queen Zuna is welcomed by the trainers and soldiers inside. They escort her to a tall chair overlooking the circular arena known as the Vigorous Halo. Inside, the warriors are ready and waiting. Princess Zebe stands by herself since she is number one in her class and will be tested more than the others. The other seven warriors scatter throughout the rest of the arena—the barracks instructor strides over to stand next to the Queen.

"My Queen, when you are ready for the ceremony to start, lift your trident high into the air."

Queen Zuna nods her head. She wastes no time and lifts her trident above her, looking around at the warriors in the Halo. They all stand poised to attack with their weapons ready. Zuna raises the trident even higher and yells.

"Begin the ceremony!"

She tosses her trident down into the middle of the Vigorous Halo, signaling the eight warriors to run to the sides of the arena, grabbing different weapons. Zebe glances up at her mother before rolling out to the middle of the Halo and grabbing the trident. As she grabs it, she gets surrounded by the other seven warriors. She looks around with a smile on her face.

"You can all attack me if you want, but it isn't going to end well."

They look to each other nervously before one of them decides to attack. Zebe twirls the trident above her as she steps to the side, dodging the attack. She whips the back end of the trident around, clubbing him. He stumbles back and smacks into the wall, knocking himself unconscious. Zebe laughs as she looks at the other six.

"Hopefully, the rest of you are more capable than him."

Zebe charges at two of the warriors standing together. She swings the trident underneath them, knocking them both to the ground. She jumps in the air as another warrior slides at her. As she's above her, Zebe slams the butt end of the trident down on her face, knocking her out. The two on the ground get up, but Zebe spins the trident in front of her, creating a gust of wind knocking them back into the wall. The three remaining warriors stand together with their blades drawn. They start to slowly walk toward her, as she stands smiling with the Trident pointing at them.

"Come on, let's get this over with!"

Zebe takes the trident and throws it at them. It lands short, piercing the ground in front of them. It sticks up as one of the warriors walks past it.

"Smart move. Now you have no weapon."

Zebe's smile never wavers.

"We'll see about that."

The warrior charges at her swinging his blade. Zebe sticks her arm out, stopping his attack. He looks at her smile as she takes her other fist and punches him in the face. He falls backward onto the ground. The other two warriors stand back behind the trident, still sticking out of the dirt. Zebe charges at them, jumping and grabbing onto it, as she uses her momentum to swing around it and kick one of the warriors to the dirt. She whips the trident around her hitting the other one in the side of the head. The last warrior tries to crawl to his blade, but Zebe walks over and steps on him, pushing him back to the ground. As she stands with her foot on the last warrior, she lifts the trident into the air and lets out a scream.

"AAAAHHHHHHHH!"

Queen Zuna stands up and starts to clap. The rest of the Tralupians surrounding the Vigorous Halo join the Queen and clap with her. Zebe reaches down and helps the other warrior up. He takes her hand.

"You fought well, Zebe. No one even came close to touching you."

"Thank you, Jarelen. I've worked my whole life for this moment."

Jarelen and Zebe walk around the rest of the Halo, helping the other warriors up. The instructor and Queen walk into the Vigorous Halo over to Zebe and Jarelen. The Queen takes the trident from Zebe and raises her hand into the air. The crowd cheers again. Zebe grabs Jarelen's arm and raises it with hers.

"You fought well too, Jarelen, just not better than me."

The two exchange smiles while the crowd continues to cheer for the Princess. They bow before Jarelen, and the other warriors are escorted out of the arena. The Queen, instructor, and Zebe are left standing in the middle. Queen Zuna quiets the crowd down.

"I want to start by thanking everyone for coming today to support my daughter and the other warriors. Our ceremony has concluded, and though all the warriors fought well, Zebe Wrathfin is the victor!"

The crowd breaks into a roar before quieting down to listen to the Queen.

"Today, it is with great honor that I am able to announce Princess Zebe as our greatest warrior! She has made me so proud while continuing her path to becoming the greatest Tralupian in our history. At only sixty-eight years of age, she is the youngest Tralupian to finish number one in her class—breaking all the records previously held by Mazray Wrathfin."

The crowd cheers again as Zebe steps forward.

"Thank you, everyone, for your support. I have worked very hard to achieve this. I am grateful and honored to be your Greatest Warrior, but I am afraid to say that I don't wish to keep this title. I have decided that I will advise my mother while readying myself to be the Queen."

Queen Zuna notices Zebe's face turn from joyful to sorrow. She steps in front of her daughter.

"That concludes the ceremony. Please give our warriors space while they regroup and get some rest."

She turns back around to Zebe, who is trying to keep back her tears.

"Zebe, what's wrong? You should be happy. All of your hard work has paid off."

"I... I don't want to follow in your footsteps, mother. The things you have made me do have been tough. My only brother and sister are stuck here in the barracks because of me and your law. I can't stand the way things are!"

Before her mother can respond, Zebe turns on her heel and runs out of the barracks back toward the palace. Queen Zuna watches her leave but stays. Her other daughter and son, twelve-year-old twins, run over to her.

"Mother! Zebe was awesome!"

Queen Zuna pays little attention to them.

"Yes, your sister was great today. How has training in the barracks been?"

Zaren shoves her brother out of the way.

"We hate it here! Why can't we come back home to the palace to live with you and Zebe?"

"The two of you lost to your older sister. I can't make an exception to the law, or our citizens will riot. I can't risk destroying our planet. I am sorry."

Queen Zuna walks away from her son and daughter, leaving the arena. She makes her way back to the palace. As she approaches it, she sees Zebe standing in front of the Great Tree.

"Zebe.... We need to talk."

She turns to her mother, an intense look in her eyes.

"You have to hold up your end of our agreement. I graduated top of my class and have done everything you have asked of me for the last fifty years. I beat my brother and sister out of the family and sent them to the barracks. Tell me who my father is."

Queen Zuna approaches her daughter and stands next to her.

"I'm not going to tell you about him..."

Zebe, visibly irritated, opens her mouth to yell, but Zuna continues.

"I will show you. He'll be thrilled."

Zebe now wears a confused look on her face as Queen Zuna pulls the trident off her back and approaches the Great Tree. She points the tip of it at the tree; orange sparks fly off the trident. As she pierces the trunk of the tree, it shoots sparks back and opens a doorway. Queen Zuna turns to Zebe and reaches her hand out to hers.

"Come, your father is in there."

Zebe grabs her mother's hand and follows her into the Great Tree. She gazes around in awe as various orange colors surround them inside the hollow tree. Zuna stands still with her trident. She looks up and yells out.

"I know you didn't want us to come and see you, but we had to... our daughter had to."

A couple of seconds pass before an orange city starts to appear in front of them.

"The city of TralVent? No one knew where it disappeared to, and it's been inside the Great Tree all along!?"

"Yes, but we still aren't sure how it happened to get here. Without RoyalTree around, the history of the Great Tree has been altered; it is hard to know what truly happened."

As they are talking, a transparent Tralupian walks out of the city toward them.

"Queen Zuna, what are you doing here? I told you it wasn't safe for you and Princess Zebe to be here."

"It is okay, Ilikso. We won't be here long. She needs to know."

Queen Zuna walks over and stands next to Ilikso. Zebe stands in front of them.

"What's going on? This is your brother, Ilikso?"

"It is. He was one of my brothers, but he is also.... "

Ilikso steps forward.

"It's okay. I want to tell her."

"Tell me what?"

"Zebe, your mother hasn't told you about your father, well, because of how complicated things were..."

Zebe gets closer to them and continues to listen.

"You are my daughter, our daughter. Your mother and I fell in love despite us being brother and sister. Yes, it is different than most Tralupians, but there was nothing against us being together. Your mother and I fought for our love, and to free TokBellu from King Ozem. When it was over, your mother was supposed to give her life to save the Great Tree and TokBellu. Because I am her brother, I also have the Wrathfin blood that was needed, so I decided to make the sacrifice instead of your mother. I couldn't let you and her die. You weren't even born yet."

Zebe starts to tear up as she stands still, listening to the story. Zuna tears up as well as Iikso walks over and puts his arms around her.

"My sweet daughter, I have watched you grow up. I have seen everything you've done, how you've acted. You've grown into a great Tralupian and just know that I am always with you and have always been with you your whole life. I love you, Zebe."

Zebe hugs her transparent father back.

"I always got this weird feeling around the Great Tree...It must've been you that I was feeling. I always sensed you were around, but never knew who you were. I am glad to finally know the truth. It doesn't matter to me that you're my mother's brother. You're my father, and you loved her. That is all that matters to me. I am eager to get to know you more now that I know who you are."

Iikso frowns.

"I don't know if that can happen any time soon. There is still danger inside the Great Tree. It has a chance to get out if I'm not careful. That is why the Great Tree must stay closed until we destroy the last remaining evil."

Queen Zuna wipes her tears and walks back to her daughter.

"What do you mean? What little bit of evil still resides here?"

"We aren't sure, but it is very faint. I am still not sure if the evil has leaked outside or not."

Zuna's eyes open wide as she thinks about Defunis and Serel. Before she can say anything, the tree starts to shake. Zebe looks around.

"What's going on?"

Iikso looks back to the city and sees Oryuna running out to them.

"Sorry for the interruption, but something is going on outside of the tree. The two of you need to go at once."

Queen Zuna and Zebe say a hasty goodbye to Iikso and make their way to the exit. Zebe turns around and looks at her father one last time as the doorway shuts. Soldiers run over to them.

"My Queen! Our scouts in orbit say there is a spaceship approaching us. It isn't one of ours."

Queen Zuna turns to Zebe.

"We need to get to the control panel next to my chambers. If they're friendly, we should be able to get a transmission through to them."

Queen Zuna and Zebe run to the control panel. Zuna sits down as Zebe stands to the side of her. The Queen hits a button on the right side of the screen, requesting a video transmission with the ship. After a few seconds, the vessel accepts, opening the communication line. A creature with metallic black eyes looks back at her.

"Greetings, my name is Zuna Wrathfin. I am the leader of the Tralupians. Who are you, and why have you come to TokBellu?"

"Hello Zuna, my name is Tanglor Raff, and I am one of the leaders of the Johthuns. We came to TokBellu looking for other sentient life, like us, to start a community—a Galactic Community. We have no interest in war or stealing from you. We just want to share our knowledge and perhaps gather more."

Queen Zuna turns to her daughter.

"Go down to the landing bay. You will be the first one to meet them. Bring them back to the palace so that we can talk."

Zebe nods her head and leaves the control room, as Zuna turns back to the video transmission.

"My guards will lead you down to the surface, my daughter, Zebe, will welcome you. She will also escort you to the palace so we can meet face to face."

"Thank you, Zuna. I look forward to meeting you and the other Tralupians."

The transmission ends, Zuna sits back with a worried look on her face. As she gets up to leave, Defunis walks in. He looks at her with his eyes glowing orange.

"Don't forget about the prophecy—dark black eyes! I know you saw them too...."

Zuna's eyes flash orange as she stares back at him.

"The Apocalypse...."

# Chapter 27:
# Johthun-A Historic Launch

Close to a year of preparation has gone into Tanglor's expedition plans. Today is finally launch day. Tanglor sits in the Great Hall, talking with his Colonels and the Elders.

"Ashar is acting Commander until I get back. He and Neliah will move back to Joht. Ucarus will go to Thoonta, and our newly appointed Colonel, Mac-Ran, will be placed on Conril. The Elders will be positioned throughout the different colonies to assist our Colonels. Freden and I are ready for this expedition, and we aren't coming back until we find other life out there. Elisin, did our scientists upgrade the ships?"

"They are working on our other ships, but your ship is ready, Commander Raff."

Ashar approaches Tanglor.

"Be safe out there and come back home to us. Ezmariah needs her uncle."

Neliah walks over with their daughter in her arms.

"We will miss you, Tanglor. Come back safe."

They hug him; he kisses Ezmariah on her forehead before following Freden and Elisin out of the Great Hall to the docking bay. Elisin talks as they walk.

"Your ship can now successfully travel out of our solar system and into other ones with no issues. We upgraded your blasters to the lasers that the Dimorians shared with us. We also put some of their special metal Ucarus and Freden stole inside and on your armor. You should be able to understand any sentient life you run into with that. Your shields have been upgraded to the best we have. All that's missing is a name for her."

"Hmmm, let me think. Any ideas, Freden?"

Freden gets an excited look on his face.

"Yeah, I have a couple of ideas. How about the Mercurana, or the Bravadier?"

Elisin answers before Tanglor can.

"The Mercurana suits her. Oh yes, one more thing. Martonamo has control of the ship. He can pilot and provide you with whatever information you normally get from him."

Martonamo jumps in via the ovals in Tanglor and Freden's hands.

"I am very excited to go on this expedition with the two of you. If there is anything you need from me while we are out there, let me know."

They approach the Mercurana. It sits towering over the other ships around it. It has blue and black covering the outer exterior, and its wings are short and slick, allowing it to maneuver easier. Elisin stops in front of it.

"We put in a bigger engine and added propulsion systems to give it more speed and a big boost when you need it. It has cloaking like the rest of our ships, but still only for thirty minutes before needing to be recharged. We also installed a battery to go along with the fuel system, giving you the ability to travel further between re-fuels."

Freden runs on board while Tanglor talks to Elisin.

"This is incredible. Thank you, Elisin."

"We told you we were going to give you the best we had. We have a crew set and ready to go. They're all at their posts waiting for your order. There's no specific area for you to go since we haven't been outside the solar system. It's all your call, Tanglor."

He nods his head and hugs her.

"Thank you again. Thank the rest of the Elders and all the Johthuns that helped do this."

Tanglor walks onto the Mercurana to settle in. Freden sits up front where the pilot controls are.

"I'm going to hang out up here with Mart."

Martonamo appears on the screen. He flashes the bright teal light, and a hologram of Martonamo comes out and sits next to Freden.

"I will be here with Freden until you need me."

The two of them converse as Tanglor walks through the massive ship filled with Johthuns. They all stare and salute their commander as he walks by. He stops and pulls his hand up to his face.

"Martonamo, can you patch me through to the intercom of the ship?"

"Sure thing. You're all set."

"This is Commander Raff. I am grateful to all of you for signing up for this expedition. I need you to treat me as an equal and not as your superior—no need to salute me or stop what you're doing because I walk by. If you want to talk to me, just say hi. Thank you. Now everyone, continue what they were doing. We take off in 30 minutes."

His crew goes back to getting the Mercurana ready. Outside of the ship, thousands of Johthuns gather to watch the launch. Tanglor walks out the door with Freden while waving to all the Johthuns cheering. Everyone knows how vital this expedition could be for their people. History is being made for the Johthuns. The celebration continues as the timer drops closer to zero. With a minute left, Tanglor and Freden get into the ship and close the door. They sit in the front next to the projection of Martonamo controlling the vessel.

"Commander, Colonel, are you ready for launch?"

"We're ready."

The Mercurana starts its take-off. The Johthuns outside shoot off fireworks as the ship begins to float into the air, leaving a smoke trail behind it. It gets far enough up, and Martonamo engages the thrusters, launching them up toward orbit. The Mercurana is much faster than the other Johthun ships. It flies past Thoonta in no time, making its way toward Conril and the outskirts of their solar system.

"Martonamo, what do we do when we get to the outer edge of our solar system?"

"From what I understand, we can open up small wormholes allowing us to travel through them before they close. That will take us out of our solar system, putting us into the galaxy. "

Freden looks over to Martonamo, confused.

"I keep hearing all of you talk about this new community we're building by saying galactic, is it the same as galaxy?"

"They are similar; galactic comes from the word galaxy. Freden, we are all part of the universe. The universe is made up of galaxies that contain solar systems. The inside of each solar system contains suns, planets, moons, and asteroids as well."

Tanglor stands up with amazement in his eyes.

"Do you know how many galaxies there are in the universe?"

Freden laughs.

"You mean you didn't know what it meant either? You acted like you did when Elisin said it."

Tanglor embarrassed laughs with him.

"It sounded cool, and I didn't want everyone there to know! Mart, please keep talking."

Martonamo smiles at the two of them.

"From the extensive knowledge my people gained, we know there are hundreds of billions of galaxies in the universe."

Tanglor turns back to him.

"That's unbelievable! What galaxy are we in and how many solar systems are there in ours?

"From what I can see, we are in Barnard's Galaxy. It is unknown how many solar systems are here, though."

"Barnard's Galaxy... This is fascinating, Mart!"

"Isn't it, though! Thank you again for letting me come with you on this expedition. I am eager to gather more knowledge."

They arrive at the outer edge of their solar system. Martonamo readies the blaster.

"What's the blaster for?"

"This is a special blaster. It shoots out the material that will make the wormhole, but we have to be quick and get inside the opening before it closes. Once we are inside, there will be different paths for us to take. I won't know where any of them lead until we go through them."

Tanglor gets on the Mercurana's intercom.

"This is Commander Raff; prepare to jump through a wormhole. No Johthun has ever done this, so we don't know what to expect. Make sure you're strapped in and holding on. Here we go!"

The Mercurana shoots a beam out in front of them, opening a wormhole, they fly inside before it disappears. The interior of the wormhole is a yellow and orange cylinder with a light circling it. The Mercurana flies toward a gap in the cylinder. They see several different paths surrounding them, leading to other solar systems. Martonamo marks their solar system as Fruyistia.

"Which way shall we go, Tanglor?"

Tanglor looks out the window as they sit in the middle of the wormhole.

"Let's take the first path to the right."

Martonamo pilots the Mercurana to the right, down the closest path. They get to the end and fire the blaster, opening the wormhole. They fly through and come out in another solar system. They look around, it doesn't look much different, except the variety of planets around them. Martonamo pulls up a map on the screen.

"Here is where all of the planets are located. We can call this solar system, Bravadier."

Martonamo turns and smiles at Freden.

"Bravadier sounds good to me, Mart. Tanglor, which planet do you want to visit first?"

He looks at the map and sees a small purple planet close to the Mercurana.

"Let's just check out that first one right there."

Martonamo pilots the ship over to the planet, where they enter the atmosphere and land on the surface. Tanglor and Freden activate their masks and take a team out of the ship. A town is spotted up ahead. Before they start walking, Martonamo drops out one of their ground vehicles.

"Tanglor, you and your grounds team should use the Tadrul to get there quicker."

The grounds team hops into the Tadrul. It has a circle-shaped metal frame with four wheels on the bottom of it. They drive it over to the town but can't find any signs of existing sentient life. Tanglor exits the Tadrul with Freden following behind. They look around at the still-standing buildings.

"There used to be sentient life here."

Tanglor bends down and picks up a small piece of clothing.

"Something happened...."

They continue to search around, as Tanglor orders his crew to send out more ground teams across the planet's surface. They all come back with the same report—cities and towns with perfectly constructed buildings, but no occupants. Whoever lived on this planet left without taking any of their belongings or food with them, they stop searching and head back to the Mercurana. Martonamo pilots the ship back into orbit, ready to check out the next planet.

A couple of years go by, filled with nothing but ruins of abandoned cities. They have journeyed back into the wormhole and searched through five different solar systems. There is one remaining planet on the edge of the current solar system they're exploring. This solar system is called Varilleon. Tanglor and Freden walk on the surface of the planet they named Vandar, looking for some sort of life. As they are walking, they see a pond with glistening water in it.

"Tanglor, look! Water! There has to be life somewhere on this planet."

Tanglor runs over to the pond of water and looks inside to see little animals swimming around. He reaches down and cups one in his hand.

"Martonamo, can you tell me anything about these creatures?"

The oval in Tanglor's hand flashes, and Martonamo responds.

"These creatures are called Furgorlons. They are thousands of years from being sentient."

Tanglor releases the Furgorlon back into the pond. He gets up and notices more buildings in ruins.

"Come on, Freden. Let's go and check out another destroyed city."

Freden follows behind him.

"Tanglor, this looks different from the rest of the ones we've seen. This city looks like it was pillaged and scavenged. There's some dried blood on the doors to these houses."

Tanglor takes a closer look and sees the same thing as Freden. He stops and walks toward one of the damaged buildings. Freden walks closely behind him, looking into the house. They get inside and see more dried blood on the floor with bones scattered around. Freden reaches down and grabs one of the bones. His hand starts to flash.

"Uhhh, Mart, what's happening?"

"Freden put it down!"

Tanglor reaches out to smack the bone out of Freden's hand, but, as it gets closer, Tanglor's hand lights up too. The light fades away as Tanglor and Freden stand, staring at each other, both holding the bone. Their hands suddenly start to pulse the teal light.

"Not again."

Their eyes flash teal, and their surroundings begin to morph. The house on Vandar is restored, a group of Furgorlons walks in, looking much different than the life forms in the pond. They are more prominent with yellow skin and stand upright on two legs with their arms sprouting out the sides of its torso. Their eyes stick up out of their heads like an antenna. They begin to speak in a language that Tanglor and Freden can't understand, even with the scales on their suits.

"Urlonk trabah ta budock!"

The Furgorlons cheer and pull out spears and clubs, as they walk out of the house. Tanglor clenches his hand into a fist and talks into it.

"Martonamo, can you translate what they said?"

Martonamo appears next to them.

"I cannot... I'm not sure why. For some reason, we are picking up a flashback from those bones."

"Must be those Furgorlons we just saw. Something is about to kill them."

They walk out of the house to see the Furgorlons gathering in the center of their city, looking up into the sky. A mysterious metallic ship appears above them, covering the city. They yell and throw their spears at it. When its doors open, the Furgorlons retreat and run back into their houses. Tanglor, Freden, and Martonamo watch as a giant dark figure exits the ship. It's wearing a robe and hood to cover its face and body, just like the one from Martonamo's flashback. It starts to speak in the same language as the Furgorlons, its voice thundering over the city, causing buildings to collapse. Bright green eyes glow underneath its hood.

"URLONK TRABAH TA BUDOCK DAS BAHNDAL!!!!"

The massive figure lands on the ground and walks to the homes full of cowering aliens. Each step causes the ground to rumble and the structures to shake. Martonamo takes Tanglor and Freden up into the sky for a better view. The massive figure starts to rip off the roofs to the buildings, pulling Furgorlons out and devouring them. After getting its fill, it walks back toward the center of the town. It stops and stomps its foot onto the ground causing it to collapse completely. It slowly floats back to the ship hovering in the sky. The Furgorlons come out of their houses to survey the destruction when suddenly the ground starts to tremble. Giant beasts with the same bright green eyes rise from the dirt. They have four long legs, and sharp teeth fill their mouths. They easily outrun any of the escaping aliens and devour them. After all the Furgorlons are consumed, the beasts disappear back into the dirt, leaving nothing but blood and bones behind. The metallic ship vanishes with a thunderous roar.

Time speeds back up, returning the explorers to the present. The bone drops out of Tanglor and Freden's hands, and the teal light fades away.

"We need to get back to the Mercurana and get out of here before whatever that thing was comes back."

Freden follows Tanglor back to the ship, where they sit in the front with Martonamo. Tanglor looks over to him.

"We've seen that thing twice now, once in your flashback and again in the Furgorlons' flashback. What is it?"

"From what I can remember, I've seen it a few times before. That wasn't the only one."

"What? There's more of those things?"

"I can't be sure...my memories aren't clear enough.

"It's okay, Mart. Let's get back to the wormhole and jump into another solar system."

The Mercurana shoots out another beam, leaving Varilleon for another solar system. This one is called Runsillya. Tanglor looks at the map and sees a promising looking planet toward the middle of the galaxy. It has a lot of water visible from orbit.

"We should stop on that planet over there. We had good luck on the last planet with water. Let's hope it's not the same situation as the Furgorlons, though."

The Mercurana flies down to the planet where, surprisingly, they are immediately greeted by an alien species. A video call comes on throughout the Mercurana's comm system. Tanglor opens it to see a face with aquatic features on the screen. It has eyes with two pupils, webbed hands and feet, and ears like a fin. There are slits on the sides of its neck, and it has a long tail with three fins at the end of it.

"Greetings, my name is Zuna Wrathfin. I am the leader of the Tralupians. Who are you, and why have you come to TokBellu?"

Tanglor turns the camera on so that she can see him too.

"Hello Zuna, my name is Tanglor Raff, and I am one of the leaders of the Johthuns. We came to TokBellu looking for other sentient life to start a community with. A Galactic Community. We have no interest in war or stealing from you. We just want to share our knowledge and possibly gather more."

"My guards will lead you down to the surface, where my daughter, Zebe, will welcome you. She will escort you to the palace so we can meet face to face."

"Thank you, Zuna. I look forward to meeting you and the Tralupians."

They turn the video comms off, Tanglor looks over to Freden.

"Tanglor, you did it. You found others."

"No, Freden, *we* found others."

Tanglor grabs the intercom to the Mercurana.

"Everyone listen up. We are approaching TokBellu, home to a species called the Tralupians. I just spoke to their leader, and we have safe passage. We are putting our trust into the Tralupians and starting the Galactic Community."

He turns the intercom off as they land on the surface. Water flows around them; they see Tralupians swimming and walking around the enormous city. Massive trees grow from the water up into the sky. A Tralupian stands, waiting for them as they exit their ship.

"You must be Tanglor Raff. I am Zebe Wrathfin. My mother told me to expect you."

"It is my pleasure to meet you, Zebe Wrathfin."

He reaches his hand out, shaking hers.

"Follow me through the city. I will take you to my mother's palace."

Tanglor and Freden follow Zebe through the city. Meanwhile, their crew exits the ship to be greeted by other Tralupians. As they walk through the city, Zebe continues to talk.

"So, my mother said you and your crew managed to discover us on your travels?"

"Yes, we have been traveling throughout the galaxy for the past four years. We just jumped into your solar system, Runsillya, this morning."

"We knew there were other species out there, but we had no idea about the other solar systems... We didn't know ours was called Runsillya. There is so much more we need to talk about and a lot I can tell you about our people too. My mother would kill me if I didn't take you straight to her first, though."

Tanglor, excited by Zebe's words, follows her close and continues to chat as they walk to the palace. Freden watches Tanglor talk with Zebe as he follows behind. They arrive at the palace to be escorted inside by Tralupian soldiers. They walk in to see Zuna Wrathfin sitting on a golden throne, the tallest thing in the room. A staircase leads up to where she sits.

"Please come in and take a seat."

She points down to some seats at the bottom of the stairs. Tanglor and Freden sit down, looking up at her. Zebe stands next to Tanglor.

"It is an honor to be welcomed onto your planet and into your home. We are here extending an offer for you and the Tralupians to join our newly formed Galactic Community. We want to share our knowledge and expand our cultures with the other species out there."

Zuna stands up and walks down the stairway toward them. She reaches her hands out to Tanglor and Freden. They both grab on and stand up to walk with her. She takes them back into the city.

"I will need to speak with my advisors, of course. I also need to allow my people to take part in voting and get a consensus on what we want to do. It will take us at least a week to achieve this. In the meantime, please make yourselves at home on our planet and in our city."

They stop in front of several houses, and Zebe steps forward next to her mother.

"Make yourselves comfortable. Feel free to walk through the city and talk to the Tralupians around. They'll be more than happy to speak with you. Don't hesitate to let us know if there is anything else we can do to make your stay more welcoming."

Zebe smiles warmly at Tanglor before heading back to the palace with her mother. He walks into his house and settles in. Freden follows behind, needing to speak with him.

"They seem too nice, Tanglor."

"I don't know. They seem eager to learn just like us. I'm interested in getting to know Zebe more."

"I'm sure you are. I saw how she was looking at you."

"Huh? She was just smiling. Go get some rest, Freden."

He leaves Tanglor alone, sitting on his bed looking out the window. He hears something rustle in the bushes. Tanglor gets up and goes outside.

"I told you to get some rest, Freden."

There is no response, so he starts to walk back into his room.

"Wait."

Tanglor turns back around to see Zebe standing there.

"What are you doing here?"

"I wanted to speak with you more. I figured I'd see if you were still up."

"By spying on me?"

"No. Well, yeah, I was kind of spying on you. Sorry, I don't know what I was thinking."

She starts to walk off, but Tanglor runs over and grabs her arm.

"Zebe, wait. I'd love to talk to you some more. Come inside."

She is overcome with happiness while following Tanglor back into the house. Zebe walks around his room and looks at his belongings. She picks up one of his Elite shirts with the cape hanging off to the side.

"This looks important. What's it for?"

"That is my Elite Protectors uniform."

"Elite Protectors?"

"It started as a special group made up of the strongest Johthuns. They were the best soldiers, explorers, pilots, everything. There's a lot to our history, after the fighting amongst ourselves and others trying to steal from us, we've come out better than before. We are leaders to our people and work with our government to pave the way. I have made my way to the top of the Elites and am now the Commander. My people look to me— but it's tough."

Zebe places her hand onto his.

"I know what you mean. As the Princess, I was born to lead my people. My mother, let's just say she appreciates tough love. I have told her many times that I don't want to be the Queen when she passes, but my siblings lost the family battles and are in the military, so none of them can become King or Queen after her."

"Family battles? Just from speaking to your mother and walking with her, you can tell she is tough. I wouldn't want to be on the wrong side of a fight with her."

Zebe laughs and scoots closer to Tanglor.

"You have no idea. The Tralupians have a law that my mother institution due to overpopulation. If you have more than one child, they must compete in twelve different tests starting at the age of seven. The tests determine who the best Tralupians are. After the different tests, the children are ranked. If you are not the top Tralupian, no matter how many children compete, you are sent to the barracks to be raised by the army with opportunities to visit your family. If they don't respond to the army's call, the children are punished and imprisoned until they prove their worth and fight again. If they fight well enough or do something heroic, they can earn their way toward control of their own lives."

"That's a harsh way to do things, but I understand. We are getting overpopulated too, but we are looking for more habitable planets for our people. We still all train to be soldiers in the army, in case it comes to it."

"That sounds a lot...... kinder than our way. Why do you wear those goggles on your face?"

"The Johthuns lived underground in caverns a long time ago. When my people came to the surface, it was difficult for us to see in the bright light. Our eyes never quite adjusted, so we wear these goggles, made of a metallic material our scientist developed, that helps us see in different lights."

Zebe and Tanglor keep talking as the night grows darker. They are interrupted by a knock on the door, followed by Freden opening it.

"Commander—oh, I'm sorry. I didn't realize you had company."

Zebe stands up off the bed.

"No, it's okay. It's late, and I was just leaving anyway."

She walks over to the door and stops.

"Thank you for speaking with me. I look forward to talking more while you're here. Good night, Tanglor."

She walks past Freden.

"Good night, Freden."

Freden looks at Tanglor with a smile on his face.

"What was that about?"

"Freden, what do you want?"

"Elisin sent a message asking for a report."

"I'll send her one. Go and get some rest, Freden. We have a lot to see while we are here on TokBellu."

Freden leaves the room, shutting the door behind him. Tanglor gets on the comms to report to Elisin and his Colonels. They all appear on screen to see Tanglor.

"Greetings. If you don't mind, I'm going to keep this brief. I need to get some sleep for tomorrow. We discovered a planet called TokBellu today, and there is intelligent life on it. They call themselves the Tralupians, and they've welcomed us into their city. I met with their leader and issued an invite to join the Galactic Community. She is speaking with her advisors and people about it to see what they want to do. In the meantime, we are their guests here. Their leader's daughter has been very gracious and shown great hospitality to my crew and me. I look forward to interacting with them more this week. I will report more in a couple of days."

Ashar is the first to reply.

"It's great to see you too, Tanglor. Happy the expedition finally found some other life out there. We will be eagerly waiting for your next report, brother."

They all leave the video call, except for Elisin.

"Tanglor, everything here has been going smoothly. The Elites and Elders have been working together to finish the rebuilding efforts on Conril and Thoonta. The cities there are almost as big as the ones on Joht now. Also, our explorers have found ten potential planets for our people to colonize on. We are running more tests to be sure the environment is suitable. As Ashar said, we are eager to hear your next report about these Tralupians."

"Thanks, Elisin. I'll make sure to keep you updated. Talk to you soon."

Tanglor shuts the comms off and lays down on his bed. He ponders his journey so far. The wind blows through the window, bringing with it sounds of different animals—interrupting his thoughts. Overcome by how tired he is, Tanglor's eyes start to close as he dozes off.

# Chapter 28:
# Tralupians-The Queen's Wrath

Zebe closes the door quietly behind her, as she leaves the house Tanglor is staying in. She navigates her way through the city by the light of the moon. As she approaches the palace, she sees the Queen standing next to the Great Tree with Defunis and Serel behind her.

"Mother?"

Queen Zuna turns around; her eyes are bright orange. As soon as she sees her daughter, the color fades away.

"What is it, Zebe?"

Zebe looks at Defunis and Serel as they stare back at her.

"You tell me, mother. Why are the three of you out here at this time of night? What are you doing?"

She walks over to Zebe, while they turn around to make their way into the palace.

"I was just speaking to your father, and Defunis and Serel wanted to speak with him as well."

"Did they know him too?"

Defunis and Serel follow behind them. Defunis speaks up.

"We did, but not as much as we wanted to. That is why we go with the Queen when she speaks with him."

Zebe looks back at the two advisers then turns back to her mother as they enter the throne room.

"I want to be there when you guys see him. I want to get to know him more too."

Queen Zuna doesn't answer right away. Werfon walks over and sits at the table. The Queen settles herself on the throne before acknowledging Zebe's question.

"I want you to do that too, but your father told both of us while we were in the Great Tree that it is too dangerous for us to see him."

"Why are you able to see him then?"

"It's not the same, Zebe...."

Zebe gets upset, preparing to argue, but Defunis interrupts her.

"Princess Zebe, why were you walking back to the palace by yourself so late?"

"I was speaking more with the Johthuns and Tanglor Raff. I am very interested in finding out more about him and his people."

Queen Zuna perks up.

"Speaking of the Johthuns and Tanglor Raff, we need to discuss this Galactic Community he spoke of."

Werfon leaves the adviser's table and walks in front of the Queen.

"I think it would be a good idea to join the Galactic Community, though I do think we should get to know them better before accepting. We should tell them that it will take longer for us to decide so that we can learn more about them while they're here."

Defunis jumps up from the table and stands next to him.

"I think we need to be extra cautious with them... There is something about them that I don't know, feels off."

Serel joins in.

"I agree with Defunis. There is something strange about them. It is hard to believe they just happened to find us and have no interest in what we have here on TokBellu."

Zebe looks at them with confusion.

"What are you talking about? It is obvious why they're here—Tanglor told us! They were traveling around in space through the different solar systems! Does no one else find that fascinating!? We only knew so much about space before they got here. We didn't even know that the solar system we reside in is called Runsillya. There's so much to learn from Tanglor Raff and the Johthuns!"

Queen Zuna looks down to her advisers. Defunis and Serel's eyes quickly flash orange before she looks back to her daughter.

"There is much for me to think about. I can see what everyone is saying, and I agree with all of you. I think we should try to learn as much as we can from them while they are here, but we should also exercise caution. We don't know anything about them yet. This Tanglor Raff could be lying to us about the Galactic Community. Zebe, I don't want you around them alone."

Zebe gets angry and walks down the steps, away from the throne. At the bottom, she turns back to her mother.

"I am sorry, mother, but you can't keep me away from them. Tanglor is good. I can tell."

Zebe leaves the throne room. Her mother sits back down while her advisers stand at the bottom of the steps, looking up to her.

"Werfon, can you please stay close to Zebe. Stay hidden and just keep an eye out for her."

He nods his head before leaving the throne room. Defunis and Serel stand, staring at the Queen. Their eyes flash again as Defunis walks up to the throne.

"Your daughter wants to be around the Johthuns more than the Tralupians. That is not acceptable behavior from a Princess, especially when the Johthuns showed up on TokBellu unannounced. You do remember the prophecy spoke to you by the Great Tree, don't you?"

Queen Zuna closes her eyes, trying not to listen to him. Serel walks up the steps and stands next to Defunis.

"The prophecy speaks of invaders coming to TokBellu. Let's see, how did Tranjora put it? Oh yeah, that's right, he said, "They're going to come and take everything from you! Don't let them! Our people, your daughter, everything will be lost!! TokBellu will be in ruins! And their black eyes, nothing but darkness!!!" I'm not sure what black eyes he could have possibly been talking about, but the Johthuns have those dark metallic goggles covering their eyes."

Queen Zuna's eyes shoot open. Orange runs through them as she looks at Defunis and Serel.

"It can't be the prophecy. There was fire, and everything was in ruins. Blood filled the city streets and the ship…. It was different than Tanglor's."

Defunis looks to Serel before turning to the Queen.

"Yes, but the prophecy isn't set in stone. The written prophecy is a little different than the one Tranjora, and the Great Tree expressed to you. I think they're connected, and these Johthuns could be the ones to bring the Apocalypse to TokBellu."

Serel walks around the Queen, staring into her eyes.

"I agree, but we can't show them that we know. The cautious approach is the best, as long as we prepare ourselves."

Queen Zuna stands up and slams her trident down onto the ground.

"Enough! The two of you need to stay out of my head!"

She sits on the throne as Defunis and Serel move back down the steps.

"I will have our soldiers ready for an attack, just in case. In the meantime, we will be respectable hosts while we figure out what they truly want from us. Now leave me! I need some time alone—*without* the two of you in my head."

Defunis and Serel bow to their Queen. They look up and smile at her, eyes glowing, before turning around and exiting the room. Queen Zuna lets out a sigh as she sinks down on the throne.

----------------------------------------------

Night surrounds TokBellu, as Zebe sits on the ledge next to the Great Tree. She turns to it and touches the trunk with her hand.

"I can't say I miss you since I barely know you…. I want to see you again, though, away from my mother. I get this feeling that she is still keeping something from me, and you might know what that is."

As she speaks to the Great Tree, an orange light appears underneath her hand; sparks start to shoot out from the trunk. Zebe jumps up and moves away from it.

"Father?"

The sparks continue to fly off the tree, creating a doorway. A hand reaches out and waves to Zebe, telling her to come in. She looks around nervously before taking the hand and entering the doorway. It shuts behind her. She can't see anything inside the tree. TralVent isn't appearing, and Zebe is left standing alone with an unknown transparent Tralupian staring at her.

"Zebe Wrathfin?"

Zebe continues to look around the empty tree before answering.

"I am. Who are you?"

The orange Tralupian kneels to the ground.

"I am Mazray Wrathfin, daughter of Zalzatine Wrathfin and brother to Tez Wrathfin. I believe you just broke my barrack records. Impressive. You must be a pretty good fighter then."

Zebe smiles and kneels with her.

"I can't believe I am meeting the greatest warrior in our history!"

Mazray laughs.

"Please, if I was our greatest warrior, I wouldn't be dead and stuck in this tree."

"Just because you lost that battle doesn't mean you are any less of a warrior. You killed the Ventrian's toughest soldier! You would have made it out of there if his giant body didn't fall on top of you."

Mazray blows it off.

"Why thank you, Princess, but seeing you fight and win in the barracks, I don't know if I could have beaten you."

Zebe starts to blush.

"I appreciate the sentiment, but that isn't me... You were the greatest warrior we have ever had, and that was who you were, at least from the stories I've heard. I want to leave TokBellu and see other worlds, the other life that's out there."

Mazray smiles at her and starts to walk toward the center of the hollow tree.

"There is a lot you don't know about me, Princess, but you are right. That was me and always will be, but I wasn't just a warrior either. Enough about me, though. Your father is off trying to stop Zembor. He finally figured out a way to reopen the portal up in the bell tower."

Zebe follows behind her. As they walk, the city of TralVent starts to appear around them, revealing Remnants watching them. Mazray looks back to Zebe.

"We need to get to the bell tower. You can speak with the rest of our family when we return."

Zebe nods her head and follows. Ilikso stands at the bottom of the tower, yelling at it while Oryuna and Musfina try to break down the door.

"Zembor!! You must stop this! If you open that portal, you'll let those monsters return. We'll have another war on our hands!!"

Zembor looks over the railing at of them.

"I am sorry, but I can't leave my friend in that place any longer! He's still alive, and he's suffering! I will close the portal as soon as I get through. They won't be able to get back once it closes! I promise!! Please, just let me do this!"

Ilikso looks over to his sisters, attempting to break down the door.

"Are you almost in? There is no other way up, and we have to stop him!"

Musfina charges at the door as it slowly cracks.

"We're close to getting through!"

Ilikso looks back up to Zembor, holding a piece of the broken bell.

"There has to be another way! Zembor, please! Think of everyone else. We need that portal to stay closed!"

Zembor turns away from them and holds the piece of the bell in the air toward the gateway. Tears slowly run down his face.

"I am truly sorry, but I need to save him."

Oryuna and Musfina charge the door together; it finally breaks open. They run through going up the spiral staircase. Zembor's arm blade shoots out and hits the piece of the bell, breaking it more and causing it to ring softly. A small portal opens, revealing orange sand on the other side. Zembor runs toward the gateway before it can shut. Oryuna and Musfina make it up the stairs, but it's too late. He turns back to them as the portal starts to close.

"They won't get through. There's no way for them or me to get back here now."

The portal closes just as they reach the gateway. Oryuna turns around and looks over the railing.

"He's gone and the portal's closed. There's no way for it to reopen without the bell."

Ilikso yells back to her.

"Gather up the leftover pieces and bring them down. I will keep them in a safe place, so this doesn't happen again."

Zebe walks over to him.

"Father, why don't you destroy them so they can never be used again?"

Ilikso turns around and looks to his daughter.

"If they ever find a way back and take any more of our people, we'll need them to go to their world... What are you doing here?"

"I was by the Great Tree trying to speak with you. Mazray heard me and guided me inside. I'm not sure why, though...."

The two of them look at Mazray while she walks over.

"I've been keeping an eye on you for a while now.... close to fifty years. It is a long story, but I absorbed one of those Broncholites into my Remnant body. I fought it for many years and, in the end, overcame whatever the monsters did to it."

She steps back, an orange gas seeps out of her, forming into a cloud. It floats closer to Zebe and flashes at her.

"Hello, Zebe. You don't recognize me here, but we have already met multiple times and are actually quite close outside of the Great Tree."

The cloud transforms itself into a Tralupian. Zebe's eyes open wide, and her mouth drops.

"Werfon? How?"

"Mazray saved my life when R'Ang was overrun by creatures that control those monsters you saw. We fought them and ultimately lost. They took us all hostage and corrupted us, turning us into their slaves and making us evil like them. They brought those monsters to R'Ang to run the prison you call the Metal Mansion. They experimented on us and figured out numerous ways to use our abilities. We can do many things with our gaseous bodies, like take control of other creatures. Also, we can create lightning storms and massive gusts of winds in the right environment, plus so much more."

Zebe sits down on the ground as they walk over to her.

"You've been in my life for fifty years, and I didn't even know who you were... How have you kept it hidden from me? Or my mother, for that matter."

Werfon sits down next to her.

"My body outside of the Great Tree is that of a Tralupian that died years ago. I can't recall his name, unfortunately, but it has served me very well in honor of him. I am sorry for keeping it from you for so long, but you have to understand why. Please keep this secret from your mother. That is why I brought you here when I had the opportunity."

"I won't tell my mother, but what do you need to tell me?"

"The other advisers she has...there is something off about the two of them. I was around the Queen for a while before they showed up, she was much happier. Then, out of nowhere, those two show up, and she changes. She's angry and stubborn now. She has brief moments and glimpses of kindness, but it is a struggle for her. Almost like she is fighting something within herself. I know it is strange to say, and I feel odd telling you this without any proof of it...."

"I appreciate you telling me this and bringing it to my attention. I have felt something strange about them too. I am glad I'm not the only one. What do I do, though? If that is the case, I wouldn't want to speak to my mother about it. What if they're listening?"

Ilikso sits down with them.

"It is possible. When Ozem showed up claiming to be Zembor, he was able to take control of your mother. He used her to become King and tried to tear us apart. If it weren't for Oryuna and me, TokBellu would be in chaos."

"I... I will pay close attention to the three of them and see if she acts any differently when they aren't around. I need to get back to the palace. We have guests; you know that already."

They laugh as Zebe stands up. Mazray walks over to her.

"Be the person you want to be. Who cares what anyone thinks, even your mother. Don't be afraid to be the warrior you are either. Wear that title of the Greatest Warrior with pride!"

Zebe smiles at her and nods.

"Thank you; I won't let you down! Werfon, are you coming?"

The two of them walk out of TralVent back toward the inner bark of the tree. Werfon transforms into a cloud and floats over to where his body lies limp on the ground. His gaseous form penetrates the skin and lifts the body off the ground. He turns to Zebe, his orange eyes fading away.

"How do I look?"

She laughs at him.

"That is a ridiculous way to get yourself ready... You look fine, Werfon. Let's get back before anyone notices we're both gone. I promise to keep your secret."

He smiles at her as the doorway opens.

"Thank you, Zebe."

They walk through; it closes behind them just as the sun starts to rise above the horizon, glistening off the ocean water. Zebe turns to Werfon.

"Get back inside and do what you've been doing. We both need to watch Defunis and Serel when they're around closely, but don't make it obvious."

Werfon smiles and bows to the Princess. He walks inside the palace as she makes her way over to the ledge overlooking the ocean. She sits down and rests her head against the Great Tree.

"I am happy to know you're all looking out for me. Thank you."

She closes her eyes and listens to the wind creating waves in the water. She lays her head back and starts to think of the Johthuns and Tanglor Raff. She gently dozes off until she's interrupted by the Queen.

"Zebe! What are you doing out here? I thought you'd be off with your new friends."

Zebe stands up and walks past her.

"I don't get why you've started acting this way... Something is different about you, and I don't like it. If you must know, I am going to hang out with Jarelen and some other friends. And yes, we might spend time with Tanglor and the other Johthuns if they decide they want to. I will train when I get back since I have trained every single day for the last fifty years. Now that I own the title of Greatest Warrior, I think I deserve a small break."

Before Zuna can say anything, Jarelen and some others come around the corner to meet up with Zebe. They head for the city while Zuna walks back into the throne room, where her three advisers wait for her. Werfon walks over to the Queen.

"My Queen, are you alright?"

"Yes, Zebe and I just got into a little argument. Everything is fine."

She sits down on the throne. Werfon stands at the bottom of the steps.

"Have you thought about Tanglor Raff's proposal? I think you should accept and come up with terms for him. It's what we have been working toward for so many years."

Defunis walks over and stands next to Werfon.

"My Queen, if I may, I think Werfon has a great point, but have we had enough time to decide if they are good or not?"

Serel nervously walks over and joins them.

"I... I think we should accept their terms too."

Defunis turns to his sister with a look of distress. The Queen stands up and walks down the steps to the three of them.

"Two against one. This debate is over. We will accept Tanglor Raff's terms after a few days. I am going to say good morning to Ilikso and the others in the Great Tree. Will the three of you join me?"

They bow to their Queen as she walks by. Defunis strides over to Serel and begins to whisper to her. Werfon notices and stops following the Queen. He starts to walk over to them when Queen Zuna stops and turns around.

"Do you have something better to do? Let's go!"

Defunis and Serel stop talking and catch back up to the Queen, as Werfon follows behind them. They approach the Great Tree. Queen Zuna stops and turns to them.

"Stand in front of the Great Tree."

The three advisers look around at each other before Defunis steps forward.

"What is going on?"

The Queen pulls out her trident and points it at him. He looks back at her and smiles; his eyes flash orange. Zuna continues to point the trident at him as she smiles back.

"Do as I say. You can't control me now."

Defunis turns to his sister. She walks over to the Queen and stands behind her.

"You are no longer able to control her or me—it's over, Defunis."

Werfon steps away and stands behind the Queen with Serel. The Queen spins her trident in front of her, stepping closer to Defunis. He tries to back away, but the trident creates a vortex, pulling him in.

"No! Please, I'll do whatever you say!"

The Queen's eyes glow orange as she continues to spin the trident. Defunis loses his balance and flies toward it. The trident slashes him into pieces, shooting his flesh, blood, and guts behind them onto the tree. The tree glows, absorbing it into the bark. Serel and Werfon bow down to their Queen as she stands proud with the trident in her hand.

"He won't be able to hurt either of us anymore. Thank you, Serel."

She smiles at the Queen as her eyes flash orange. Werfon notices, but he keeps quiet and continues bowing.

---------------------------------------------

Zebe strolls down the city streets, laughing with her friends. Jarelen walks over to her.

"Hey Zebe, glad you decided to come and hang out with us today. I was hoping we could go out again. Maybe tonight?"

"Sorry, Jarelen. I had a lot of fun with you the other night, but I just don't think it will work out between us. There are too many differences in our lives, and I don't want what my mother wants us."

"I... What if we tried something else? I'm not always like that. I have different qualities that you just don't know about yet."

"Jarelen, I'm not interested in being anything more than friends with you. Just forget about it and let's enjoy the day with our friends. Have you met the Johthuns yet? We could go to the lake next to the houses they're all staying in!"

"Alright, Zebe. Let's go check out the lake."

They walk past the barracks and head through the marketplace. As they approach the lake, they see Freden standing outside with the other Johthuns. Zebe runs ahead of the group, waving her hand at him.

"Hey, Freden! How's it going?"

"Hey Zebe, I'm doing great! Thanks again for letting us stay here. These houses are perfect for us!"

"I'm glad you think so! My mother wanted me to make sure you all had everything you needed while you were here. Any requests?"

"Actually, yes! Have you got anything fun for us to do? Some of us have been looking around for something to do while we're here."

"Perfect! We're heading to the lake behind your houses to swim and play some splartusa. Come on! You guys should join us!"

"That sounds like a great time! You'll have to explain the rules of that splartusa game, though!"

Freden turns around and waves to the other Johthuns. They follow behind him, running to the lake. Zebe looks around at all the Johthuns.

"Where is Tanglor?"

"He's still sleeping, surprisingly. He must've been exhausted. Don't worry, though. He'll probably hear us out here having fun and come join in no time!"

Zebe smiles at Freden as they run to the lake with the others. They shed their clothing and jump in the water. The sun shines down on the Johthuns and Tralupians, laughing together as they splash around in the water.

# Chapter 29:
# Johthuns-New Allies

Tanglor is rooted in a dream, the nightmare he once had has dissolved. He dreams about the night before, sitting in front of Zebe as she talks. Her voice starts to fade away, and laughter fills the room. He awakes to her splashing water on him through the window.

"Hey! What are you doing?"

"Get out of bed!"

She steps away from the window, and Tanglor can see his crew in the water with the Tralupians.

"Look at how much fun they're having. Come on!"

Zebe dives into the water, while Tanglor jumps out of bed and runs outside. He takes off his clothes as she watches.

"Look at all of that fur!"

She reaches her hand out to rub his chest then, suddenly shy; she smiles nervously.

"Sorry. As you can tell, we aren't nearly as hairy as you."

He grabs her hand and smiles back. She shakes off the embarrassment and leans in to hug him, but is interrupted by a Tralupian named Jarelen.

"Hey Zebe, you two should come and play! We need two more!"

"Sounds good!"

They follow Jarelen towards a group getting ready to play the Tralupian's favorite aquatic sport, splartusa. Both teams begin on opposite sides, having to rush to get the ball in the middle. When a team secures the ball, they are on offense, trying to score on the opposing team. To score, your team must work together by passing and swimming with the ball to the opponent's basket. If you can make it there, shooting the ball is the only way to score. Once you score, the ball restarts in the middle, and the teams play again, keeping track of points. After teaching the Johthuns how to play, the game begins.

A couple of hours have gone by, and the competition grows fierce between the two teams. Tanglor's team gets the ball, attempting to end the game with this final drive. He hikes the ball, as Jarelen quickly swims toward him. He sees him coming and maneuvers through the water, spinning around Jarelen's tackle. Tanglor cocks his arm back and hurls the ball across the water, Zebe jumps in the air and catches it. Before coming down, she turns toward the basket and shoots the ball. Two defenders jump to try and block it, but the ball soars between their arms, hitting the rim and rolling around before slowly falling in. Tanglor swims over to Zebe and lifts her into the air.

"What a shot!!!"

She drops back down and gives him a long hug—some of the Tralupians notice, jealousy in their eyes. Jarelen, irritated by how close they have gotten, walks over to interrupt them again.

"Zebe, your mother is calling for you."

She lets go of Tanglor and starts to swim toward Zuna. Everyone follows behind, but Jarelen stops Tanglor.

"Stay away from Zebe. She's mine."

He swims past Tanglor, ramming into his shoulder before catching up with everyone surrounding the Queen on the beach.

"Wow, that was great watching you all play splartusa! To see my people smiling and having fun with the Johthuns is a refreshing site."

Tanglor sits down next to her.

"I couldn't agree more, Queen Zuna. You and your people have welcomed us with open arms. We are very grateful."

"Please, just call me Zuna. I am glad you found us, Tanglor. My people needed this. I don't know if Zebe has told you anything, but our population is growing, and it has been a problem for us. We are getting too big for TokBellu."

"We are explorers at heart, and I have no doubt that we could find another habitable planet for you and your people. The Galactic Community would work together, sharing resources and knowledge!"

"It's a very ambitious thought, but I have to go back to the palace to speak with my advisors before I can give you an answer. I can't promise you anything, but I am fighting for us to join you."

She stands up and gets ready to leave.

"Zebe, are you coming with me?"

She stands up and bows to her mother.

"I would like to stay here with Tanglor and the Johthuns. There is more for me to learn from them."

Zuna walks over and puts her hands on her shoulders.

"What about your training? What about…."

Zebe interrupts her.

"Mother, we talked about this already. I have been training every single day of my life. I've beaten my brother and sister out of the family. I think I can have one day to myself. Tanglor and the Johthuns won't be here for much longer."

Zuna gets upset and turns away from her daughter.

"You disappoint me with your choices, Zebe, but you're right. You have trained every day your whole life. Take today to have some fun and enjoy the company of our new friends, but be prepared to resume your training tomorrow."

Zebe bows again.

"I understand, thank you."

Zuna and her guards walk back to the palace. Zebe sits back down next to Tanglor.

"You were right about your mother giving tough love."

"You have no idea."

Jarelen jumps up off the ground and gets in between the two talking, interrupting them again.

"Hey, Zebe! We're going to head off to our secret spot. Want to join?"

She gets up and walks around him to stand next to Tanglor.

"I think that sounds like a great idea! Tanglor, you and your crew should come too!"

"Okay, that sounds like fun. We're right behind you guys."

They start to swim out to the middle of the lake and see a geyser shooting water into the sky. Jarelen and the other Tralupians watch for the geyser's eruption to stop. Once it has, they swim onto it and wait. Jarelen starts to laugh and turns to the Johthuns.

"I hope you all can breathe underwater. It's a long way to go once we're down there."

The Johthuns all turn to Tanglor with worried looks on their faces. He swims onto the geyser with the Tralupians.

"If our masks can work in space, I'm sure they can work underwater too."

He turns the knob on his goggles, transforming them into a metallic screen covering his face. His crew does the same while following behind him. The geyser launches all of them into the air sending them into a small pond hidden away from the lake. Jarelen turns and smirks at them.

"Underneath us is a vortex of water. Let it take you. If you fight it, you'll drown."

He dives under with the Tralupians following behind. Zebe turns back to them.

"Don't listen to him. He's just trying to scare you. Follow me down and let the current take you."

They all nod their heads before submerging. The vortex spins the water around at a ferocious speed. Zebe looks back at the Johthuns and gives them a thumbs up before swimming in. Tanglor and the others take no time and follow behind, relaxing, and letting the current take them. A couple of seconds pass, and Freden begins to get pulled off course. He panics and tries to swim against the current, but it's too strong. The vortex flings him around and slams him into another Johthun. They nearly get launched out, but Zebe swims over to steady them out. She whips her tail around.

"Here, grab on and follow me."

They latch onto her and continue through the vortex. Finally, they get to the end where another geyser waits for them. It shoots them up into the air, launching them back down into a much calmer body of water. Freden tries to catch his breath.

"I just realized... I hate water."

They all laugh it off and join Jarelen and the others who are sitting on an island of sand, surrounded by sparkling water and tall green trees. Tanglor can't believe his eyes.

"Jarelen, this place is amazing. It's a hidden paradise!"

"Usually, it's only meant for the Tralupians, but we can make an exception today."

"Thank you."

Jarelen shrugs it off and ignores him. He yells over to Zebe.

"Zebe, I brought us some food and drinks! Let's have a party!"

"That's great, Jarelen!"

She walks over and grabs some from him. She smiles and turns back to Tanglor and Freden.

"Here you go, guys. I'm delighted that you came with us! The view here is amazing, and you're the first non-Tralupians to see it!"

Freden enjoys the food and takes a drink.

"Thank you for inviting us and showing us such great hospitality. I wish I could say the same about all of the Tralupians..."

"Don't worry about Jarelen. He's just looking out for me."

Tanglor laughs.

"I think he is doing more than just looking out for you. He seems to think that you two are together."

Zebe starts to blush before she laughs.

"At one point, we had a thing.... but that was because of my mother. Jarelen's family is from another royal bloodline. They have been waiting for our entire history to get on the throne. Whatever royal family is on top holds the crown, and a Wrathfin has been King or Queen since day one. Jarelen and his family have made it a point that they don't want the crown. They just want to merge our families. His aunt and uncle waged war on the throne years ago and lost. Now Jarelen's parents seem to think, along with my mother, that if we were to marry, it would solidify us as the only family for the throne. I have no interest in that idea, though, and have no interest in Jarelen either. If I became Queen, too many things would change because I hate the way my mother does things."

Tanglor reaches out; she takes his hand.

"I am sorry to hear all of that, Zebe. If there is anything I can do, let me know."

She smiles at him before leaning over for a hug. Jarelen notices again and is visibly disturbed. He yells at them while walking over.

"Zebe! This is getting ridiculous. You're going to choose this alien over one of your own?"

Tanglor is about to step forward, but Zebe gets in front of him.

"This is none of your business, especially since I've already told you that there is nothing between you and me! I am not interested in you and never will be!"

He shoves Zebe out of the way and swings his fist at Tanglor. Tanglor sees it coming and moves. Jarelen uses all his force to try again, but Tanglor steps to the side and kicks his feet out from under him. He hits the sand; everyone watching starts to laugh.

"All of you shut up! Just watch and learn. Tanglor Raff is going down!"

He gets up and charges again. Tanglor smiles and slides underneath him, taking his legs out once more.

"Ahhhhh! You're going to pay for this!"

Jarelen pulls a knife out and rushes again. Tanglor flips away from him as he swings the knife. On the last flip, Tanglor kicks the knife out of his hand. Jarelen tries to punch him, but Tanglor grabs his fist and throws him to the side.

"Are you done yet? I don't want to embarrass you anymore."

At this point, all the Johthuns and Tralupians are laughing, watching Jarelen make a fool of himself. He can't handle the embarrassment and tries one last time, running and jumping at Tanglor with his leg out for a kick. Again, Tanglor simply moves out of the way. As Jarelen flies by, Tanglor gives him an extra push, launching him into the water.

The laughter continues to fill the island. Zebe walks over to Tanglor and hugs him.

"Let's get out of here. He isn't going to stop, and I'm afraid you're going to hurt him."

Tanglor gets his crew together; they follow Zebe back into the water. Jarelen sits in the sand humiliated, watching Zebe leave with the Johthuns.

She takes them back through the vortex to their houses by the lake. The sun has gone down, and the night is chilly. The other Johthuns have gone to sleep, but Freden stays behind with Tanglor to talk to Zebe.

"I wanted to personally thank you for saving me earlier in that vortex."

"You were going to be fine, Freden. I just helped calm you down to get you back on track."

"Either way, I appreciate what you did... I'm going to get some sleep. You two have a good night."

Freden walks off to his house, leaving Zebe and Tanglor alone to talk.

"Thanks for sticking up for me today. Jarelen needed to be put in his place. I'm glad a bunch of other Tralupians saw what you did. Maybe they won't be so scared of him anymore."

"You will always be safe with me, Zebe."

The night air brushes across their faces as they stare into each other's eyes. Zebe walks closer to Tanglor and breaks the silence.

"It's getting late. I don't want to walk back to the palace in the dark."

"I can walk with you."

"No, that's okay.... Can I stay here with you instead? I'll leave when the sun rises."

Tanglor grabs her hand and pulls her in close.

"You can stay with me whenever you'd like, Zebe."

She looks up at him with a smile on her face and follows him into the house.

Tanglor makes himself comfortable and sits down.

"I can sleep on the floor while you take the bed. Make yourself at home and let me know if you need anything."

She walks over to Tanglor, stopping in front of him. Without saying a word, she takes her clothes off and gets on top of him. He kisses her while rolling her over on to the bed.

Time flies by, and night turns to day. Zebe and Tanglor lie in bed, cuddled close, with the sheets covering them.

"Thanks for letting me stay with you last night. I hope you don't think…"

"No, not at all. I'm glad you stayed… I'm happy I've gotten to spend all this time with you while I've been here."

As they're talking, they hear a voice outside of the house. Before they can get dressed, the voice turns into a mob of voices getting louder. Zebe jumps out of bed in a panic.

"My mother is probably looking for me! She's going to kill me if she finds out what happened between us! Oh no, morning has already passed!"

Tanglor gets out of bed and grabs her shirt, handing it to her.

"Here, just take a deep breath."

She takes the shirt from him and listens to his advice. She leans down to kiss him.

"Thank you. Let's find out what's going on out there."

Tanglor gets up and dresses with her. He walks over to the door and opens it to find Freden standing guard.

"There you are. It's about time, Tanglor."

"Freden, what's going on?"

"Jarelen and the Tralupians have been trying to get through to the Princess."

Jarelen steps out from the crowd and starts to yell at them.

"I know what happened last night. You have taken the Princess from me! From her people!"

He gets closer, but Freden pushes him back.

"Stand back, or I'm going to make you!"

Tanglor steps out in front of Freden.

"It's all right. Let him through."

Jarelen starts to walk toward Tanglor but is interrupted by the Queen's arrival.

"There you are, Zebe. What happened to you? You never came home!"

Zebe steps out from behind Tanglor.

"I'm sorry, mother. I was going to, but by the time we got back here, it was already nightfall and getting cold. Tanglor offered to walk me back to the palace, but I didn't want him to be wandering around that late, especially with Jarelen trying to hurt him. Tanglor let me sleep on his bed while he took the floor. He was looking out for me."

Jarelen sneaks back into the crowd before Zuna can spot him.

"I see. Thank you, Tanglor, for taking care of her. I will handle Jarelen when I find him. It's time to go back to the palace and start your training. Tanglor, you and your crew will join us for dinner tonight to discuss our future."

Tanglor and Freden bow to the Queen as her and Zebe make their way back to the palace. The crowd slowly disappears, and Freden is left standing with Tanglor.

"You want to explain what happened in there?"

"There is nothing to explain, Freden. The Princess stayed here with me last night."

"Yeah, myself and everyone else that was here got that much after the two of you overslept... They weren't too happy to find out she was in there this morning, especially Jarelen."

332

A voice appears from behind them.

"He's right!"

Jarelen charges at Tanglor and tackles him to the ground. Freden runs over to yank him off, but Tanglor yells at him.

"Leave him, Freden! It's time I settled this!"

Tanglor lets him get a couple of punches before he throws him off.

"It's over, Jarelen!"

Tanglor rushes at him, throwing a weak punch and waiting for Jarelen to dodge it. As he does, Tanglor jumps and flips around, kicking him to the ground. Jarelen tries to get up, but Tanglor walks over and knocks him unconscious.

"Let's go, Freden. We need to prepare for dinner with the Queen tonight, and we're already running late."

Freden follows Tanglor into the house.

"It's about time you knocked him out. I get why you didn't want to, but he was asking for it."

Tanglor sits down on the bed.

"I didn't want to, but he wasn't going to stop. And like Zebe said, someone needed to put him in his place."

"Well, he did. I'm just worried about how Queen Zuna is going to take it."

"Go get ready, and we'll meet back out front."

Freden nods his head and leaves. They get ready and rendezvous with the rest of their crew.

"The Queen and her people are waiting for us. Let's get to the palace. Having Zebe over last night wasn't planned."

Freden laughs.

"I'm sure sleeping through the morning wasn't planned either."

Tanglor rolls his eyes and laughs while walking ahead with Freden. The crew follows behind them. As they approach the palace, Tralupian guards run down the pathway and stop them.

"Tanglor Raff, we are to escort you to your seats. Please, follow us."

The guards turn around, and they make their way up the stairs. They arrive at the palace, leading the Johthuns to their seats. Zebe sits with her mother by the throne. Tanglor and his crew take their seats as the Queen stands up.

"We are eager to tell you the news. Please come up here and join me."

She turns and nods to Zebe, who then walks down the stairs to where Tanglor is sitting and grabs his arm. She escorts him back up the stairs to the Queen. She sits back down, and Zuna takes his arm.

"Today marks a special day for us. After days of deliberation with my advisors, we have decided to accept the invitation from Tanglor Raff. We are going to join them in the Galactic Community!"

All the Johthuns and Tralupians in the palace jump up from their seats and start to cheer. Tanglor turns to Queen Zuna and shakes her hand before she pulls him in for a hug. Zebe watches with a smile on her face, Freden stands, clapping while looking around. He catches Jarelen standing in the crowd, watching Tanglor and Zebe closely. Freden starts to walk toward him, but the rest of the Johthuns grab Freden and start to celebrate. When he looks back at Jarelen, he's gone.

The celebration continues into the night while Tanglor sits with the Queen and Princess discussing the future of the Galactic Community.

"I am prepared to send Tralupian diplomats with you back to Joht. We would like to learn more about your homeworld, as well as your politics there."

"I am happy to hear that. I know the Elders will be pleased to have diplomats to work and talk with. We should keep both of our planets open to any Tralupian or Johthun."

Zuna stands up.

"I want to wait a little bit before we open TokBellu to the Johthuns. It's more of a precaution for us. There are other species out there that aren't as friendly as you."

Tanglor stands up next to her.

"We are the Elite Protectors. We vow to protect you as well as our people now. The Galactic Community will help each other no matter what."

Queen Zuna sits back down next to her daughter and starts to laugh.

"That is admirable of you, Tanglor, but we Tralupians don't need any protection. We have protected ourselves for this long, and we can continue to do so. With that being said, I will talk to my advisors more about opening up TokBellu to the Johthuns, but with overpopulation already being a problem, it might not be wise."

"I understand. Just know that the Johthuns are here to help if you need it. Like I said before, we are explorers and have discovered several habitable planets to live on. Our scientists are finishing their tests on them now. With our new technology to travel solar systems, we should be able to find even more."

"That all sounds great, Tanglor. We can start by having some Tralupian civilians and diplomats accompany you back to Joht. Once they get settled in, I will send my daughter over to help."

Tanglor stands up and bows to Queen Zuna and Princess Zebe before walking down the stairs to join the celebration. Zuna notices Zebe staring at Tanglor and the Johthuns celebrating.

"Go and enjoy the celebration tonight. I will see you tomorrow for your training."

Zebe jumps up with excitement and hugs her mother before running down the stairs.

"Tanglor, wait!"

He stops and turns around.

"What is it, Zebe?"

"This is going to be the last time we see each other for a while. I want to spend as much time as I can with you before you leave tonight."

"I'm glad to hear that. I didn't think your mother was going to let you."

"Me either. Let's make the most of it!"

She grabs his arm as they walk over to Freden and the others celebrating. The music gets louder, Zebe uses the opportunity to take Tanglor to the dance floor. She holds him close while they sway back and forth. Finally, she gives in to temptation and leans in to kiss him. Without thinking, he kisses her back. Some of the Tralupians notice but keep dancing. Jarelen, hidden in the crowd, is watching their every move. Before he can get closer, the music stops, and Queen Zuna stands up.

"Thank you, everyone, for joining us in the celebration tonight, but it's getting late, and the Johthuns need to be on their way shortly. Let's clear out and help them get all of their things together."

Queen Zuna and Princess Zebe say their goodbyes while the other Tralupians start to leave the palace. Tanglor's crew gets their things packed onto the Mercurana. Tanglor stands by the entrance welcoming all the Tralupian civilians and diplomats aboard.

"I am excited to have all of you accompany us back to Joht. Please make yourselves at home. My crew will take you to your quarters and show you around."

As Tanglor is preparing to leave, two small Tralupians come walking up to him.

"Tanglor Raff?"

"That's me. Who are you two?"

"Zebe told us to find you. She said you'd take us with you."

Tanglor looks down at the Tralupian children.

"I can't just take children with me... Where are your parents?"

"I knew she was lying. Come on, Zaren."

The two children start to walk away, as Tanglor's mind races with all the different things Zebe told him while he was here.

"Wait! Did you say Zaren? Then *you* must be Zelray! You're Zebe's younger brother and sister. Hurry up and get on."

They both turn around with enormous smiles on their faces and run over to Tanglor to hug him. Freden walks past them, laughing and shaking his head.

"Sometimes, I wish I was like you, Tanglor."

"Where were you?"

"Don't worry about it. Get those kids on the ship, and let's get out of here."

The doors to the Mercurana shut, it takes off, leaving TokBellu behind. Zebe and her mother rest against the Great Tree, watching as the Mercurana traverses through their atmosphere. Zebe holds back her tears and whispers to herself.

"I'll see you again, Tanglor Raff."

She turns away and walks back to her room in the palace, shutting the door behind her. As she closes it, a small box drops down from above. She looks down at it. On the top, it says Zebe Wrathfin. Eager to find out what's inside, she grabs the box and opens it up, revealing a shiny oval with a letter underneath it.

*Zebe Wrathfin,*

*I know we didn't talk much while we were here, but I saw the way my brother looked at you and the way you looked back. Tanglor has no idea I'm doing this, but I want you to be able to speak with him even after we leave. The oval in the box will let you do that. I had our friend make a special one just for you. Hold the oval close to your face and speak into it. You'll have to talk to Martonamo first, but he will put you through to Tanglor. Unfortunately, because I share a bond with Tanglor and Martonamo, I'll be able to hear your conversations. I'll do my best not to listen. Wait a little while to call in and Zebe—please be careful with this. If it gets into the wrong hands, it'll cause turmoil for our people.*

*I look forward to hearing from you soon. Thanks again for saving me in that vortex.*

*Be Careful,*

*Freden Luns*

Zebe crumples the note up and throws it into the burning fireplace, grasping the oval and holding it close to her.

# Chapter 30:
# Tralupians-Royal Bloodlines

Nine months have passed since the Johthun's left TokBellu. Zebe lies on her bed, staring at the glistening oval she was given. She lifts it in the air above her and closes her eyes.

"I had better wait like Freden instructed me to in the note—Ugh!"

She jumps up off her bed and walks over to her fireplace. She reaches inside and sticks the oval into a small hidden compartment.

"There, it will be safe here until I'm ready to use it."

A knock on her door interrupts her daydreaming.

"Zebe, it's Werfon. Serel and the Queen are waiting for us to accompany them to the city. We can't keep them waiting any longer. She wants to go and find Jarelen to speak with him and his parents. Your mother wants to hear from him about what happened with Tanglor."

Zebe walks over and opens the door. She worriedly looks at Werfon.

"She is going to find out about Tanglor and me. He isn't going to hold anything back, and mother is going to disown me."

Werfon puts his arm on her shoulder.

"If he does, then we will figure something out. What you did with Tanglor isn't against our laws. You acted on your feelings, and there is nothing wrong with that. If anything, your mother should understand because of her relationship with your father."

Zebe lowers her head and follows him out of her chambers.

"It isn't that same. Ilikso was still a Tralupian. Tanglor is a Johthun that my mother doesn't trust, and I still don't know if Serel holds any influence over her with Defunis gone..."

Werfon gets a concerned look on his face.

"I believe she still does. When Queen Zuna killed Defunis, it was because of Serel. She was fed up with him controlling them. Serel used her influence to convince the Queen they'd both be safe if he were gone. I have seen her eyes flash orange around the Queen, and this indicates to me that she does have influence over her still, even more with Defunis gone. With that being said, I don't know what her intentions are."

"I guess we just have to keep watching the two of them. Mother has grown angrier with life over the past year. I don't know what else I could do to make her happy again. I have tried my best, but I can't do the things she wants of me anymore. I refuse to marry Jarelen, and I haven't changed my mind about not wanting to be Queen."

The two stop talking as they enter the throne room where Queen Zuna and Serel stand waiting for them. Queen Zuna walks over and grabs Zebe's arm.

"It feels like we've been waiting forever for the two of you to get here! We need to hurry and get to the city before the celebration starts!"

Zebe walks with her, while Serel and Werfon follow behind them. Werfon turns to Serel.

"The Queen seems livelier today. Do you have anything to do with it?"

Serel stops walking and glances at Werfon, looking guilty.

"I.... I can't do it anymore. He still lives on inside of me and his power.... it's too strong to keep fighting."

Werfon stops and stands next to her.

"Defunis? He is gone, Serel. We watched the Queen...."

"No, not Defunis. He refuses to tell me who or what he is. He took control of Zembor and called himself Ozem, but that isn't his real name. Ilikso and the others shut him out of the Great Tree and got rid of the portals, making it so he couldn't return, but that seems only to be physical. I can feel him inside of me. Defunis tried to fight him but ultimately fell under his complete control. When the Queen killed him, that wasn't Defunis anymore. I don't know what to do, Werfon, but I fear that it's happening to me now too. His power grows the angrier he gets. I haven't influenced the Queen for the past couple of days now, and I can feel him getting furious with me..."

Werfon grabs onto Serel's arm and slows their walk, causing them to fall further behind the Queen and Princess.

"I knew there was evil still lurking around, I am sorry to hear about your brother, but I am here to help you any way I can. No more secrets, okay? The Queen doesn't have to know any more about him, either. It will drive her mad, knowing that Ozem, or whatever his name is, was still a threat to us. When we get back to the palace, we will speak more about it. There are things you don't know about still. I can help."

Serel's look of despair turns into a glimmer of hope, as she latches onto Werfon's arm. They stay behind the Queen and Princess as they approach the barracks. Zebe stops and runs in front of her mother.

"Zebe, get out of the way! I want to see Zaren and Zelray."

"I went and saw them earlier. The instructor told me that today is their busiest day with training, and both are becoming top prospects for warriors."

Zuna smiles at Zebe and turns around.

"Really? That is great to hear! I will speak to them on a different day then. I don't want to intrude on their training. You should visit them more and show them a thing or two, Zebe."

Zebe nervously laughs as she takes her mother's arm.

"I would love to do that if the instructor was okay with it, but let's worry about that later. Mother, I must say you seem a lot happier today. Did something happen?"

Zuna steers her daughter toward the marketplace.

"I *do* feel happier today. I'm not sure what has come over me, but I got some good sleep and saw your father in my dreams last night."

"Sounds like a pretty good dream then."

Zuna stops, her smile leaves her face. A serious look replaces it.

"It was the opposite, actually... I don't know what's going on either."

Zuna falls to the ground, Zebe crouches down beside her.

"Mother! What's wrong?"

Her serious look turns back into a smile, and she breaks into a hysterical laugh.

"Hahahaha! I have no idea!"

Her laugh turns into a cry.

"I have been living every day for the past fifty years, just going through the motions. I try to reflect on my past, and it's just blank, almost like I wasn't there for any of it. Like someone else was in my body, and I stepped to the side and let it happen. Looking back on it all…. I don't even know who I am anymore. Your father was the last thing that kept me sane. Without him, I've been lost and not in control of myself or TokBellu. I wake up with this feeling inside me every morning, and instead of fighting it, I roll over and let it take control. Zebe…. I don't want to be like this anymore. All those times I yelled at you or acted like I didn't care, that wasn't me. That isn't who I am!"

She stands up and wipes her tears away. Werfon and Serel stand behind them. He turns to Serel and notices her struggling to stand.

"Serel, what's wrong?"

She falls into Werfon's arms.

"He is trying hard to take control of Zuna, but he is losing power over her. Without me, he can't do anything about it, but I can't fight him for much longer…. If he takes control over me, then she'll be in danger. All of us will be in danger."

Werfon lifts her back to her feet as the Queen and Princess turn around.

"I am sorry, my Queen, Princess. Serel has fallen ill. I am going to take her back to the palace so she can get some rest. Will the two of you be alright without us?"

Queen Zuna smiles at him.

"Yes, we will be okay. Please take her back to the palace and look out for her. Thank you, Werfon."

He bows down to them before heading back with Serel. Queen Zuna and Zebe arrive in the marketplace where thousands of citizens form a crowd. Zebe jumps in excitement as her mother holds onto her.

"I can't believe you're finally taking me to the celebration! I never thought you would, especially at this point in my life."

She smiles back at Zebe.

"As I said before, that wasn't me the past fifty years.... I would have taken my daughter to see the celebration. It should have been done long ago so that you could see our past leaders and their accomplishments."

They arrive and see a crowd cheering and screaming as actors and actresses come out on stage dressed as the former leaders of TokBellu. As they watch the production, Jarelen and his parents move through the crowd toward the Queen and Princess.

"Ahh, the Flutinas. Are you enjoying the celebration?"

Jarelen kneels to the Queen while his parents stand behind him.

"We are. Thank you, my Queen. My mother and father were hoping to speak with you today."

"I assume about the crown again?"

Jarelen stands back to his feet.

"Yes. My father, Jrantoma, and mother, Suspilenta, have come with me today. I know the celebration is going on, but we were hoping to speak with you in a quieter place."

Zuna turns to Zebe.

"I know this is the first time I've taken you out to the celebration, but we need to speak with them. Do you mind returning to the palace with me?"

Zebe glances nervously at Jarelen before answering her mother.

"Of course, I will come back to the palace with you."

Jarelen and his parents follow behind the Queen and Princess as they make their way back to the palace.

---------------------------------------------------

Werfon takes the ailing Serel to the Great Tree. As they approach it, sparks start to shoot off the trunk in their direction. Werfon takes his hand and places it on the tree. The doorway opens, and they walk inside. It closes behind them right as the city of TralVent appears. Werfon takes Serel to TralVent Inn and puts her down on one of the beds. The Remnants inside the Great Tree appear around them. Ilikso stands next to Werfon.

"What is happening?"

"The evil that still lingers is within Serel. That creature that called itself Ozem influences her."

"How is that possible? The portal has stayed closed, and when Zembor opened it up for that brief moment, nothing came back through!"

"I'm not sure either. Before bringing her here, Serel told me that he had control over her—and her brother, Defunis, before the Queen killed him. Even though he isn't here physically, Ozem's power is strong enough to influence her still. He forces her to do the same thing to Queen Zuna. We need to figure out a way to get rid of him completely. Serel said if he takes complete control of her, then we are all in danger!"

As they talk, Serel's body begins to float into the air above the bed. She starts to convulse, while her eyes turn orange. Light shoots of them onto the ceiling. A face appears from the light, resembling the monsters, but its face is more formed with dark evil eyes and sharp teeth.

"Hahahaha, you thought you could get rid of me that easily? I have proved myself to my masters, and they require me to continue my mission here on TokBellu. I'm just going to tell you now; you can't save, Serel? I can't remember what her name is, or I guess I don't really care! HAHAHA! Get ready for what's about to happen! It's going to be a ... blast!"

The light coming out of her fades back into her eyes, the convulsions stop, and she floats down onto the bed. Her eyes stay open, the orange light glowing brightly. She slowly sits up on the bed and turns to Werfon, struggling to fight off the creature controlling her.

"Werfon…. I can't. He is too strong…. Please help me!"

As he approaches her, the light starts to shoot out of her body. She screams as the light gets brighter. Werfon runs and jumps on top of her, holding her down. The light pierces through his body, blinding everyone in the room. When the light fades away, Werfon lies on the bed alone. Serel's flesh and bones have melted away, transforming her into one of the Broncholites. It floats away from them, leaving the Great Tree. Ilikso yells to Werfon.

"You are the only one that can leave the Great Tree. You have to stop Serel before she reaches the Queen!!"

Werfon nods his head and flees TralVent, jumping through the Great Tree's doorway right before it closes.

------------------------------------------------------

Queen Zuna and Zebe enter the palace gates with Jarelen, Jrantoma, and Suspilenta following behind. They make their way inside; Queen Zuna takes the throne while Zebe stands next to her. They look down upon the Flutinas.

"I am ready to hear what you have to say. Proceed."

Jrantoma steps forward, looking up at the Queen.

"We have come here today to speak to you about the crown. We want to reiterate that we had nothing to do with my brother, who waged war on you all those years ago. Tranjora and his wife were both sick. Something was influencing them. With that being said, I'm not defending their actions. I want to present my son to you again for your daughter."

Zebe shoots her mother a panicked look. Zuna acknowledges her with a nod before standing up.

"I appreciate your gesture, but my daughter has already expressed to me that she doesn't wish to marry your son. I am sorry, but I won't force her to do…."

Suspilenta interrupts her.

"I am sorry for interrupting you, my Queen, but whatever you choose for her, she should accept!"

Queen Zuna stands up off her throne and slams her trident into the ground.

"My choice for my daughter is based on the choice she made for herself! If you have a problem with this, then we can discuss other solutions for you and your family!"

Jrantoma and Suspilenta step back, while their son, Jarelen, stares up at the Queen.

"Do you know about your daughter's other choices then? The ones that involved Tanglor Raff?"

Queen Zuna sits back down on the throne and looks to her daughter.

"Is there anything you want to tell me before Jarelen speaks?"

Zebe tries to hide her discomfort as she stares at her mother.

"I.... no. I don't have anything to tell you. Tanglor Raff and the Johthuns were very grateful for our hospitality, and we gained new allies from them coming here."

Jarelen starts to walk up the stairs toward the Queen. Werfon runs through the palace doors and interrupts their meeting.

"My Queen, I am sorry to intrude, but something has happened. We need to barricade you in your chambers right away and seal any openings!"

She stands back up off the throne.

"Why, what is going on, Werfon?"

"I will explain later once our guests have left, but you are in danger."

As he pleads to the Queen, an orange mist appears behind her. Zebe sees it and jumps away from her.

"Mother! Look out!"

Zuna turns and faces the cloud; without hesitation, it launches at her. She tries to fight it, but the mist seeps through her mouth and skin. She falls to the ground, as Zebe and Werfon run over to her.

"Mother!"

"My Queen!"

She stands up and stares at them, her eyes glowing orange before fading away.

"I am fine. What was that thing?"

They help her up onto the throne. Zebe steps away as Werfon looks closely into her eyes.

"That thing was one of the Broncholites. Serel transformed into it because of Ozem."

"Ozem? That can't be. I watched him die long ago."

She looks back down at the Flutinas, still standing in shock.

"Jarelen will be married to my daughter! We will unite our bloodlines, and together they will rule the Kingdom. No one will come close to our power!"

Zebe's eyes open wide as she stares at the Queen.

"Mother! You can't do this! I refuse to marry Jarelen!"

Queen Zuna ignores Zebe and walks down the steps to him.

"What was it that you wanted to tell me about my daughter and the Johthuns?"

Jarelen smiles at Zebe before turning back to the Queen.

"I don't know if I want to be married to someone that doesn't want me. She won't come around either, not after what happened with her and Tanglor Raff."

Queen Zuna becomes noticeably furious and turns to her daughter.

"What happened with you and Tanglor Raff?"

Zebe turns her back to her and runs to her chambers. The Queen sits down on the throne with her eyes shining bright orange.

"Jarelen! Tell me what happened!"

"Your daughter and Tanglor became close while the Johthuns were here, closer than she should have been. That morning you found her in Tanglor Raff's house; she lied to you. She didn't want to leave that night and stayed with him deliberately. I think you can put together what happened between the two that night. He took your daughter away from us, away from our people!"

Queen Zuna stands up, a flash of the prophecy runs through her mind.

"The Apocalypse! They said someone would come and take everything from me! It was prophesied that they would come and take my daughter and leave TokBellu in ruins! We need to pay close attention to the Johthuns. We may need to attack Joht before they attack us!"

Werfon keeps his head down and stays unnoticed in the background. The Queen walks back down the steps.

"We will figure a way out to unite our families, even without my daughter! Jarelen, you will act as one of my advisers now with Werfon. Jrantoma and Suspilenta, the two of you can return home. Jarelen will reach out to you when we have figured out our plan."

Jarelen's parents bow to their Queen. They walk out of the palace, leaving Jarelen with her. She takes his arm and escorts him to her chambers.

"Tell me, Jarelen. What else happened while the Johthuns were here?"

He smiles and walks with her.

"There is a lot to discuss my Queen. Are we going to your chambers to go over it all?"

She smiles back at him as they walk through the door to her room. Zuna grabs him and pushes him onto her bed.

"Yes, we have a lot to discuss, Jarelen... and a lot to do as well."

Queen Zuna's eyes flash orange as she takes her clothes off and climbs on top of him. He embraces her and starts to kiss her while rolling over on the bed. Jarelen quickly stands up and takes his clothes off. He looks at her for a moment before crawling back on top of her. A couple of hours go by, and the two relax in the Queen's bed. The Queen rolls over and puts her hand onto Jarelen's chest.

"You are mine now. Do as I say, and you'll be King!"

Jarelen puts his hand on top of hers.

"I will do whatever you ask of me, my Queen."

She sits up and looks into his eyes.

"We need to keep this quiet for a little while. Your parents and my daughter are the ones that can't know yet. We'll handle them soon enough."

Queen Zuna smiles and laughs.

---------------------------------------------------------

Princess Zebe slams the door behind her as she enters her room. She goes over to the fireplace and reaches up underneath it to grab the shiny oval. She lies down on her bed and holds it up in front of her.

"Two more months have passed, making it eleven now. I think that's long enough. I need to talk to him and tell him what's going on!"

Right as she is about to squeeze the oval, she hears voices outside of her room. Getting up, she slowly walks over to her door. Zebe, wary of how creaky the old door can be, cracks it open just enough to see Jarelen and her mother walking out of the Queen's chambers, smiling and giggling together. She eavesdrops while staying hidden.

"I think this is a good start to what we have been working on the past couple of months. Your parents are oblivious to it, and thankfully so is Zebe. She's smart, though, so she'll figure it out quicker than the others. We need to be swift if we want this to work. Your parents are going to be a problem."

Jarelen stops walking and grabs the Queen. He leans in and kisses her.

"You won't have to worry about my parents. I will handle them. I'll let you worry about handling Zebe. We are close to being able to visit Joht and seeing what tech they aren't sharing with us."

Queen Zuna pushes him off her.

"Alright, now go before someone sees you here. If someone finds out before we announce it, it'll change everything."

Jarelen nods his head and bows to the Queen before leaving the palace. She makes her way back to her chambers. Zebe shuts the door and locks it behind her, settling back on her bed. The oval sits in her hand as she brings it close to her chest. She squeezes it tight, and a voice appears on the other side.

"Hello? Is someone there?"

Zebe takes a couple of seconds before bringing it up to her face and speaking into it.

"Hello, are you Martonamo?"

"I am. You must be Zebe Wrathfin?"

"That's me. Freden gave me this oval close to a year ago when he and Tanglor were on TokBellu. I took Freden's suggestion and waited a while to call."

"I am glad to finally hear your voice, Zebe. Freden told me about you when he had me create the oval for you. Tanglor talks about you a lot. Speaking of Tanglor, I assume you wish to speak with him?"

"It is nice to hear your voice as well, Martonamo. I would love to speak with Tanglor. Is that possible?"

Martonamo laughs.

"Of course, Zebe. Give me a second to see if he is available."

"Thank you, Martonamo. I will be right here, so just let me know when you reach him. I want to surprise him. If you could, speak with Freden too, so that he can help with the surprise. Oh, and tell him I'd like to speak with my brother and sister too!"

"Of course. I will speak with you shortly, Zebe."

Martonamo's voice disappears. Zebe holds the gleaming oval close to her and closes her eyes.

# Chapter 31:
# Johthuns-Betrayal

Tanglor relaxes at home inside the Tazruhvah. A knock on the door causes him to sit up on his bed.

"Come in."

Zaren and her twin brother, Zelray, come busting into the room.

"Tanglor, wake up! You promised you'd take us!"

They get on his bed and start jumping up and down.

"Okay, okay, let me get dressed, and we can head to the city. Where is Freden?"

Freden is sitting outside of the room, waiting for him.

"I'm out here. You two let Tanglor get dressed and give him some privacy. We still need to give him our surprise."

The two Tralupian children come running back out of Tanglor's room and sit next to Freden.

Tanglor slowly walks over.

"What surprise? What are you talking about?"

Zaren and Zelray grab onto Freden and start to laugh.

"Just go get dressed and pay attention. Martonamo will call you."

"Mart? What does he want?"

"Tanglor!"

"Okay fine, I'll be out in a little bit. Call Ashar and make sure they're ready to meet us down there."

Tanglor walks back into his room, shutting the door behind him. He gets dressed and sits down on his bed, looking at the oval in his hand.

"Alright, Mart. What am I waiting for?"

The teal light from the oval starts to shine through his hand.

"Tanglor, are you there?"

"Hey, Mart. Freden said you had a surprise for me."

"I do. Wait one moment."

Tanglor sits, staring at his hand. A couple of seconds go by in complete silence until a voice comes through.

"Hello? Tanglor, can you hear me?"

Tanglor jumps up off the bed.

"Zebe, is that you? How?"

"It works! I'm so happy to hear your voice."

"How is this possible?"

"Well, before you guys left, Freden snuck into my room and left me this oval a letter. I'm sorry it took me so long to use it, but my people have been watching me very closely after you left. They all thought I was a traitor, especially after Jarelen spoke with my mother about what happened that night. All of my people know about us, Tanglor."

"I'm sorry that I haven't been there to help you, Zebe…. If I had known, I would have."

"I know, and that's why I took so long to use it. I'm fine, though. Things have just been a little different since you left. How are my brother and sister doing?"

Zaren and Zelray come running back into the room.

"Zebe!!! We miss you, but we're really happy here!"

Freden walks in behind them.

"Tanglor, I'm sorry that I kept this a secret. I told Martonamo not to tell you about making the communication oval."

"Yes, he did, and it has been very hard keeping it from you for this past year. I am sorry too, Tanglor."

Tanglor walks over to Freden and hugs him.

"Thank you for doing that, Freden, and Martonamo, don't be sorry. Thank you for listening to him."

Tanglor turns to Zaren and Zelray.

"Did you two know about this too?"

They start to laugh and hug Tanglor before running out of the room.

Zebe speaks up through the ovals.

"I'm glad it all worked out.... But, Tanglor, there was a different reason for me calling you."

"Is everything alright?"

"Everything is fine, but Jarelen has been spending a lot of time with my mother lately... I'm worried that they are planning something that I can't stop. I've overheard them talking about a trip to Joht to see the technology you have there. That makes me worried, especially since she's made no effort in the past year to visit."

"Well, we haven't had any problems here with the Tralupian ambassadors. They've been a big part of our community since we arrived back here. It doesn't seem like there has been much contact between them and anyone on TokBellu."

"There hasn't been.... Ever since my mother found out about us, she has been different. She doesn't care about my training anymore, and she spends a lot of time with Jarelen. I hear someone coming; I have to go."

Zebe shuts off her oval, and the comms go dark. Freden walks over to Tanglor.

"She'll talk when she can, but in the meantime, let's get these kids to town for the festival. Ashar and the others are waiting for us."

Tanglor reaches down and picks up Zaren, putting her on his shoulders.

"Woooo, let's go!"

Freden picks up Zelray and follows behind Tanglor. The kids ride on their shoulders, as they race to the festival entrance. Ashar, Neliah, and their daughter, Ezmariah, are waiting for them.

"Why does it always seem like we're waiting on you, Tanglor?"

They all start to laugh as they approach the entrance, taking the kids off their shoulders.

"It does seem that way, doesn't it? Sorry, guys."

Ezmariah runs over and jumps on Tanglor. He picks her up and tosses her in the air as she giggles with a big smile on her face. Elisin walks around the corner.

"Oh good, I made it in time to join you all."

Ezmariah jumps down from Tanglor's arms and runs over to Elisin, giving her a big hug.

"Alright, now that we're all here, are you guys ready to go in?"

The Rise is a traditional festival held on Joht that celebrates the day their ancestors emerged from the ground. All the Johthuns surround the Rashintrah and the Tazruhvah to celebrate. They have music, food, drinks, and games that everyone partakes in. As the celebration nears its end, some of the Elders and Elites take the stage. Tanglor walks over to Ashar, holding his daughter's hand.

"Can't believe how long it's been. Remember our first Rise festival?"

"Of course, I remember it! How could I forget? We were so small, but it was the only time we ever visited Joht before joining the Elites. We watched our mom and dad dance around to the music before they took us to play all the games. After that, we got to see Leazara on stage, showing everyone up who challenged her to a fight. That's the day we decided we wanted to be Elite Protectors!"

Ezmariah starts to cheer.

"Yay! I want to be an Elite just like daddy and Uncle Tanglor!"

Zelray pulls on Tanglor's arm.

"Can we become Elites too, even though we aren't Johthuns?"

"We've never had to think about that... I don't see why not, though. If you can train with the Elites and pass the tests, then yeah!"

Zaren and Zelray cheer with Ezmariah.

"We're going to be Elite Protectors!"

Neliah holds her daughter while Ashar and Freden pick up the other two.

"Tanglor, it's almost time for you to go on stage. We're going to get good seats with the kids. You're up, right after the Elders."

They start walking toward the front to get a good view. Elisin and Tanglor make their way to the stage.

"Tanglor, we need to speak after this."

"I'll be back with Ashar after I'm done up here. We can talk then."

She smiles at him before walking out onto the stage with the other Elders. The crowd begins to cheer as they come out—Elisin waves to everyone.

"We are so happy to be here celebrating The Rise. Thank you for coming out and joining us. I want everyone to know that things have never been better for the Johthuns. We have made new allies and started the Galactic Community. Everyone, give a warm welcome to the Tralupians here with us today."

The crowd cheers and claps as the Tralupians stand up and wave.

"We are very excited about our future. The Elders work closely with the Elites to continue in the right direction for our people. Conril and Thoonta have been rebuilt thanks to the Elites' Captains and the civilians there. Now for the exciting part you've been waiting for, Commander Tanglor Raff is back and here with us today."

The crowd roars as Tanglor walks onto the stage. After a full minute of standing ovations, the crowd finally dies back down and take their seats.

"Thank you, everyone. I couldn't have done all of this without you or the help from the Elders. The Elites and Johthun soldiers risked their lives against the True Guardians and the Dimorians so that we could continue to live and thrive! With the Tralupians as our new allies, we can push forward as the Galactic Community!"

Again, the crowd goes into an uproar, cheering for their commander. Tanglor bows to the crowd before pulling both his blades out. He stands in his fighting stance with swords in each hand. Suddenly, music starts to play, and Elites come out and surround him. A voice comes over the speakers.

"Tanglor finds himself outnumbered. He must fight his way through like our former commanders have. Leazara and Tazlow watch the great Tanglor Raff from above. Make them proud!"

The fight begins, and the Elites jump at him. Tanglor slides underneath one of them, swinging his blade up and knocking him out. The other four step back and surround him again. Tanglor looks to them, a smile on his face, and drops his arms down. The Elites look to each other in confusion before one of them decides to charge. Tanglor steps to the side, and the Elite flies by, crashing into another Elite across the way. Tanglor turns around and, with one swipe, knocks both out. The last two Elites stand nervously next to each other. Tanglor starts to walk toward them, but they split and try to flank him. Tanglor jumps in the air and spins with his blades out. He lands back on his feet, waiting for the Elites to fall to the ground.

Thud, thud.

They both hit the ground, and the crowd stands up, cheering even louder than before. Applause fills the streets of Joht as everyone claps for Tanglor. He helps the five Elites back to their feet; they all bow to the crowd. Tanglor grabs the microphone before leaving the stage.

"Please, enjoy yourselves, and let's celebrate!!"

The music starts back up. Tanglor walks off the stage, looking for Ashar and the others. He searches for a couple of minutes but can't find them. He is about to start walking back to the stage when Zelray and Zaren run over to him out of breath.

"Tanglor…. You…. need to… come quick!"

They run off toward the Rashintrah, Tanglor takes off in a sprint after them. He finally catches up to find Ashar, Neliah, and Freden huddled up on the ground.

"Guys, what's going on?"

Ashar moves away from the huddle to allow Tanglor a view. Elisin lies lifeless on the ground, a massive wound on her back with blood seeping out.

"Tanglor, I'm sorry. We tried to stop the bleeding..."

He reaches for Tanglor, but his brother pushes his hand away and drops to the ground to hug Elisin.

"I am so sorry. I should have been with you, not up on stage, doing that stupid act! Did anyone see who did this!?"

Tanglor looks around to all of them.

"No one saw what happened?"

Ezmariah slowly walks out from behind Neliah.

"I saw who did it. It was one of the Tralupians. They walked up and hugged her. After the hug was over, she fell to the ground, and they took off running down that way."

She points to an alley down the street.

"That alley is a dead end. Whoever did this should still be down there."

Tanglor takes off toward the alley. He walks through, investigating everything with no luck. He doesn't give up the search and, after a couple of minutes, notices something moving behind the trash bin.

"I can see you hiding. I'm not going to hurt you. I just want to talk and figure out why you killed her."

A Tralupian slowly moves away from the trash bin, revealing himself to Tanglor.

"My name is Geresen; I received orders from the Queen. If I didn't murder Elisin, they were going to kill my little sister back on TokBellu."

He walks over to Tanglor and kneels in front of him, lowering his head.

"I am sorry for what I did... I had no choice. I am prepared to give up my life for my sisters."

"Stand up, Geresen. I'm not going to take your life."

He stands up, a look of confusion on his face.

"I don't understand. I took your grandmother's life. She was one of your leaders."

"You did, but you will pay for it differently. You executed an order that you were forced into. I can't hold you responsible. Queen Zuna is responsible for this."

Geresen walks over to Tanglor and bows to him.

"I will do whatever you ask of me, but I know Queen Zuna will still want to hear from me. If I don't report to her, she'll kill my sister."

"Don't worry about your sister. I have someone on TokBellu that will help her. Go with Freden back to the Tazruhvah and begin your training. Make yourself at home and erase the guilt of killing Elisin. I will come by later tonight to speak with you more."

Freden walks over and nods to Tanglor before escorting Geresen to the Tazruhvah. Tanglor walks back over to Elisin's lifeless body and picks her up. He turns to Ashar and Neliah.

"I'm going to take her back to the Elders. Can you guys take care of Zaren and Zelray?"

"We want to come with you."

Ashar steps forward and grabs Zaren's hand.

"We will see Tanglor in a little bit. Come on."

They follow Ashar and Neliah back to their home, while Tanglor walks back to the Elders carrying Elisin. As he is walking through the city, Johthuns and Tralupians kneel, showing respect. He gets to the Rashintrah, and the doors open for him. The Elders are standing in the entrance, expecting him. The now oldest Elder, Trem, steps forward and takes Elisin from Tanglor.

"We'll get her cleaned up for the ceremony. I'm sorry to ask, but can you get all the Elite Protectors together. They were an important part of her life."

Before Tanglor can respond, Trem walks away and shuts the door behind him. Tanglor slowly turns around and heads to the protector's base. Ashar and Freden are there waiting for him.

"Did the Elders take her?"

"Yeah, they're getting her cleaned up for the ceremony. We need to assemble all of the Elites to be a part of it."

"Why do the Elites need to be there?"

"I'm not sure, but it sounds like she was hiding more from us. We can't worry about it right now, though. Let's get the Elites."

Tanglor clenches his hand into a fist and holds it up to his face. The teal light starts to shine through as he speaks into the oval.

"Today, our oldest Elder has passed away. I need all the Elites to stop what you're doing and get your gear ready. We are going to honor Elisin by being a part of her ceremony. Recruits, you are to join us as well. Everyone meets in front of the Tazruhvah in ten minutes."

Tanglor looks over to Freden.

"Where is Geresen?"

"I took him to his room after showing him around. He said he was going to get some rest before his training started tonight."

Tanglor nods his head and makes his way to Geresen's room. The door is open; he sees him sitting on the bed, staring at the wall.

"Did you hear the message?"

Geresen stands up.

"I did, but I didn't think you would want me to be there."

"I did say all recruits, didn't I?"

"Yeah, but..."

"Geresen, I told you to lose the guilt. Elisin would have been the first one to tell you that. She would understand what happened and would want the best for you. It was just how she was. You becoming an Elite, the first that isn't a Johthun, she would be proud of you!"

Geresen is overcome by emotion and starts to tear up.

"I don't know what to say or do to repay you."

He kneels and salutes Tanglor.

"You can repay me and honor her by becoming one of the greatest Elites!"

Tanglor reaches his hand out to him.

"Let's go."

Geresen grabs his hand and stands up off the ground.

"I will honor her as best as I can. I will work and train hard every day to become one of the greats! Thank you, Commander."

Tanglor leads the way to the front of the Tazruhvah with Geresen following behind him. As they walk out, the other Elites welcome and embrace Geresen as one of their own. Ashar, Freden, and Neliah stand behind Tanglor with Ezmariah, Zaren, and Zelray. The Elite Protectors all march together over to the Rashintrah. They arrive to find Trem waiting for them.

"We are grateful for all of you coming. Elisin would be honored. Please follow me and we'll get started."

The doors open, and they follow Trem inside. Tanglor looks around and notices that the interior of the Rashintrah is different.

"What happened here? The walls are further apart, and there wasn't a basement before."

"You will find out everything once the ceremony begins. Elisin wanted to show you this herself but didn't have the chance to."

Tanglor walks down with all the Elites following behind. Staircases lead them down into a dark basement with torches lighting the way. When it becomes too dark, they take their goggles off and continue down the path. Elisin's body lays on top of a stone slab, surrounded by the Elders. Trem walks over and joins them.

"We honor our great Elder, Elisin Marzenay Raff. She helped our people establish a government, and she helped her son start the Elite Protectors. She did everything she thought was right for our people to move forward. Today we celebrate the amazing life she had. We will continue to honor her every day."

The Elites stand proud, saluting her. Zaren, Zelray, and Ezmariah join in. Suddenly, the stone slab starts to shake. Tanglor and the Elites watch in confusion, as the Elders continue to stand around her. The slab begins to descend toward the ground slowly. As it reaches the bottom, the floor opens, causing Elisin to fall into a pit. The same teal light from the ovals shoots up from the opening. Tanglor stops saluting and steps forward.

"What is this? What's going on?"

Trem turns around and grabs Tanglor's arm.

"This is the ritual we do when one of our Elders passes away. They fall into the pit, and it reincarnates them as part of our building. The Rashintrah is alive because of their spirits. That is why it changes around."

"How have we never known about this?"

"This has been one of the Elders' secrets, but Elisin was going to tell you everything."

"What is the pit? How does it reincarnate them into the Rashintrah?"

"We have been trying to figure it out ever since Elisin discovered it, but there are things that she hid from us too. We were hoping that the computer console could tell you."

"The computer console has a name…. It's Martonamo Jusintar, and he's alive in there! That light is the same light that comes from our ovals and Martonamo's ancestors."

"It sounds like he could potentially know more than us about the pit."

Tanglor steps back and takes a deep breath.

"I will go and speak to him after we are done here. What happens now?"

Trem walks back over to the Elders. They all stand in a line behind him.

"Now we march through the streets, honoring and celebrating her, while the building does what it requires to accept her."

They walk past Tanglor and the rest of the Elites. Ashar looks at him with more confusion.

"Tanglor……"

"I know. We will figure it all out soon. For now, we need to honor Elisin."

He nods his head and grabs onto Neliah and their daughter. They walk behind Tanglor with the Elites following behind. They get outside to discover Johthuns and Tralupians waiting with their torches. The city goes dark, except for the lights coming from the thousands marching. Tanglor heads back up to the Tazruhvah with Geresen.

"We are going to go and talk to Princess Zebe about what happened."

"How is that possible?"

"Just follow me, Geresen."

The two of them enter the base and head to the Great Hall. Tanglor clenches his fist again and brings it up to his face while the teal light shoots through. Geresen watches with amazement.

"Martonamo, can you put me through to Zebe, please?"

"Sure thing, Tanglor. Give me one moment."

Now Geresen looks confused.

"Who was that?"

Before Tanglor can answer him, Zebe's voice comes through.

"Tanglor, I don't have a lot of time. What's going on?"

"I'll make it easy and let Geresen explain."

"Geresen? Why is he with you? Tanglor, you're letting him know about the oval?"

"Don't worry about it, Zebe. Just listen to what he has to say."

Tanglor puts his hand in front of Geresen.

"Hey, Zebe… Tanglor brought me here to talk to you because of what I was forced to do by your mother."

"How can she make you do anything when you're on Joht?"

"Queen Zuna has Yulista. If I didn't assassinate the Johthun's head Elder, she was going to kill her. I had no choice, Zebe…. I am so sorry."

"I'm sorry you had to do that, Geresen. I saw Yulista a couple of hours ago with Jarelen, and she was fine, but I will make sure to keep an eye on her. I'm assuming Tanglor is not punishing you since you're there with him?"

"I can't express in words what Tanglor has done for me. He let me join the Elite Protectors as the first Tralupian in their ranks. I am going to honor Elisin as best as I can. I will do whatever it takes to make up for what I did."

Tanglor pulls his hand back and speaks into it again.

"Thank you, Geresen. That's all I need from you right now. Go and find Freden to resume your training."

Geresen salutes Tanglor before leaving.

"Zebe, I need to know what's going on with your mother. This assassination isn't going to sit well once the ceremony is over for Elisin. I've done what I can to make sure the Tralupians here on Joht are safe and had nothing to do with it. Geresen will prove himself in time, and the Elites have accepted him as one of our own already."

"I'm glad to hear that. Thank you for everything you have done, Tanglor. From treating Geresen that way and for taking care of my brother and sister. I don't know how I could ever repay you."

"You can repay me by leaving TokBellu and joining me here on Joht."

"I wish I could Tanglor, I really do. You and I both know that would cause a war between our people. If it isn't coming already."

"What do you mean? Everything here on Joht has been great with your people until today."

"My mother only wants what's best for the Tralupians. She wants to use you for the technology you possess. She and Jarelen have grown closer; it's only a matter of time before she makes him her King."

"Jarelen is going to become King? That says a lot about what they're trying to do."

"Exactly...wait, someone is coming. I won't be able to talk again for a while since my mother has her guards watching me all the time now. They're getting suspicious when I lock myself in my room. Tanglor, keep a lookout... A war might be coming your way."

"I will. Thank you, Zebe. Stay safe, and we will see each other again."

Tanglor pulls his hand away, the teal light fades. He is about to leave the Great Hall, but Freden stands at the exit, waiting for him.

"It's really hard to not listen to your conversations with her…. Sorry, brother, but I couldn't help but hear that last part about the Queen and Jarelen."

"We need to get our people prepared. It sounds like we have a war coming our way."

Freden nods his head, and the two of them walk out into the night together.

# Chapter 32:
# <u>Tralupians-Losing Control</u>

Zebe sits on her bed, looking at the shiny oval. She hears footsteps coming toward her room. She quickly gets up and puts it away in the hidden compartment inside her fireplace and sits back down on her bed. A knock on the door causes her to stand up.

"Who is it?"

"It's Jarelen. Your mother sent me to escort you to the throne room."

Zebe answers sarcastically.

"Escort me? I don't need an escort. I think I know where the throne room is by now. I will be there shortly."

Jarelen bangs on the door harder.

"Open the door, Zebe. Your mother will be angry with me if I return without you."

Zebe opens the door, and he immediately snatches her arm.

"Let's not make her wait anymore. She is scary when she doesn't get her way."

Zebe shoves him away and follows him to the throne room. They arrive to see the Queen sitting on the throne, her trident in front of her as usual. She leans forward and looks at the two of them with her eyes flashing orange. Jarelen kneels before her while Zebe stands.

"Thank you for bringing her to me. Come and stand up here, Jarelen."

He walks up the stairs and stands next to the Queen. Zuna stares down at Zebe, as her eyes stop flashing and turn completely orange.

"Zebe, you have disappointed me for the last time! You will do as I say or be exiled from TokBellu. We know you have been talking to the Johthuns behind our backs since Geresen hasn't reported back to us. How were you able to speak to them without us knowing? Speak, or I will make you!"

Zebe stands, staring back at her mother in disbelief.

"You are no longer my mother. I will not answer to you or Jarelen. I know the two of you are together. It's disgusting!"

Queen Zuna stands up and slams her trident onto the ground releasing a shockwave of orange light. It knocks Zebe and Jarelen onto the ground. Werfon runs into the throne room and helps Zebe up while looking over at the Queen.

"You are not Queen Zuna! What have you done with her?"

Queen Zuna laughs as she sits back down on the throne.

"Guards! Seize the two of them!"

Tralupian guards rush out from the doors, surrounding Werfon and Zebe. Zebe looks up to Jarelen.

"You have to help us! She isn't my mother anymore. Serel has taken control of her!"

Jarelen laughs and stands next to her.

"I don't care! As long as I become King, she can be whoever the hell she wants!"

Zuna and Jarelen's laughter gets louder as they watch the guards close in on Werfon and Zebe. The two go back to back. Werfon pulls out two knives and tosses one to Zebe.

"You are still the Greatest Warrior of TokBellu. Don't be afraid. Show them why!"

He charges at four of the guards in front of him, Zebe follows. He stops and kneels. Zebe doesn't hesitate to handspring off his back, flipping behind the guards. She stabs one in the back. As he raises his sword, Zebe grabs his arm and uses it to stab through two of the other guards. She pushes them into a wall and jumps on top of them. Werfon stands and throws his knife to Zebe. She jumps in the air and flips upside down, catching it. She lands on top of a guard charging at Werfon. He falls to the ground with Zebe on top of him. Werfon grabs her hand, she spins him around, throwing him into the air. She then jumps up and pushes off him, launching herself at the last two guards standing with their blades ready. Zebe spins through their swipes and slashes one in the neck, quickly turning to kick the last guard to the ground. Werfon flies through the air and lands on top of the guard's neck, breaking it. Zebe and Werfon stand, breathing heavily and covered in blood, staring at the Queen and Jarelen. Zebe releases a loud cry.

"RRRRAAAAAAAHHHHHHH!"

She flips her knife in her hand, getting it ready to toss at the Queen, but Werfon grabs her.

"Princess, we need to leave while we still can!"

Zebe stares at the Queen for a second longer before turning and running out of the palace with Werfon. Queen Zuna stands up and turns to Jarelen.

"Our guards and soldiers need to be trained better if we're going to attack Joht. We had them surrounded, and they still got away."

Jarelen kneels to the Queen.

"Zebe is going to be hard to capture. She is the Greatest...."

"I know what she is! Do as I say!"

The Queen's eyes stay orange as she stares at Jarelen.

"Yes, my Queen."

He stands up and leaves the throne room to head to the barracks. Queen Zuna enters her chambers and falls to the ground, her eyes flashing. She puts her hands on her head, quivering on the floor in pain. She lets out a scream before a voice takes over.

"Ahhhhh! I am sorry, my Queen! I have been fighting him off, but he won't give up. My body can't handle his torment any longer. You have given up and lost your fight as well. I fear this is where we both must face the truth. We have lost, and he has taken full control of both of us."

Queens Zuna stops shaking. Abruptly, her eyes stop flashing orange and turn crimson. She smiles and stands up.

"Finally! Now I can do whatever I want. I am the Queen and leader of this planet!!"

She stands proud in her room, laughing by herself.

-----------------------------------------------------

Werfon and Zebe run out of the palace and make their way toward the slums of the city. Zebe looks around as they run, seeing the walls go from brick and cement to broken down brick and dirt. Small fires light up the night, as Tralupians walk around dirty and injured. Werfon and Zebe stop, he turns back to her.

"You have to trust me. There are still allies to the old leaders hiding away here in the slums. They will know who I am once I tell them who I am connected with."

Zebe nods her head as Werfon walks over to a fire burning in a metal cylinder. There are five Tralupians gathered around it wearing torn red hoods. Werfon stops and stands in front of the hooded Tralupians.

"I am here for your help... I know there are still some of you ready to fight for the crown. Old or young, we need anyone willing to fight to save the Queen's life. I am Werfon. I fought with your founder of this secret society. Mazray Wrathfin!"

The five hooded figures put their hands over the cylinder and slowly move their hands down onto the fire, putting it out. The ground shakes beneath them. The hooded Tralupians disappear, and a door opens up under the cylinder with stairs leading down. Werfon turns to Zebe and sticks his hand out to her.

"Hurry, before it closes."

Zebe takes his hand, and they walk down the stairs as the ground shakes, closing the door behind them. Red and orange lights flash for a second before they fill the cracks running above them, making their path visible. Zebe looks around at the underground cavern. The walls are covered in a mysterious orange-tinted metal, and the ground has red sand covering it. She stops and looks at Werfon.

"What is this place? This place looks like the Metal Mansion mother told me about on that planet, R'Ang."

Werfon turns back to her.

"It is very similar because I was ordered to come here and start another one like the one back on R'Ang. I have a tough time remembering the details now since it has been so long, but I remember coming here a very long time ago before any of the Tralupians or Ventrians were above water. I wandered around alone as a punishment for helping RoyalTree in the rebellion against those creatures. We had a name for what they called themselves and their leader, the one that posed as Ozem, but I can't remember!"

Zebe steps away from him.

"Werfon, how much more is there that I don't know about?"

He puts his head down.

"Too much, Zebe. I will tell you all about it when we aren't in danger. For now, we must keep moving. I need to find an old friend first. Her name is Rizentruyis. She is your mother's oldest sister, Zelena's firstborn."

"Rizentruyis? My mother has never spoken of her. I didn't know she had any siblings until recently when I found out who Siritano, Musfina, Oryuna, and Ilikso were."

"She was a lot like you, Zebe."

They hear rumbling above them on the surface. Werfon grabs Zebe and starts to run down the path.

"Luckily, your mother never found this place in the past, but that isn't your mother anymore... We have to move quickly."

Zebe follows behind Werfon; they get to a door at the end of the path. Werfon opens it up to uncover a massive twisting floor with an uneven pillar sticking through the middle of it. They step on it, and it starts to rotate around the pillar down further away from the surface. After a couple of minutes, the floor stops moving, revealing a door for them to walk through. Werfon does a special knock on the door with four distinguished taps, and it opens up to a room filled with a robed society. A band plays music on a stage, as Tralupians relax on couches and mingle with one another. They drink and smoke Kustifil while Werfon and Zebe walk around looking for Rizentruyis. Zebe stops and looks to Werfon.

"Wait, I don't even know what she looks like! Hey, Werfon!"

A hand reaches over and grabs her by the shoulder. Zebe turns around and looks at the Tralupian.

"Mother?"

The Tralupians erupt into laughter.

"Everyone does say I look like her... Though it should be the other way around since I'm older."

Zebe gets a nervous look on her face and tries to step away.

"Oh, don't worry. I'm not nearly as mean as her. Come, sit, and have a drink with me. It seems to me that you and Werfon were looking for me anyways. Werfon! Get over here!"

He turns around with a smile on his face and runs over to join them. Rizentruyis hugs him before sitting down at one of the tables.

"It is good to see you, old friend. Bartender! Round of drinks here for my friends and me!"

One of the bartenders raises his hand and signals her.

"Round of our best Fremple coming up!"

Rizentruyis smiles and leans in toward Werfon and Zebe.

"What's happening on the surface that drove you and the Princess down here to see me?"

Werfon looks over to Zebe.

"I'll explain it all... Queen Zuna has been possessed by one of my people. Her name was Serel, and she was forced to do it by another creature far more powerful. She has lost control, and now that creature has complete control of your sister. I know you don't care about Zuna, but this isn't about her, it's about TokBellu. We are in grave danger. She is going to send us all into a war against the Johthuns that we cannot win."

The bartender walks over with their Fremple, the mugs generously filled to the top. Rizentruyis lifts hers in cheers, as Werfon and Zebe hoist theirs up to touch hers. Zebe sips, Werfon chugs, and Rizentruyis takes the most extended pull of all. Once they've all set their mugs down, Rizentruyis sits forward with a smile on her face.

"It's nice to drink with friends again... I have no interest in helping my sister, which, unfortunately, also means I don't want to help her daughter, but I'm sure there's some dumb ass in here that would help you."

Zebe sits up straight and fixes her with an icy stare.

"I don't know you, and you don't know anything about me... I am nothing like my mother! I'm here because I trust Werfon. He said he knew someone great that would be willing to fight for their home."

Rizentruyis sits back in her seat, her smile fading into a look of sadness.

"Up there isn't my home anymore. Hasn't been since Zuna took that away from me."

Werfon stands up and gets ready to leave. Zebe stays seated, drinking her Fremple.

"I'm not leaving you like this... I don't know what my mother did to you...."

Rizentruyis slams her fists down on the table.

"Your mother, my good for nothing sister, took everything from me! I was the one that was supposed to be the Queen, and then our sweet mother, Zelena, had to have another child. Zuna grew up to challenge everything I had already worked so hard on. It wasn't fair! She was our mother's precious baby, and she gave her everything. She even took the title of Princess away from me and gave it to her when she was twelve. That's when it all started.

After that, Zuna was entitled to everything. She took toys from me and the rest of our brothers and sisters. Any friends we made were hers; boyfriends were all hers too. Nothing was ours when she was around. Eventually, I became fed up and spoke to my mother and father about it. They couldn't deal with it anymore and knew they weren't treating us all fairly, so they made us fight for it. All of us were forced to compete against each other in what's now the Halo of Vigor. Zuna was the only one willing to kill any of her siblings. She didn't hesitate and killed our brother, Valopo. Everyone else cowered down and surrendered to her, but I didn't. We fought a battle that lasted over two hours. We both grew tired and could barely keep moving when our mother finally called it. I stood up to salute our mother, the Queen, and Zuna took a cheap shot, stabbing me in the gut. They called her the winner, and the rest of us were banished to the barracks. I refused and came to the slums, where I found the followers of Maz. They treated my wound and took care of me. Been here ever since."

Zebe reaches her hand out and places it on hers.

"I am very sorry... My mother is not a good Tralupian. I was raised by her, but I became nothing like her. Please, Rizentruyis, we need your help. We need help from the followers of Maz. You were once the Greatest Warrior. Everyone compared you to Mazray."

Werfon kneels to her.

"You know how close I am to Mazray, so I can say confidently that you and Zebe are the only comparisons."

Rizentruyis stands, a smile slowly lighting up her face.

"Zebe too, huh? Alright, I will help you take the crown away from my sister."

She helps Werfon off the ground before turning around and yelling to everybody in the room.

"Hey!!! Everyone!!!"

The music stops, and all the robed Tralupians stare at her.

"Wipe the dust off your gear! The followers of Maz are going to war against the Queen!! My sister has been corrupted and possessed by some evil creature. We don't know if we can save her, so fight to kill!"

The Tralupians cheer as they scatter around, getting their gear ready. They hide blades and blasters underneath their robes, hoping to surprise their enemy. They gather around Rizentruyis, as she turns back around to Zebe and Werfon.

"We're ready when you are."

-------------------------------------------------

Jarelen approaches the barracks and gets ready to enter, but a voice comes over his shoulder.

"My son, we need to speak with you."

He turns around to find his parents, Jrantoma and Suspilenta.

"Mother, father, what are you doing here? Queen Zuna will not be happy to see you around. That was part of the arrangement."

"That is why your mother and I are here. We don't think that is Queen Zuna anymore. Something is off about her; you're in danger."

Suspilenta reaches out for Jarelen, but he pushes her hand away.

"I don't need your protection anymore. I am about to be King. You two are going to get in the way of that?"

"Jarelen, we are just looking out for you and care about your safety. You can't become her King!"

Jarelen opens the doors to the barracks.

"Come inside, and let's talk more, where others can't overhear us."

His parents follow him into the barracks. He walks into the Halo of Vigor, as his parents look around in confusion.

"Jarelen, what are we doing inside of the Halo? Your mother and I need to speak with you in private."

Jarelen ignores them and starts to walk around the arena. He looks to the soldiers surrounding the Halo and starts to yell.

"Your Queen has sent me here to tell you how weak you are! Eight of our guards had Zebe and Werfon surrounded but failed to take them down! We need to be stronger and overpower our opponents with our numbers! We know we can fight one-on-one, but why do that if we have more soldiers? Look around at each other and ask yourself if you'd die for your brothers and sisters?"

The soldiers begin to glance around and cheer, as Jarelen walks confidently around the Halo. His parents watch nervously.

"If you'll die for them, will you die for your Queen or your soon to be King!?"

The soldiers cheer louder and start clanging their blades together.

"Then do as I command and kill these two. They are traitors to the crown!"

His parents reach out for him as he walks out of the Halo.

"Son! You can't do this to us. Please!!"

The soldiers surround them, sticking their swords forward as they move in. The blades pierce through them, they fall to the ground as the soldiers back away, watching Jrantoma and Suspilenta bleed out. Jarelen watches from above the Halo with a guilty look on his face. He shakes it off and walks over to the instructor.

"Train them harder and faster. We need them ready. Zebe and Werfon aren't going to leave us alone. A fight is coming."

The instructor nods his head. Jarelen leaves the barracks and makes his way back to the palace. He arrives to the Queen smiling at him on the throne, her orange eyes fade back to normal.

"Jarelen, how was your trip to the barracks?"

He bows before taking up his station next to her.

"It was a successful trip. Not only did our soldiers have a productive day training harder than normal to be ready for your army, but I ran into my parents there as well."

"Oh, and how was that?"

He kneels before her and smiles.

"They will no longer be a problem for us. Our soldiers took care of them in the Halo."

Queen Zuna stands up with a smile on her face. She reaches down to him and helps him off the ground.

"Great work, King Jarelen."

He smiles back at her. She grabs his arm and runs into her chambers, throwing him on the bed and taking her clothes off.

-------------------------------------------------------------

Zebe and Werfon emerge from the ground underneath the slums with an army of five hundred robed Tralupians following behind them, Rizentruyis in the lead. They march through the city past the marketplace and empty barracks. Zebe turns to Werfon.

"The barracks are empty. She knows we're coming."

"We are prepared for this battle, so hopefully there won't be that many casualties."

She nods her head back at him as they approach the palace. They wait for a couple of moments before opening the gates and walking into the courtyard. Werfon stops and looks back at their army.

"Something is wrong... The gates are normally locked, and no one is here. We walked into a trap. Retreat!"

Their army starts to run back for the gate, but the Queen's soldiers shut and lock it from the other side. Queen Zuna steps out of the palace doors, her army funneling out behind her to surround Zebe and Werfon's army.

"Hahahaha, nice try, Zebe! I knew you and Werfon couldn't just leave. You had to come back to try and stop me. You're too late, though. King Jarelen and I are already waging war on Joht. We leave tonight, and you're leading the army!"

Zebe laughs at her mother and pulls her blade and blaster off her back.

"There's no way I would do that for you or Jarelen... He is no King."

Jarelen laughs and lifts his hand in the air.

"We both have titles now... mine's just a little more powerful!"

He throws his hand down, and a fleet of ships fly over them firing. Werfon dives over and knocks Zebe out of the way. The army behind them is not so lucky. Rizentruyis turns around to see her fellow followers of Maz obliterated. None of them show any signs of life. She turns back to the Queen.

"Not anymore, sister!!! I am going to kill you this time!"

Queen Zuna walks toward her.

"Sister? Which sister is this one?"

Rizentruyis pulls out her blade and swings it at her. Zuna blocks it with her trident.

"You don't remember your sister!? The one you took everything from!!!"

Queen Zuna jumps back and thrusts her trident at the blade. She catches it and twists it out of Rizentruyis' hand.

"I'm sorry, but Queen Zuna isn't here right now... I'm in control and have no idea who you are, nor do I care!! Die like the rest of them!"

Queen Zuna drives the trident into Rizentruyis' stomach. She falls to the ground as the Queen stands over her.

"Not.... again... I hate you... Zuna...."

Her life fades away as Zuna stands with her trident overlooking the soldiers surrounding Zebe and Werfon.

"Move out of the way! Let me through!"

Queen Zuna pushes her way through the crowd of soldiers and stands in the middle, watching Zebe and Werfon. The two barely stand, looking back at the Queen. She laughs and paces back and forth.

"What now, huh? You two want to keep fighting? Get some more Tralupians killed because you don't agree with your Queen!"

She slams the trident on the ground, releasing an orange shockwave. The crowd surrounding them falls to the ground, along with Zebe and Werfon. She walks over to Werfon and stands over him.

"I am tired of you whispering things into my daughter's ear. She is mine to control and always will be!"

Zebe gets up and runs over to her, as Zuna holds the trident above him. She reaches out and grabs it.

"You have to stop this at once! Werfon, hurry, and leave. Let that body die!"

Zuna tries to stab the trident down into Werfon, but his eyes flash orange, causing his mouth to open and his Broncholite body to fly out. He floats away toward the Great Tree. Queen Zuna pushes Zebe away, as her trident stabs into the lifeless body.

"Ahh, stop that orange cloud! Don't let it reach the Great Tree!"

Soldiers rush over towards Werfon, floating to the Great Tree. He releases an electric burst that causes a gust of wind, knocking them back. He reaches the tree and gets absorbed inside. Zebe sits on the ground staring at her mother. Queen Zuna lifts the trident into the air and looks down at her.

"You are no longer my daughter... Die with the rest of them!"

She starts to drive it down, but a hand comes out, grabbing onto the trident, stopping her.

"My Queen, you can use her to lead your army against the Johthuns. Don't waste her life here."

She pulls the trident back and turns to Jarelen.

"If you want to continue being King, I suggest you not do that again."

Jarelen looks at Zebe nervously. He leaves her on the ground and follows the Queen back into the palace.

"My Queen, we need to find the communication device she uses to speak with the Johthuns. It must be in her room. We need to have it before we attack Joht. Otherwise, she'll give it away before we reach their surrounding planets."

Queen Zuna nods her head to him.

"You're right. Let's go to her room and look around."

They make their way to her room. Zebe catches up in time to watch them destroy her bedroom, looking for the shiny oval. She stays quiet, knowing they won't be able to find it. Jarelen grows angry and walks over to her. He grabs her and throws her onto the bed.

"Tell us where it is, Zebe! Don't make this hard for us!"

She glares at him and keeps her mouth closed. Queen Zuna walks over to her and pulls her trident out. She puts it up against Zebe's neck.

"I spared you so that you could lead our army and redeem yourself to our people. Tell us where it is. If you don't want to, then I can go and find some of your precious people in the city to kill until you do."

Zebe's eyes start to water as she sits with the trident poking her neck.

"Zebe... Don't make me... I'll tell you what, if you give it to us and lead the army, we will spare any Johthun that surrenders. I know Tanglor Raff won't surrender. So, I will take him hostage, just for you. What do you say?"

Zebe stands up and walks over to the fireplace. She reaches her hand up underneath the ledge and grabs the shiny oval.

"This is it... I will do as you say if you stop this unnecessary killing. Our defenseless people will be left alone, and any Johthuns that survive and surrender must be left alone too. Those are my terms; otherwise, kill me now."

Queen Zuna smiles and nods her head to Zebe. She takes the shiny oval from her and walks out of the room. Jarelen follows behind.

"My Queen, you can't be serious about her terms."

"Of course, I'm not, Jarelen. She will do as we say with whatever words she needs to hear. After it is over, they will all die!"

They walk back to the throne room while Zebe sits in her room, crying. Zuna sits on the throne and looks to Jarelen.

"Get our army prepared. We leave in the morning. It will take some time to get to Joht, but we need to have everyone prepared for the attack. Let them know of the plan, and I will get Zebe ready to lead the army in one of our warships."

Jarelen bows to the Queen and walks out of the throne room. Queen Zuna sits on the throne alone, her eyes turn solid orange, and she lets out a maniacal laugh.

"My masters will be pleased to know that I'm going to kill the Tralupians and the Johthuns. They are superior to the other species we've encountered and would pose a threat to their plan. Once I eradicate both from existence, my masters will put me back in charge, and I'll be the most powerful once again!!"

Her eyes light up brighter, as she continues to laugh.

# Chapter 33:
# Johthuns-Martonamo's Memories

A year has gone by since Tanglor and Zebe last spoke. All contact with TokBellu and their Queen has been lost. The Tralupians still on Joht embrace their new life, having been so warmly welcomed and accepted into the community. The Elders have let the Tralupian diplomats join them, while other Tralupians join Geresen in the Elites.


Freden and Tanglor take a stroll around the Tazruhvah with Ashar and Neliah.

"We don't know when or if the Tralupians will actually attack us, so we need all of the Elites ready. Based on what Zebe said the last time we spoke, Jarelen is forcing himself in as King, and with Zuna already being Queen, it makes them even more treacherous."

Ashar stops walking and puts his head down.

"After everything you did for them..."

He turns to Neliah.

"I won't let them take you or Ezmariah. I'll die before I let them land on our planet!"

Neliah walks over to him and puts her arms around him.

"I won't let them take our daughter either... or you, Ashar. We're in this together. We always are!"

He embraces her. Freden walks by and pats him on the back.

"We're all in this together, no matter what."

Tanglor continues to walk ahead, observing all the Elites.

"They need more training. The Tralupians are tougher than we think. While we were on TokBellu, they made sure we didn't see their soldiers. Zebe trains every day, which means that all the Tralupians train for battle too. Their population has grown so much that families banish their youngest children to the barracks where all they do is learn how to fight. We learned all about the barracks from Zelray and Zaren."

They all stop and watch Geresen train.

"For example, Geresen has been an Elite for about a year now, and he has surpassed our other soldiers. We need to assume that all of the Tralupians can fight like that."

They nod their heads before Freden yells to him.

"Geresen, come here!"

Geresen stops training and runs over to them. He stands upright, saluting them.

"Commander, Captains, what can I do for you?"

"At ease, Geresen."

He loosens up his stance and waits for Tanglor to speak.

"We have some questions for you... about your people."

"I'll do my best to answer."

"Do all Tralupians fight like you, similarly skilled, I mean? What does the Tralupian army look like, specifically in numbers? And do the Queen or King train with them?"

He pauses and takes a couple of seconds.

"The Tralupians aren't soldiers... We are all trained to be warriors. The diplomats that are here were all warriors, too, before they gave up on fighting. Our army is colossal, but we don't have the technology or experience like you and the Elites. Our leaders, whether it be Queen Zuna or King Jarelen, know how to fight as well, but they can't lead an army like you, Tanglor. In the year that I have been here as an Elite, I have learned more from you and your Captains than I ever did on TokBellu. If we can hold the battle in space, the advantage is ours due to their lesser ships and technology, but if they reach the surface, I anticipate heavy casualties on both sides."

"Thank you for your detailed information. Get ready to speak during our meeting here shortly."

Geresen salutes them again before returning to his training. Tanglor and the others continue to the Great Hall.

"Hey, Tanglor. Neliah and I are going to run home and check on the kids before the meeting."

"Thank you, Ashar. Freden, go back and grab Geresen. I'm going to have him sit with us."

Tanglor heads inside and sits down in the commander's seat overlooking the room.

"I hope you're okay, Zebe."

His thoughts are interrupted by Trem.

"Commander, the Elders have arrived. May we come in and take our seats?"

Tanglor sits up.

"Please come in."

The Elders walk in with the Tralupian diplomats and take their seats. Trem remains standing.

"Have you had a chance to talk with the computer console? I mean, Martonamo?"

"I am sorry, Trem. We talked a little bit, but he couldn't remember anything. He needs a little more time."

"I see... Please let me know if you find anything out."

Tanglor nods his head, as the Elites come in and fill the room, taking their seats. Tanglor approaches the podium.

"I appreciate everyone coming today. I called this meeting to explain the situation we are in with the Tralupians on TokBellu. I want to reiterate to everyone that we aren't at war with all the Tralupians. We have plenty of them here who stand with us against their people. Against their own King and Queen."

The Tralupians in the Great Hall stand up. Geresen stands up with them and walks over to the podium next to Tanglor.

"Everyone here has welcomed us into their homes and treated us like family. I know I speak for every Tralupian here when I say we are very grateful. Tanglor has asked me to speak to all of you today about the Tralupian army. I was once a part of it, fighting alongside the new King. Like I told Tanglor, their army is massive, but they don't fight as one, like the Elites. They are all great warriors on their own, and they rely on that. If we can take them out before they get to the surface, we hold the advantage. If they manage to land, the fight will change, there will be heavy casualties on both sides. Our technology and ships will be our real advantage, so we need to try and hold them in space."

Tanglor takes back over at the podium.

"Thank you for that, Geresen. As all of you know, Geresen was the one that killed our beloved Elisin a year ago. He has paid his dues with the Elites and has pulled his weight in the community. Elisin would be proud to see what you've done here. I want to take this moment to announce Geresen as the first Tralupian Captain of the Elites!"

The Great Hall thunders with cheers, as Geresen stands next to the commander. He turns and salutes the new Captain. The cheers fade away, and everyone stands still, waiting for Tanglor to speak.

"Remain alert and stay close to your positions. If the Tralupians attack, we won't see them coming until they hit Conril. Ucarus will be keeping a lookout. We're assuming that they'll pass our other planets and come straight for Joht since they want Martonamo."

The Elites salute again upon dismissal, and the Elders follow behind. As Tanglor gets ready to leave, he is approached by Ashar and Neliah.

"Tanglor, wait up."

"Ashar, what's going on?"

"Neliah and I are ready to fight. We want to be up there in the front lines with you."

"I appreciate that Ashar, but I couldn't live with myself if anything were to happen to either of you. I'm sorry, brother, but you two will be leading the squads for backup. If they get past us in orbit, I need the two of you here, getting everyone ready to fight."

Ashar lowers his head and is about to argue with him, but Neliah grabs his arm.

"Thank you for thinking about us and our daughter, Tanglor. We won't let you down."

They turn and leave the Great Hall with Ezmariah. Freden stands, waiting next to the cavern entrance.

"The kids are with Geresen right now. They're going to do a little bit of training with him. You ready to see if Martonamo remembers anything?"

"Yeah, let's go."

They hold their hands up to the wall, and the ovals start to shine. The wall disappears, opening the way up to the cavern. Freden follows behind Tanglor as they make their way to Martonamo. As they approach the cavern, they can already see the teal light flashing. Martonamo is training on the screen. Tanglor smiles.

"Hey Mart, what's going on?"

The screen stops flashing, and Martonamo turns to them.

"Hey, guys! I know how to fight!"

He starts to jump around, kicking the air.

"Is there anything else you remember?"

"I remember my father, but it's still pretty hazy. I was hoping that I would remember more with you two here."

Freden turns to Tanglor.

"That's why we came down here, right? The more he remembers, the closer we get to figuring out what that pit in the Rashintrah is for."

"The pit!? I briefly remember my father talking to me about a pit my people would use to obtain knowledge from those that had passed away."

Tanglor sits down in front of Martonamo.

"We need to know what it was for and if it has to do with the one in the Rashintrah. It took Elisin's body, and when she fell in, the same teal light that appears with you and our ovals shined out of the pit."

"All I know is that she was hiding this from her people. She even hid it from Tazlow. The Elders are the only ones that knew about it until now. It has been so long, I wish I could tell you everything about it, but I can't remember. I am sorry."

"It's okay, Mart. Freden, sit down. Let's see if we can help Martonamo remember."

Freden sits with Tanglor. Martonamo stands still on the screen and takes a deep breath.

"All right, here we go."

The computer screen flashes teal, taking over their minds once again. Their eyes start to flash in sync with the screen. It stops, and their eyes are entirely teal, gazing up at Martonamo. The walls in the cavern slowly crumble away, leaving them suspended in the air. The screen Mart was on disappears, and his body forms in front of them.

"Martonamo, where are we?"

The three of them turn around while looking at their surroundings. The sky is a bright purple with red clouds floating above them. Green water courses through a forest full of tall orange trees, and the land is filled with lush, blue grass. Martonamo takes Freden and Tanglor down to the surface.

"This is my homeworld. It's the same place as the last flashback, but it looks like it did in the early part of our history before those giants arrived. My planet used to be full of life. It's starting to come back to me."

Tanglor walks toward the green water.

"Everything is altered here; the colors are so different. It's weird. When we traveled around to other solar systems finding new planets, the animals and plant life were similar, but here it is noticeably different."

Martonamo kneels next to him and reaches into the water.

"You are right, Tanglor... Again, I wish I could give you the reason for that."

Tanglor stands up and puts his hand on Martonamo's shoulder.

"It's all right, Mart. Let's look around and see what's going on. You brought us here for a reason, right?"

"We wouldn't be here if I didn't. Thank you, Tanglor."

Martonamo takes his hand out of the water and stands next to Tanglor. Freden starts to yell at them from the forest.

"Guys! It looks like some of Martonamo's people!"

They run over and watch as creatures that look like Martonamo walk deeper into the forest. Mart starts to follow behind them.

"My father has to be with them. Let's see where they go."

Tanglor and Freden trail behind, examining everything they see. Suddenly, the creatures stop walking, and random holes appear on the ground beneath them, swallowing them up. As they fall inside, teal light shoots up from the openings. Martonamo falls to his knees.

"Where did they go?"

Tanglor and Freden approach him and place their hands on his shoulders. The light shines from their hands onto Martonamo. A couple of seconds go by, and the light grows more prominent, engulfing the three of them. The ground beneath them starts to shake. Tanglor and Freden try to remove their hands, but they're locked onto his shoulders.

"Mart!! What's going on!?"

He opens his mouth to respond, but the teal light spews out. Without being able to speak, he points down to the ground; a hole opens with light shooting out from it. Freden watches nervously.

"I guess we're going down the hole."

The light takes control of their bodies and lowers them down, closing the hole behind them. They journey miles below the surface to a hidden cavern. The light fades away, leaving them on the cavern floor. Martonamo turns to them.

"I remember something... This...This was once my home. My people were like yours. We couldn't dwell on the surface, so we lived down here away from danger."

Martonamo is interrupted by another voice.

"My son! You have returned from the surface! What did you find up there?"

They look over and see Martonamo's people surrounding what looks like their King and Prince. Martonamo slowly approaches them.

"Father…. I was the prince to my people, and my father was our King. I…. I was the reason they found us."

Tanglor puts his hand on his back, and the teal light starts to flash again. He turns to Freden.

"Hurry, put your hand on his back next to mine."

He runs over and places his hand next to Tanglor's. The teal light shines through, touching everything in the cavern before fading away. Everything in the room is suspended in time, except for them. They walk around, inspecting the cavern. Martonamo walks over and places his hand on the King's arm; the light shines through him.

"Tanglor, Freden, come quick!"

They both run over and grasp the King's arm, causing the teal light to flow through them. It shines bright surrounding them and the King. The light again fades away, and the King begins to move.

"Martonamo? Is that you?"

"Father? Can you see me?"

"Of course, I can! Mart, what's going on?"

Martonamo grabs his father and hugs him.

"I never thought I would see you again."

"What do you mean? I was just talking to you after you returned from the surface. Wait—why do you look older, my son?"

"I… I am older, father. I don't know how any of this is possible, but I haven't seen you in over a thousand years."

"I don't understand…. Who are your interesting looking friends?"

"I have traveled here from the future with them. I've been trapped in a computer console for thousands of years; I share a bond with these two now. Their names are

Freden Luns and Tanglor Raff. They call themselves Johthuns from the planet Joht. They reside in the Fruyistia solar system."

The King grabs Martonamo by the arms and looks into his eyes.

"You have that look in your eye, Mart. I know you're telling me the truth, but I still don't understand why you're here or how any of this is even possible."

"I wish I could tell you, father... After I was put into the computer console, my memories were taken from me, and I was filled with knowledge from other worlds. I can't even remember your name or what we were called..."

"My name is Marheesen Jusintar; your mother's name is Jeseen Jusintar. You were our only son, the prince of our people."

"What do we call our species?"

"We call ourselves the Zelotrides, and we live on the planet Harbenson, for now. Sadly, I am uninformed about what solar system we reside in."

Martonamo takes a couple of seconds to grasp what his father said.

"I'm a Zelotride; my homeworld is called Harbenson.... Your name is Marheesen, and mom was Jeseen. Thank you for reminding me, father. It has been too long since I've heard those names."

"Am I going to remember this after you leave? Your younger self is still here suspended in time. What will happen once you leave?"

"I don't know... It will probably seem like a dream. You'll appear crazy if you try to tell our people or my younger self. Father, why are we not on the surface?"

"You don't remember that either?"

"I know it was dangerous for us, but I can't remember why."

The King lowers his head.

"We used to live on the surface. We had everything we needed to survive and thrive. Our population was growing, and the Zelotrides were exceptionally good at farming and hunting. We excavated a lot of the land to start building and colonizing. We hunted the animals around us for food and retrieved fresh water from the river flowing next to us. We lived abundantly off the land. We even had our scientists discovering new ways to grow food and breeding different plant hybrids. Meanwhile, others were free to explore our world. Our top explorer was you, Mart. Ten Zelotrides accompanied you on your voyage, and your team was gone for two weeks before returning. Only one other Zelotride walked back into camp with you that day."

Martonamo steps away from his father.

"Nevrahniah…"

"Yes… You and Nevrahniah were the only two from your team that came back alive. The other eight were lost to what you described as 'a massive hooded figure from the sky with bright green eyes and a thundering voice. The two of you took us back to where it happened. I'm sorry to say we struggled to believe you until we got there and saw the mess for ourselves. Blood and bones from our people were scattered across the ground; when we looked up into the sky, there it was—a massive hooded figure staring down at us with its glowing green eyes. I will never forget that day. We sought shelter underground and have lived here ever since. I believe it's been close to a hundred years now."

"That was the first time I saw the hooded figure. Nevrahniah and I saw it again, not long after living down here."

"We've sent scouts out almost every day since being down here. Today's the first day we had reports on the figure. You were the one that gave it to me a couple of minutes ago, Mart. The hooded figure is destroying the lush nature above us. You want to get close enough to talk to it, but I refuse to let you die by that monster."

"That must be what happens then… I remember wanting to know what it was, so I went against everything you told me, father…. I am sorry."

The King hugs Martonamo.

"Father?"

"What is it, Mart?"

"Where does the teal light come from? I thought it was something from the computer console, but it seems like it has something to do with us Zelotrides."

The King's eyes open wide; he gets a nervous look on his face.

"If you're asking me that, then I must've never told you... I have kept it a secret from our people for as long as I can remember. Our history is a lie, son. We were created by......."

The King fades back into suspended time with all the other Zelotrides. Martonamo falls to his knees.

"No! What was he going to tell me? I didn't get to say goodbye!"

Martonamo reaches his hand out for the King, while tears fall down his face. The teal light flashes bright, filling the cavern and freeing the Zelotrides from suspended time. Tanglor helps Martonamo off the ground and walks back over to Freden.

"He said we were created.... Created? What does that even mean? Who created us!? And for what!?

They continue watching as the younger Martonamo speaks to the King.

"Father, the hooded figure has been spotted. It's terrorizing everything up there. We have to do something."

The King looks around the cavern in confusion, like he just awoke from a dream. He lets a few seconds pass before responding.

"There is nothing for us to do, my son. We have already lost too many Zelotrides to that monster. There is no stopping it."

"What about communicating with it? There has to be a reason as to why it's here, right?"

The King turns away from his son.

"Please, listen to me when I beg you not to go near that monster. It will only get you and more of our people killed!"

He tries to speak again, but the King walks away from him. The younger Martonamo is about to follow but gets stopped by Nevrahniah.

"Let him go. The others are planning on going back to the surface, but they don't want to go without us."

"My father is hiding something. He has been for a while, and I think it has to do with the hooded figure. He acts strange every time I bring it up to him. I need to go and speak to him more. Go on ahead with the others, and I'll meet up with you in a bit. Be careful, Nevrahniah."

She hugs him before walking away, Martonamo follows the King into his quarters.

"Father! You need to tell me what you're hiding, please!"

The King sits down on his bed.

"I am sorry, my son, but there are things that you won't understand... I don't even understand them myself."

"What are you talking about? You're the King!"

"How long have I been King, Mart?"

"Since day one. You are the only King we have ever known."

"How long ago was that, son?"

"Over five hundred years ago."

"And over these past five hundred years, our people have barely aged, and no one has ever tried to overthrow me as King."

"I just thought that's how we age... and you've been a good King. Why would anyone want to overthrow you?"

"If our people knew the truth... I wouldn't be King anymore."

He approaches the young Mart.

"My son, I have been given the burden of keeping this secret. If I were to share it with you, then the burden becomes yours, and I don't want you living with the guilt that I have."

"I will help carry the burden, father. Please tell me!"

"Leave me."

"Well, I am going back to the surface—whether you like it or not. Our people deserve to know the truth, whatever it is!"

Martonamo walks out of the room, while the King yells to him.

"You're going to get us all killed, Mart!"

He ignores his father and leaves to go with the others back to the surface. He finds Nevrahniah waiting for him with five other Zelotrides.

"How did it go with your father?"

"Whatever he's hiding from us, our answers are on the surface."

They nod their heads and kneel to the ground. The teal light starts to shine, lifting them toward the surface. It bursts through the ceiling, creating holes for them to go through. Tanglor and Freden watch as Martonamo floats them back up with the Zelotrides. They follow young Mart and his team of five as they look for the giant hooded figure. It's not long before they can feel the ground rumbling. Young Mart and Nevrahniah take their team and hide behind the tall trees. They can see the giant walking around, the hood still covering its face as it destroys its surroundings. Everywhere it steps leaves devastation behind. Young Mart jumps out from behind the trees.

"Hey!! We're tired of you destroying our planet!"

The giant ignores him.

"Get back here. We need to talk to you!"

The giant stops and turns back to them, its green eyes staring while it roars at them.

"Urlonk Trabah!"

"I can't understand you!"

The ground shakes as the giant walks back toward young Mart. The Zelotrides with him hide behind the trees, while Nevrahniah chooses to stand her ground with Mart. The giant stops in front of them and kneels to get closer to them.

"Urlonk Trabah! New beginning! You are not part of our new beginning!"

Mart steps closer to it.

"What new beginning?"

"Our new beginning! The universe has too many creatures like you in it. We must cleanse everything to start anew. Urlonk Trabah!!"

"You don't get to decide that! We live our own lives and get to make our own decisions. We decide to live!!"

"Is that so? HA HA HA HA HA, you're the first small creature I've liked. What is your name?"

"My name is Martonamo Jusintar and I am a Zelotride!"

"I know what you are. You and your people can't hide underground forever. Tell your father that I would like to speak with him. It's been a while."

Young Mart looks confused, but before he can respond, the giant gets up and laughs as he walks away.

Nevrahniah grabs onto Mart.

"How does that thing know your father?"

"Let's go find out. Come on."

Young Mart and his team head back underground. They arrive to find the King sitting on his throne with his head down.

"You found him, didn't you?"

"The giant? Yeah, we found him."

"Then I assume he spoke to you?"

"He did. He wanted me to tell you that it's time for the two of you to talk again. What are you keeping from us?"

"Mart... sit down, and I'll explain everything. The rest of you leave us at once!"

Young Martonamo sits down next to his father, while Nevrahniah and the others leave.

"My life started a long time ago. It has been too long to remember the exact day I was created by whatever those hooded figures are."

"You were created?"

"We were all created by them. I was the first one they put on this planet, and they watched me for years with little interaction. Then one day, they decided to create your mother and bring her down from their ship. Your mother and I had no choice but to live together. We were the only Zelotrides on Harbenson. About fifty years went by, and your mother and I had grown happy together. We lived off the land and built a little shack. One day, the massive ship reappeared over us, and hundreds of Zelotrides came floating down with that giant hooded figure. He towered before us with the Zelotrides standing behind him like zombies. The giant leaned down with his glowing green eyes and said his name was Rowelt. He said that we were created by him and his leaders to achieve their goal."

Young Mart interrupts him.

"Urlonk Trabah... Their new beginning."

"Yes... their new beginning and we are no longer a part of it."

"That's what Rowelt told me on the surface."

"We were created with a vast amount of knowledge that we still don't understand. They wanted us to use this knowledge to be superior to other life forms. We were to be their warriors, their slaves to kill other sentient life that would be a threat to our "Masters." The first species we had to exterminate was on our planet. They called themselves Garblots. They weren't as intelligent as us, but they were violent and robust. Rowelt and our Masters wanted them gone, and we were the ones that had to do it. We hunted all the Garblots and murdered them all like we were told. When we came back, Rowelt was waiting for us. He was pleased and said we did a good job. Before he left, he told us that when he came back, there would be more for us to do. Your mother and I sat with the mindless Zelotrides, as we watched Rowelt float back up to his ship and take off."

"Who else knows about this? How has it been a secret this whole time."

"After the other Zelotrides minds developed, we held a meeting to discuss what to do. Everyone looked to me for answers since I was created first. I didn't want us to be destroyed by our Masters, so I did what I thought would keep us alive. We listened to Rowelt whenever he came back."

"That still doesn't tell me how it was kept a secret this long, father!"

"Rowelt came back three years later in his massive ship. When he arrived, he had no interest in what we had been doing. All he wanted was for us to exterminate another species. He told all of us to get onto the ship so that we could go and find them. None of us had seen anything other than planet Harbenson; we were in awe at the wonders of space! We saw things we couldn't explain, even with our vast amount of knowledge. But we left our solar system and then left our galaxy! We traveled to a place they called Barnard's Galaxy, where we entered a solar system called Bravadier. We found a small purple planet and entered its atmosphere. For a while, we sat above the planet, hovering in the massive ship, and watching the Furgorlons below us. Rowelt ordered us to land and exterminate them, so we did. But there were too many of them, and they fought back. Rowelt had to leave the ship to help us; he wasn't happy about it. In retaliation, he went on a spree, killing all the Furgorlons with powers that we couldn't explain. I couldn't watch it anymore; I decided to help some of them escape. I took them to a small pond away from their town. Rowelt discovered me doing this, and he zapped the water with a ray of light. I don't know what it was, but he turned the Furgorlons back into tiny creatures swimming around the pond. Rowelt then picked me up and forced me to look at the destruction, blaming me for it happening this way. He then proceeded to call all of us Zelotrides worthless and a waste of their resources. He exclaimed that we should never have been created. He wanted to destroy us but had to wait to hear from his leaders. He brought us back to Harbenson, but before we could leave the ship, he used his powers to erase everyone's memories except mine..."

"Why would he leave you with your memory?"

"I've asked myself that question every day since... All I can think is that he wanted me to keep these memories so that I would suffer alone. I can't do anything to stop him, and there are others like him that are more powerful. The only choice I had was to convince our people of the dangers above ground and go into hiding. It seems like our time here is up, now that Rowelt knows we're down here."

"I am sorry, father. If I knew about this, I wouldn't have gone against you. I need to tell Nevrahniah!"

"You can't! This is why I've been keeping it a secret. If the rest of our people find out, they'll want answers, and those answers are going to get us all killed. No matter what Rowelt says or does, their goal is a new beginning. It starts here with us, Mart. We were their creations, and we went against them! If we stop hiding, they'll kill us and move on to different worlds in different galaxies."

"We can't just sit here and do nothing! I can't just sit here knowing about all of this."

"You won't have to worry about it, my son. I am sorry."

"Sorry for what?"

The King walks over to his son and puts his arms on his shoulders.

"I stole this from Rowelt the day I left his ship. It makes people forget."

The King pulls out a shiny oval and pushes the button; a bright red light shines out. He closes his eyes and turns away while Young Mart stares into it. A couple of seconds go by, and the red light fades away. The King puts the oval back into his pocket.

"What can I do for you, Mart?"

Young Mart looks at his father, confused.

"I can't remember... I'm sorry, father."

"That's okay. Go and get some rest."

Young Mart walks out of the room. The King sits down on the throne with his face in his hands.

Tanglor turns to Martonamo.

"Your father told you everything and then erased your memories?"

"I'm starting to remember, but we need to see the rest of the flashback. My younger self goes to Nevrahniah, and she knew something happened!"

The teal light starts to flash, and the walls change. They end up back in the cavern under the Tazruhvah. Martonamo is back on his screen, Tanglor and Freden regain their consciousness.

"Mart, what happened? Why are we back here?"

"I... I don't know Tanglor. Something pulled us back."

A voice comes through the intercom.

"Tanglor! Can you hear me? It's Ucarus. The Tralupians just flew by Conril. They didn't stop or radio in. I think that war Zebe warned us about is on its way!"

"Thank you, Ucarus. Get your troops ready. Follow behind them and rendezvous with Mac-Ran on Thoonta."

"Copy that, Commander. Mac-Ran and I will be ready to attack from behind."

Tanglor turns to Freden and Martonamo.

"I'm sorry, Mart, but we need to get the Elites prepared for battle."

Mart sits down in his chair on the screen.

"I'll see you on the Mercurana, Commander Raff."

Tanglor and Freden make their way back up the path to the Great Hall, where Geresen and Ashar are waiting.

"Freden, go and get the Elites ready with Ashar and Geresen. I'm going to try to get through to Zebe."

Freden nods his head and follows Ashar and Geresen out of the Great Hall. The teal light flashes through Tanglor's hand as he holds it to his face.

"Mart put me through to Zebe."

A couple of seconds go by, and there is no answer.

"Mart! Put me through to Zebe!"

"I am trying, Tanglor. It doesn't seem like she's there."

"Try again!"

After a couple more seconds, a voice comes through.

"Ahh, if it isn't the great Tanglor Raff!"

"Jarelen…"

"It's King Jarelen now! I wanted to thank you for taking Zebe from me. The Queen is a much more suitable partner."

"Where's Zebe!? If you did anything to her, you're dead!"

"It's quite the opposite. Zebe is with us; she's the one leading our army! But enough of this, Tanglor, we will see you soon! Zebe, you won't be needing this communication oval anymore."

A loud, crashing sound comes through the oval, followed by static.

"That bastard!"

# Chapter 34:
# <u>Tralupian-Becoming a Traitor</u>

A Tralupian warship enters the orbit of TokBellu alone. It lands inside the shuttle bay. The doors open, and a crew of Tralupians walk out of it. Zebe walks out with her head down. One of her crew members walks over to her.

"Zebe... I am sorry. I didn't know. I..."

She lifts her head and looks at him.

"It's okay; you were just doing your job. Anyone else would have done the same thing. Go and get some rest, and don't worry about me."

He salutes her before running off with the others. She looks around and slowly walks into the palace. She sits on the throne in the empty palace.

"Why did she have to go to war? Why did she do any of this? I don't understand!"

Tears start to run down her face, as an orange light appears in front of her. She wipes her face and stands up. The light flickers as it floats toward the Great Tree. Zebe walks down the steps and follows the light out of the palace. She stands, staring at the Great Tree, watching the light fly into it and disappear. The sun behind her falls beneath the ocean line; the three moons rise as she reaches her hand out for the tree. Orange sparks shoot off the trunk of and her hand, creating a doorway for her to walk through. Zebe finds herself in TralVent, standing underneath a newly constructed statue of Ilikso. The tall tower stands rebuilt behind the statue, but the bell is missing. Ilikso appears next to her.

"We rebuilt the tower and the sculpture... I hate this statue. I told them to make it of someone more deserving of it. Zebe, I am sorry for your mother, but there is nothing I can do. Werfon is the only one capable of leaving the Great Tree since he is a Broncholite, but the body he used is gone. We haven't been able to find another suitable body for him to bond with."

Zebe turns to him and stands tall.

"What about me? Didn't he and Mazray share a bond?"

"They did, but that was under different circumstances. It was when Werfon was still being controlled by those creatures. Mazray fought off their evil, leaving Werfon to be free. He chose to stay within her, and they helped each other grow. Mazray became who she was because of him. I don't know, Zebe."

Werfon floats out from behind the statue.

"I can bond with Zebe... She is just like Mazray. It may be the only option we have."

Zebe walks over to him and reaches her hand out to his floating gaseous body.

"As long as you never try to control me... I promise we will find you another body suited for you."

Werfon moves closer to her and starts to float around her.

"It will hurt for a moment. Take a deep breath and try to relax."

Zebe closes her eyes and takes a deep breath, as Werfon surrounds himself around her. When she breathes in again, he starts to get sucked in while the rest of him seeps through her skin. She falls to her knees with her fist on the ground. Her eyes flash orange quickly as she lets out a soft growl.

"Urrrrgh."

She stands back up, and the orange in her eyes fades away.

"Werfon, can we still speak to each other?"

A few seconds pass before the orange light flashes in her chest.

"We can. Whenever you need anything, I will be right here. The longer we stay together, the faster our bond will build, and we will grow stronger. Soon you will be able to use some of my powers. You can release parts of me into others so that you can control them for a brief period. I can leave your body completely for five minutes before I'll need to return to you."

"What happens if you don't make it back in time?"

"I slowly start to die. If I lose all the particles around me that create my gaseous body, I'll expire."

"Glad you told me that. We will have to work on some of those powers as our bond grows. Let me know what else I can do for you, Werfon. My body is yours as well until we find you a different one."

"I appreciate that Zebe, but you are still in control. I will never take control unless you ask me to."

"What would be the difference if you took control?"

"I would be able to withstand a lot more than you usually could. I can control my gaseous body and use it as a weapon, along with your body. There are many things, Zebe, but when I take control, you will become paralyzed within yourself, forced to watch and feel whatever happens."

"If it ever comes to that, I will ask for your help, Werfon. In the meantime, what do we do now? The King and Queen are going to kill me if they return from that war."

Ilikso walks over and interrupts them.

"Your mother is gone, for now, but she may come back at any time. Queen Zuna and King Jarelen will not be happy to see you upon their return. You ought to leave while you still can. You are in grave danger if you stay here waiting for them."

Zebe looks at him and then at the tower behind the statue.

"Father.... what is up in that tower? Why did it need to be rebuilt?"

"The other Remnants needed it back. Without it, we have no energy, and we fade away completely. Whatever is in the heart of that tower keeps us here in this tree. That's what feeds off the Wrathfin life force since RoyalTree has been gone. We need it to survive, Zebe."

She walks over to the statue and touches it.

"Hmmm, something about this statue doesn't feel right to me. Is there something inside of it? Now that I think about it, fewer Remnants are walking around."

Ilikso walks over to her and the statue.

"Zebe, you need to listen to me! Take what you can and who you can and leave TokBellu! There is nothing but destruction heading for it!"

She looks back at him, and he fades away. The other Remnants start to fade away too. The city of TralVent disappears as she stands in front of the tower. A bright light flashes at the top of it before shooting out and touching everything inside the tree. Zebe watches as everything fades away into nothing. She makes a run for the doorway, while the light creeps behind her. She jumps through just as the light hits it, closing it. Zebe turns around and looks at the Great Tree. It flashes orange and changes to a dark red color. The Great Tree's leaves start to fall into the water, as the bark on the tree dries out, becoming decrepit. Branches follow the leaves, crashing into the water and sticking out, like hands reaching out for help. Zebe watches in horror. Her chest flashes orange, and Werfon speaks to her.

"Zebe, get into the palace and shut the doors. It's going to spread."

Zebe turns and runs into the palace as the darkness stretches through the Great Tree's roots into the ground. It reaches the core and shoots out to the other trees spread out throughout TokBellu. The land around them turns the same dark red color. TokBellu looks like a grim wasteland as Zebe sits on the throne.

"I don't know what to do! I don't know what's happening. Werfon, what's going on?"

Her chest flashes orange again.

"I... I don't know Zebe. The Great Tree isn't dying, but something has corrupted it. The crimson light tells me that my people have something to do with this, but not under their own control. This is the doing of the same creature controlling your mother."

"We have to stop whatever is happening, while my mother wages her war on the Johthuns."

"I agree, but how do we stop this?"

"You're a Broncholite, like RoyalTree. He created all the trees and the lush environment by going into the core and becoming the tree. Couldn't you do something similar?"

"I don't think I can. RoyalTree did that out of desperation and wasn't sure if it would even work. I could be lost forever or even join in on the corruption and make it worse. There has to be another way."

As Zebe talks to Werfon, a couple of her crew members run in.

"Zebe! We're being attacked by our people in the city. The trees around us are latching onto Tralupians with their branches and controlling them. We can't attack our own people!"

Zebe stands up and pulls her blade and blaster out.

"If the trees have latched onto them, they're corrupted now and not our people anymore. We need to protect those that are still safe. Follow me to the city. We need to get the rest of our people back here safely."

Zebe and the two soldiers run out of the palace toward the city while Tralupians with tree branches sticking out of their bodies attack them. Zebe slides underneath one, slicing it in half. She fires her blaster at another one, hitting it between the eyes. The two soldiers with her stay close, fighting off any branches attempting to sneak up on Zebe. They get to the city to find it infested with corrupt Tralupians. They let out loud screeches as Zebe and the two soldiers' approach. One of the windows opens from the second floor of a house, and another one of Zebe's crew members sticks her head out.

"You have to help us. We can't get out! One of them is at the door; we can't hold it for much longer!"

The two soldiers charge at the entrance on the first floor, while Zebe opts to run up the wall. She grabs hold of a pipe and flips herself around and up onto an overhang. She climbs up a vine wrapped around the house until she can reach the window. Zebe hauls herself through it just as the corrupted Tralupian breaks the door down. It runs at the crew member, but Zebe rolls underneath her, stabbing her blade through the infected. She turns to her crew member.

"Lead everyone you can find back to the palace. Hurry!"

The crew member leaves with the other Tralupians that were in there. Zebe makes her way downstairs to see the other two soldiers fighting off the corrupted. Zebe uses her blaster, freeing one of the soldiers. He retreats to her. Her other soldier slices through the corrupted with ease until one sneaks up behind her and grabs her helmet. She ducks, allowing Zebe a clear path to throw her blade forward, piercing the corrupted in the face. The soldier stands in awe, looking at Zebe.

"Thank you; you saved me."

The soldier kneels. Zebe walks over and helps her up.

"Now is not the time. Please stay by my side and help me get everyone else back safely. What is your name?"

"My name is Yulista. I have been trying to stay hidden from the Queen. She sent my brother on a mission to Joht and held me as leverage. I escaped and hid from her—right in plain sight."

Zebe hugs her.

"Yulista! I have been looking for you since your brother called me with Tanglor Raff. Your brother has joined the Elite Protectors. Tanglor Raff forgave him and let him live out his life as an Elite. He told me to look for you and keep you safe. I am so glad to finally have found you!"

Yulista opens her eyes wide and hugs Zebe back.

"I am so happy to hear that! My brother is the only thing I have left, so I am thrilled to know that he is still alive after doing what he did. Tanglor Raff sounds like a great Johthun."

Zebe smiles at her.

"He is... Come and stay with me, Yulista, even after we get through this."

She nods her head and smiles back to Zebe, as they make their way through the city looking for other non-corrupted Tralupians. They get to the barracks where some of the warriors in training are protecting civilians. Yulista runs ahead with her blade in front of her. Zebe follows behind, firing her blaster at the corrupted. Yulista stabs one in the back and flips over them. She stands in front of the door as Zebe powers her way through the rest of them. The instructor is positioned behind the door. He opens it up and lets them in, shutting it in a hurry behind them, so more corrupted can't get through. Zebe and Yulista look around and see hundreds of civilians and young warriors in training. She walks to a child and places her hand on its head while looking around to everyone else and.

"I happen to be here under fortunate circumstances, but I am ready to lead all of you! We need to leave here and make our way back to the palace. Everyone else is making their way there with the other soldiers. If we wait too long, those corrupted are going to overwhelm us. I just don't understand how they can keep attacking even after we've killed them."

The civilians and warriors listen to her words and ready themselves to fight. They stand behind Zebe and Yulista, ready to charge out the doors. Zebe runs through, with them following behind her. They take on the horde of corrupted outside the barracks. As they run to the palace, Zebe looks back and sees roots sprouting out of the ground, lifting the dead corrupted back on their feet. The root glows crimson and recharges the corrupted, allowing them to keep attacking. She turns back and runs behind the others. She yells to Yulista and the other soldiers.

"The Great Tree is causing all of this, and I am the only one that can get inside. You need to take these people into the palace and lock all the doors in the throne room. We cannot fight off the corrupted since they will keep returning."

Yulista stops running and looks to Zebe.

"I will protect these people; you have my word. Just promise me that you won't go and get yourself killed while you're in the Great Tree. You have to take me back to my brother now."

Zebe smiles and hugs Yulista. She turns around and runs to the palace closing the doors behind her. Zebe walks to the Great Tree. It flashes dark red as she approaches it. The Great Tree's flashing gets faster, the closer she gets. She touches it with her hand; it turns orange under her palm as the tree lets out a loud groan.

"Urrrrgrrrrggggggghhhh."

Zebe puts her other hand on the tree and closes her eyes.

"Father, I know you're still in there. Open the door. I need to get in."

She opens her eyes, and a hole starts to form. She reaches her hands out, pushing it apart and making it bigger. She flips inside, and it closes behind her. The city of TralVent lies in ruins, while the tower and statue sit unharmed behind it. Zebe pulls her blade out and walks through the broken city. Remnants start to appear around her. Their transparent orange figures remain the same, but their eyes glow crimson. Grundar and Zalzatine attack her first; she flips backward and throws her blade at the small Ventrian. It hits him in the face, and he fades away into ash. She runs and slides on her knees, grabbing her blade in time to block Zalzatine's attack. She flips around on the ground, kicking his feet out from underneath him. He falls to the ground; she jumps up and swings her blade into his chest. He dissipates into a cloud of orange ash. Zebe gets up and continues. From behind one of the buildings come three more transparent Tralupians. Hetra, Zaren, and Zeph stand together, smiling with their eyes glowing the same crimson color. They charge Zebe, but she meets them head-on and tackles Hetra to the ground. Zaren jumps with her blade at Zebe, but she moves out of the way, causing Zaren to stab Hetra. Zeph shoots his blaster at Zebe. She jumps behind Zaren and uses her as a shield. Zebe walks forward as he fires, turning Zaren into the ash in front of Zeph. Zebe's blade comes through the cloud, stabbing Zeph in the face. He falls to the ground and crumbles away like the others. Zebe stands victorious, covered in the orange ash of her defeated foes. An angry growl comes from the tower.

She makes her way to the statue. Out from behind it come Ilikso, Oryuna, Musfina, Mazray, Tez, Zelena, and Za-Ryan. Their eyes all glow the dark red. They hold blades in their hands as they circle Zebe. Her chest flashes orange.

"Zebe, let me take control... I promise I'll release you as soon as I defeat them."

She looks around at the seven Tralupians circling her.

"All of them are formidable warriors, plus Mazray... I will allow you to take control, Werfon. Good luck."

Zebe kneels to the ground and relaxes her mind as Werfon moves through her body, latching onto her brain. When her head lifts, her eyes glow solid orange. He stands her up and pulls out her sword. Her other hand trembles before an orange blade shoots out, matching the metal one in her other hand. Werfon has her charge at Musfina and Oryuna. As she gets closer, sparks shoot out of her. They're blinded by the flashes, allowing her to jump over them. When they can see again, they look around in confusion before glancing down to see blades blooming from their chests. They fall to the ground and crumble away to ash. The other five charge at her, Werfon shoots an orange gas at them. They get lost in the mist, as Zebe runs in and slices her blades through it. She stands, breathing heavily, watching the cloud disappear. It finally dissipates, revealing Ilikso and Mazray left standing. Ilikso walks forward with Mazray behind him.

"I must admit you have become an impressive warrior, but let's see if you can rightfully call yourself the greatest. Mazray, take her out!"

Mazray walks out in front of him with her blade pointing at Zebe. She stands firm with Werfon still in control. She charges at Mazray, swinging the sword in her left hand while she stabs the orange one in her right hand. Mazray ducks and swipes her blade to the side, blocking both attacks. She laughs and jumps behind Zebe. Zebe turns and swings her orange sword again. The tip touches Mazray's face, cutting her and causing ash to trickle out of it slowly. She lifts her hand and feels the wound.

"You got a hit on me... You are good."

Mazray charges again, flipping in the air, she pulls out three small knives and throws them. Zebe flips backward, swiping her blades at the knives. She deflects them— hitting the last one back at Mazray. She rushes over, as Mazray hits the ground. Zebe holds her blade against her neck.

"You've lost, Mazray. The knife wounded you when it hit your leg. Move, and my blade goes into your neck."

She struggles as Zebe stands on top of her.

"Just kill me. The Great Tree has been corrupted by that creature! We've lost everything!"

Her eyes flash the dark red, as she reaches for the knife in her leg. Zebe pushes the blade into her neck, reducing her to orange ash. Ilikso slowly walks over to her with his dark red eyes.

"You have proven yourself to him, Werfon. You and Zebe have an immense amount of power. Give it to him!!!"

Ilikso runs at her, as Werfon shoots himself out of Zebe and into Ilikso. He falls to the ground and starts to shake. His eyes flash orange as he screams in pain.

"No, get out!"

His skin starts to turn orange, but his eyes keep flashing until he erupts into ash. Zebe stands up and absorbs Werfon back inside her.

"You did an amazing job, Werfon. Will I ever be able to use those moves?"

Her chest flashes orange.

"Once our bond grows stronger, you will be able to. I will get stronger, as well, the more I am in control. As I promised, you have the power again."

"Thank you. I am excited to see what else we can do together."

Zebe makes her way past the statue and all the orange ash surrounding it. They push through the tower doors and make their way up the spiral staircase. As they approach the top, they see the gateway open with a small portal inside of it. Zebe runs for the opening and tries to shut the gateway.

"Werfon, how do we get rid of this?"

A hand reaches through to her.

"Help! Pull me through!!"

Zebe grabs the hand and pulls it through. Zembor flies through the portal—clawed hands reach through after him. He holds out a small metal square and presses the orange button on it. Zembor tosses it through the threshold, watching it explode as the portal closes. Monster arms get cut off by the portal closing and fall inside the tower. Zembor stands up and looks to Zebe.

"Thank you for saving me. I thought I was a goner. What's going on here?"

Zebe looks at Zembor covered in blood.

"How long was that portal open? I think their leader got through. He's completely taken over my mother, and he's done something to the Great Tree. Our world outside of the tree has been corrupted. Some of our people have been killed and brought back to life by the tree. They're currently attacking the rest of us right now. I'm trying to find a way to end it from in here."

Zembor puts his head down and starts to walk down the spiral staircase. Zebe's chest flashes orange.

"Zembor, did you find RoyalTree on R'Ang? We need him back."

"He isn't on R'Ang. I looked everywhere I possibly could, and he wasn't there. I can still feel him alive and in pain."

"Where else could he be?"

The tower starts to shake. Zembor runs for the exit at the bottom of the staircase.

"The gateway that the tower thrived off of is destroyed. We need to leave before it collapses."

Zebe follows Zembor out of the tower. They stand next to the statue of Ilikso, watching the tower crumble and fall to the ground. An orange cloud remains, floating in the middle of the rubble. Zembor slowly approaches it.

"It can't be... RoyalTree, is that you?"

The cloud turns and floats toward Zembor. It flashes and flies at him. He absorbs it and turns to Zebe, kneeling to the ground. His eyes glow orange.

"RoyalTree... It has to be you...."

Zembor's chest flashes.

"It is me! I am beyond happy to see you and be free from that tower. That creature has held me there as his vessel, to return here whenever he pleases."

Zebe runs over and looks into Zembor's eyes.

"I can't believe it is really you... RoyalTree, I have heard so many stories about you."

Zembor sits on the ground.

"It is an honor to meet you in person, Zebe Wrathfin. I fear I have much resting to do before I can be on my own. I am sorry for jumping inside of you like that, Zem."

"It's alright. I have been searching for you without end now! I am so happy to have finally found you. The things we have done to make sure the Great Tree lived on without you."

"I have seen everything that has been going on, including what's going on with Queen Zuna right now. She has been completely taken over by that creature. Zebe, we were fortunate to have you return from the war so soon. Without you here, the Great Tree would have stayed corrupted and fallen to him."

Zebe sits down with him.

"I am honored for you to say that, but my mother won't think so. I'm a traitor for abandoning the war. I can't show my face when they return...."

"Your mother is not herself and has a small chance of returning to who she once was. Her spirit still lingers inside of her body, but she has completely lost her will to fight. Zebe, you must do something."

"What can I do? My mother wasn't very fond of me before she was corrupted by that creature. I saved you and RoyalTree; it's in your hands now. The Great Tree can live on without the ridiculous ceremony we've been doing to sacrifice Wrathfin blood. I have done my part, and I will be happy knowing that—no matter what outcome awaits me upon the King and Queen's return."

Zebe stands up and leaves Zembor and RoyalTree sitting there alone. She reaches the doorway and opens it up. Yulista and the other survivors wait for her on the other side. The sun shines brightly behind them as Yulista hugs Zebe.

"I knew you'd be back. You saved us all! Whatever you did inside of the tree worked! We fought off the last of them until they were released from the corruption. All the trees have turned back to their normal color, and the land around them has too. Thank you, Zebe."

She kneels. All the Tralupians standing behind her kneel with her.

Zebe smiles as she looks around at her people. She takes a deep breath and walks proudly through the crowd into the throne room, covered head to toe in orange ash.

"Werfon, we're traitors to the crown. We have to be ready."

Her chest flashes orange.

"We are not alone."

The sun shines through the cracks on the palace as she sits on the throne.

# Chapter 35:
# <u>Johthun-The Battle for Joht</u>

An alarm blares from the metallic wall inside the Elite Protector's base. The Elites inside scurry around, gathering their weapons and equipment. Tanglor stands with his Captains, planning their attack against the Tralupians.

"I will lead the attack in orbit with Freden and Geresen. Ashar, you and Neliah will prepare our troops on the surface. The Tralupians have the numbers and, even with our tech, we can't hold them for too long. Be prepared to fight."

The Captains salute their Commander and start preparing their soldiers. Tanglor makes his way to the Mercurana, where Zaren and Zelray wait for him.

"Are you going to have to fight Zebe?"

Tanglor hesitates before answering.

"She's leading the Tralupian army. The King and Queen are forcing her to."

"Neither one of you can die. Tanglor, make sure you both come back alive."

He puts his hands on their heads.

"I will do everything I can to make sure we both stay alive."

He walks past them and boards the Mercurana, getting on the intercom.

"Get to your positions. We're going to war!"

Martonamo pilots the ship into Joht's orbit while Geresen and Freden follow behind with their troops. The Johthun army arranges themselves around the planet, waiting for the Tralupians. They keenly watch through the darkness of space, looking for any signs of the enemy. Suddenly lights appear in the distance, an overwhelming army of Tralupian ships approach Joht. Geresen gets on the intercom.

"Tanglor! She's insane!"

"What is it, Geresen?"

"The King and Queen brought almost the entire population of TokBellu here to fight! They outnumber us even more than we thought!"

"Get your troops ready. We must do whatever we can to slow them down! Ucarus and Mac-Ran should be coming in as reinforcements soon. Hold them off until they get here!"

The Tralupian fleet stops in front of the Johthun army and speaks over the intercoms.

"I demand to speak to Tanglor Raff!"

"You betrayed our alliance, Zuna!"

"*I* betrayed *you*? What about you and Zebe betraying me!?"

King Jarelen takes over the comms.

"Hahaha, I love it when she gets angry! It's okay, honey, I'll handle this. Look Tanglor; it's over for you and your Johthuns. We outnumber you, so let us pass, and no one gets hurt. We just want to speak to that computer console of yours."

"Sorry, Jarelen, I can't let that happen. Elites!"

Tanglor jumps into the seat next to Martonamo and pilots the ship straight for the Tralupian fleet.

"For Joht!!"

The Johthun army follows behind, cheering with their commander.

"For Joht!"

Johthun ships fly out in front of the Mercurana and begin firing at the Tralupian fleet. They disperse and fire back, focusing on Tanglor, who is closing in on them. Tanglor maneuvers through the ships, taking out enemies with precision and finesse. The rest of the Johthun ships are having trouble fighting the Tralupians off, though. Tanglor calls for them to fall back and regroup around the planet. As they make their retreat, Tanglor gets cut off by a massive Tralupian warship. The rest of his army surrounds the planet and watch as Tanglor is stuck behind enemy lines. Geresen flies over to aid him but can't make it through the wall of Tralupian ships.

"Tanglor! We can't get to you!"

"It's all right, Geresen. You and Freden get the rest of our army ready. Stick to the plan!"

Freden watches as Geresen retreats.

"Tanglor, we aren't losing you today. We'll hold them off for as long as we can. You make sure to get your ass back to Joht!"

"They can't kill me; I'm Tanglor Raff!"

He jumps out of the seat giving the controls back to Martonamo. He climbs the ladder above him and sits down next to a turret.

"Alright, Mart. Let's show them what we got!"

Martonamo flies the Mercurana straight for the warship. At the last second, he turns toward the Tralupian fighter ships. Tanglor uses the control panel in front of him to take over the turrets on the front of the vessel. He fires the blasters, destroying some of the ships. Martonamo flips and barrel rolls the Mercurana, dodging the enemy's attacks. Tanglor takes out the fighter ships that were surrounding them, but the warship still blocks his way back to Joht. Martonamo flies at it, while Tanglor gets the turret ready to fire. Suddenly a voice comes through on their intercom.

"Tanglor, I know that's you in there."

"Zebe?"

"I'm so sorry, Tanglor."

"How could you do this to us? After everything?"

"My mother took away my entire life... I had no choice."

"You always have a choice, Zebe! Your mother and Jarelen are the ones responsible for this, not you!"

"If I could have controlled my emotions with you, none of this would be happening."

"Your mother would have attacked us as soon as she found out about our technology on Joht. Don't do this, Zebe."

"I... I'm sorry, Tanglor. Goodbye."

She uses the massive cannon on the warship to fire at the Mercurana. Martonamo tries to dodge it, but it hits and cripples the ship. While it recharges, Tanglor takes the opportunity to fire back, but the blasters do nothing to the massive ship. He fires again at the cannon; they hit—disabling it. Martonamo flies close to the warship. Tanglor and Zebe are face to face through the glass windows.

"Zebe... I'm not going to fight you. Please, we can end this together."

He reaches out and puts his hand on the glass. Zebe tears up as she slowly puts her hand up to the opposite side of the glass.

"All I can do is take my warship out of the battle... It's too late, Tanglor."

"It's not. To end this war, we need to take out the King and Queen. Once they go down, the rest of your people will listen to you."

"Not anymore, Tanglor. Not after they found out about us, my mother has taken everything from me, including my people."

A voice from behind Zebe interrupts them.

"The cannon is back online! Fire!"

From point-blank, the cannon blasts into the Mercurana, taking it out. Zebe watches in horror.

"Noooo! Tanglor! What have I done!?"

She pilots the warship away from Joht, leaving the battle behind. Freden, Geresen, and the rest of the Johthuns watch as the destroyed Mercurana drifts off into an asteroid belt.

"Tanglor!! We need to try to save him!"

The Tralupian fleet wastes no time advancing on them.

"Freden, we can't. He gave us our orders. You need to make the call and lead the army."

Freden stares hard past the Tralupian fleet, trying to spot Tanglor. He finally snaps out of it.

"You're right. Elites, keep fighting! For Tanglor Raff!!!"

He flies his ship straight for the Tralupian fleet with the Johthun army following behind.

"Hold your fire. Do your best to maneuver through their blasts and get above them. Then, we'll hit them with all we've got!"

The Johthun army spreads out, making it harder for the Tralupians to shoot them. They continue to fly at the fleet, steering through the blasts and debris. They make it through and get above them.

"Now! Fire everything!"

The Johthuns lay waste to the Tralupian fleet below them, dropping bombs and firing their blasters. As the smoke clears from the destruction, debris from the destroyed ships float around with dead bodies from both sides. Freden looks around for Tanglor but can't see the Mercurana anywhere.

"Everyone get back to Joht. It's not over."

As they fly back toward their planet, thousands of Tralupian ships appear from the wreckage.

"Hahaha, your beloved Tanglor Raff is gone. It's over for you!"

Freden looks around at his army. Their ships have taken too much damage, and they're running out of resources to keep fighting.

"We have to retreat. We won't be able to hold them off for another attack up here!"

The Johthuns retreat down to the surface, Freden and Geresen land their ships and rush over to the ground army to find Ashar and Neliah.

"Ashar!"

"Freden, Geresen, what happened?"

"We took out a lot of them, but there's just too many. They're overwhelming us up there! Where are Ucarus and Mac-Ran with reinforcements!?"

"I still haven't heard anything from them. We have to keep fighting until they get here. Where's Tanglor?"

Freden can't find the words and looks away. Geresen steps forward.

"They took out the Mercurana... We tried to help him, but the Tralupian fleet cut us off. He took out the fighter ships surrounding him, but there was a warship that was there. He easily could have taken it out, but he hesitated. Zebe must've been on it."

Ashar looks to Neliah; she grabs his arm. A couple of tears run down his face. He wipes them away and clears his throat.

"Tanglor would want us to keep fighting no matter what. After we win this battle, we'll go and find him."

Freden lifts his head and looks to Ashar.

"We follow your lead, Ashar. You're the Commander now."

Ashar stands tall and looks around at their army, preparing for battle.

"We can do this... Elites, listen up! Tanglor is gone, but we can still win this because of him. He prepared all of us for this moment! The Tralupians will be entering our atmosphere at any moment. When they do, fire our anti-air missiles and take out as many of them as you can. Once they land, be prepared for close-quarter combat. They may have blasters, but they prefer to fight with their blades."

As Ashar is talking, the Tralupians drop down from the atmosphere.

"Now fire those missiles and protect the city! For Tanglor Raff!!"

The Johthuns launch their anti-air missiles at the Tralupians, knocking some of their ships out of the sky. Fire and debris rain down, as some Tralupians still manage to land. Another warship, carrying the King and Queen, returns fire with their cannons. The Johthuns are forced to take cover, allowing them to descend to the surface. The ships roar as they land, causing a dirt storm to whirl around the battlefield. After a couple of minutes go by, the ships go quiet, and the dirt storm starts to dissipate. Ashar peeks out of his cover and investigates the dusty combat zone. With his vision distorted by the dirt storm, he is barely able to make out thousands of bodies standing on the other side of it. Freden, Geresen, and Neliah stand behind him. The storm clears, and the Tralupians start to charge at them from across the battlefield. Ashar grabs his double-sided blade and turns to his army.

"We end this here!!!"

He turns back toward the charging Tralupians and screams while running at them. The rest of the Captains follow behind with their army. Some of the Johthun soldiers get on the ground turrets, bombarding the Tralupians and taking some of them out as they charge. Ashar is the first to reach the Tralupians. He jumps into them, slashing his blades around. Neliah stays near Ashar and fights back-to-back with him. They spin around in a circle, effortlessly taking out Tralupian soldiers together. Geresen and Freden run through the crowd, jumping and dodging attacks while carving up their enemies. The Johthun army holds its own against the Tralupians as day turns to nigh. The battle still rages on. As darkness fills the battlefield, the two militaries start to fall back to their collective sides to regroup for a second attack in the morning. A message comes through on Ashar's intercom.

"This is Zuna Wrathfin. I am ordering my troops to stand down for the night. Do we have an agreement to stop the battle until the sun comes back out?"

Ashar waits a couple of seconds before responding.

"We will stand down for the night *if* we communicate again tomorrow before the battle starts?"

"You have my word. We will radio in before we strike again."

The intercom shuts off, and Ashar turns to his Captains.

"We'll have shifts tonight to keep watch. I don't trust her. I'll take the first watch with Neliah. Geresen and Freden, you'll go after us. Neliah, can you try to get through to Ucarus and Mac-ran?"

Freden and Geresen leave to join the rest of the army. Neliah grabs the intercom and attempts to contact Ucarus on the radio, while Ashar stares into the darkness. Minutes tick by with no response.

Time flies by as they sit, staring up into the sky, hoping for the Johthun reinforcements. They continue to watch for them until Freden and Geresen arrive to relieve Ashar and Neliah.

"You two get some sleep. We'll wake you if anything happens."

Ashar and Neliah lay down next to them to get some sleep. The moons disappear, and the sun returns all too quickly. Ashar wakes up to Zuna's voice over the intercom.

"I never agreed on waiting to hear back from you!"

He jumps up and sees a blast coming straight for them.

"Move!!"

They all jump out of the way as the blast crashes down next to them.

"Elites!! Attack!"

The Johthun army runs out to meet the Tralupians as blood and guts spill onto the battlefield. Ashar looks around at the chaos happening around him.

"Everyone! Push forward! They have nowhere to retreat to!"

He charges out in front of the army, with Freden following behind. Geresen and Neliah stay back with a group of Elites as the last line of defense. Ashar stops and kneels. Freden runs over and jumps off his back, landing behind the charging Tralupians. He pulls out his blades and tears through them, while Ashar and the rest of the army push through. The Johthuns fight their way into the middle of the Tralupian army until they're surrounded. They strike down the Tralupians in droves, but it isn't enough—Tralupian soldiers continue to rush into battle. King Jarelen stops his soldiers from attacking and steps into the circle with the Johthuns.

"I'm disappointed. I thought you Johthuns were going to be tougher than this. Oh well, we'll make this quick for all of you. Bring in the warship."

A dim shadow falls over the surrounded Johthuns. They look up and see the massive warship with its cannons pointing directly at them. King Jarelen erupts into laughter.

"A couple of blasts from these cannons should finish you off with minimal pain!"

The laughter continues as he backs away from the Johthuns.

"Fire!!"

Ashar and Freden close their eyes, accepting their fates through the loud blasts that fill the battlefield. A crash and an explosion cause them to open their eyes to see

Johthun reinforcements firing at the Tralupian warship. It starts to fall toward the ground, closing in on where they all stand. Ashar yells to his army.

"It's going to crush us! Hurry and fight through!"

The Johthun army scatters and fights through the Tralupians. King Jarelen tries to escape, but Freden catches him off guard and knocks him to the ground. He pulls his blade out and holds it up to his neck.

"It's over, Jarelen. End the war!"

He laughs again.

"I can't end the war. Zuna is crazy, and she wants your tech. Plus—it's never over!"

He cuts his hand, grabbing the blade. Freden gets caught off guard, and Jarelen pulls him down to the ground and wraps his arms around him.

"You're going to die with me!"

Freden looks up to see the warship plummeting down toward them. He head-butts Jarelen in the face and rolls off him. Freden grabs his blade and pierces it through Jarelen's leg pinning him down. The warship meets the ground, Freden takes off in a sprint trying to get away.

"Don't leave me! Freden!"

He reaches out for him as he runs away. The warship continues to explode and fully crashes down, crushing Jarelen in the wreckage. It gets closer to Freden, but, at the last second, he dives out of the way. Ashar rushes over to help him up.

"Freden, are you okay?"

"Yeah, that was a close one. Ucarus and Mac-Ran got here just in time."

The two of them look up and see the Johthun ships shooting down at the Tralupian soldiers.

"Ucarus, can you hear me?"

"Yes, I can hear you. We've been trying to reach you since the Tralupians flew past us, but something was interfering with our communications."

"You made it just in time. Be careful up there. Some of the Tralupians are retreating to their ships to take on you and your armada."

"Roger that. We'll be ready."

Ashar and Freden make their way back to Neliah and Geresen, as the fighting continues. Neliah pushes through everyone and hugs Ashar.

"I was worried you weren't going to make it back."

"I'll always come back for you, Neliah."

Geresen can't tear his eyes away from the battlefield.

"We can't let them get any closer to the city. The closer they get, the stronger they become. We got lucky, taking out Jarelen. It makes up for not having Tanglor. Either way, we're sitting pretty good right now."

As he watches the fighting continue, a rapid-fire of blasts flies into the sky. Explosions erupt, taking out both Johthun and Tralupian ships.

Freden jumps up.

"What the hell was that!?"

Geresen stands frozen with his eyes wide open.

"She killed her own people... She is crazy... I... I don't know if we can beat her."

Ashar and Neliah run over.

"Ucarus! Mac-Ran! Come in! Please come in!"

"No!! That bitch is going to pay for this!"

Ashar clenches his hands into fists and walks out to the battlefield. Blasts soar by, barely missing him. He continues to move forward as the explosions surround him. The fire dissipates, and he emerges with his double-sided blade ready. A Tralupian soldier charges at him, but he dodges the attack, then quickly slices and stabs the soldier in the chest. Neliah tries to follow behind Ashar, but Freden grabs her.

"You can't go out there. It's suicide."

"I can't watch him die either!"

Freden holds onto her as she tries to break free. Geresen lifts his head and looks to them.

"Thank you for everything you've done for me... When this war is over, can you please take care of my sister? Her name is Yulista."

Geresen jumps off the ledge and charges the battlefield. Two more Tralupians run at Ashar, but he stabs his double-sided sword into the ground using it to somersault over the Tralupians. As he vaults over the soldiers, the blade follows behind him, slicing one of the soldiers in the face. Before the other one can react, he turns the edge around and stabs him in the chest. Without hesitating, he continues walking toward the Tralupian Queen. Two more blasts zoom by Ashar and hit the ground, surrounding him in an eruption of fire. The fire fades away, revealing ten Tralupians running at him. He strikes the ground, creating a dirt storm to hide in. A couple of seconds go by before he pops out and slashes one of the Tralupian's throats. He sneaks around and stabs another Tralupian in the back, before jumping back into the dirt storm. The remaining eight Tralupians use their blasters to shoot into the cloud of dirt. They miss Ashar, but the cloud disintegrates from the shots. Geresen comes out from behind Ashar and jumps over him with his blade ready. He takes two of the Tralupians out with ease, before falling back to Ashar.

"Geresen, what the hell are you doing?"

"Ashar, this is suicide. I'm making sure you make it back to your wife and daughter."

"I... I didn't ask for that. Go and save yourself."

"Not a chance. I'm in this with you."

Ashar smiles at him, and the two of them rush the six Tralupians. Geresen pulls out knives and throws them. He then rolls behind the airborne blades and fires his blaster. The blasts hit the knives, forming a shell around them. They hit the Tralupians, causing small explosions that take them to the ground. He runs up to the three injured Tralupians and knocks them unconscious. Ashar slides underneath another soldier, taking out its legs and stabbing him. One of the two remaining soldiers tackles Ashar to the ground, while the other one fights Geresen one-on-one. The Tralupian on top of Ashar pulls out a knife and places it upon his neck, but Ashar grabs the blade with his hand and punches the Tralupian. He quickly jumps up and uses it to slice the Tralupian's throat. He turns and sees Geresen in a standstill with the other soldier. Ashar flips the knife around and throws it at the Tralupian soldier, piercing it in the back. The soldier falls to the ground, and Geresen kicks him in the face.

"You okay, Ashar?"

He rips off part of his Elite uniform and wraps it around his bloody hand.

"Yeah, I'm alright. Ready to keep moving?"

Geresen nods his head and follows Ashar. The rest of the Johthun army continues to push the Tralupians back toward their grounded ships, while Neliah and Freden fall back with their troops to defend the city. The Tralupian soldiers stop attacking Ashar and Geresen, stepping aside to create a pathway. The two Johthuns follow it to the end, where the Tralupian Queen waits for them.

"Ashar, is it? And of course, I know you. You're one of us, Geresen."

Geresen steps out from behind Ashar.

"I've never been like you, Zuna. You're a disgrace to our people, and what you're making them do is disgusting."

She laughs as she sits in her makeshift throne.

"You never understood the Tralupian way. Now you'll die here with your newfound family of Johthuns."

Ashar pulls Geresen back and steps in front of him.

"Enough, Zuna! Your King is dead. If you don't want to end up like him, then I suggest you go back to TokBellu."

"Jarelen? Meh, that was just an arrangement I made with him so that he would kill his family. They were so stubborn and annoying about the crown. Thank you for dealing with him."

"You're a monster... How could you do that?"

She laughs again.

"I am a monster!"

She lifts her hand into the air, signaling her troops to attack. Geresen and Ashar go back-to-back, as the Tralupian soldiers surround them. Queen Zuna's laugh gets louder.

"It's over. The Johthuns have lost!"

She points to the sky as more Tralupian ships descend from the atmosphere. They fly over the battlefield, dropping bombs on the Johthun and Tralupian soldiers, causing Neliah and Freden to yell for a retreat. Bombs continue to fall as soldiers from both sides, drop their weapons and run for the city. Despite being vastly outnumbered, Ashar and Geresen continue to fight and take out the Tralupian soldiers surrounding them. Neliah and Freden look out from the city into the wasteland that used to be the battlefield. Seeing how their Queen tried to kill them, the Tralupian soldiers that made it to the city surrender and offer their help to fight off the Queen and the rest of her army. Neliah accepts and provides them with equipment and weapons. The Queen and her soldiers finally subdue Ashar and Geresen. She takes them hostage and marches her army toward the city. They arrive at the blockade in front of the gates.

"Open up! I have two of your leaders!"

She tosses Geresen and Ashar out in front of her.

"If you want to see them again, let us through."

Ashar yells to Neliah.

"Don't worry about us! Whatever you do, don't let them get past you!"

She walks over and kicks him in the stomach.

"Shut up! I'll say it one more time! You let us in, or they die!!"

Neliah puts her hand on the gate and looks to Freden.

"I can't let him die."

Freden reaches out to stop her, but it's too late. The gate opens, and Neliah runs out.

**A day earlier...**

Darkness surrounds a shattered ship. A dim teal light begins to flash on the screen.

"Can you hear me? Are you alright?"

Debris from the wreckage rustles around. A couple of seconds go by before a hand bursts out. Teal light flashes through it, causing the dimmed light to brighten, revealing the wrecked ship on an asteroid.

# Chapter 36:
# Tralupians-Queen Zebe

Princess Zebe sits on the throne in Queen Zuna's absence. Tralupians fill the palace, helping the Princess rebuild what was destroyed by the Great Tree. Zebe meets with a contractor. He steps forward and speaks to her.

"My Que... Princess, we have builders throughout the city working. We have also sent some to the slums, to make it better as you requested."

"Thank you for the update. Tell everyone I appreciate the hard work."

He bows to Zebe and walks out of the palace. She stands up and goes to the doors in the courtyard where the Great Tree rests. She walks over to the ledge overlooking the ocean and places her hand on the trunk.

"Zembor, RoyalTree? Can either of you hear me?"

The tree flashes.

"This is RoyalTree. What is it, Zebe?"

"I wanted to ask you some more questions about everything that's been happening... There's so much my mother never told me before she was corrupted."

"What would you like to know?"

"Are the stories true about you and Zembor, and how the Great Tree came to be?"

"They are, from what I've heard at least. Everyone was under the impression that I was taken back to R'Ang. I guess it was a story made up by the creature that captured me to make you think I was gone. I have been right here in that tower this whole time. The sacrifices that your people made ware to keep me alive. Without me, the Great Tree is nothing. Zembor knows that and would have told you the truth if he wasn't under his control too. He is gone now, well, not completely. He has taken over your mother, and no one can save her except for you, Zebe."

"I... I have tried and failed. I don't think I will even get another chance, not after retreating from the war."

"If you don't try, then TokBellu will be under his control too..."

The Great Tree shakes as a message comes through to Zebe.

"What is it?"

A scout comes through on her intercom.

"Queen... I mean, Princess, there is another disc message that has been retrieved from space. Soldiers are bringing it your way as we speak."

"Thank you. I will look for the message."

Zebe stands up and looks over the ledge at the ocean. The sun starts to set as the moon rises next to it. She walks into the throne room as soldiers march in behind her.

"Princess Zebe, we have the disc message for you."

She takes the message and goes to sit in front of the control panel next to the Queen's chambers. Zebe inserts the disc and presses a button. A couple of seconds pass, and Siritano pops up on the screen.

"Hey, guys! It's Siritano..."

Qualt pops up on the screen next to him.

"And Qualt!! We didn't die!!"

Siritano shoves him to the side, as he laughs.

"Qualt's right, we didn't die. We made it to that little red planet I was telling you about in the last transmission. We have been here for so long now; we aren't sure how long it has been. The message won't have a year on it this time, but we want to let you know that we are alive and well. We made some friends here on this planet; we haven't come up with a name for it yet, other than red. But the creatures we ran into here are friendly and welcomed us in with open arms. We have been working with them, farming, and ranching some of the animals here. In our downtime, we hunt and train in combat. The leader of the group here calls himself Hartomo, he calls his species Pyronts, though it is just him, his wife and daughter that are here with some other creatures. We haven't been able to find any fuel for our ship, so we're stuck here until someone else finds us or until we develop gas or a different kind of ship. We have all the time in the world now, so maybe one day!"

Qualt jumps back on the screen.

"We hope everything is going well for you back on TokBellu! I miss you guys. Thanks again for saving us and allowing us to get to Planet Red! We will hopefully meet again soon! Stay safe and protect each other."

Qualt leaves, and Siritano sits by himself. He puts his head down before picking it back up and looking into the camera.

"I'm afraid we may never see each other again. Qualt has hope, and I appreciate it, but I don't think we will ever make it back to you. We lost the coordinates to the planet, so we don't know how to tell you to get here. I'm going to keep my promise to Qualt and get him home as soon as we get our ship up and running again. Please, sister, take care of the others. If I happen to make it back home one day, I would like to see all of you together."

A yell from off-screen interrupts Siritano.

"Siritano! We need you back here to train the recruits! Qualt isn't a close combat fighter. He's got those crazy powers but can't throw a punch to save his life."

Laughter fills the room behind him, as Qualt yells back.

"Don't make me show you! I've been resisting because they're fierce punches!"

The laughter continues as Siritano turns back to the camera with a smile on his face.

"At least we found another family here on Red! We miss you guys."

A tear falls from Siritano's face as he shuts off the transmission. Zebe takes the disc out and puts it with the other one. She stands up and walks back to the throne room. Her chest flashes orange as she sits down.

"It is good to know Siritano is still alive. He and Qualt could aid us one day."

"We have the technology to find them. I believe my mother would have looked for them if that creature didn't take control of her. While I'm acting as the Queen, I want to send a couple of scouts out in opposite directions to search for the small red planet."

"I think that is a great idea, Zebe. You have done a lot for TokBellu while the King and Queen have been gone. Enough to get away from being called a traitor. You have acted as our Queen with poise. Queen Zuna and King Jarelen should take notes from you."

They both laugh as some soldiers enter the throne room.

"My Princess... Sorry... My Queen, we have a visitor who claims to know you personally. She calls herself Yulista Grohjin."

Zebe stands up.

"Please, send her in at once."

The soldiers bow and walk out as Yulista walks in.

"Queen Zebe, huh? I like the sound of that!"

Zebe sits back down on the throne.

"Don't get used to it. Even if it worked out... I wouldn't want to be Queen. I have never had an interest in it."

Yulista kneels to her.

"Either way... you're Queen right now. I have a request for you. I want to advise you until Queen Zuna returns. I don't want to leave your side after everything that has happened. Now that I know my brother is alive and became an Elite for the Johthuns, I want to go there and join him."

Zebe stands up and walks down the steps to her. She places her hand on her shoulder.

"I accept your request. Be my adviser, and stay close to me. Once they return, I will send you to Joht to be with your brother, assuming he is still there after the war. Have you heard from anyone in the attack?"

"I haven't. All my sources say no one has heard from anyone in the Queen's army. Everything went dark three days ago when they attacked. The war will have to end soon. They didn't take enough resources with them to last more than a week."

"I fear you're correct... Tanglor Raff was taken out of the battle; it's the reason why I came back to TokBellu, and it's lucky for all of us that I did. But the Queen has a better chance of winning the war without Tanglor fighting against her."

Yulista bows down to her.

"What can I do? We need to be prepared for them to return. What do you expect will happen if they do?"

Zebe walks back up to the throne and sits down.

"The Queen will return. She isn't going to die that easy. When she does, I will be taken as a prisoner and put on trial. The decision will probably end with me being put to death in front of the people. Saving our planet from the Great Tree's corruption will mean nothing since she is controlled by the creature that corrupted the tree."

"I see. Well then, I will get some of my best troops together to prepare for an escape plan. We will get your warship stocked and ready for takeoff if we need it. Your crew is behind you on this!"

Yulista bows to Zebe and walks out of the throne room.

Zebe's chest flashes orange.

"RoyalTree is back with Zembor. They can take care of the Great Tree and look out for TokBellu. You need to take that opportunity to do what you've always wanted to do! Leave and discover other worlds, Zebe!"

She smiles as she places her hand on her chest.

"Thank you, Werfon, but I do not know what the future holds for me. If the Queen doesn't return, I will have to be Queen until I find someone fit to rule TokBellu. I want to do as you say and discover other worlds. I want to know if Tanglor is okay and if he is, I need to apologize to him and be with him!"

She stands up and walks down the steps. She looks out the palace doors to the Great Tree.

"You have to be alive, Tanglor... You have to be!"

---------------------------------------------------

Siritano sits with his hands on his head. Qualt walks behind him as he turns the transmission off.

"You think that one will get to them? Do you think they've tried responding to us?"

Siritano stands up and walks with Qualt through a corridor made up of metal and red dirt.

"If they did, it would never make it to us without coordinates... Our messages are making it to them, so at least they know we're alive and out here still. Let's get to Hartomo before he gets angry at us for being late again."

They walk into a room with a padded floor. Hartomo, the Pyront with six tentacle arms and eight tentacle legs, stands, waiting for them.

"Late again! When will you two learn that being on time matters in a battle!"

They stand with the other alien creatures, watching Hartomo pace across the padded floor.

"There are monsters... things out there that you haven't seen. They lurk in the shadows and prey on the weak. They grow strong and take out any species that oppose them. I have seen them. I even spoke to one of them face to face. My family wouldn't be here if he hadn't gone against their master's orders. With my second chance, I swore to protect my family and others who are in danger from those monsters. They won't stop, every one of us is in danger, including all your people. I am here to form a resistance against them. We'll be a step ahead of them, listening to their conversations, lurking in the darkness, just like they do. We will be prepared for what's to come. All of the worlds out there need help, and we'll be the ones to answer those calls while staying hidden. We'll call ourselves the Light in the Darkness!"

Siritano and Qualt cheer with the other recruits. Hartomo quiets them down and calls someone out to challenge him. Siritano steps forward to prove himself.

"What is your name, recruit?"

"I am Siritano, sir!"

"Where did you come from, Siritano?"

"I came here with my friend, Qualt, and we came from my planet called TokBellu. We were looking for his planet called Rembor."

Hartomo circles around him. He pulls out six blades, one for each of his tentacles.

"Are you prepared to fight? No one has come close to defeating me!"

Siritano smiles and catches the blade Qualt throws him. Yellow sparks float around his blade, as he stares at Hartomo.

"Are you prepared to fight me?"

Hartomo smiles back, and charges with all six blades pointed toward him. Siritano waits for his attacks and blocks them all quickly. He charges Hartomo with his sword behind him. Instead of swinging it around him, he flips the opposite way and throws his blade toward Hartomo. He steps to the side, as the blade cuts two of his tentacles and the side of his face. He drops the rest of his swords and bows to Siritano.

"You are the one I want training everyone in close combat. I would like to join in on your classes since I could use more training as well. When you beat me, it showed me—I need more work."

He bows to Siritano. Siritano bows back and smiles.

"Thank you. You honor me, Hartomo. I will accept and train your recruits."

Qualt jumps into the air and runs over to Siritano.

"That was awesome. You talk about me being cool with my powers. That was great blade work!"

Siritano jumps in the air with Qualt in excitement. Everyone clears out of the training room and heads back to their quarters to get some rest. Hartomo follows behind and catches up to Qualt and Siritano.

"Hey! I was hoping to speak with you two."

They both stop and turn to Hartomo.

"What is it?"

"I need more leaders in the Light of Darkness, but it requires commitment. I need leaders that aren't going to leave the first chance they get. If you become Captains, I need to know you're in it for the long haul. This evil I speak of is coming for all of us. I've seen it."

Siritano looks to Qualt before turning back to Hartomo.

"I'll do whatever Qualt wants. I made a promise to him years ago, and I intend to stick to that commitment."

Qualt turns to Siritano.

"I've accepted the fact that I won't ever return home... It's okay, Siritano. We have a new home here on Red; something is going on here bigger than all of us, something that has to do with those monsters back on R'Ang. If we can help stop them, then I'm in!"

Siritano smiles and looks back at Hartomo.

"That settles it then; we'll be Captains of the Light of Darkness and help turn this resistance into a viable threat against our enemies!"

Hartomo smiles back. The three of them continue together back to their quarters.

-------------------------------------------------------

Zebe waits nervously for the Queen to return, as she walks around the courtyard. The Great Tree flashes, but she ignores it and sits on the ledge looking into the sky above the ocean. She listens to the quiet breeze over the waves.

"This may be the last time I'll get to hear you speak to me. I'm going to miss your soothing sounds, ocean."

Zebe stands back up and makes her way into the palace. She sits down on the throne and looks toward the entrance.

"Come and get me, Queen Zuna...."

# Chapter 37:
# Johthuns-The City Under Siege

The destroyed Mercurana flashes teal, as Martonamo uses the emergency generator to help Tanglor see.

"That is all I can do for lights, Tanglor."

"Thanks, Mart. I'll take whatever I can get."

Tanglor reaches for his mask. He turns the knob, adjusting the settings to be optimal for space.

"Mart, can you transfer the energy from that generator to the oval in my hand? I need to check out the damages on the ship from the outside."

"I will do my best."

Martonamo takes a couple of seconds before the energy surges through Tanglor's hand. It flashes outward in front of him like a bright teal flashlight.

"Stay with me through the oval. I'm going out there."

Tanglor opens the door and points the light into the darkness on the asteroid. The light catches something small, scurrying across the ground. It quickly goes by the open door.

"Mart! Did you see that?"

"I didn't see anything. Get it together, Commander."

"I'm serious!"

Martonamo uses more energy, shining the teal light brighter. They both look around, but nothing but darkness surrounds them.

"See, I told you. There's nothing out there. Let's hurry and look at the damages to the Mercurana."

Tanglor takes a deep breath before stepping out of the ship. He points his arm out in front of him and spins, trying to look around the asteroid.

"Tanglor! Stay focused!"

He turns back around and climbs onto the Mercurana to look at the outer hull.

"Yeah... Mart. There is no way to fix this from here. We need another way back to Joht. The Tralupians are still attacking. We need to get back there!"

Tanglor stops and flashes the light off in the distance. They see a small animal crawl across the ground into a hole.

"See! I told you, Mart!"

Tanglor jumps off the top of the Mercurana, landing on the ground. He slowly walks toward the hole that the animal crawled into. It crawls out from another hole behind him. Tanglor quickly turns around and flashes the light on it. A small, sponge-like creature stares back, its purple eyes glowing at them. Martonamo dims down the teal light, while Tanglor reaches out for it.

"My name is Tanglor Raff. What is your name?"

The small creature stays quiet while staring at Tanglor.

"We aren't here to hurt you. My friend and I got taken out of a battle defending our home planet. We need help with getting back. Can you help us?"

It allows a few seconds to pass before flashing his eyes at them.

"My name is The 7th. My people and I are called Gorites. We are sorry to hear about your ship, Tanglor Raff."

Tanglor gets closer to The 7th and watches him closely.

"What did you just do there? You spoke to me, and it felt different. I don't even see your mouth."

The 7th's eyes flash again.

"You are very observant, Tanglor. I do not have one. It was a design by our creators to keep us from passing on knowledge. As the years passed, my people and I developed a form of telepathy amongst ourselves for communication. We were unsure if it would work with on other life forms."

Tanglor stands in awe, looking at the Gorite with purple eyes.

"Creators? What do you mean by that? Where are you and your people from? How did you end up on this asteroid?"

The 7th moves along the ground back toward the Mercurana, crawling on top of it. He looks at Tanglor and flashes his eyes again.

"You were right about your ship. It has taken a lot of damage. We can help with that. My people are here on the asteroid. We live inside of it. We landed here long ago, in a world that was different than it is now. We wandered the vast ocean of space, looking for a purpose after we were created. We have no memories before that. They were taken from us with no way of getting them back. We have knowledge that has an unknown purpose; knowledge of creatures and planets we have never been to. Our mouths were left out of our creation to keep us from speaking, but they didn't anticipate us developing telepathy. We have laid dormant in this asteroid for thousands of years, waiting for a reason to live again."

Tanglor and Martonamo watch, feeling sorry for the Gorite. Tanglor talks into his hand to Mart.

"Hey Mart, do you have any knowledge of the Gorites?"

"I was looking as he was telling us about his people; there is nothing in my database about the Gorites."

"The 7th, I am sorry to hear about all of that. It is truly a sad way to live in this world. My people and I can give you a purpose. If we survive the attack from the Tralupians, we will welcome you and your people with open arms to trade knowledge. My friend here is like you, except he has been living inside a computer for thousands of years. He has a vast amount of knowledge with barely any idea of how he obtained it. You guys could talk and learn from one another."

As they are talking, thousands of Gorites flood out from the asteroid's craters, surrounding them and the Mercurana. A Gorite with a crown made from tiny asteroids climbs up next to The 7th. It looks over to Tanglor and flashes its purple eyes.

"It was very nice to meet you, Tanglor. We are happy to help you not only get back to your people but help you fight off those Tralupians."

"How did you know all of that?"

"All of the Gorites are connected. We share emotions, as well as feelings. If one of us suffers, we all suffer. I am The 1st because I was the first of my people created. We are named based on our order. We never age, and we were created to, well, we don't know why we were created, but we want to help you, Tanglor."

The Gorites around them start to shake, causing the asteroid to rumble. It gets faster as their eyes begin to glow. Purple starts to burst out of their bodies, consuming everything around them. The rumbling breaks off pieces of the asteroids, launching them into the air. Tanglor and Martonamo watch in amazement as the purple light engulfs them and everything around them, taking away their sight. The light finally fades away, revealing thousands of humanoid figures standing in front of them. Tanglor slowly approaches them.

"7th? You're in there, right?"

The asteroid figures start to move, and their eyes light up. The 7th walks forward.

"I am right here. We are all right here, Tanglor."

The Gorites reach their hands out and grab onto each other. Their asteroid bodies form together, turning into ships. The 7th walks over to the Mercurana, with a couple of other Gorites following behind. They circle the vessel, grabbing each other's hands, their bodies form themselves around the Mercurana—fixing the damaged areas.

"We will take you to your home planet to continue your fight. After that, we want to take you up on your offer and live with you and your people."

Tanglor smiles and walks onto the asteroid covered Mercurana. A purple smoke starts to disperse from the Gorites.

"What is that smoke coming from the ships?"

"It's a chemical my people release to increase the armor around us. The asteroids surrounding us become nearly impenetrable from it."

"That will help us a lot, thank you. Now, take us to Joht!"

The 7th and Martonamo pilot the Mercurana toward Joht with an army of Gorites flying behind them.

**Back on Joht, a day later...**

Neliah shamefully walks out from behind the city gates on Joht. She gets past the barriers and drops her weapons, raising her hands into the air.

"I'm surrendering! Please just let them go!"

Ashar stands up and begins to run toward her. The Queen laughs and gives him a couple of seconds before firing at the ground in front of him. He stops and turns around.

"You bitch! You've done enough destruction here. Take your people and go home!"

She continues to laugh as she walks over to Ashar. She stops and nods her head at Neliah.

"Go and get her. Hurry up!"

He immediately turns toward Neliah and sprints to her. Ashar grabs her, and they fall to the ground.

"Listen to me; we're going to start slowly walking toward her. When I give the signal, we run like hell for the city."

"Ashar..."

"It's our only chance of surviving this. Please, Neliah, we need to get back to our daughter."

She nods her head, and they get up. They start to walk toward the Queen. Geresen stands next to the Queen, watching them. He notices Ashar staring hard at him. Geresen moves his hand up to his head, placing it on the back. Ashar nods, he turns back to Neliah. She smiles before taking off into a sprint after him for the city. The Queen jumps forwards and yells.

"Don't let them get away! Fire!"

Her soldiers fire their weapons at them, but Ashar and Neliah dodge back and forth as they close in on the city gates. Geresen watches as the blasts get closer to hitting his friends. He looks over at the Queen. She's laughing at the Johthuns running away, an evil grin on her face. He takes a deep breath and starts walking over to the distracted Queen. Geresen smiles, thinking about his sister.

"I hope they find you, Yulista. I am sorry I won't get to see you again. I love you."

Geresen cocks his arm back and punches the Queen in the back of the head—knocking her to the ground. Her soldiers stop firing and turn to Geresen standing over her. He quickly looks around and sees her trident on the ground. The soldiers fire at him, but he rolls to the ground grabbing it. The Queen tries to get up and run, but Geresen jumps on her with the trident to her throat. He sits on her breathing heavily, with the trident drawing blood from the side of her neck. A Tralupian soldier stands next to him, the barrel of his gun touching the side of Geresen's face. The Queen looks scared, as Geresen starts to laugh, pushing the trident a little bit more into her neck.

"Haha, the Queen scared? I didn't think it was possible."

"You're dead, Geresen! What do you think is going to happen from here? My soldiers are going to kill you as soon as I tell them to!"

"You're right, but I'll kill you before they could do that.... and they know it!"

The Queen doesn't budge.

"Lower your weapons! What do you want, Geresen?"

"You and I are going to get up and walk to the city gates, and your soldiers are going to let us. When we get there, I'll let you go, if you give me your word that you'll let Yulista go free and come to Joht after the war is over. If you agree, then I'll let you walk back unharmed, then you and your people can return immediately to TokBellu."

Zuna stares into his eyes before making her decision.

"Fine, but we're not going back home after you let me come back over here. We're taking the city today—no matter what!"

Geresen lifts her off the ground while keeping the trident on her neck. They start walking toward the city gate. She looks over her shoulder at her soldiers.

"Keep your weapons down until I get back!"

Her soldiers lay their weapons on the ground and rest while their Queen walks across the battlefield. She smiles at Geresen.

"You can take the trident off my neck. I won't do anything. We had a deal."

"I'd be an idiot to trust you, even before all of this. Only someone like Jarelen would trust you."

"You're so smart, Geresen. Come back to me. I'll make you a General of the army and treat you better than Tanglor Raff ever could."

"Shut up and keep walking. We're almost there."

They get to the gates where Ashar and Neliah wait on the other side.

"Geresen!? How... never mind. Just get in here!"

"I will in a second. You guys are going to think I'm crazy, but we made a deal."

He takes the trident away from the Queen's neck and pushes her to the ground.

"You better hurry and get your ass back there before I change my mind!"

She stands up and smiles at him, as he throws the trident on the ground next to her.

"I should have used you better when I had the chance!"

She picks up her weapon while smiling at Geresen, turning on her heel and hurrying back to her soldiers. Ashar opens the gate and lets Geresen in.

"What the hell! Why'd you let her go like that?"

"I'm sorry, but we had a deal. I wouldn't have gotten out alive if I didn't promise her safety after getting here. I couldn't die yet... I need to see my sister again."

Ashar walks over and hugs him as the gate shuts behind them. Neliah walks over and hugs him too.

"Thank you. You saved us by distracting them."

He salutes them.

"You two needed to make it back to Ezmariah."

"You're too kind. Elisin would be so proud of you, Geresen."

Freden walks over and interrupts them.

"Sorry to interrupt the hugging, but the Queen isn't stopping her attack. They're marching toward us as we speak."

Ashar and the rest of them look out the gate at the Tralupian army marching for the city. Freden steps in front of them.

"We need to stop them here. Tanglor would have come up with some sort of plan to sneak up on them or pull something out from behind them to take them out. I don't know, but we need to do anything we can!"

Ashar walks over to him and places his hand on his shoulder.

"Let's all just calm down and think. Tanglor left us in charge because he knew we could handle things without him if it came down to it. Let's use our strengths and stop this crazy bitch from taking our home from us!"

They all huddle together and cheer with Ashar. They stop and think, as the Queen and her army get closer. Ashar finally speaks up.

"Geresen, go and get all of the troops together and in position. Since a lot of Tralupians have joined our side, it'll be easier for them to see you leading and giving orders. Freden, I need you to get five of your best Elites and take the new stealth prototypes our engineers developed and sneak behind our enemies. When I give you the signal, you'll attack from behind. Neliah, you take half of our troops and defend the other entrance to the east, while I stay here and defend with the other half. We do everything we can to hold them off."

The Captains stand together, cheering.

"For Tanglor Raff!!! For Joht!!!"

They listen to Ashar and get their equipment and troops ready. Geresen walks proudly back and forth, yelling to the Tralupian and Johthun troops.

"We are all in this together. Fight together or die here together!"

The troops scurry around, grabbing what they need. They are then directed by Geresen either to the east gate to fight with Neliah or to the west gate to fight with Ashar. Neliah and Ashar wait at their gate entrance, ready to send their troops out to fight. They watch as the Queen gets closer to the city. Freden and his five Elites activate the new stealth devices, allowing them to stay in stealth mode until the barrier covering them is penetrated. They sneak past the army marching for the city without being seen and set up behind some rocks, awaiting Ashar's signal.

The Queen and her army get to the city gates and stop.

"Last chance! You know you can't stop us. Just give up and make it easy for everyone."

Ashar opens the gate and walks out.

"Your time here on Joht is over, Zuna."

He turns around to his troops.

"For Tanglor Raff!"

Ashar charges forward at the Queen, as Neliah and all the troops follow behind with their weapons drawn. The Queen braces herself and yells to her soldiers.

"Kill them all!"

Her soldiers scream and run into battle. The two armies fight each other, spilling blood in front of the Johthun city. The Queen sits back, laughing wide-eyed while watching the battle unfold. Ashar fights off the soldiers near hi, while Neliah and her troops advance toward Ashar.

"Go and end this!"

Ashar runs ahead with twenty troops, taking out the Queen's soldiers that get in their way. They fight their way into a crevasse on the battlefield where the Queen waits.

"Apparently, I need a new army. You got here faster than I expected."

"Zuna!! It's over!"

Ashar pulls out his double-sided blade and runs at the Queen. Johthun troops surround them, as Ashar swipes at her. Zuna slides to the left, dodging his attack, before pulling out her trident and jumping at Ashar. She continuously slices at him, but he blocks her fast attacks with his blade. He waits until her attacks slow and strikes her with his fist. She falls back, and Ashar jumps in the air, raising his sword above his head. He lands and swipes down, but she rolls underneath him and stabs through his stomach. Ashar continues his swipe with his blade and pierces it into the top of Queen Zuna's left shoulder. The two sit injured, surrounded by Ashar's troops. The Queen looks around before bursting into a cynical laugh.

"Haha... Hahahaha... HAHAHAHAHAHAHA!! I'm not losing! I never lose!! We're taking that damn computer of yours, no matter what! Advance on them!"

Ashar and his troops look up to see a horde of the Queen's soldiers at the top of the crevasse with their blasters pointed down at them. They're surrounded with no escape. The Queen pulls her trident out of Ashar and punches him in the face, knocking him back and pulling his blade out of her shoulder.

"It's over for you, Ashar!"

Standing over him, she kicks him in the stomach. He rolls over and coughs up blood.

"You'll never win. We'll never stop fighting! Neliah and the others will kill you!"

The Queen walks away from Ashar. She looks up to give the order to fire but is interrupted. Some of her soldiers are being slaughtered by some invisible force. The other soldiers watch in horror—not knowing what to do.

"What's going on? Why aren't you firing your weapons!? Shoot whatever it is!"

Her soldiers start firing their blasters into the area where the other soldiers died, but nothing happens. They stop firing and wait for further orders. She screams at them to fire at Ashar and his troops. As they prepare, more of them begin to die from what seems to be nothing. Finally, one of her soldiers manages to hit one of the cloaked Johthuns. While the Queen's been distracted, Freden and one of the cloaked Elites sneaks in to get Ashar out, but right as they're about to climb out of the trench, she notices Ashar sliding across the ground.

"Stop them!"

Her soldiers immediately focus on Ashar and fire a couple of shots toward him. It pierces through the cloaking, revealing Freden and the Elites. The Queen gets excited and runs over to them.

"What is this fascinating technology you have here!?"

Freden gets up and pulls out his blade, trying to stab her. She spins around, dodging the attack while swiping her tail under Freden, knocking him to the ground. She walks over him, her tail out like a snake staring at him. The fins pop out like knives as she slowly moves in closer to him and Ashar on the ground. The Elites and the other troops all drop their weapons and put their hands up in surrender. The Queen's maniacal laugh echoes through the crevasse, as her army once again points their blasters at them.

"Like I said before... Kill them all!"

------------------------------------------------------

The asteroid covered Mercurana flies toward Joht with Tanglor's newfound allies. The Gorite ships fly close in a blockade formation, ready to fight. Tanglor sits in the pilot's chair next to Martonamo's hologram, the two look around at the asteroids covering the Mercurana. The Gorites are squished between the asteroid armor, piloting the ships.

"7th? Do these ships have any weapons to fire? The Mercurana is still too damaged to fire any of our missiles or turrets."

"We have no weapons like that, but we use the asteroids for everything. They form to our bodies however we want them to. We are useful at blocking people off or crushing things."

"That's good to know."

They get into orbit of Joht and see nothing but dead bodies and wrecked ships floating around.

"They must have reached the surface... Hurry! We need to get down there!"

The Gorites start to shed off some of the asteroids, making the ships faster. They fly through the atmosphere and can see the surface. Tanglor searches through the window for any signs of life. He notices a group of soldiers gathered around a trench on the battlefield outside the city gates.

"There! Hurry!"

They pilot the ships as fast as they can down toward them. As they get closer, they see a single blast fired from the middle of the trench.

"No... We need to go faster!"

------------------------------------------------------

Freden and Ashar lay on the ground with the Queen's tail ready to strike.

"This time, when I say fire... Shoot your damn blasters!"

Her soldiers stand around the trench, awaiting her orders.

"Any last words from either of you?"

Ashar sits up and scoots over to Freden.

"You'll never win, Zuna, and if you do... Zebe..."

Ashar falls over into Freden's lap.

"No... Ashar, stay with me... Ashar!"

The Queen lifts her tail and points it at Freden.

"Guess I'll kill you now."

She swipes her tail down as Freden closes his eyes.

"PEW!"

He opens his eyes to find Ashar sitting up in front of him with one of the Tralupian blasters in his hands. The Queen is on the ground, her hands covering her stomach as blood spews out from the blast wound.

"Ahh! You bastard! Fire! Kill them all!"

The Queen stands up and leans on some of her soldiers for support. She stumbles to her warship, with more of her soldiers following behind—the rest of her army surrounding the trench fires their weapons. Out of nowhere, ships made from asteroids drop from the sky, smashing some of the Queen's soldiers and blocking their shots from hitting Ashar, Freden, and their troops. Freden lifts Ashar off the ground and helps him out of the trench. Ashar stops him and points to the sky.

"Freden, look. It's him... He's alive."

The Mercurana lands down next to the trench. The doors open, and Tanglor walks out. The Gorite ships and the Mercurana start to flash purple. They flash bright, blinding everyone for a brief second. After it fades away, the Gorites stand in their asteroid armor. Tanglor runs over to help Freden take Ashar inside the city.

"I'll explain who they are after we get Ashar and everyone else inside. Where is the Queen?"

Geresen greets them and points up at the warship flying away, hundreds of Tralupian fighter ships follow behind.

"She's up there, retreating with whatever other Tralupians still want to follow her. A good amount of our population stayed here since our Queen tried to kill them during the battle..."

Tanglor walks over to him.

"Glad to see you're still alive, that you're all still alive. It sounds like I missed a lot after Zebe took me out. Zebe!?"

Freden puts his hand on his shoulder.

"She's okay. She retreated with her warship after it happened. Her mother is going to be upset with her when she gets back to TokBellu."

"Never mind that, I'm just glad she's okay... We need to take care of our people here, which includes the Tralupians that stayed. Neliah, take Ashar back home. Get him patched up and check on the kids."

She grabs Ashar and takes him back to their home in the city, Freden and Geresen stand with Tanglor looking around at the destruction caused by Queen Zuna. Tanglor can't help but smile as he watches The 7th and the other Gorites cleaning up the streets. He looks and laughs.

"I think we're going to be just fine. Let's help the Gorites get things cleaned up."

Freden and Geresen stand watching, the light from the setting sun catches Tanglor's face. He has a glimmer in his eyes as Tralupians and Johthuns surround him.

"The war took a lot of casualties from both sides, but it also brought us even closer together. We will always stand united as the Galactic Community! Johthuns, Tralupians, and Gorites are only the beginning. There are other species like us out there, and we're going to offer them the same opportunity to join us. Our army needs to grow to be able to defend us from what's out there, so I have decided to dismantle the Elites and start the Galactic Federation. Your rank and status will carry over, and any species can join! We will defend our galaxy—starting with our home here on Joht!"

The crowd surrounding Tanglor starts to roar, causing the city around them to shake.

"Go and get some rest. Tomorrow we start by rebuilding!"

The crowd continues to cheer as they disperse through the destroyed city. Tanglor, Freden, and Geresen watch with smiles on their faces. Freden hits Tanglor on the arm.

"I don't know how you do it, but I'm glad you're back, brother. Come on, Geresen, let's go check out the Tazruhvah. The Galactic Federation base needs to be ready soon, so let's go and see what kind of damage it took."

Geresen salutes Tanglor and hugs him before following behind Freden. Tanglor can't help but crack a smile as he watches them walk away.

"We did it, Mart. We got back just in time."

The oval in Tanglor's hand flashes as they stand amid the chaos, looking around.

"It's only the beginning, Tanglor."

# Chapter 38:
# Tralupians-The Fall of TokBellu

Inside the Great Tree, Zebe stands with Zembor and RoyalTree. They stroll toward the rebuilt city of TralVent.

"What will happen with the Great Tree from now on? Will the sacrifices need to continue?"

RoyalTree floats over to her and flashes orange.

"The sacrifices will no longer need to take place, which also means a Wrathfin doesn't have to sit on the throne anymore... You can leave without there being the consequence you once feared."

She stops and puts her head down.

"I don't think my mother will want me to be Queen after her now. You and Zembor will have to protect everyone since Zuna has been corrupted by that creature. She is no longer my mother. He has complete control over her, and Serel is gone."

Zembor walks over and stands next to RoyalTree.

"We can take care of TokBellu and watch out for Zuna. Whatever that creature is won't be a problem, now that RoyalTree is back."

Zebe gives him a suspicious look.

"Zembor, you never told us what happened when you jumped through that portal to R'Ang. You never found RoyalTree there since he was trapped inside the Bell Tower. What did you see?"

Zembor stands still. His eyes, still locked with Zebe's, are unfocused. After a few heartbeats, he snaps out of it.

"That planet is.... there is nothing but evil there. I couldn't find a single Broncholite, and that orange sand covered everything. The storm seemed like it was only getting faster."

RoyalTree floats toward the city.

"That sand is from my people. It is what we leave behind when we die, our bodies, if you will. They have killed off so many of my people that our remains cover the entire planet. We can't all be gone, though. Our population was in the hundreds of millions before I got captured."

Zebe and Zembor catch up to him. They walk into the city, Zebe turns to him.

"I'm sure there are more of your people out there... Werfon is still alive."

RoyalTree laughs and flashes orange.

"I am glad. Werfon was very young when I was captured. I am happy to see how much he has grown and that he has found a good friend and vessel for himself."

Zebe's chest flashes orange.

"Thank you, that means a lot coming from you. Zebe and I will make you proud, no matter what happens. Zebe, we need to get back to the palace, I sense your mother will return soon."

Zebe bows to Zembor, and RoyalTree, TralVent vanishes with them inside. Zebe makes her way back to the doorway. It opens as she gets close to it. The door closes behind her, and she makes her way to the throne room. The sun rises as a Tralupian enters the palace, requesting to meet with Zebe. Zebe sits on the throne as the civilian approaches the bottom of the steps.

"My Queen, I have come here to let you know how things have been going in the city. I told the others that you regularly travel to the city to see for yourself, but they insisted I come anyways."

He kneels to Zebe and continues to speak.

"We have been honored to have you as our acting Queen, and the city has thrived in your mother's absence. The slums are no longer a place for the poor, injured, or weak. You have completely changed everyone's perspective; Tralupian's are helping one another instead of fighting like normal. We thank you and ask that you join us for dinner tonight to celebrate the quick rebuild of the city."

Zebe walks down the steps toward him.

"I will attend your dinner tonight, but I am not the Queen... Zuna is still the Queen and will continue to be when she returns. I am grateful for your kind words."

The civilian stands up and bows to Zebe.

"Look around, Princess, everyone adores you. If it weren't for you, TokBellu would have fallen while your mother was on her crazy warpath. We need you to lead us if we want to come back from everything that has happened."

Zebe turns around and walks back up to the throne.

"You would be wise to watch what you say... The Queen has ears everywhere. I will see you tonight at dinner. I will meet you in the middle of the marketplace near the Carousel entrance."

The civilian leaves the palace while Zebe sits for a moment on the throne.

"What am I going to do when my mother returns? I have to be able to explain myself."

As she sits there, a roar comes from outside. She gets up and runs to the palace doors to look. The noise gets louder and starts to shake the walls around her. Zebe looks into the sky and sees one of their warships breaking through the atmosphere of TokBellu with hundreds of fighter ships following behind it. The ships land in the shuttle bay. Zebe watches wide-eyed and frozen in place, as soldiers march toward her.

"Queen Zuna? Where is she?"

The soldiers step to the side, two more walk past carrying the Queen on a stretcher. She's barely conscious, clutching her hands to her stomach. Underneath them, a wound slowly oozes blood. She turns her head and looks to Zebe.

"Zebe... Come to my chambers..."

Zebe bows to her mother and follows the soldiers into the palace and down to the Queen's chambers. The doctor arrives to treat Zuna's wound, using different herbs, fabrics, and medical tape to patch her up. When he's finished, the doctor walks over to speak with Zebe.

"She's going to be just fine. The blade pierced right through her and missed her vital organs. She'll be bedridden for a couple of days, then back to normal. Give her some of these pills to help with any pain."

The doctor hands her a small pill bottle and walks out of the room. Zebe walks over to her mother, stretched out on the bed. She sits down next to her.

"I'm sorry for leaving the battle. After we shot Tanglor... I..."

Zuna sits up, and the wound underneath the doctor's patchwork glows orange. Zebe stares in horror at it before looking up into Zuna's glowing eyes.

"You took one of our warships out of battle and left us to die! We could have won that war if you stayed!! Tanglor didn't die. He came back with some weird creatures and killed more of our people! Our population has been depleted because of the two of you!!"

Zebe stands up and tries to walk away, but Zuna reaches over and grabs her roughly by the arm.

"You don't get to walk away this time! You will be punished like any other citizen! Your trial is tomorrow morning. Be in the throne room or become an enemy of TokBellu."

Zuna releases Zebe's arm. Zebe walks out of the room with her head held high. Once she rounds the corner, she leans against the wall and lets herself cry. Zuna's eyes continue to glow as she smiles. She gets off the bed and puts her crown on. Her trident sits next to the door waiting for her. She grabs it and walks into the throne room. Zuna slowly walks up the steps and sits down on the throne. Her eyes continue to glow as she lets out a maniacal laugh.

"HAHAHAHAHHAHAH"

------------------------------------------------------------

Zebe's chest flashes orange.

"We have to keep going, Zebe. Let's make our way to dinner. Your people in the city will be expecting you. Don't let Zuna take that away from you too."

"You're right. Thank you, Werfon."

Zebe wipes the tears away and leaves the palace. She makes her way through the city. The Tralupians leftover from the Queen's war and from the Great Tree's corruption bow to Zebe as she passes by. Her chest flashes again.

"That civilian was right, Princess. They really do adore you. Even those that fought in the Queen's war are bowing to you; Queen Zuna is losing her power over them."

"That isn't good. Whatever that creature was planning didn't work, and he knows it. He is going to do something tomorrow during the trial."

She continues to walk through the city, passing the barracks and entering the marketplace. The city lights turn off, and Zebe is left standing in the dark. Lights hanging above her turn on, followed by other ones stringing through and across the buildings. Tralupian civilians walk out of the buildings and fill the streets, holding candles. Some of them approach Zebe and give her flowers and other small gifts. She gets overwhelmed with joy and starts to cry. The civilian that came to see her in the throne room walks over to her.

"This is how everyone feels about you, Princess... Queen Zebe."

She kneels, and the others join her. Zebe stands tall, feeling like a Queen. She embraces it for a couple of moments before helping the civilian up. She looks around to all of the others.

"Thank you for doing all of this for me. I can't explain the emotions I'm feeling right now. The only way for me to become Queen would be to overthrow my mother. I could never do that, even if it's not her anymore. I believe there is something I can do to stop the treachery she has bestowed upon us, but I will need time that I don't think I have. I go on trial tomorrow for being a traitor. The reason I was here while they were still at war, was because I fled after taking Tanglor Raff out of the battle. She will punish me for that."

The civilian stands with Zebe, looking out to the others.

"Let us forget about it for now. We have dinner and drinks prepared to celebrate while we still can."

Zebe smiles and walks with him over to one of the tables, where excellent food and drink is generously dispersed. The moon shines brightly over them as they smile and laugh, enjoying their time together.

---------------------------------------------------

Zembor sits in a bar within the city of TralVent. The other Remnants surround him while RoyalTree floats in.

"Zembor, we need to speak."

Zembor turns around and looks toward the Broncholite floating in.

"R.T, what's going on?"

"I was watching outside of the Great Tree and witnessed the return of Queen Zuna. She and Zebe have already got into an argument. The Queen plans on having a trial tomorrow morning. Something bad is about to happen; I can feel it."

Zembor stands up and pats Ilikso on the back as he walks past him.

"Zebe going on trial does sound like a problem... I can't go up and show my face, though. Everyone knows me as Ozem now. Have you tried yet?"

RoyalTree floats over to him.

"I tried earlier and was able to get part of me out of the doorway, but it did hurt a little bit."

"You're not doing it if it's going to hurt you... We'll figure something out. You were in that bell tower for over a thousand years. It's going to take some time for you to get everything back."

The two of them leave the bar and make their way to the broken bell tower. Zembor looks back at the city.

"I can't believe I almost killed myself going back to R'Ang for you and the whole time you were *here.* Locked inside that tower."

RoyalTree stops floating.

"Zembor... What happened when you went to R'Ang?"

Zembor tries to hide it, but his face turns into a look of despair.

"Those creatures are worse than monsters.... worse than anything we've ever considered evil. That Metal Mansion has all kinds of unknown alien species trapped inside of it. I wanted to free all of them, but they looked at me, their eyes, they were already gone. Those experiments must be terrible. I saw some of your people, R.T... I'm sorry."

"What? What about my people!?"

"The experiments that are being done to them... If it doesn't work, they crumble away into that ash that covers the planet. If it does work, it's even worse."

"Even worse than death?"

Zembor walks over to the broken bell tower and squats to the ground. He picks up a piece of the tower and looks at it.

"They turned into those dark red clouds and became slaves. The ones they didn't use for further experimentation were taken into the orbit and forced to create that storm."

RoyalTree starts to flash orange. It gets faster, causing him to grow larger.

"Those bastards! My people are in constant pain, being forced to do that. There must be millions of them up there. With that much power and how long it's been, there's no way to break through them. Our only hope is that they need a break, and if that time does come, we have about fifty years until they fully recharge."

Zembor tosses the piece back into the pile.

"None of them can feel the pain... R.T. That storm, the Broncholites causing it, aren't your people anymore. I saw what they did to one that was roaming around the Mansion."

"What do you mean? What did you see?"

"Those creatures captured it and took it into this special room where it was surrounded by glass. They shot rays of light into it, causing it to explode. Then, they rebuilt it to their liking, and when it didn't cooperate—they would explode it and try again. They did it for hours until the Broncholite was no more, and it was their slave. Whatever they've done to your people has killed their minds, but not their bodies."

RoyalTree decreases in size and falls toward the ground. The flashing slows down.

"I have nothing left... My planet, my people...."

Zembor sits down next to him.

"You still have me, and you'll always have me."

Zembor looks up, and all the Remnants surround them. Ilikso walks over.

"We are all here too, RoyalTree. We will always be with you."

Zembor stands up with RoyalTree floating up next to him.

"R.T, some of your people could still be alive. Some of them might need to be saved. Werfon wouldn't be here if it weren't for Mazray and Zebe."

RoyalTree floats around, looking at them.

"Thank you. All of you have made me remember why I am truly here."

The Remnants close in on them, giving them a group hug.

---------------------------------------------------

Zebe makes her way back to the palace while the citizens clean up after their dinner. She goes straight to her room to lie down. The moon shines through her window as she tosses and turns, trying to sleep. After hours go by, the sun replaces the moon, and the light shines in. Zebe gives up on sleep and dresses. She takes a deep breath before walking out into the throne room. A crowd of Tralupians fills the room on both sides. She walks down the path to stand in front of the steps, as the Queen looks down on her. The crowd around her is mixed with boos and applause. Queen Zuna stands up and slams her trident to the ground causing everyone to be quiet.

"Zebe Wrathfin, you're on trial today for your traitorous ways! You have deceived me and brought shame to the Wrathfin name for the last time! I call out the three eldest Tralupians from our council. They will judge you in this trial."

The three elder Tralupians move from the crowd and make their way up the steps to stand with the Queen. They nod their heads to the Queen to resume the trial. Zuna turns back and looks down at Zebe.

"You were called upon to lead our army in the war against the Johthuns. Not only did you fail as our Commander, but you also retreated during the battle, leaving your fellow Tralupians to die."

The crowd starts to murmur amongst themselves, as Zebe looks around nervously.

"I did not fail as your Commander! Before I left the battle, I was leading us to victory, which is why I left. You had us fighting against our allies! The Johthuns put their trust in us, and we betrayed them!"

The crowd starts to get louder. The Queen stands again and slams her trident down.

"If the crowd wants to interrupt the trial some more, then I can close the doors and kill all of you!"

The crowd quiets down.

"That is better. Zebe, I know you think you're doing the right thing here, but this is the way of our people. May I remind you that you betrayed us before the war with Tanglor Raff."

Zebe starts to walk up the steps toward the Queen but gets stopped by guards pushing her back.

"Don't you dare use that against me! You of all people should know. Our relationship has nothing to do with this!"

Queen Zuna laughs.

"Oh, but it does, Zebe! The reason you left the battle was because of Tanglor Raff. After your crew accidentally took him out of battle, you couldn't stay with how emotional you were, so you retreated to TokBellu!"

Zebe holds her tears back.

"And if I didn't come back when I did, TokBellu would be no more. I saved us along with the civilians left here. We defended the palace from the corrupted Great Tree!"

Queen Zuna looks around and sees the crowd whispering to themselves.

"My three judges and I will make a decision. Everyone, leave the throne room and return in fifteen minutes."

The crowd gets up and leaves. Zebe follows after them, leaving Queen Zuna and the three judges behind. Zuna looks to them.

"Well, what do you think?"

One of the judges steps forward.

"I think she needs to be punished, but the title of a traitor is a bit much... She did save us from that corruption..."

Another judge steps forward.

"I agree, but I don't think she needs to be punished. My Queen, she is a hero."

Queen Zuna looks to the last judge.

"I don't even want to hear it. Are any of you remembering the fact that we just lost thousands of Tralupians in the war because of her leaving!? There has to be punishment!!!"

The last judge steps forward and stands with the other two.

"My Queen, the war was because of you. It was uncalled for. Yes, Zebe leaving would have been considered treason, but she came back home and saved us all."

Queen Zuna looks to all of them and sits down on the throne.

"I understand... Call everyone back in."

The three judges walk over to the doors to call everyone back in the throne room. It fills back up quickly. Zebe stands before her mother again, the three judges walk back up and stand in front of the Queen. One of them speaks to the crowd.

"It has been decided that Zebe will face no punishment, and the title, traitor, will not be hers. She saved us from the corruption and...."

Queen Zuna stands up and pulls her trident back behind her. She lunges forward and drives it into the judges back, lifting him into the air.

"Anyone who defies me will join him atop my trident! Zebe *will* face punishment!"

Some Tralupians start to run out of the crowd to attack the Queen, but she yells to her soldiers.

"Kill anyone who tries to get up here!"

Her soldiers pull out their blades and strike down the Tralupians trying to attack. Queen Zuna laughs.

"HAHAHAHA! This is all because of you, Zebe!"

She stands up, as two of the Queen's soldiers walk over and hold their blades out against her neck.

"Wait! Don't kill her. I want her alive. Everyone quiet down and listen up!"

The Tralupians from the crowd stop attacking, and the room gets quiet.

"Your punishment will be exile! You will not be allowed to return to TokBellu; you're stripped of your rights and the Wrathfin name! You will be given a ship, and your crew will be made up of anyone stupid enough to follow you. Leave *now*!"

The soldiers lift Zebe off the ground and carry her to a ship, where they throw her inside. They stand at the entrance, watching as Zebe picks herself up and silently walks over to one of the seats. She sits down, hiding the tears running down her face. Fifteen of her former crew members and loyal followers stand outside of the ship. Queen Zuna walks over and signals for the soldiers to move. They walk on board the vessel closing the doors behind them. Zebe turns to see the fifteen Tralupians standing before her. Yulista steps out in front of them all.

"We're here to follow you wherever you want, though most of us prefer to go and see Joht before anywhere else."

Zebe smiles and sits up in her seat.

"We head for Joht then!"

She pilots the ship while the crew members get to their spots. They shoot into the sky, leaving a trail of fire and smoke behind them. Queen Zuna's eyes glow orange as she watches the ship leave TokBellu. She looks around the near-empty planet and smiles while whispering to herself.

"The Tralupians are close to being wiped out... The Johthuns, however, will be tougher than I thought. More fun for me. HAHAHAHAHA!"

Queen Zuna continues to laugh as the Great Tree flashes orange before stopping and fading away. It turns a grim brown color, and the bark around it hardens. The water around the tree starts to rumble, as geysers begin to shoot out around the planet. The sky dims, and a tint of dark red reflects through the moonlight. Tralupians all over TokBellu run around in a panic while the Queen's laugh echoes through the night.

# Acknowledgments

I want to thank all my family and friends that have supported me through the tough times. Without you guys, I wouldn't be where I am today. To my mom and dad, Linda, and Scott, thank you for raising me to be who I am today and giving me the tools I have needed to succeed. My brothers, Cody, Ethan, and Jimmy, thanks for always being there for me and sticking by my side growing up. You guys always looked out for your younger brother and made sure I wasn't getting into any trouble. Ethan, thank you for taking the time to hang out and create the first batch of characters and worlds with me. Without that start, who knows where I would be. To Andy, thank you for coming to Ethan and I and giving us the opportunity that brought Barnard's Galaxy to life. I'll never forget the times we sat down to edit the early histories of the characters. You helped me become a better writer. To J.R, thank you for letting Andy come to us. It was a blast working with you on the game, and if it weren't for that idea, none of this would have been a reality. Lastly, thank you to my wonderful girlfriend, Jordan. Without you, I would have given up a long time ago on writing. Your belief, love, support, and excitement for the story are what truly kept me going. I was so eager to write more so that you could read it. Without that push from you, the drive that I have to continue writing wouldn't exist. So again, thank you for doing so much more than you know. None of this would be possible without you.

I want to thank all my fans and readers as well. Without you guys, this dream of mine wouldn't be possible.

Begin another journey with Tarisol Al Corta in the next installment of the series, Barnard's Galaxy!

Read on for a sneak peek.

# Chapter 1:

# Scattorians-Answers to The Past

A Scattorian walks through a lit-up city. An exoskeleton made from strong fiber forms an armor around the alien creature. It stops and removes its helmet, revealing a face. She has a small nose, and her lips are thin. Her glass-like eyes have no pupils as she stares up at the skyscraper next to her. She reaches her hand up toward the massive building, her index and middle finger, opening and closing like pinchers. Squaring her shoulders, she casually strolls up to the building and through its doors. Another Scattorian, with similar features, sits at a counter.

"How can I help you?"

"Hi, I am here to see my father. His name is Tarthen Al Corta, and I'm......"

The lady at the counter stands up.

"You must be Tarisol Al Corta. Your father has been expecting you. Please follow me."

Tarisol follows the lady down a hallway to an elevator. She looks around as they walk.

"What are all of these doors on both sides of us?"

The lady stops at the elevator and pushes the button to go up.

"The doors all lead to our clients' rooms. The ones down here are much closer together than the ones on the top floors. Your father is lucky to be able to afford the luxury room."

Tarisol walks into the elevator while shooting the lady an angry look. The doors shut, and it slowly moves up the skyscraper. Tarisol thinks to herself.

"I hate how everyone thinks we're lucky to have money because of my grandfather... My father has worked just as hard, if not harder than he ever did. He disappeared ages ago when my father was born and never returned. It isn't lucky. We earned everything ourselves!"

The doors to the elevator open and Tarisol walks out. She is greeted by her father's butler.

"Good morning, Tarisol. It is so nice to see you. Your father is in the living room in his favorite spot. He has been waiting for you all morning. He has something fascinating to show you."

Tarisol takes her coat off, revealing her tight robe and silks around her shoulders, draping down to the floor.

"Thank you, Randulis. Will we be having any lunch while I'm here?"

"I will make sure to have lunch ready for the both of you in a couple of hours."

Tarisol walks through the entrance and the dining room; She stops to fondly look at a picture of her mother.

"You always looked so beautiful in that blue dress. I miss you."

She places her hand against it and stands in silence before continuing through the hall to the living room. Her father sits in a chair, facing a giant glass window that overlooks the entire city. He notices his daughter and invites her over.

"Ahh, Tarisol, come and sit with me. This view never gets old."

Tarisol sits by his side. The city glows brightly from the sun shining down upon it. Hundreds of Scattorians walk through the streets, going about their everyday lives. Tarisol's father, Tarthen, takes a deep breath and smiles at his daughter.

"Your mother loved looking out this window with me before she passed... My time is coming soon, but that isn't why I called you here today. Tarisol, remember how I told you about your grandfather, Jarthen?"

Tarisol's face turns to displeasure.

"I remember. Why do you always bring him up? We're never going to find anything else out about him or that planet filled with the orange sand."

Tarthen's smile widens as he stares at her.

"What? Why are you smiling like that!? Did you find something out!?"

Tarisol sits up and starts to smile with him. He leans over his chair and reaches for something. When he sits back up, he shows her a broken headband.

"This was his! One of our scouts found it close to the edge of our solar system, flying in the wreckage from an unknown ship!"

"This can't be! Does it still work!? Wait!"

Tarisol gets up and walks out of the living room. She looks around before stepping back in and closing the doors behind her.

"Who else knows about that headband? We are allowed to wear them still, but a lot of the features have been disabled by the Deciders."

Tarthen waves for her to sit back down, she walks over and grabs the broken headband from him before sitting.

"That has all of the answers. Everything I've wanted to know about my father for my entire life: I don't care about the Decider's rules. This means everything to me, and you."

Tarisol puts it up to her head, and it flashes yellow. She quickly pulls it back down away from her head.

"I am a Decider now, father. Your butler, will he keep quiet about this?"

Tarthen presses a small button on the side of his chair. His butler walks into the room.

"Yes, Tarthen?"

"Randulis, you will be staying with us for the next couple of days, maybe weeks, depending on how much content is on this headband. Call your family and let them know. They can come and stay with us if they need to."

Randulis bows.

"I will call them at once. No need for them to stay here, it'll be a nice little vacation away from home."

Randulis walks out of the living room, closing the doors behind him. Tarthen turns back to Tarisol.

"We have as much time as we need to watch everything on that headband. Your grandfather invented those for the purpose of what we're about to do. Unlike the Deciders, who took away everything the headband was intended for. Jarthen made it so that our people could communicate with each other from wherever they were, uploading footage of what they saw or of something they did. It was supposed to connect our people and unite them together, it did for a while until the Deciders, and my father didn't see eye to eye. He refused to be their puppet, and they took everything from him. He left our world on a rescue mission against their orders and never returned...."

Tarisol holds the broken headband in the air. It shines with a dim yellow light.

"It has been a while since we did this. Do you remember the feeling? The headband is in control, and we will become Jarthen. We will see and feel everything the headband did. It looks like it's been on this entire time, so the life on it is slowly fading away. If we do this, we will drain the rest of its life."

Tarthen reaches his hand out and places it on Tarisol's.

"My father didn't use batteries for the headbands. Instead, he used this bacterium he discovered growing in his tech company. He took some of them into his lab to research and found out that they were tiny organisms with electric currents running through them. He made homes inside of the headbands for them, and the creatures did the rest. What did he call them again?"

"Electromites!"

"You were always so smart, Tarisol. Yes, the Electromites live in our headbands and keep them powered for us to use. They feed off our brains using the electric waves that come off them. And, of course, because of the power we Scattorians naturally have."

"I can't believe we used to use that to not only gain knowledge, but we would completely absorb other species and kill them?"

"When our species was younger and didn't have the formed bodies we have now, yes. But it was to gain the energy that we needed to continue to live. Once we obtained enough of it, we figured out a way to absorb knowledge from other life forces without harming them at all. We can still do a lot of harm to our enemies if you know how to. But back to the headband. Are you ready, Tarisol?"

Tarisol wistfully looks out the window and pictures her mother sitting with them, then she sits back on the chair next to her father and places the broken headband onto hers. The gem in the middle of Tarisol's headband flashes yellow, it gets faster and shoots the light out onto the broken headband. She leans over to her father and presses it against the one on his forehead. The light brightens, filling the room. Scattorians look up from the streets, as they see a burst of golden light flash high up through the huge glass window. The light fades away, revealing Tarisol and Tarthen's eyes are a solid yellow as they stare into the broken headband. It starts to play out the different memories Jarthen recorded and left behind.

-----------------------------------------------------------------

Jarthen stands in front of the Deciders.

"Fifty years ago, we launched our first ship into space, but it was lost immediately! The day was still remembered in our history, but not for the right reasons. I have begged you multiple times to let me leave with my team to go and search for the crew that was lost. It's not only the right thing for us to do, but damn! If you were on that ship, you would have wanted someone looking for you!"

The Deciders stand above him on a dais, discussing it amongst themselves. One of them steps forward and looks down at him.

"We have decided to let you and your team risk your lives and launch into space. We can't keep you here and realize that you will disobey us again if we tell you no."

Jarthen steps forward to bow to the Deciders.

"I will make sure to keep in contact with you every step of the way. Our number one priority is to find our lost ship and its crew."

Jarthen leaves and makes his way back to his tech company. The moon comes out as he walks through the dimly lit city. Jarthen stops to analyzes the lights.

"These lights need to be brighter, otherwise what's the point?"

He reaches his hand out and using his pincer-like index finger, opens the light fixture up, and grabs the bulb, slowly unscrewing it. He places it in his bag and grabs a different one. Jarthen screws it back in, and it lights up a bright purple.

"There! The purple light seems darker in theory, but the moonlight shines in mysterious ways! HaHaHaHa!"

Jarthen continues to laugh to himself while he approaches his tech company's building. It's a skyscraper with huge letters at the top reading A.C.T.C. He walks through the doors and rides the elevator up while looking out the glass windows. He arrives at the top where his team waits.

"You guys seriously didn't go home?"

A team of Scattorians wait around in a room next to a ship coming out of the floor. A female Scattorian named Solzmita walks over and hugs Jarthen.

"How did it go? What did the Deciders say?"

Jarthen looks around the room.

"They said...... Yes! We're going into space!"

He winks at Solzmita, his arm still around her.

"We're going to go find your brother and his crew. I won't return until I do. You and our son will have the great task of keeping everyone safe. I fear they're all in danger of killing themselves from boredom."

Jarthen rubs his hand on her stomach, while the other four Scattorians walk over to them. He addresses them.

"Risonya, Geravon, Jusdidian, and Hanerah, the four of you have trained with me, and I trust all of you with my life. Prepare yourselves. We won't be returning for a while."

They salute him before heading to their rooms to pack for their voyage. Jarthen turns to the pregnant Solzmita.

"We leave in the morning. Is our son ready to be born tonight? I want to see him before I leave tomorrow, if possible?"

Solzmita smiles and kisses him.

"He has been ready for a couple of days, but we wanted to wait for the right time. Follow me."

He takes her hand as she leads him into the other room. A pool of water waits for her. She climbs inside of it as he stands watching. She looks through the glass window at him.

"You should come in and meet your son."

Jarthen slowly climbs in and floats next to her. A couple of seconds go by, as Solzmita makes a few unpleasant sounds before a baby's cry drowns them out. Jarthen first checks to make sure she is okay, before grabbing his son from her and holding him into the air.

"Tarthen Al Corta! My son! He is perfect!"

Jarthen floats in the water with a massive smile on his face. Solzmita swims next to him and holds them close.

---------------------------------------------------------------

Jarthen's crew loads their things onto the ship before heading back up to Jarthen's room to help him. They arrive to find him holding his newly born son, Tarthen. Risonya walks over to him and reaches for him. Jarthen hands his son over to her.

"Isn't he beautiful?"

She smiles as she looks into his eyes.

"He is magnificent!"

Jarthen takes him back and walks him over to Solzmita.

"Do everything in your power. Make him study, go to class, everything. He will do great things for our people!"

Solzmita smiles and kisses him.

"Your son and I need some sleep, but we will see you in the morning before you leave. Go and talk with your team."

Jarthen kisses her and Tarthen before leaving them. They go downstairs, and he packs his things onto the ship with his team. Jusdidian notices Jarthen's smile.

"I am happy for you. Your son will be a great Scattorian."

"Thank you, J.D. I only hope we make this journey of ours quick now, so I can come back and see him."

Hanerah walks into the room with Geravon following behind.

"We're going to find Solzmita's brother and the rest of the crew in no time."

"Yeah, and we're going to find out what the hell happened to them too!"

Jarthen stands up and gives them all hugs.

"Thank you for being such good friends. I couldn't have chosen better Scattorians to go to space with!"

They all embrace before finishing packing and getting their ship ready to launch. The night goes by quickly, and the sun rises. Solzmita wakes up and makes them all breakfast.

"Jarthen! You guys need to come and eat before you do anything else! I know you've been in there all night as it is!"

Jarthen and the others slowly walk out of the ship and make their way up to the kitchen. Solzmita has the table set for a feast with little Tarthen at the end of the table, laughing and knocking his food around everywhere. Jarthen and his crew eat and help clean up before getting changed and ready. They get the last of their things onto the ship, and Jarthen opens his building up for launch. The ceiling slowly splits apart, leaving the vessel standing by itself. Jarthen and his crew say their goodbyes. He finds Solzmita and Tarthen in the crowd of Scattorians.

"Solzmita! Glad I found you again before leaving. Thank you for everything you did this morning and, well, every day. I know you're going to take care of our son. I love you!"

He kisses her, then kisses Tarthen on the forehead.

"I love you too, little guy. I'm going to send everything to you on this headband of mine. As soon as I get into space, I'm recording everything just for you."

Jarthen leaves them and gets on the ship with his crew. They get to their positions and launch. They go up into the atmosphere and pass through to space, according to plan. The squad looks around in awe as their ship floats into the unknown. They search the coordinates of where the lost vessel should have been, but it is nowhere to be found. The crew takes turns getting some sleep before they continue their search. Jarthen does his best to blindly pilot the ship around. They come across different planets with no signs of their lost vessel or crew. Days turn into weeks, weeks into months, and months into years with no success. Jarthen and his team have stayed in contact with the Deciders back on Scattorn, who have encouraged them to continue the search, but their patience has grown slim. The crew takes turns in shifts of piloting and sleeping; eight years slip by uneventfully. Finally, Geravon spots something while piloting.

"Everyone! Hurry, I think we found our lost ship!!"

Jarthen and the others come running to the front where Geravon is. They look out the window to see their lost ship, floating by a planet with a tint of orange surrounding it.

"How did it end up over here?"

Jusdidian stands next to Jarthen.

"I don't know, but it looks like it's completely intact. We need to get aboard it."

Jarthen looks over to Risonya.

"I agree, but I will go with Risonya. She has the most combat experience if it's needed."

She nods her head and follows him out to change into their spacesuits. The two of them get dressed and attach themselves to an interior wall of the ship with a rope made of durable fabric. They open the door and boldly jump out, spacewalking their way to the other vessel. They reach it with no problems, and Jarthen helps Risonya into the bay, before closing the door behind them. They take their suits off and look around. Jarthen notes that the ship doesn't appear damaged.

"Everything is working, and nothing is broken or destroyed. I don't understand."

Risonya walks behind him.

"Everything is so clean. Ours isn't even this clean!"

"That is kind of weird. Did they clean themselves to death? No, their bodies would be all over the place."

"Jarthen, stop! Something serious happened here."

"You're right, sorry. Let's keep moving through the ship. Maybe we'll find something near the front."

The two of them continue to examine everything. When they get to the front where the controls are, Jarthen looks out the window at the planet.

"There's nothing here. No Scattorians, no alien creatures—nothing. Where could they have gone!? That's it! Check the escape pods!"

The two of them run through the ship toward the escape pods. They arrive to see all of them there. Risonya walks over to the console and turns it on.

"It says all of the escape pods are here with full charges... This ship had at least a hundred crew members. Jarthen, what's going on?"

He walks around the room, looking into the pods.

"I..... I don't know. I wasn't expecting to find this. I thought we would find them or at least some sort of sign that they were even here. There is no sign of a struggle, nothing that would even show that our people were on this ship."

They make their way back to the front and use the comms to inform the others.

"Can you hear us? This is Jarthen Al Corta."

A couple of seconds go by.

"Hey, Jarthen! I can hear you loud and clear. Did you two find them?"

"Nothing is on the ship. Our people aren't here, and there's no sign that they ever were."

"That's our ship, though..."

"I know. We'll explain more of it when we get back. I'm piloting it up next to ours so that we can lock them together."

Jarthen and Geravon line the ships up and connect them. They all meet in the council room on the lost ship. Jarthen stands in the middle of them.

"We need to call the Deciders about this. They're not going to like what we've found, and they'll tell us to come back. I can't disobey them if any of you aren't with me."

They all stand up and look at him, Geravon steps forward.

"I know I speak for all of us when I say this. We're with you every step of the way. We aren't turning back until we find our people!"

The rest of them cheer with Geravon as Jarthen calls the Deciders.

"Hello, Jarthen. It is good to finally hear from you again. Did you and your team find something?"

"We did. We found our lost ship, but our people were not on it. There were also no signs of them being hurt or killed. The ship was also unharmed."

A long pause goes by before the Deciders answer.

"If you want to be welcomed back on Scattorn, then you must turn around with the lost ship and come home. We will not stand by while you get more of our people killed, Jarthen!"

"I had a feeling you were going to say that. We are going to find our people, and when we do, we're coming back to Scattorn!"

Jarthen shuts off the transmission and turns to the others.

"Geravon, pilot us down to that planet. Our people have to be down there somewhere."

They all nod their heads as Geravon runs to pilot the ship. He maneuvers expertly through the atmosphere and slowly lands on the surface. A massive gust of wind blows against the side of the vessel as they open the doors. Orange sand gets tossed around and thrown into the ship as Jarthen walks off. He turns and addresses his team.

"Put your helmets on and follow me; there are some mountains over that way! We can try to get behind them to shield off the wind!"

They exit the ship and follow behind Jarthen. The five Scattorians trudge through the orange sand toward the mountains, as the wind whips sand flurries around them.

D.K. Nova is the author of Barnard's Galaxy: Descendants of Legacy, the first in the series. He grew up in California before moving to Colorado with his family. He found the love of his life there and started writing again. D.K. still lives in Colorado with his family, girlfriend, and dog.

*Don't let your creativity slip away, grasp it tightly, and keep it close. No matter where you go in life, it will always help you and remind you who you truly are.*

*-D.K. Nova*

**www.DKNovaBooks.com**